Louise Voss has been in the music business for ten years, working for Virgin Records and EMI, and then as a product manager for an independent label in New York. More recently she has been Director of Sandie Shaw's company in London. She lives in south-west London and has one daughter.

Louise Voss is the author of two previous novels, *To Be Someone* and *Are You My Mother?*

Acclaim for

ARE YOU MY MOTHER?

'An exhilarating emotional ride through love, friendship and loss'
New Woman

'A heart-warming story which covers the complicated and emotional themes of being orphaned and adopted and searching for birth parents'
Hello!

'Strong characters, a meaty plot and a satisfyingly unexpected twist transforms Emma's journey of self-discovery into a very good read'
Woman & Home

'Utterly believable . . . Highly emotional . . . it's also a complete tear-jerker'
Heat

www.**booksattransworld**.co.uk

Also by Louise Voss

TO BE SOMEONE
ARE YOU MY MOTHER?

and published by Black Swan

LIFESAVER

Louise Voss

BLACK SWAN

LIFESAVER
A BLACK SWAN BOOK : 0 552 77155 4

First publication in Great Britain

PRINTING HISTORY
Black Swan edition published 2004

1 3 5 7 9 10 8 6 4 2

Set in 11/12pt Melior by
Kestrel Data, Exeter, Devon.

Black Swan Books are published by Transworld Publishers,
61–63 Uxbridge Road, London W5 5SA,
a division of The Random House Group Ltd,
in Australia by Random House Australia (Pty) Ltd,
20 Alfred Street, Milsons Point, Sydney, NSW 2061, Australia,
in New Zealand by Random House New Zealand Ltd,
18 Poland Road, Glenfield, Auckland 10, New Zealand
and in South Africa by Random House (Pty) Ltd,
Endulini, 5a Jubilee Road, Parktown 2193, South Africa.

Printed and bound in Great Britain by
Cox & Wyman Ltd, Reading, Berkshire.

Papers used by Transworld Publishers are natural, recyclable
products made from wood grown in sustainable forests.
The manufacturing processes conform to the environmental
regulations of the country of origin.

For the beautiful and
inimitable Gracie T. Voss

Prologue

I caught him as he was on his way out of the front door, with the abstract yet focused look in his eyes he always got when his mind had raced ahead of his body.

'I've got something to tell you.'

My hesitant words seemed so clichéd; marginally better than the pure soap opera corn of 'we need to talk', but not a lot. It occurred to me how much like a soap opera the last year of my own life had been.

'In a bit of a hurry, baby, can it wait?'

'No. Sorry. It can't.'

He turned in the doorway, alarm framed on his face as I stood there, terrified, with my box of carefully prepared props under one arm. As ready as I'd ever be. I pictured my lies as the dark shapes of goldfish, previously undetected in an algeous pond, all rushing up at once and breaking through the slimy surface.

I'd written down my excuses. I'd wanted to use index cards, to try and pretend it was some kind of skewed business presentation: bullet points and headers, neat captions. But I hadn't been able to find any index cards. The only vaguely suitable writing material I'd been able to lay my hands on was a book of post-cards depicting famous tennis players of the twentieth century. I'd ripped them all out, one by one, hearing the small squirty sound of their perforations tearing:

shuffling Nastase's frown of concentration and Borg's headband, Agassi's smash and Sampras's serve. The world of tennis seemed so pure somehow, a distillation of energy, ambition and talent, worlds away from the messy, complicated confession I had to make.

I was in a pop video once. You could say it was the highlight of my acting career – a depressing thing to have to admit. I had been in loads of plays too, sometimes in the lead role, usually not. But this video was for a very famous country act, a slightly cross-eyed nouveau cowboy called Dwight Unsworth. I'd played his girlfriend. I didn't recall the story, but what I did remember about it was having to stand stock-still for ages as crowds of extras flowed past me. The director had later speeded up the film so it looked as if the people were rushing like water, streaming around me as I remained motionless, waiting for Dwight.

That sense of standing still while things happened around me – that was exactly how my life had felt for a long time. Until I'd met Adam and Max, and everything had changed.

Now it was all changing again.

Part One

1

EIGHT MONTHS EARLIER

'Anna, please, come round as soon as you can. It's an emergency. I don't know what to do. Please? I need help.'

I'd just got in from a run, and had to force myself to breathe quietly enough to listen to the message on the answering machine, before letting the remaining gasps of air out of my lungs in a panicked exhalation.

It was my great-aunt, Lil. Guilt stabbed me in the side, worse than a stitch, because I'd run past her house not fifteen minutes earlier, and I could have checked on her then. But the truth was, apart from stilted hellos if I'd seen her around, I hadn't been able to face Lil for ten months. I'd crossed the street and looked away, averting my eyes from her neat front garden, and the beautiful purple pansies blooming in her window boxes. Purple was the colour of healing, I'd once read. I hated purple, it reminded me of something strangulated, of blood which couldn't flow properly. More like the colour of hernias, in my opinion.

The blood in my own body was flowing around me with no problems, my legs felt like jelly, and my T-shirt was sticking to my back, but I turned straight back around and ran out the door again, not bothering to double-lock it. Quicker to jog than to take the car during rush hour. I barged past dog-walkers, trying

11

both to avoid and yet not see all the prams and pushchairs. It was just about possible to force my legs to keep up a rhythm fast enough for me not to be able to look at the faces within, at the chubby cheeks turned like petals towards the sun.

Eyes front, Anna, I thought. Don't do it. I was getting quite adept at avoidance tactics. It was just self-preservation, I decided, blocking out the sound of Aunt Lil's hurt voice from all her earlier answerphone messages.

Please don't let her be injured or in danger, I prayed as I hurtled around the corner into her street and puffed up to her front door, sick with dread. I'd never have forgiven myself. There was no smoke billowing out of her bedroom window, no fire-engines or ambulances, no groups of concerned passers-by on the pavement; but that hadn't assuaged my fears. Maybe she'd slipped into unconsciousness, I thought, pounding on the knocker of number twenty-one.

'Hello, dear,' Lil said, opening the front door with my hand still attached to the knocker. 'Do come in. I've just put the kettle on.'

I stood rooted to the spot with disbelief, my ribcage heaving and my forehead dripping sweat (I'd only recently had the energy to take up running again, and I was still far from fit).

'What is it?' I gasped, scanning her for signs of distress. The sides of her dove-grey hair were pulled away from her face and, I noticed as she bent down to pick up a sweet wrapper which had fluttered onto her doorstep, fastened with a clip at the back of her head in a jaunty style. Her pale coral lipstick couldn't have been more neatly applied if painted on by a make-up artist; she wore a lavender wool suit and smart steel-coloured court shoes. She looked perfectly fine. No, more than that, she looked immaculate.

'Well, hurry up, Anna,' she said, straightening up with the litheness of a woman twenty years younger, 'you don't want to stand around out there all day, do you? I'll get you a towel, and you can rub your hair dry. This much exercise surely can't be good for you!'

No, it bloody can't be, I thought. Not to mention the near heart attack she's just given me. I allowed her to usher me inside, where I leaned against the banisters, still panting loudly in the quiet hall.

'So there's nothing wrong with you at all, then, is there?' I said, once I'd got my breath back.

Lil smiled disarmingly – at seventy-nine, she still had the most amazing teeth – and handed me a small burgundy towel, which I rubbed across my face and the back of my neck.

'Well, I really didn't know what to do. And I do need help – there's a lightbulb stuck in the fitting in the pantry, and I need somebody strong to twist it out for me. I'm always worried that I'll break it and then have to spend hours in Casualty having shards of glass tweezered out of my fingers. So anyway, I just happened to be looking out of the window when I saw you jogging past a while ago and guessed you were on your way home.'

I buried my hot face in the towel. It smelled of the inside of her airing cupboard: yeast, rosemary and rose-petal, tweed, and something unidentifiable from my childhood. She knew that I couldn't resist the scents of the past. I felt a rush of emotion: anger, guilt, affection, grief.

'Very clever,' I said, following her into the kitchen and flopping down on one of the orange Formica stools she'd had in there since the seventies. I used to love the fact that Lil's house had a breakfast bar and stools; it was so different and exotic.

The stools were quite high with long varnished wooden legs as if they aspired to being imitation plastic. When I'd sat on them as a kid, I'd felt like a solo artiste on *Top of the Pops*: Mary Hopkins, perhaps. All I'd needed was the guitar and the cheesecloth dress and the blonde curtains of hair. My little brother Olly and I used to balance on them, relishing being so high up, legs dangling unsupported. We would sit and eat our tea with our heads down, facing the wall. 'You look like horses at a trough,' Uncle Norm would say when he got in from work to find us there.

Now Norm was dead, and I worried that Lil would break her hip some day, trying to get on or off one of the stools.

'What do you mean, dear?' she asked innocently.

I didn't know what to say. I stuck my left forefinger through a rip in the slippery vinyl covering of my stool, feeling the yellowy crumbling stuffing inside. That rip had been there for years, and it was always a temptation to pull at the foam, like picking a scab. But it was deceptively tough and unyielding, clinging to the stool's wooden seat like a limpet to a rock. It reminded me of Lil herself.

Lil placed a cup of thick brown tea in front of me, incongruous in a delicate china cup and saucer, and a large glass of cold water, which I immediately gulped down. When I replaced the empty glass on the counter, she reached out and put her hands over mine.

'You live less than a mile away. We used to be such good friends. I'm pleading with you, Anna, don't shut me out any more. I miss you. It's been months now – getting on for a year – and you know how awful I feel about it too . . .'

I bit my lip, unable to meet her eyes. Part of me felt that I couldn't possibly cope with this, not at nine o'clock in the morning in my damp sweaty running gear; but a bigger part of me was relieved that she'd decided to take matters into her own hands. The same thin hands which now covered mine, with their bluish veins and constellations of liver spots. Those hands had pulled so many souls into life.

'It's not you . . .' I managed.

'I know. But it won't help, your not talking to anybody about it. You aren't talking to anybody, are you?'

'I went to that shrink for a while,' I mumbled, feeling the steam from the tea heat my already burning cheeks.

14

'What about that support group, SANDS?'

'Went a couple of times. Couldn't handle it. All those people expecting me to cry, just because they were crying. Telling me they knew how I felt, like that made it all right.'

Lil got up, put on a flowery apron and her Marigolds, and painstakingly began to wash a pot which had been sitting in the sink. She rinsed it, put it on the drying rack, then peeled off the gloves again and lifted the noose of the apron carefully over her head, hanging it back on the nail on the back of the pantry door. Even in the misery and awkwardness of the moment, I couldn't help marvelling at somebody who would do all that, just to wash up one pot. That's what I'd missed about her, I thought.

'I'm sorry,' I said, finally.

'So am I, darling,' she replied, holding out her arms to me. 'So am I.'

We hugged. I feasted on the scent of her lavender wool and leaned into her shoulder, without looking up to see if she was crying. I'd seen her cry once, and I never wanted to again. It was such a relief, to be held by her, surrounded by her tall, gaunt frame.

'So what's new?' she asked later, in the post-hug rapprochement. After I'd changed her lightbulb for her, we had adjourned to the living room, where we sat facing one another in her deep flowery wing-back armchairs.

I shrugged, feeling the black veil of depression drifting gently over me, cloying and cobwebby.

'Nothing. Nothing at all. There's no work around. I've got an audition tomorrow, for a soap, but it's only a cable show, filming in Bristol or somewhere.'

I was about to add: 'I won't get it, anyway,' but just in time I realized how self-pitying this sounded, and made a colossal effort to lighten my tone. I didn't want Auntie Lil to feel any worse than she already did.

'But at least it's something,' I said vaguely instead.

'And I've started seeing Vicky a bit more, though, now that it's getting easier for me to see the kids again. They all came over on Saturday. She's finding it really tough, with two.'

Lil nodded sympathetically. She had always really liked my friend Vicky (largely, I thought, because Vicky used to do uncannily accurate impressions of Thora Hird, Lil's favourite actress). 'Do send her my love, won't you, when you next see her?'

'I will. In fact I'm meeting her and Crystal later. I'm going to a fifth birthday party at a bowling alley with them. Vicky's dreading it, so she's asked me along to keep her company.'

'That sounds fun, dear,' said Lil, dubiously. 'And how is Ken? Still working far too hard?'

I sighed. 'Yes. I only see him last thing at night most nights. He's even working weekends now too, you know, either travelling or entertaining executives from the different territories. When he's not out playing tennis, that is – he's in the First Division of his club's league now. Takes it all very seriously.'

I looked around the room, feeling its stillness. The only sound was a radio with the volume down low, murmuring classical music. Something seemed different, although for a few moments I couldn't work out what. Then I realized.

'Your baby table's gone,' I blurted out. Where before there had been dozens of framed photographs propped up, the majority of them black and white, of tiny babies and toddlers in clumsy hand-knitted garments, there was now just a gleaming empty mahogany table. Its surface was blank and smooth and somehow threatening, like deep brown polished ice.

Aunt Lil gazed at me, and I admired her for not looking away. 'I took them down some months ago. You just haven't been in this room for a long time.'

'But why?' I asked, knowing exactly why, but not being able to stop myself. 'You loved those pictures.'

'Yes. I still have them. But I just didn't want to see

them every day any more. All those babies are grown up now. Most of them have babies of their own . . .'

I felt the pain physically, starting in my sternum, then sneaking around my shoulderblades to close in on my chest. I nodded.

Aunt Lil had been a midwife for six decades. That was an awful lot of babies: hundreds and hundreds of them over the years. The extraordinary thing about it was that she'd managed to keep in touch with so many of them; with the mothers at first, of course, and then later with the babies themselves. Lil's babies, they were called. Some of them had even got to know one another, members of an exclusive club. Lil's babies were lawyers now, mothers, jugglers, teachers, priests. A couple were even grandmothers themselves, which blew my mind.

Ever since I'd been a teenager, I'd told Lil I wanted her to deliver my babies too. I wanted to have them at home, with only her and my future, as yet unseen husband present.

And this was what happened, although in the end there was another midwife there too, a young, plump Irish girl called Teresa, because Lil thought we should have the extra back-up. In case anything went wrong. At the time I imagined Teresa at the start of her career, thinking of all the baby souls she'd deliver safely into their earthly bodies to become 'Teresa's babies', and wondering if she'd keep in touch with them as Lil had been doing for half a century.

Lil did deliver our baby. We called her Holly, and she was indescribably beautiful. But she stopped breathing twenty-seven minutes after she was born, and all Lil's efforts to resuscitate her failed. She died before the ambulance arrived. We never found out why – the autopsy was inconclusive.

I later discovered that, shortly after Holly's death, Teresa had given up midwifery and gone to work at Barclays in the High Street. I found it hard to imagine her out of the blue midwife's uniform and in a pencil skirt and neat blouse. I tried hard not to imagine her at all.

'I'd better go,' I said, standing up abruptly. 'I've, er, got loads to do. Got a neighbour coming round to lunch and I need to do some shopping first. Then there's this kids' party . . .'

Later, when I remembered the comment about the neighbour arriving for lunch, it occurred to me that perhaps lying had always come more easily to me than I'd thought. I used to believe that those sorts of lies were simply words that made things more palatable for other people, as if I was doing them a favour by lying – the 'no, of course your hips don't look wide in that dress' school of white lies. I genuinely hadn't wanted Lil to know that I'd be going back to an empty house. But now I realized that lies were just lies. They started small, like two rubber bands twisted together, and got bigger and bigger until the bundle became a ball the size of a grapefruit, and each lie had to stretch further and further around its circumference.

Lil stood up too and clasped my hands in hers again. That had been the thing I'd dreaded most about seeing her: I'd thought I'd never be able to cope with the raw emotion of seeing those large hands again; the hands which, in the end, couldn't help the one baby she'd most wanted to usher into the world.

But as we stood at the door saying goodbye, I felt instead an overwhelming wash of gratitude that Lil had made that false emergency call and physically got me round there.

It wasn't her fault anyway, I thought as I left, really believing it for the first time ever. Holly just hadn't been ready for us, that was all.

2

When I got home again, the house was still and empty. Of course that's what I'd been expecting, but I wasn't sure why it always gave me a split-second's worth of bafflement, as if people ought to have crept in in my absence and decorated the place for a party, and should be hiding behind sofas and chairs, about to jump out and shout, 'Surprise!' Wishful thinking, I decided miserably, trailing up the stairs and peeling off my clammy running gear at the same time.

It wasn't only Ken's absence which I felt so keenly in the silence – after all, I was used to that. My abiding impression of my husband, at least for the past four years of our lives, had been of a man on his way out of the door. He always seemed to be leaving the house: going to work, to tennis, to a gig; as if home were some kind of mandatory holding pen to be escaped from as soon as possible, so that his real life could begin. Maybe it had something to do with the fact that his family had been asylum seekers; in the 1970s they'd emigrated to England from Uganda, to get away from Idi Amin's regime.

'I've got to run,' he said, only that morning. I sometimes thought he never stopped running, and it had got much worse since Holly died. We didn't talk about her, although I'd have liked to. 'I'm going to squeeze in a quick set with Chris before I get my train. Take it easy today, OK?'

As I put the plug in the bath and turned the taps on full, I thought of Ken on the tennis court, his lovely legs dark brown and muscular in his white shorts and his top riding up to expose his hairy tummy when he served. We used to like making love in the mornings, but that hadn't happened for a long time. More often than not, Ken left the house while I was still asleep.

Then I imagined him on the train, showered and glowing with slick black wet hair, his BlackBerry bleeping quietly in his jacket pocket like a small electronic animal, or a Clanger perhaps. I thought of him getting newsprint on his fingers from somebody else's abandoned copy of *Metro*. What I didn't like to think of was all the female office workers who might be staring at him with admiration, surreptitiously checking to see if he was wearing a wedding ring, and then feeling disappointed when they saw that he was.

I climbed in the bath and lay there for a long, long time. The only sound in the house was the slow steady plink of the cold tap dripping into the water, and a bluebottle whizzing around the bathroom, so fast it was a blur. I tried to focus on it for a while, watching it zigzag, and then fly in concentric circles, as if being spun from a string on the ceiling. No wonder it kept bumping into things – at that speed, how could it possibly see where it was going? And when it crashed into the window, how come it didn't knock itself unconscious?

In many of the 'inspirational' life-after-death books I'd read in the past ten months, people who had lost loved ones were graced with the presence of, say, a rare bluebird, or a butterfly in winter, hovering or fluttering around them and making them feel the spirit of the deceased was with them still. I put the word 'inspirational' in inverted commas because those books depressed the hell out me. Why hadn't *I* ever got visitations from a beautiful but unfamiliar cat, who would appear just when I was feeling at my lowest? All I got was this big fat irritating bluebottle, and I doubted that it had any messages of eternal wisdom with which to succour me.

I contemplated getting out, but closed my eyes instead and sank back under the water, letting it close over my head and face, feeling the tickle of my hair on my cheek as it floated around me. I had nothing else to do, not until the party that afternoon. I supposed I could have run through the script for my audition the following day, but I couldn't be bothered. It was only a part in a West Country cable soap, nothing huge.

The character I was up for was the glamorous but tired mother of twin babies – which was a little close to the knuckle. My agent, Fenella, sounded like she was walking on broken glass when she told me about it, full of apologies and qualifications: she knew I might not feel up to it, but it was decent money for a cable, and it would probably do me good to have some regular work. But then, having to hold babies . . . I wasn't sure.

I wondered how Ken felt about me going up for an audition. In the old days he'd have helped me go over my rehearsal piece, prompting and encouraging me, bringing me cups of tea and sending me little break-a-leg cards to wish me luck. I couldn't even remember if I'd mentioned this one to him or not. He certainly hadn't referred to it lately, if I had. He just told me to 'take it easy', and buggered off to play tennis.

Ken assumed that because I spent so much time lolling around the house, 'taking it easy' was a treat for me. He didn't realize that it was actually my idea of Purgatory: empty house, time on my hands, frustration, boredom, depression. And the guilt . . . I knew I ought to have gone to the gym, or the supermarket, or for a walk; but I'd rather be bored and cloistered at home than be out during the day, because daytime was when the mothers roamed. They were everywhere, and with such an array of equipment: prams, buggies, papooses, car seats, scooters, push-along trikes. 'It's like being roadie to the world's smallest rock star,' Ken used to joke, when he thought he was going to be a dad. But I didn't think that joke was funny any more. Anything could set me off: the squeak of a pushchair's wheel, a tiny dropped sock, trickles of melted ice-cream running over a dimpled chin.

If I went out during the day, my hands felt limp and loose at my sides without anything, or anyone, to push or carry, and it just made me want to crawl indoors again.

I lay in the bath and watched the bluebottle until my eyeballs ached with the exertion of darting around the room after it, and the water was almost stone cold. Suddenly I really wanted the part in the cable soap. I wanted to have my hands full of baby again. With a watery swoosh I climbed out of the bath and dried myself with a towel which probably ought to have been washed about three weeks ago.

The phone rang just as I'd got back into our bedroom and was knotting the belt of Ken's towelling bathrobe around my waist. I picked up the extension by the bed.

'Hello?'

'Hi, Anna, just ringing to check you're still on for the party today. Crystal can't wait to see you! And thanks again for Saturday, by the way. It was fun.'

'Oh, hi, Vic; yes, it was,' I lied. 'Thanks for coming.'

We'd had Vicky and her husband Peter over for dinner. Maybe it was just that we were somewhat out of practice in hosting dinner parties, or maybe it was the presence of my goddaughter Crystal and her baby brother Pat, but the whole thing had been hideously unrelaxing. Vicky and Peter's babysitter had pulled out at the last minute, and Vicky had entertained the fanciful notion that her children would go to sleep at our house instead. Fat chance. Both Crystal and Pat had decided that fighting and crying for Vicky's attention was a far better way to pass a few hours away from home, way past their bedtime.

The fact that neither Ken nor I really like Peter very

much wasn't very helpful, either. Peter has this great thick mass of reddish hair, and freckles, and in my opinion doesn't pull his weight with the kids nearly enough. Every time I see him it reminds me of the words of my favourite childhood book: 'Anything to me is sweeter/Than to see Shock-headed Peter.' Crystal is the image of him but, being four, she still manages to be incredibly cute.

Much as I adore Crystal, I had only recently been able to face her again; to actually want to spend any time with her. It still hurt, seeing each new thing she did and said and learned. I couldn't help thinking about my little Holly, and how left behind she'd got. She would have looked up to Crystal so much. Crystal could have taught her all her bad habits. Given her lessons in Advanced Hypochondria, Primal Screaming, and of course, Tantrum Throwing II – The Full Monty.

This was a bit unfair, although Crystal was going through a bit of a difficult phase. She was fine around me, but she didn't half give poor Vicky a hard time; the expression 'drama queen' could have been minted just for her.

'What did you do yesterday?'

I tried to remember. 'Um. Not much. Ken played golf with some people from the office. I went over my audition script.'

'What audition? You didn't tell me you had an audition! When? For what?'

Vicky sounded slighted, and I felt too lethargic to protest that I had definitely brought up the subject of the part. 'It's tomorrow. Only a regional cable soap, plus I'd have to be away filming for days at a time, most weeks, down in Bristol. I'm not sure I want it.'

'Oh, Anna, go for it. I'd kill for a part like that – regular work, and fame, but only regional so you don't get papped every time you're seen rolling out of a bar with your skirt stuck in your knickers and your lipstick sliding off.'

The wistfulness in Vicky's voice gave it another edge:

a hologram of longing. She was dying to get back to work, but hadn't been offered any parts since she got pregnant with Pat. It was hard enough for her to get away for the auditions, let alone to commit to any sort of theatre run or filming schedule.

'Yeah. I suppose I could handle being famous in the West Country.'

'That's the spirit. Anyway, see you at four for the party, yeah? Come round to me and we'll go in my car.'

Ten minutes after we hung up from each other, I was still sitting in Ken's bathrobe on the unmade bed. Eventually I roused myself enough to trudge downstairs, fill the kettle, and half-listen to a heated radio phone-in, something about congestion charging. I let the different voices wash over me and remove me from myself, like sleep. The kettle boiled, but I didn't notice. I forgot about the audition. I made myself switch off, click, like the kettle, and just sat. It was something I'd done a lot in the past ten months. Instant numbness, like a mobile epidural. I craved it, and I'd become quite adept in achieving it. I looked on it as a technique to be perfected, like a Stanislavsky exercise, or yogic breathing.

I really thought I'd only been there for ten minutes or so, until I looked at the clock and realized with a lurch that almost an hour had gone by, and I hadn't moved. No wonder I felt stiff. Time treated me strangely these days. It was either stretched out into endless skeins of sticky minutes that I didn't know what to do with, or it compacted itself into hard little atoms which moved so fast I couldn't keep up with them.

I wished that I didn't have to battle with time like this. I shouldn't even have been aware of it, that's what was so unfair. Right then, I ought to have been making pipecleaner butterflies with felt-tip decorated wings, or sticking cork flooring down in a Wendy house. Having other children round to play; sewing name tapes into coats; washing sticky hands; polishing small fingerprints off the French windows; or any of the dozens of things that Vicky moaned about having to do. If things had been different, I wouldn't have had the time to sit motionless on a stool in the kitchen for an hour, still in a dressing gown.

Still, I thought, at least Lil and I were friends again. Got to try and be positive about something.

I was just concluding a more successful attempt to make myself a cup of coffee when I heard a sickeningly loud grinding sound from outside. The bin men! If their cart was churning, it meant that they'd already picked up our neighbours' black bags and were getting ready to leave for another week.

I sprang into action – it was almost a relief to make a sudden move – leaping out of the front door, throwing the lids off the bins, and charging into the road, two full binliners in each hand. The bin men cheered half-heartedly as I tossed the bags into the cart's grinding maw, and I smiled equally half-heartedly back again, before turning to plod back to the house in the warm and intensifying drizzle.

It really was about time I got dressed. Even I thought it was a bit shaming to be outside in just a dressing gown and sparkly flipflops – but then the neighbours already thought we were slatterns. Our house was a lovely tall Victorian semi, but neither Ken nor I had had the heart to do anything to it, despite the elaborate plans we'd made when we first moved to Hampton, when I was seven months' pregnant. Wisteria choked the gutters and covered the upstairs windows at the back; the once-white paint on the front door and the garage door was as patchy and flaky as psoriasis, and weeds sprouted enthusiastically from the gravel in the drive. I bent down and yanked out a dandelion, as if this might atone for my state of public undress.

The neighbours never mentioned Holly. They hadn't known me well enough to come over and commiserate when it had become apparent that there was a bump and then no baby; and as time had gone on, it had clearly become harder for them to address the issue. So they'd never bothered. Consequently we hadn't made any friends in the street. Ken didn't care, of course, because he was never there; but there were times I thought it would have been nice to have someone over for coffee and a chat about the poor quality of the street lighting in Grosvenor Drive, or the copious amounts of dog poo on the pavements.

As I was chucking the weed behind our now-empty dustbins, the postman cycled up. His long lank hair was tied into a ponytail, and the ever-present roll-up stuck to his lips like it was part of the uniform. He parked his red bike by the gate, rootled around in his bag, and handed me a pile of envelopes of different sizes, the top one softened and damp from the insidious rain, its address blurred.

He never spoke, this postman, but nodded and smiled at me instead, which made the roll-up between his lips flap up and down and occasionally scatter ash. Our post always smelled of cigarette smoke, but at least he was friendlier than most of the neighbours.

'Thanks,' I said, wiping dandelion milk off my fingers onto Ken's dressing gown before thumbing through the stack: subscription *Vogue*; bookclub magazine; Air Miles junk; a postcard addressed to both of us from my brother Olly, who was travelling with his boyfriend Russ and now appeared to be living it up in Ibiza; and a letter for me: a thick, real envelope, hand-written in unfamiliar writing. My brain clunked through the various processes of elimination one made when receiving unexpected correspondence, discounting all the potential candidates: Agent? No, she'd have rung. Party invitation? Possibly, although the envelope wasn't the right shape for an invite. Distant relative? Unlikely – I recognized most of my relatives' writing.

There was something vaguely thrilling about receiving a proper letter in an email age. I hoped it wouldn't turn out to be something tedious like an invitation from my doctor for a smear test.

Back indoors, I sat on the bottom stair and examined the envelope. There was no forwarding address on the back, and I couldn't make out the postmark. The writing was fat and loopy; unusual. I had no idea whom it might be from.

Relishing the experience, I slid my thumb underneath the glued-down flap and ripped, slowly, pulling out two folded sheets of lined paper – covered, curiously, with handwriting different to that which was on the envelope. It appeared to be from the Gillingsbury Adult Education College, which confused me even further – until I began to read.

27 July 2002

Dear Mrs Sozi,

You don't know me – us, I mean. My name is Adam Ferris, and my son's name is Max. He's four years old – coming up to five – and the reason I'm writing to you now.

Two years ago, Max was extremely ill with Acute Myeloid Leukaemia. You saved his life with the bone-marrow donation you so generously gave him. As I'm sure you're aware, the Anthony Nolan Trust do not permit any contact between donor and recipient for at least two years after a transplant, but I've wanted to get in touch ever since Max got the all-clear eight months ago. I put a note in my diary to remind me of the exact date at which I'd write this letter to you, because it makes me so happy, and so grateful, to be able to do so.

I could fill pages with thank yous, but it still wouldn't come close to expressing my gratitude to you. You have given my little boy's life back. You have given him back to me, when I thought he was going to be taken away – oh hell, and now of course I'm crying, writing this . . . ! How could I not? Max

27

means everything to me, you see. He's my only child. My wife and I are separated and, although I know she loves him very much too, she handles things differently. We haven't seen her for some time. Anyway, I'm sure you don't want to hear about that! I suppose I just feel sort of close to you, now that you are a part of my son – the part which saved his life.

I know nothing at all about you, Anna (I hope you don't mind me calling you that), not even your actual address – as you will see, this letter will have been forwarded to you by the Anthony Nolan Trust. You may well have a family of your own; in which case, you will certainly understand the extremes of fear and joy I've been through since Max was diagnosed as he was turning two. I must admit that I'm very curious, and would love to get to know a little more about you. Of course we will respect your wishes if you decide not to be in touch with us – at the Trust they tell me that this is quite common, understandably, especially in cases where the transplant fails. Time will tell with Max, but at the moment, thank God, he is most definitely in remission, and as healthy, happy and bouncy a kid as you could ever meet. So if you do fancy writing back, or emailing, please do (address at top of page: it's my work email; I teach pottery and ceramics. Not full time, but it gives me plenty of time to be a dad). Max and I would both love to meet you one day to say thanks in person.

Yours truly and eternally gratefully,
Adam (and Max) Ferris

I was barely aware that, as I slowly read each word of the letter, I had walked up the stairs, along the landing, and into the smaller of our two spare bedrooms. It wasn't intended as a spare bedroom, but I'd insisted that the elephant and butterfly frieze, matching curtains and primrose-yellow walls be obliterated by yards of bland biscuit-coloured emulsion. The carpet was still the same blue one we'd bought for Holly, though. The only visible reminder of the nursery, and the only freshly decorated room in the house. There was a brand-new bed in there, but nobody had ever slept in it.

I missed that elephant frieze; the walls still seemed bare without it. But I didn't regret the decision to rip it off. Some people kept their children's bedrooms as shrines, but that made no sense to me. I suppose it might have been different if the room had held memories of Holly herself, but she'd never even got to see her elephants and butterflies.

I dropped the letter onto the soft blue carpet, then slid down the wall next to it, putting my head in my arms. I couldn't hear anything except the blood roaring in my ears, and the faint sound of a plane high in the sky.

Gradually, I became aware that I was beginning to smile. I reread the words two, then three times, and even as my throat was constricting, my smile got slowly wider. It was the first time I'd smiled in that bedroom since it had been redecorated.

3

'I think I've died and gone to hell,' Vicky yelled over the din, as we stood in the entrance hall of Ultra-Bowl. Even Crystal, usually so confident, clutched my hand and shrank into my legs. The noise was intense: slot machines bleeping and crashing; snooker balls cracking on ten tables to our left; teenage boys with shaven heads crouching in the saddles of stationary motorbikes, their eyes glued to the screens and their bodies swaying as they roared around one-dimensional corners of non-existent speedway tracks . . . I began to feel out of place for not wearing an oversized death-metal band T-shirt or body piercings.

'Perfect place for a five-year-old's birthday party, isn't it?' I said.

'Nooo, Auntie Anna, it isn't,' said Crystal, appalled. 'Mummy, don't make me have *my* party here. I want to go home!'

'I'm only joking, darling, don't worry. I'm sure Mummy will stick with the bouncy castle and Polly Mixtures the clown, won't you, Vic?'

Relieved, Crystal turned her attention to picking a scab on her elbow. 'Where's the party, Mummy?'

Vicky pointed towards a sign saying 'Kiddies Korner' in flashing neon. 'Over here, I think. Don't pick it, Crystal, or it won't heal.'

We weaved around a cluster of slot machines, over the casino-patterned carpet and up a short flight of steps, where the noise changed. The clamour of the machines faded to a mercifully dull roar, but it was supplemented by the sugar-fuelled screams of six children's birthday parties all taking place simultaneously, each in its own truncated bowling lane. Score monitors above each lane blared out more noise, and over the top of it all some distorted but thumping pop was hovering, like a toxic emission.

Crystal stood uncertainly in her party dress, clutching her gift for the birthday girl. The raw pinkness of the skin under her picked-off scab made my throat hurt, it looked so vulnerable.

'At least it's not bleeding all down her party dress,' said Vicky, catching my gaze. 'Look, Crystal, there's Lottie!'

Lottie was a sturdy child with pierced ears. She was wearing crimson nail varnish, high wedge heels, an armful of sponged-on tattoos, and pink lipstick.

'Happy birthday, Lottie,' said Vicky as Crystal handed over the gift. Lottie snatched it without a word and dumped it on the pile of other presents under a bench, before marching back to the top of the bowling lane, elbowing Crystal out of the way.

'She's the only five-year-old with cellulite that I've ever seen,' Vicky whispered to me. Then: 'I'm sure Lottie will love your present,' she added, bending down to comfort Crystal. 'She's just over-excited.'

'I still want to go home,' said Crystal mournfully.

After the inauspicious start, though, things eventually improved. Crystal watched the other children roll bowling balls down metal ramps into the lane, and after a few minutes she allowed me to lead her over to them and show her how to do it. We scored a strike immediately, which cheered her up no end, so I left her there, happily joining the back of the queue for her next triumph.

'That's my girl,' called Vicky, giving her the thumbs-up.

31

'Bowling's good fun, really, isn't it?' I commented. 'Pity about the racket though.'

'And the . . . *pond life*,' added Vicky snobbishly.

We were sitting on a wobbly bench at the side of the lane, watching the children all become noticeably more hyperactive as they slurped lemonade from huge paper cups brought over and distributed by Lottie's mother. I hated seeing Crystal drink that crap, but I knew I couldn't say anything to Vicky. Nor could I, however, prevent myself from muttering, 'I wish they at least had a choice about what to drink.'

'Anna, it's supposed to be a treat. It's a party – it's practically inevitable that Crystal will get hopped up on additives. Anyway, I bet if there was a choice, it would only be between Coke, Diet Coke or 7-Up. They don't do organic elderflower cordial in these sorts of places.'

Well, they should, I thought, just about managing to button my lip. I wished it had occurred to me to bring a bottle of mineral water.

Vicky changed the subject. 'So how's things? All set for your audition? I'm so envious.'

'Mm,' I said, although I wasn't thinking about the audition. I was thinking about the letter from Adam Ferris, tucked in the inside pocket of my handbag. I looked at Vicky, at her familiar, tired but pretty face. Part of me really wanted to tell her – I had a thrilled yet fearful excitement in my stomach, like the butterflies on Holly's frieze – but another, bigger part made me keep quiet. Maybe I'd tell her later, once I'd decided what to do. Some things were too big to tell; at least until you'd got them sorted out in your own head first. That was how I felt about Max.

'Don't be jealous. I'm sure I won't get it.' Now it was my turn to change the subject. 'How's my little Pat?' I took a long slug of Crystal's lemonade, thinking that the more of it I drank, the less it would be able to poison Crystal.

Vicky sighed. 'He's hideously clingy at the moment. I

can't put him down. When I left him next door before you came round, he screamed so loudly I thought the windows were going to blow out.'

For a minute I thought she was about to cry, but when I reached a tentative hand over to squeeze her knee, she moved her leg away, so I withdrew it again.

I thought about Pat, thirteen months old and utterly adorable. If he were mine, I wouldn't care how clingy he was. How wonderful, to be that loved. I couldn't say that to Vicky either.

We sat in silence for a while, watching as Lottie lugged a large ball to the top of the metal chute and shoved it down. When it knocked down six of the pins, Lottie did a little Indian war dance of delight, her bottom wobbling. She ran around and hugged all the nearby children, a podgy Beckham who'd scored a goal for England. I turned to remark on this to Vicky, but her face had that closed-down expression on it again.

'Oh look, what fresh hell is this?' I said instead, as the children's food arrived.

The party tea consisted of plastic baskets of brown, hard, cold chips and some breaded bullet-shaped nuggets of indeterminate origin. I hadn't been expecting a nice fresh green salad or anything, but you'd have thought they could run to a slice of cucumber or two, or a few carrot sticks . . . although perhaps that was being too optimistic. The kids probably wouldn't have touched anything that healthy with a barge pole. We got up to help the other parents distribute it.

'What do you suppose that is?' I asked, pointing at one of the unappetizing nuggets with distaste.

'I have no idea,' replied Vicky. 'It looks like something my cat would produce.'

We were joined by another of the mothers, an attractive, slim woman with wavy blonde hair and an ankle bracelet. 'I think it's supposed to be chicken. Although I wouldn't swear to it. I'm Diana, by the way, Susie's mum – that's her over there with the stripy dress.

33

Whose mother are you?' She addressed the question to me, but Vicky butted in.

'Crystal's; there, the one without bowling shoes on. They didn't have any tens left, so the boy said she could wear her sandals – just as well, really, since she hasn't got any socks on. I didn't like to think of her feet in those strange shoes, I'm sure she'd have got blisters from them.'

I made myself snap back to attention, becoming aware that the plastic basket in my hand was at a perilous slant.

'And who knows what else, too. I'm glad Susie's wearing socks.' The woman turned back to me. 'So, whose mother are you?' she repeated.

There was a pause. Vicky's eyes met mine, then dropped away.

'I'm Crystal's godmother,' I said eventually. 'I'm just here to provide moral support. Is there a bar in here? I'm gagging for a gin and tonic.'

'I don't think so. Soft drinks only, as far as I can see.'

I rolled my eyes. 'This place is a nightmare. All this noise, and no booze? It's a shame, isn't it – bowling is such a fun thing to do.'

Clearly relieved that the crisis seemed to have been averted, Vicky joined in. 'Yeah. You know, someone should open a middle-class bowling alley. No slot machines. Chilled Sauvignon and canapés.'

Susie laughed. 'Classical music piped in instead of this Euro-disco nightmare stuff.'

'Members only, and you have to be proposed and seconded . . .'

'Elderflower cordial for the kids – organic, of course.'

I caught Vicky's teasing expression. I supposed I'd asked for it, with my earlier criticism about the lemonade, but all of a sudden I found I couldn't keep up the banter. The depression which I usually managed to keep in check in public rose up like a swirling tide, threatening to cut me off. 'I'm just going to the loo,' I said, walking away. I knocked a discarded

34

basket of chips to the floor and although I picked up the basket, I didn't bother to collect up the dropped chips.

The Ladies was back through the amusement arcade and out the other side, next to those machines where you dropped ten pences in and tried to shove the existing ones off a ledge. It never worked; the ledge of money just got thicker and thicker and more and more teetering, from what I remembered of youthful seaside forays into arcades. Pressure, building up and up – that was how I felt most days. Getting closer and closer to the edge but stopping just short of it. For the moment. It was ten months since Holly died, but it still felt like yesterday.

When I got into the Ladies I just stood in front of the mirror, staring at my reflection in the artificial light. Everything was artificial here, I thought. The light, the lemonade, the food. My ability to act normally.

The door opened and Vicky came in, bringing a blast of slot-machine noise with her. She joined me at the basins.

'Are you following me?'

'Not entirely. I need a wee too.'

'Where's Crystal?'

Vicky gave me another look. 'That woman Diana's keeping an eye on her. She's fine. What's wrong, Anna?'

'Nothing. Honestly. Nothing new.' It was true, I thought. I'd had some wonderful news. Why did I feel so mixed up about it? Besides, it was Vicky who, in my opinion, was keeping something from me. She was behaving more strangely than I was – sullen and seeming ill one minute, hyper and hearty the next.

'Well, you know where I am if you ever need to talk.'

'Thanks.' I considered saying the same back to her but, with Vicky, there was no point. She'd tell me whatever it was when she was good and ready, and not before.

Vicky prodded the greyish puffy flesh beneath her

eyes, looking despondently at her reflection under the harsh fluorescent light. 'Look at the state of me. I look terrible. I'm so bloody tired, and this place has given me a headache.'

It was true that Vicky wasn't as attractive as she used to be, but everyone knew that once you had children you didn't have so much time to spend on your appearance. Perhaps I could persuade her to get her roots done, I thought, and maybe have a massage too. That always helped. I wished she wouldn't moan quite so continually about being tired, though. I would never moan, if it were me. As far as I was concerned it would be a small price to pay for two beautiful children. It wasn't as if I got a lot of sleep either, unless I knocked back industrial amounts of tranquillizers first, but then I always felt muzzy and cross for hours the next day.

'Why are you so tired? Pat's not ill, is he?'

'No, although he's still got that cough. He woke me up four times last night, and then Crystal decided to get up at quarter past five. I keep telling her she has to stay in her room till seven, but she won't. Then she wakes Pat up, and that's it. I don't know how they keep going all day – I'm shattered by noon.'

I still didn't really understand. Surely sleep was something to which you acclimatised? Those perfect little bodies could jump into my bed at whatever time of night they wanted. I'd never turf them out, never. The memory of the small hot arms twined around my neck, that time I had Crystal for a sleepover, were forever imprinted on my consciousness. Her small clumsy pats on my face had been like the best kind of gift.

I kept offering to have Crystal again – Pat, too, if Vicky and Peter wanted to go and have a night in a hotel somewhere. I'd have been happy to have them both, even with Pat's clingyness and Crystal's present obstreperousness. But Vicky kept putting me off. In fact, we'd almost had words about it – Vicky grumbled that Crystal didn't want to sleep in her own bed any more, and couldn't understand why Mummy and Daddy didn't let her sleep with them, like Auntie Anna had.

'Does Peter still never get up with the kids in the night?' I asked, knowing the answer.

Vicky snorted. 'Um . . . let me think . . . No. Well, occasionally at weekends. But you know, being a carpenter's a pretty stressful job . . .' She turned and went into a cubicle.

'You should ask him to help a bit more. Maybe just on alternate nights. You've got to do something, if you feel this wretched.'

The sound of Vicky sighing floated over the top of the cubicle door, followed by the sound of the toilet flushing. 'I'm sure it'll get better eventually,' she said, emerging wearily. 'In about sixteen years' time.'

I took out my make-up bag and reapplied my lipstick. I knew it wasn't very charitable of me, but sometimes I couldn't shake the thought that, apart from on the subject of Peter, Vicky was making a fuss about nothing: her kids were healthy and gorgeous. What else could she possibly ask for? Even if she looked a bit jaded, she didn't have any stretchmarks or cellulite, and her stomach was flatter than mine.

'Come on, then,' said Vicky, shouting over the noise of the hand-drier. '"Once more unto the breach, dear friends, once more . . ."'

By the time we finally left UltraBowl, Vicky wasn't the only one with a headache. She and Crystal were having a heated contretemps – Crystal had spotted a kids' indoor adventure playground in the corner of the arcade and demanded to go in it; and the ensuing din on top of everything else was making my brain throb against the sides of my skull.

'Over my dead body,' Vicky muttered to me. 'God knows what kinds of viruses are lurking in that ball pit.' She turned to her daughter. 'No, darling, we've got

37

to go and pick Pat up from next door. He'll be missing us by now!'

In the end we had to carry Crystal, screaming and expostulating, to the car, where she proceeded to bang her cheek on the car door. Vicky tried to placate her with the slice of thickly iced but leaden birthday cake that UltraBowl provided in their party bags.

'Ah-ah-ah-auntie Anna?' sobbed Crystal, spraying cake crumbs around the car. 'Sit in the back with me? My cheek hurts so much!'

'No, darling, grown-ups sit in the front,' Vicky began, but I was already climbing over Pat's empty baby seat, squeezing myself in the gap in the middle of the back seat, and cuddling Crystal. I found it so hard to say no to her.

I heard Vicky tut to herself, and felt a little guilty; it was true that Crystal was already the most monumental hypochondriac, and I supposed that me making a huge fuss of her might make her worse. Heaven forbid Crystal ever got anything seriously wrong with her – she'd probably go into a total decline. As it was, she harped on about the most minuscule of scratches, insisting that they necessitated the application of cream and glow-in-the-dark plasters. Crystal would have sold her soul for a Band-aid.

I'd started to administer homoeopathic remedies to her at the first sign of any symptoms: sore throat; bumped head; 'strummock hake' (as she called it when she was younger); and although Vicky said that she didn't mind, I'd noticed that she didn't show any inclination to use them on the kids herself. I extracted the bottle of Arnica tablets from my handbag.

'Ooh, yummy,' said Crystal. 'Medicine! Can I have lots, Auntie Anna, because my cheek really, *really* hurts.'

'No, just two tablets. Stick out your tongue for me.'

Vicky turned the key in the ignition, but it took three attempts before the elderly Escort would start. 'We desperately need a new car,' she muttered.

'Mummy, new cars are very, very expensive,' Crystal said through pursed lips.

'What are you now, the finance director?' Vicky snapped, as she drove slowly over the speedbumps outside the bowling alley.

Crystal drew herself up to her full height on her booster seat and spoke as if she were trying to explain something very simple to someone very stupid: 'Mummy. I'm half fairy. How could I *possibly* be a finance director?'

It was the first time Vicky had smiled all day; but her face immediately settled back into stern lines again and I sensed conflict.

'Anna,' she said.

'Yes?'

'Going back to the arnica: it's not that I disapprove of homoeopathy, you know that I don't; but those pills taste sweet, and it does kind of reinforce her belief that if she makes a fuss about her bumps and ailments, she'll get lots of attention. She's started asking for them when there's nothing wrong – even by her standards . . .'

'Sorry,' I said, feeling slighted. I put the arnica back in my bag. 'Only trying to help'.

'Can I have some more medicine?' asked Crystal.

Vicky indicated left off the roundabout, leaving the industrial estate which was the proud home of UltraBowl. Her mobile rang just as we were about to turn onto the main road, so she pulled over and switched the engine off again.

'Shall I get that for you?' I asked from the back seat, already delving into Vicky's cavernous shoulder bag, rummaging around amid packets of babywipes, two dummies, a spare pair of Crystal's flowery knickers and Vicky's make-up bag to try and locate the small silver phone. I managed to pass it to her just before it went over to voicemail.

'Hi!' said Vicky into the phone, suddenly animated again. 'How's it going?'

It's Katriona, she mouthed back at me. I nodded, then looked out of the window. I disliked Vicky's NCT friends, for no better reason than the NCT was one group I was now excluded from, despite having attended the meetings all the way through my pregnancy.

Crystal had become momentarily distracted by trying to peel an 'I SAW THE LIONS AND LABYRINTHS OF LONGLEAT' sticker off the inside of the car window by her seat, so I took the opportunity to knock her chunk of plastic additive-laden cake onto the floor of the car, where I trod on it, just to render it extra-inedible. I had some raisins in my bag, which might just act as a panacea. I wondered if Adam Ferris let Max eat crappy food. His being a pottery teacher gave me the idea that he probably wouldn't. I imagined him as very tall and skinny, with a hairy hand-knitted jumper and a beard. He probably fed Max on nothing but the purest organic vegetables. I hoped so. Poor little Max had doubtless had enough poison pumped into his system with the chemotherapy. Still, it had done the trick. That, and my bone-marrow donation.

Vicky was laughing now, and looked much brighter. 'Yeah, I know,' she said. 'I've been fantasizing about one all day; with candles, and music – the works. This is definitely the hardest time, isn't it? The endless three hours before bed . . . I can't bear it.'

'Where's my cake?' screeched Crystal.

I turned my attention back to her. 'Sorry, darling, it fell on the floor. Yuck, it's all dirty now. Never mind. Let's play I-Spy instead. You can go first.'

Crystal's face folded in on itself, like an old lady who'd removed her false teeth. 'I – WANT – MY – CAKE!'

'Better go,' said Vicky, over the din. 'Yes, of course I'm on for tomorrow. See you there at eleven.' She snapped shut her mobile and turned round, the long-suffering expression on her face directed as much at me as at Crystal.

'Can't you just let her have the cake?' she said.

'No. Look at the state of it, it's all mashed. Here, can I give her some raisins instead?'

'NO RAISINS! CAKE!'

Vicky sighed. 'You can have some cake when we get home, sweetheart.'

'So, are you having an affair or something?' I asked casually, knowing that she wasn't, but not liking her having in-jokes with friends other than myself. Vicky looked gratifyingly horrified.

'Of course not! What on earth made you say that?'

I grinned. 'Well, what were you saying to Katriona then, that you were fantasizing about? Candles and music?'

'Oh, honestly, Anna, I was talking about having a *bath*. On my own, with no waterlogged starfish bean-bags or naked Barbies, or worse, slippery little children prodding and commenting on every inch of my body, and climbing all over me. I'm counting the minutes.' She laughed bitterly. 'An affair! As if I'd ever have the energy for an affair.'

In a sudden fit of rage, Vicky turned the radio up loud to drown out Crystal's yells. 'Up next we've got the Audio Bullys,' the DJ shouted at us, 'with a song called "Real Life".' Appropriate on both counts, I thought, as noise thrummed around the inside of the car, but Crystal merely increased her own volume accordingly. In a battle of wills, I thought, Vicky didn't stand a chance. She punched off the radio again.

'Steady on, Vic,' I ventured from the back. 'Listen, if you're feeling really stressed, why don't we go to a spa for the day sometime soon? Or maybe even a night or two. Grayshott Hall's lovely.'

Vicky snorted. 'Yeah right, like *that'll* really happen,' she said, and I didn't know whether she doubted I'd ever get it together to arrange it, or that Peter would let her go.

She pushed her foot down harder on the accelerator, and we shot through the deserted streets of the industrial estate, Crystal and I exchanging worried looks as we were rocked from side to side, the car screeching around corners, its front wheels banging up onto kerbs. I half expected her to start scattering dustbins and swerving up alleys, *à la* Starsky and Hutch. I reached out to put a tentative hand on her shoulder, which turned into a heavy clamp as I saw a teenage skateboarder wobble out of nowhere towards us.

'*Vicky!*'

'Mummy!'

Vicky stamped on the brake, swerving the car and narrowly avoiding the skateboarder. He swore loudly at her, giving her the finger whilst scooping up his board and slouching back onto the pavement, yanking at the belt loops of his outsized flares.

'Is there any chance that you could drive, Anna?' Vicky mumbled at me. 'I don't feel very well.'

'What's a fucker, Mummy?' Crystal asked, right before Vicky flung open the door, staggered out and vomited into the gutter. I scrambled out of the car and put my arm around Vicky's shoulders, holding her hair back from her face.

'I think I might be pregnant again,' she whispered to me, chalky-faced.

4

Back home, I felt lower than I had done for weeks. Vicky had sworn me to secrecy, at least until she'd done a pregnancy test and found out for sure – although she seemed pretty sure already. She'd almost bitten my head off when I had congratulated her, with a mixture of genuine and forced enthusiasm. I thought of the trapped look in her eyes.

'It would be a fucking *disaster*,' she'd hissed at me with such vehemence that I'd taken a step backwards and almost fallen off the kerb. I felt a thread of pure rage run through me. We'd parted on awkward terms, with her saying shortly that she'd ring me when she'd done the test.

I flopped down onto the sofa, phone in hand, and dialled Lil's number.

'Hello?' Lil always used to recite her telephone number as her opening gambit on the phone, and I missed her doing so. Nobody did it any longer, I mused. I wondered why not.

'It's me, Anna.'

'Anna!' I heard the smile in her voice, and instantly felt better. 'How lovely. How are you, darling?'

I paused, letting my eyes follow the pattern of the ceiling rose round in its ornate shabby circle. 'OK. Ish.'

'Is anything the matter?'

I began to wish I hadn't rung her – how could I say what was wrong without breaking Vicky's confidence? Instead I remembered the letter in my bag.

'I've had this letter,' I blurted, and told her all about Max and his dad, and how much I wanted to meet them.

'That's wonderful!' she said. I pictured her cradling the phone between her ear and shoulder, so that she could press her hands together; a gesture rarely seen in anyone other than of her generation. I'd missed seeing her do that too. 'I often wondered about who you gave that donation to, and whether you'd ever know. Of course you must meet him!'

I'd really like to restore that ceiling rose, and the cornicing, I thought idly. They had been painted over so many times that what had once been bunches of grapes were now just vague undefined bumpy shapes. If you stuck wads of cotton wool soaked with paint stripper onto them, that was meant to do the trick. But surely it would take weeks. And I found it hard enough to clean my own teeth most days, let alone take on a project that labour-intensive.

'Anna?'

I forced myself to answer. 'Oh Auntie Lil, I just can't.'

Without me having to tell her why I was so afraid, she understood. 'Is he still healthy?' she asked.

'Yes. But what if . . .'

'We're so alike, you and I,' she said. 'That's exactly what I would worry about, if I were you. It's the what-ifs that'll get you every time.'

'I want to know him so badly. But I don't want him to know who I am. And his dad didn't give their home address, just the college where he's a tutor. He teaches art classes, adult education. What would you do, if you were me?'

There was silence while Lil thought for a moment. 'Gillingsbury's not that far. Since you aren't working at the moment, why not go down there and ask for a meeting with the father, pretend that you want to enrol

44

in whatever art class it is that he offers. Obviously he's not going to start talking about his little boy there and then, but you could just – what is it called these days – *suss it out*? Maybe ask him where he lives? Oh, I don't know. I've always rather fancied playing detective.'

I laughed. 'That's a terrible idea, but thanks anyway,' I said. 'And besides, I've got that audition tomorrow. Who knows, I might be back in work soon.'

We didn't talk about Max after that, although I felt a lot better for having told Lil about him. It was as if he'd become a real little boy to me now, having Lil's magic breath blown into the sketchy frail body I imagined, like Geppetto animating Pinocchio.

'Break a leg, darling,' said Lil at the end of our conversation, and once again, I felt so relieved to have her back in my life.

'We'll let you know,' said the director the next afternoon, after I'd made a fairly poor attempt at a West Country accent, reading several pages of script for my screen test. I wasn't optimistic about my chances. Despite Lil's good-luck wishes, I'd found it hard to concentrate, although I wasn't sure if it was because I was out of practice, worried about Vicky, or – the most likely reason – because my head was filled with images of Max, like a grainy cine-film spooling through my mind when I ought to have been concentrating on the script.

They were clichéd images, I knew: in my imagination, Max wore a cowboy hat and fired a cap gun. He had freckles, like the Milky Bar Kid, although I gave him ginger hair instead of a blond thatch. Even though he wasn't yet five, he had an other-worldly wisdom about him. He appreciated life. He wasn't a bit whingy like Crystal, who moaned that her 'calflings' hurt if she had to walk more than ten yards. Vicky had to pretend to time her with the second hand of her watch to get her to walk anywhere: 'Right, from here to that lamp-post: Go!' and Crystal would then sprint off, leg pains miraculously vanished. In my imagination, Max never griped or behaved like a prima donna. He would be so used to pain after all his invasive treatments, I assumed, that he didn't have anything left to complain about.

Yes, OK, I knew this was unlikely. It was another reason that I really ought to meet him, I thought, so I could dispell these fantasies. Kids were kids. They all moaned; none of them was perfect. I wished Adam had put a photograph in the letter, so at least I wouldn't have had to imagine what Max looked like.

I was shocked at how badly I wanted to meet him. I could feel the longing in my empty womb; and it felt like negative space: a hungry space defined by my body surrounding it, like Giacometti's wiry sculptures of people with holes in their middles. Or like the redundancy of my hands without a buggy's handlebars to push.

Either way, it seemed a lot more important than a stupid audition.

I was in bed before Ken got home that night, worn out with the unaccustomed commute into London and the stress of the audition. It was a hot evening, and the bed had rapidly lost its initial appealing coolness. The duvet was pressing against me, so I stuck my leg out of the side, contemplating removing the quilt from its cover altogether, but feeling too exhausted to do so.

'Thought I'd find you here,' Ken said, coming into the room and sitting heavily on the bed to kiss me. He smelled like a photocopier salesman, of lager, trains and Xeroxed reports, and his mouth was warm and stale against my lips. I was pleased to see him, though, and tentatively reached out my toothpaste-fresh tongue to meet his. Perhaps I wasn't so tired, after all . . .

'Mmmm,' he hummed softly, kissing me back. 'I'm sorry I didn't get back in time for dinner. There was a leaving drink for Colin in promotions, you know?

The one who got caught with a topless temp in the conference room that time.'

'Oh right,' I said, not having a clue who Colin was, but deciding that since he had just left the company, there wasn't much to be gained from admitting so. Ken occasionally talked about his work colleagues, albeit in soundbites, and I always nodded and pretended I remembered who he was talking about. If I was entirely honest, I didn't even know exactly what Ken did all day, other than have a lot of expensive lunches.

'So what have you been up to today?' He stood up, peeled off his shirt and threw it towards the laundry basket in the corner. It missed, but he let it lie where it landed.

'I went into London for that audition. You know, for the soap.'

Instantly full of contrition, he paused in the middle of undoing his shoelaces. 'Oh, Annie, I'm sorry, I forgot. How did it go?'

'I don't know, really. The usual. But at least I wasn't nervous. I didn't care one way or the other, so we'll see. It films in Bristol, though, so I'd probably have to get digs there during the week.'

I waited for him to protest, but he didn't.

'Well,' he said. 'Ring me as soon as Fenella lets you know. By the way, you haven't forgotten about tomorrow night, have you?'

I looked blankly at him, frantically scrolling through a mental rolodex of upcoming events. 'Tomorrow . . . ?'

He sighed. 'The Cherries showcase. That band I signed a couple of months ago.'

My heart sank; yes, it was all coming back to me now. The Cherries: three nubile coffee-skinned girls with legs up to their nipples and a haughty air of cultivated superiority at the ripe old age of seventeen. I'd heard the demos and seen the Polaroids: they couldn't sing, but so what? They looked spectacular.

'It starts at six-thirty, so we should have time to grab

a curry afterwards, if you want. I don't think I have to do dinner with them.'

'What shall I wear?' I asked, out of habit, although I didn't know why I even bothered asking this question. Not once, in six years of marriage, had I ever received a serious answer. I so longed for Ken to frown, stride across to my wardrobe, pull it open and contemplate its contents. 'Let's see now, how about that lovely Whistles dress with your purple boots?' he'd say, and my dilemma would be instantly solved.

'Oh, go as you are. You look fine,' he said predictably, slipping his hand underneath the top of my Marks & Spencer's short checked pajamas. 'Maybe with stilettos too.'

He ran his other hand along my bare leg, which was still sticking out from under the duvet. I suspected that he was thinking about me in high heels. His fingers were working magic: thumb and forefinger tracing parallel tracks up and down my thigh in an almost abstracted way. It tickled, and made me shiver. I reached up and touched his face, looking with sympathy at the grey bags under his eyes and the way his thick black hair was sticking damply to his forehead. He'd aged so much in the past year. But then, so had I.

I pulled him towards me. 'You look as exhausted as I feel. Perhaps we need to wake ourselves up.'

He nuzzled into the space between my neck and my shoulder, clinging onto me in a way which was suddenly utterly non-sexual, as if he needed somebody to hold on to; as if I were his mother. I thought again of Max – why had his mother walked out on him? And his poor dad: Adam. Although maybe Adam had met somebody new by now. I hoped that Max got on with her. Could another woman ever replace the warmth of his mother's arms though?

'What are you thinking?' Ken was lying on top of me now, kissing my face, back in sex mode. He was sweating, but I felt slow prickles of arousal tingling my skin, like a distant memory of pleasure. We so rarely made love any more.

'Nothing,' I said, sliding my hand into his trousers and banishing Max.

We fooled around for a while in silence, but instead of getting more lost in it, I could tell that Ken was becoming less so. He hopped out of bed and peeled off the rest of his clothes and then, as if he needed the extra stimulus, rummaged around in the wardrobe (oh, if only he could do so when I needed his advice on what to wear!) and produced my highest and shiniest pair of stilettos. He reached under the duvet for my feet and crammed them into the shoes, before flopping back in bed beside me, smiling faintly with anticipation. Me wearing high heels in bed was his biggest turn-on. At least, of the turn-ons he'd admit to, anyway. I didn't mind, it *was* pretty sexy when you were in the mood.

I dragged my spiky heels dutifully along his chest for a couple of minutes, but I could tell that he was feeling anxious and unrelaxed again, and this in turn made me lose any desire I'd started out with. I tried to get it back for both of us, to *make* him want me: whispering sweet nothings, stroking him and kissing the prickly bit on the side of his neck, touching him – but his erection had vanished, and I felt faintly foolish, as if my touch was inappropriate and embarrassing.

'What's the matter, baby?' I said.

He instantly rolled off me, as if I'd given him permission to stop, and lay on his back, his arms crossed over his face.

'I can't,' he said, his voice muffled. 'I'm sorry. I just can't.'

'It doesn't matter,' I replied, but at the same time tears tightened behind my eyes. Suddenly I wanted to get out of that stuffy, sad bedroom. I kicked off the shoes, flung back the bedclothes, grabbed my dressing gown and ran downstairs, unlocking the back door and walking into the night air. It felt good to stand on the cold grass of the lawn, my hot bare feet connecting with the damp earth and the scratch of the patchy stalks.

I could hear the faint sound of rap emanating from the house whose garden backed on to ours. Must be coming from the teenage daughter's bedroom – her parents certainly didn't look the types who would be into a bit of Ja Rule, I thought vaguely.

I wondered if Holly would ever have got into rap. Would Ken and I have been the sort of parents to shout at her to turn it down, she was disturbing the neighbours? Or would we have remembered our own teenage years and the importance of one's small acts of rebellion and liberation: the covert cigarettes out of the bedroom window; the unsuitable outfits; the clandestine fumblings with the dozens of frogs necessary before you found your prince. If we did ever have any more children, I decided I'd prefer a boy. You didn't fear so much for boys.

Even as I thought this, I knew it wasn't true. Perhaps Ken was right, to be so scared of going through it all again. What if we did have another baby, actually succeeded in giving life, for him or her to develop leukaemia like Max had? There was no way we could go to another funeral with another small white coffin.

Ken came out and walked towards me, back in his boxer shorts. He put his arms around me and pulled me towards him. His skin was almost burning hot, and the thick hairs on his chest felt comforting.

'I'm sorry,' he said again. 'It's not that I don't fancy you, or want you. You know that, don't you?'

'I know,' I said. 'Don't worry.'

We stood in silence as the deep bassy thump-thump, ker-chink of the music floated over us and away into the cloudy night sky, more of a feeling than a sound.

5

By the following night I still hadn't heard from Vicky.
I'd left two messages for her, and, while it wasn't
unusual for her not to return my calls straight away,
I was worried about her. Her ancient answerphone
tape had stretched her voice on the message out to a
slow, miserable drawl which, illogically, seemed to me
another indication of her state of mind.

I'd go round there the next day, I decided, as I sat
with Ken in a reddish fug of backlit cigarette smoke, at
a small table on an empty balcony at his gig. My glossy
lips felt like flypaper, and I was leaving big sticky
prints around the rim of my cocktail glass. But at least
I was there, smiling brightly, being the dutiful executive wife.

Ken was talking to the head of Human Resources
from his office, who was small and blonde, and who
scrutinized me intently for signs of manic depression
(she'd sorted out the details of my post-natal bereavement counselling with the private health insurance
people, so probably felt she already knew me). While
they chatted, I thought: *This* is his real life, the
one which challenges and stimulates him, the one
where he's respected and admired, where people
routinely laugh at his jokes and feel honoured to
have lunch with him. Where he doesn't have to worry

about getting it up, or miscarriages, or dead babies.

This was the life where he had close friendships with at least four people, three of them women, with whose names I was familiar but whom I'd never met. Through throwaway snippets of overheard phone calls, and Ken's rare pieces of volunteered information, I knew about Corinne's commitment-phobic boyfriend, the fleas in Julie's eye-wateringly expensive carpets, and Marie-Therese's battle to give up smoking, but I wouldn't have recognized them if they'd passed me in the street.

I'd already asked Ken if they were coming tonight, but apparently none of them were. It was odd, I thought. For all I knew, any or all of them could have been madly in love with him. They certainly spent more time with him than I did.

It was boiling up on our balcony, and the tabletop was metal, cool and inviting-looking. I had a sudden urge to pull up my T-shirt and lean forwards on it, embracing its soothing metallic smoothness against my hot bare breasts. Imagining the horrified reactions from Ken and his employees made me smirk.

'That was a secretive little smile,' Ken said, signalling to the waitress to bring over more frosty drinks.

As soon as he said 'secretive', I thought of Max. Then I thought how strange it was that Max was a secret, when, logically, he shouldn't have been. Tell Ken, I told myself. It was only a letter. It both bothered and reassured me, the fact that he hadn't even asked why I was smiling secretive little smiles. What if I had had a secret? Not just Max, I meant, but a real, deep and sordid secret. A lover.

'Ken,' I began. The tone of my voice made him look cagily at me.

'Yes?'

'Do you believe that old Chinese saying, that if you save someone's life, you become responsible for them?'

But before he could answer, a tall, thin woman in a

brown suede mini burst onto the balcony, grabbed him, and kissed him effusively on both cheeks.

'Kenneth, darling! How *are* you? So glad you could make it – the girls were delighted to know you're here. You will come for sushi with us afterwards, won't you?'

'Hello, Shawna. This is my wife Anna. Anna, this is Shawna McKenzie, the Cherries' manager.'

I smiled as heartily as I could manage. 'Hello,' I said, and stuck out my hand, but Shawna had already given me my allocated nanosecond's worth of attention, and had gone to drag a chair away from the other empty table to join ours. She perched on the edge of it, leaning keenly forwards, her knees touching Ken's leg. They began a lengthy and involved chat about marketing budgets, of which, due to the loud R & B in the background, I caught only the odd word here and there: 'recoupable', 'royalty break', 'studio time'. I tried to listen and nod interestedly, but after a few minutes it was clear they'd forgotten I was even there.

As the tiny venue filled up and the noise increased, floating up to our balcony as if borne on the thick clouds of cigarette smoke, I stopped stressing about Ken and his impenetrable conversations, and drifted back to Max again, a far more pleasant subject.

How could I do it? How could I get to know him? All I knew is that I didn't want to go about it in the way that Adam would be expecting – a straightforward reply to his letter. I realized it was over-complicating matters, but I had to protect myself. I *had* to. If I was merely to write back, then it was obvious what would happen: we would start a self-conscious correspondence. Like in his first letter, Adam's every word would be infused with the knowledge that he owed his son's life to me. I didn't mind being responsible for Max – in fact, that was why I wanted to meet him so badly, to fill the emptiness in my hands and head and soul – but the important thing was that nobody else, including his dad, *knew* that I was now responsible for him.

After the self-conscious correspondence, which

53

would probably have been upgraded to email chats and maybe a couple of phone calls, we would inevitably make an arrangement to meet. In a café or a park, I expected; possibly – nightmare – in the presence of a photographer on behalf of the Anthony Nolan Trust, in whose quarterly magazine we would then feature; a small photo of the three of us grinning awkwardly. Then it would be there, in full colour, for everyone to see: I, Anna Sozi, was the person responsible for this child's life.

Perhaps to anybody else it would simply have been a source of pride, but for me it felt like an unexploded bomb. It was all well and good whilst he had pink in his cheeks and plenty of strong white blood cells, but who knew how persistent his disease might be? It could be hiding in the secretive shadows of his body, biding its time to emerge and take us all by surprise.

Then I'd have let him down, and everybody would be hurt. Including me.

I supposed the obvious solution was to just let it go. Tear up Adam's letter and get on with my life. I already had one small ghost haunting me, the brief wave of tiny furled fingers and struggle of walnut-sized lungs far stronger in my dreams than they ever were in her half an hour of real life. I didn't need another one.

But on the other hand, I honestly believed that in some strange way I *was* now responsible for Max. Obviously I wouldn't be able to swoop down to Wiltshire in my Superwoman outfit and materialize in front of him if he ever decided to chase a football into the street, but I needed to know him. So that if I ever could protect him in any practical way, I would. I'd saved Max's life. A part of me had settled into his body and made itself at home, and now he was alive, and healthy again after being ill for years.

I couldn't stop feeling, well, faintly *triumphant* about it. And then, immediately afterwards, guilty for gloating, and after that, terrified again. What if this was only a temporary respite for him? What if his body ultimately rejected the transplant, and he died? It would be the third time that I'd have caused another person's death, however indirectly.

I knew what Vicky would have said, if I could have brought myself to tell her about it all: 'Don't be so melodramatic. He's been given the all-clear, hasn't he? He's no more likely to die than the rest of us.'

But doctors weren't infallible, and children were such fickle and fragile creations, easily sucked under by the beckoning finger of the undertow.

'Oh, for heaven's sake,' Vicky would say. I heard her voice in my ear as clearly as if she had been sitting next to me. She'd point at Crystal, with her sturdy scabby knees and chunky crossed arms. 'Look at her! Fickle, yes. *Fragile?* Ha! You must be joking.'

Vicky, of course, had no idea how lucky she was, to have that sort of confidence. It was why I didn't want to tell her about the letter.

By eleven-thirty we were in a pre-booked black cab on our way home. I felt tired again, but not as unhappy as I'd felt the day before. Sometimes the very act of appearing 'up' in public had the knock-on effect of making me feel better for real. Ken was checking his emails on his BlackBerry and talking on his mobile at the same time, telling someone in LA what a huge success the showcase had been. I leaned against his shoulder and let the headlights of the oncoming vehicles blur and dance together. Eventually, with the series of beeps and chirrups which had practically become a part of my husband's vocabulary, an electrical extension of himself, he put away his gadgets.

'Are you OK, baby? What did you think of it?'

'I'm fine. I enjoyed it. They're great.' I thought about whether I really meant any of that. My T-shirt was sticking to my back, so I pushed the cab window down enough to let some of the sultry cloudless night into the taxi. As a blast of exhaust-scented air blew my hair out of my face, I decided that 'I'm fine' was debatable; 'I enjoyed it', true; and 'They're great', a patent lie.

For, in a way, I had enjoyed it. I'd enjoyed being out of the house. I'd enjoyed the glamour, and the sequinned hopes of the young band. These were the halcyon days for them, when everybody was making a fuss about their talent and their looks. When expectations were packed at their feet but without the pressure of results pushing down on top, like trying to close an overstuffed suitcase. The pressure would come later, when the single bombed or the album barely troubled the murky lower reaches of the charts – unless they were extremely lucky, of course. I was no expert, but something told me that this might well be as good as it was going to get for the Cherries.

It was, I reflected, a bit like being pregnant – for those fortunate women who'd never suffered miscarriages, at least – the blissful optimism, the plans, the excitement of it all. Once you were past the three-month danger zone and began to relax into it a bit more, faith in the outcome was what became essential. You knew, technically, that things could and did sometimes go wrong, but not for a second did you ever allow yourself to believe they would. Ken would never have sat down to a band like the Cherries and said, 'Well, I'm afraid you probably won't be all that successful. It's an impossibly difficult market and, actually, you aren't very good singers.'

Some women who'd miscarried babies were cautious and superstitious throughout their viable pregnancies, buying nothing except maybe a pack of plain white newborn sleepsuits, and then having to rush frantically around at the last minute, decorating nurseries and test-driving pushchairs. I had been like that for the first three months with Holly, but once I got the all-clear, even after what had happened before, I just didn't have it in me to hold back. I wanted to enjoy my pregnancy after the earlier miscarriages, and I did, even the shitty stuff: sciatica, nosebleeds every day for six months,

56

itchy shins. It had all been wonderful. I'd been so, so sure that Holly was the one – and she had been, I suppose, insofar as she made it full term.

The doctors hadn't known that Holly would not live; any more than Ken had any idea whether his band would be successful or not.

6

'Darling, it's me, Fenella. It's about your audition . . . So sorry, they've just rung to say that you were soooo close for Trina, but in the end they decided to go back to their original idea of having her as a redhead. The babies are gingery, I understand. Lord knows how they're going to manage with twins on set – I mean, what will they do for stand-ins? Anyway, I'm sorry, darling. Hope you're not too disappointed.'

'I could have worn a frigging wig,' I said, a dark mood stifling me like a mass of synthetic orange curls. 'I mean, that's the lamest excuse I've ever heard! *Hair* colour?'

I heard my agent spark up a cigarette, inhale, then exhale. I imagined the smoke billowing out of the receiver into my face and resisted the urge to cough. It was only ten o'clock in the morning and, as I lay in bed, I could still faintly smell the previous night's smoky club on my own skin and in my hair. The thought of it in my lungs made me feel sick.

'Well,' said Fenella. 'If you ask me, they knew who they wanted all along. I did tell them not to waste my time, or yours, but you know what the politics are like with these people.'

'Whatever,' I said. I pushed back the duvet and got out of bed, moving across the room to stand in front of the bedroom mirror in my pants, where I examined the faint silver stretchmarks on my belly. You could only see them in a certain light. 'So, have you got anything else for me at the moment?'

Another inhalation, a nicotine sigh. 'I promise you're top of my list if anything suitable comes up. How do you feel about doing panto this year?'

I could have cried. It made me shudder even to think of it: the forced jollity and fake fairy-dust, the thigh-slapping and stupid hats. The tedium of bad puns twice a day for two months.

I climbed wearily back into bed again. 'You know I loathe panto.'

'Yes. Just thought I'd ask, though. So that's a no, is it?'

'That's definitely a no. I'd rather be on the dole.'

After we'd said our goodbyes – mine somewhat grumpily – I rang Ken at the office to tell him that I hadn't got the job. But his voicemail clicked on, after what seemed like an eternity. I hated leaving messages on his machine, it was such a palaver: press '1' to do this, press '0' to terminate the call (why on earth wouldn't you just hang up, if you wanted to terminate the call?); listen to Ken himself running through a variety of options – i.e. ringing his secretary on this number, trying him on his mobile on that number. Then eventually, by the time I'd lost the will to live – or at least forgotten what I was ringing to tell him in the first place – I'd be offered the chance to leave a message. I hung up long before that. It was hardly important, after all.

The day stretched ahead of me as all the others did, with not even the promise of the distraction of work. No lines to be learned, no research to be done, no cast to meet. I didn't have the energy for a run. Lil had said she was going on a coach trip with her Women's Institute friends up to the National Gallery and, besides, I didn't want to get too reliant on her company now that we were friends again. I thought of visiting

59

Vicky, but then remembered that Thursday was the day she took Pat to his toddler group.

So I decided to get up and go for a drive instead. I liked driving, it was a great de-stresser. I hadn't left the house for ages after Holly, and had missed my car so much that once I was back behind the wheel again (Ken having discreetly disposed of the brand-new ladybird-print car seat), I found myself going out more and more. I could listen to CDs or the radio, and it somehow felt far more productive than doing the same sitting at home. I was covering miles, swallowing distance. And I admit, the first few weeks I went out there was more than a niggle of a self-destructive element to it: I was testing God. Or myself. If I pushed up to ninety along this stretch, what might happen? Might I lose control, spin over the central reservation? Would I care? Might it just be the easiest way out?

I felt that less now. I took fewer risks on the road, although that was mostly because I was afraid of causing death or injury to somebody else. Somebody who, unlike me, was a hundred per cent sure that they wanted to live.

I honestly hadn't set out to drive to Gillingsbury. I'd just decided that I needed a change of scenery, I wanted to get out of the house, and I had my Ryan Adams CD to listen to. The bottom of the M3 was only a couple of miles from where we lived, and I often drove down there – if you went against the traffic, the road was rarely busy, and the scenery wasn't bad, either. It was miles to the first junction, which I liked. No option but to keep going.

By the time I reached Fleet, I remembered – consciously, at least – that the M3 was the route to Gillingsbury. My mood had lifted a little: I'd had plenty of rejections in my acting career, and this was just another one; but the thought of visiting Max's town grabbed me under the armpits and hauled me right out of my slough of despond. Aunt Lil's words rang in my ears: 'You could just . . . *suss it out.*' It was the first time

I'd taken those words seriously. The idea really had seemed preposterous when she'd said it, so casually, but I found myself getting more and more excited at the thought of maybe meeting Max's father. How sad and empty was my life, I thought to myself, that this was so thrilling to me?

The first sign to Gillingsbury took me off the motorway and onto the A303. 'Salisbury 24, Gillingsbury 17', it said, and my left foot tapped with excitement against the floor of the car. There was a storm brewing to one side of me; the sky had turned an amazing lowering sort of yellow, and everything seemed so clear – I could see individual leaves on trees fifty feet away, and felt as if I was looking into the eyes of the reclining cows in the fields.

It took less than an hour and a half. The town of Gillingsbury lay in a valley, and as I approached it, I thought: Max is down there somewhere, with a part of me having rooted and blossomed inside of him, helping make him well again. The yearning to meet him was so strong that it was literally a hunger – my stomach rumbled with anticipation.

I stopped at a petrol station on the outskirts and asked directions from the man in the glass booth. It was easy, he said, handing me change for the two chocolate bars I'd purchased in the hope that they would take my mind off the nerves and the longing fluttering inside me: halfway around the ring road, then first left. It was another five minutes' drive to the college, by which time all the chocolate was gone.

With a cloying sweetness on my tongue and coating my teeth, I parked the car and got out, marching far more confidently than I felt towards the main reception.

Gillingsbury Adult Education College looked like most modern colleges seem to, as if the architect's brief had been to make the building look as anonymous and nondescript as possible. I couldn't pick out a single notable feature; it was more like a multi-storey car park

61

than a seat of learning. Yet somehow this reassured me: I was just an ordinary person going into an ordinary building. I had as much right as anyone else to be there: as much right as that elderly woman with fat arms bulging out of short sleeves over there, or that group of Middle-Eastern looking men sitting smoking on a wall, nudging each other and gazing at my . . . Damn! I glanced down at my clothes. Having not planned this impromptu expedition, I wasn't best equipped for it. I was wearing saggy black jersey trousers and a very small, very tight sleeveless fuchsia T-shirt, with no bra. I slung my bag over my shoulders – luckily it had a long handle – so that its strap covered one of my nipples, and self-consciously fiddled with my ear so that my left elbow hid the rest of my chest. The men snickered and muttered to each other.

I pushed through swing doors into a shabby, lino-lined lobby. A bald middle-aged man in a brown suit, with a bushy moustache and a polka-dotted bow tie, was standing behind a long countertop, behind which were a couple of desks sporting two old grey computers.

'Can I help you?'

Be strong, I told myself. You're an actor, you'll pull it off. 'Could I see a prospectus, please?' There was no law against walking into a college and enquiring about its courses, was there?

The man waved his arm expansively in the direction of a wobbly and uneven stack of A4 sized books on the floor behind me. I walked over and picked one off the top. *Gillingsbury Adult Education College*, it said in fat letters. *'Be all you can be!'* Inside were pages and pages of course listings, in tiny black script, mostly sounding fearsomely dull, or else in some kind of arcane code: EFL with IT, TESOL Certificate Training, BCS ECDL. There were a few intriguing ones too, I noticed, particularly on the General Interest page: *Classic Roasts, Haircutting for Children, An Introduction to Geology, Street Dance for Beginners, Intermediate*

Parchment Craft . . . In a moment of escapist madness I had an urge to register for everything under General Interest, but then I remembered why I was there. I sat down on a polished wooden bench, like a church pew, and quickly scanned down through the subject headings until I found *Art and Craft Department*. Page 117. I flipped through to the right page, and saw a small black and white photograph of an earnest-looking man sitting at a potter's wheel, his palms embracing the wet clay. For some reason it reminded me of the way Ken had shaken my hand when we first met. I supposed I *had* been like putty in his hands.

I wondered if the picture was of Adam. It didn't say, but looking down the listings I found A. Ferris next to several courses: *Life Drawing Beginners*, *Life Drawing Intermediate*, *Basic Pottery*, and *Mosaics for Beginners*. They were all daytime courses, starting at different dates in September – there were evening classes in the same subjects, but taught by a P. Rumbould. Adam must turn down evening work so he could be there for Max, I thought, my chest swelling with a completely unjustifiable pride. I just knew Adam was a good dad.

Oh, stop being so ridiculous, I countered. For all I knew, Adam kept his evenings free to indulge in his coke-dealing activities or run his lap-dancing club. But somehow I felt that I was right.

I went back to the man with the bow tie. He had begun to eat a very messy tuna salad sandwich, and was reading the job section of *The Guardian*.

'Excuse me? I'd like some more information about some of these courses.'

'Which ones?' He took a large bite of sandwich, dropping a blob of grey tuna onto the lapel of his jacket.

'Um. The art ones. The daytime art ones.'

I had to wait a few seconds while the man chewed exaggeratedly, jabbing a forefinger towards his mouth to indicate that he wasn't able to respond just at that moment. Eventually he swallowed. He hadn't noticed the spillage.

'I beg your pardon. If you'd like to take the second left along that corridor behind you, you will find the Art Department. The departmental secretary's name is Pamela Wilkins. She should be able to help you with any questions.'

'Thanks,' I said, glad that Adam taught arty subjects and not something nerdy and complicated like Applied Maths or Computer Aided Technology. As I walked off down the corridor, I couldn't help but feel excited. That secretary knew Adam. May even have met Max. I slowed my pace, to give myself time to think of what to say.

I put my head around the open door of the Art Department. It was a big, messy room, covered in a grey film of clay dust. Scarred melamine-topped tables were arranged in a horseshoe formation around the edge; charcoal nudes and some abstract tapestries hung on the walls – rather good, I thought, not that I was any judge of artistic merit. I couldn't draw the most basic of dogs without it looking like a donkey.

There was nobody about, but just as I stepped inside I heard brisk footsteps behind me in the corridor. I hadn't really given it much thought, but I supposed if anyone had asked me, I'd have imagined that the secretary of an Art Department would be small and slight, elfin, and would waft around distributing pastels and putting away paintbrushes, dressed in a variety of floaty, probably crocheted garments in hues of rainbow.

Pamela Wilkins, of course, could not have been more different.

'Are you looking for me?' she cried heartily. 'Sorry. Just popped out to the little girls' room.' She pushed past me through the doorway. 'Come in, come in.'

I surveyed her, impressed at how any woman could care so little for her appearance. She was about four foot two, late forties, perhaps, with thick stubby legs and enormously wide hips, across which a fantastically horrible bright blue pleated and patterned nylon skirt sat, a good six inches higher round the back. She had long dull black hair, a visible, almost luxuriant black moustache, and wore not a scrap of make-up. I suppressed a vision of her leaping naked through a bluebell field, paintbrush in mouth, hair whipping around her head, stopping every now and then to daub colour onto a large canvas nearby . . .

'If you're Pamela Wilkins, then yes, I'm looking for you. The man on reception suggested I come and talk to you about the art courses.'

'Ah, poor Wilf. Yes. I'm sure I can tell you anything you need to know about this place – been here for twenty-eight years, since it was first built, I have. People say that I must have been dug in with the foundations! Dug in with the foundations!'

Her foundations did indeed look extremely solid, although it seemed an odd thing for 'people' to say. I suspected that she had coined the phrase herself. I also felt like asking her why Wilf was an object of pity, but decided not to push my luck straight away. There were other, more pressing things I needed to know.

'Right. Well, I'm a total beginner at art, but I quite fancy something practical – mosaics, maybe?' I had no idea what one might make out of mosaic. Lamp bases, perhaps, or maybe that was a bit ambitious. I quite liked the idea of smashing plates and reassembling them in different formations – there seemed something so gloriously pointless about it.

Pamela nodded vigorously. 'Yes, yes, the mosaic courses here are excellent. Excellent. I mean, all the courses we offer are very good, but an outstanding teacher really makes all the difference.'

I felt strangely joyful. 'What's the teacher's name?'

'Adam Ferris.'

Questions bubbled up in my throat, and I had to swallow them firmly back down. There was no reason that the departmental secretary would know much about Adam's private life. Still, there was no reason she wouldn't, either.

'Has he taught here for long?'

Pamela's face lit up, and instantly I knew that she was exactly the right person to talk to about Adam. I sent a silent thank you winging its way to Auntie Lil – it could not have been easier.

'Several years now, since his little boy was born . . .'

Bingo! She couldn't wait to tell me, conspiracy was collecting in the corners of her mouth and in the sideways, excited look in her eyes. Maybe my naked need to know was dragging the information out of her, like a magnet's pull.

'How old's his little boy?' I asked innocently. Reel her in, Anna, I thought.

'Nearly five now. Adam's really been through it with him. Terrible time, he's had. But he's almost five now.' She had the really irritating habit of repeating the same information in a slightly different way.

'Why? Is he badly behaved or something?'

She looked shocked, as if I'd blasphemed. 'Oh goodness no, he's an angel. Angelic, he is. No' – she lowered her voice – 'he nearly died. He was in and out of hospital for two years. Leukaemia, it was.'

I tutted. 'That's terrible. But he's OK now?'

Pamela beamed. 'Fit as a little fiddle. You'd never guess he'd been so ill.'

'His poor parents,' I said, hopefully.

Again, I hit the target, bull's-eye. As Pamela opened her mouth to spill the beans, I wondered if she was this indiscreet about the private lives of all the art faculty. But she must have realized the same thing at the same time, because her lips clamped shut again, and my window of opportunity closed.

'So, anyway, I would thoroughly recommend the Beginners' Mosaics class. Eleven until one o'clock on a Tuesday.'

'Right,' I said. 'What kinds of things would we make?'

'Whatever you like, really. Most students do small

pieces at first: tiled photo frames or mirrors, or perhaps tissue boxes. Whatever you like.'

I could think of few items less appealing than a tiled tissue box. *'That's* lovely,' I said, pointing at a beautiful mosaic tabletop in the corner of the room.

I hadn't noticed it before, and walked over to examine it. It was circular, with symmetrical patterns of broken flowery china embedded in swirling, flowing lines which seemed almost fluid. The china was minty green and sugary pink on white, colours which would probably look horrible to eat one's dinner from, but were fresh and vibrant when rearranged, like atoms, into different patterns.

'I'd love to make something like that.'

Pamela frowned and shook her head. 'We-ll, that's a piece that one of our more advanced students has just completed. I think you'd have to talk to Adam about doing something so ambitious, I'm not sure whether he'd think it suitable for a beginner.'

'I could ask him. Might there be a chance to speak to him before the start of the term? Are there spaces left on the beginners' course?'

Pamela swayed across to a shelf at the side of the room, her hips grazing table edges as she passed them. She reminded me of the Queen of Hearts in *Alice in Wonderland*. She'd have looked perfectly natural with a large tricornered wimple affair strapped under her chin.

'Yes, I think there are still a few spaces. And I'll just have a look at the diary, to see when Adam's next in. You could ring for a chat.'

'I don't suppose I could have his home number?' Maybe Max would answer the phone, I thought longingly. But I'd pushed too far.

'Oh no,' Pamela said, in a more shocked tone than I felt strictly necessary. 'We never give out staff telephone numbers. Now, let's see . . .' She flipped through the pages of a large desk diary, liberally smeared with dried clay thumbprints. 'Adam, Adam, Adam.' She said his name so tenderly that I almost laughed out loud. If this woman wasn't in love with Adam Ferris, I'd eat that lump of plasticine on the table next to me.

'Yes. He'll be here doing some course preparation next Tuesday. Give him a ring on this number. I'll tell him to expect your call, shall I?'

She waited, pen poised above the rectangle of diary space. For a moment, I couldn't think what she was waiting for. 'Could I have your name please?'

Panic. Name. I couldn't say Anna Sozi, obviously . . . 'Anna Valentine,' I said, giving my stage name, unable to prevent a deep blush spreading across my chest and up into my face. Some actress I was! But I'd be better prepared next time. I'd make up an address and give my mobile number and—

Wait a second, I thought. *Next* time? For the first time I realized that I was actually giving serious consideration to the possibility of enrolling on one of Adam's courses. No matter that it was over ninety miles from my house. That I was only doing it because I wanted to meet the tutor's four-year-old son. That I couldn't tell my husband otherwise he'd think I'd gone off my head. That I'd therefore have to lie about where I was going every Tuesday for weeks on end . . .

All I could think about was how excited Auntie Lil would be when I told her that I'd actually done it.

7

Getting home again took a lot longer. There must have been an accident on the motorway, because the London-bound traffic suddenly slowed to a five-mile-an-hour crawl, and I found myself stuck behind a Volvo estate with two bored children strapped into the rear-facing seats in the boot, making hideous faces at me out of the back window. It was remarkably difficult not to keep catching their eyes, since they were directly in my line of vision, so I tried to switch off, letting thoughts trail through my mind: what Max looked like; how Vicky would cope with another child; whether I'd ever get a job; whether I *wanted* a job; if Ken and I would ever have sex again . . .

As I looked to my left – the children were now pointing at me and squealing with laughter – I noticed a road sign to a village whose name sounded familiar. I couldn't work out why for ages, until eventually I remembered that when we were first together, Ken had taken me to a hotel there.

He'd still been with Michelle then, his first wife. Michelle was his PA from his first Marketing Director job at Range Records. She was younger than him by six years: twenty-two to his twenty-eight. She'd wooed him and flattered him, even though for two years – by his own admission – he had treated her like dirt, dating other women but keeping her hanging on. Then something had changed. I still wasn't sure what; maybe she'd just worn him down. She was American, and didn't take no for an answer, whilst being sensible enough to realize that ultimatums would cut no ice with Ken. He didn't like to be pressured.

They ended up getting married. She'd managed to persuade Ken that she would make the perfect wife for a career man such as himself; but within six months he said he realized it had been a mistake. She'd given up work the second he'd proposed, and seemed to do nothing but play tennis, spend his money, and try to organize his life the way she'd organized his appointment book when she worked for him. It was she who'd first got him into his tennis obsession – he probably only learned because he hated anyone being better at anything than he was.

Michelle was there the first time Ken and I ever met. Vicky and I had both been in a production of Arthur Miller's *All My Sons* in Reading, and Ken and Michelle had come for the weekend, visiting Ken's mother. Michelle had talked Ken into coming to the theatre – I could just imagine the complaint: 'We never do anything cultural!' – and I grudgingly respected her for managing that, since Ken was just not a theatre sort of person. He still didn't come to many of my productions.

It was the last night, and Vicky and I were in the bar afterwards with the rest of the cast. Ken and Michelle were sitting at a small table in the corner of the bar, her with her back to me.

'Check him out, he's gorgeous,' said Vicky, nudging me and jerking her head in his direction. 'Bet you I can pull him.'

I looked. He was lovely. 'What's your definition of "pull"? A date, a phone number, a snog?' I asked. I knew she wasn't serious – she and Peter had only recently got together, but there was nothing she loved more than a good old flirt. 'Besides,' I added, 'he's with that blonde woman.'

At that moment, Ken caught us staring at him. He looked straight at me, and even from across the room I could see how thick his eyelashes were, that his hair was black and shiny as a top hat, and his skin the burnished brown of a conker. His features were perfect, apart from a smile-shaped scar that ran from the left corner of his mouth to under his cheek. It reminded me of the punctuation mark in an old-fashioned hymn book, the one under the end of a line to tell you to keep singing without taking a breath. I was instantly dying to know how he'd got it, but managed to contain my curiosity until our second date. I was sure that everyone else always asked him about it, and I didn't want to be like everyone else. (He was bitten by a Jack Russell dog when he was eight. He still hated Jack Russells, which was a shame, because they were about the only sort of dog I liked.)

I smiled at him, and he smiled back. His smile made my stomach flip, and Vicky poked me with annoyance. 'Oi! I saw him first.'

'You're spoken for,' I said dreamily.

'So is he, by the look of things,' she commented, as Michelle got up and tottered out of the room, heading for the Ladies.

Ken had immediately sauntered towards the bar, carrying their two empty glasses. Vicky looked at my love-struck face and sighed. 'Oh, go on then,' she said grudgingly. 'Your need is greater than mine.'

'Well,' I said, draining my own glass and standing up. 'I *am* quite thirsty.'

I arrived next to him just as Crispin the barman took his order. Ken was the sort of person who always got served straight away.

'Hello,' he said, beaming at me again. 'I'm Ken. You were brilliant. Can I buy you a drink?'

'Thanks. I'm Anna. White wine please,' I said, half to him and half to Crispin, who gave me an unsubtle wink. I took Ken's outstretched hand and didn't want to let it go again. His handshake was like a hug, the way he cradled and embraced my own hand.

'Do you live in Reading?' I managed, instantly cursing myself for asking such an inane question. I could see Crispin smirking as he poured out the drinks.

'No. My mother does.'

'Don't tell me *that's* your mother,' I joked, jerking my head in the direction of the Ladies. 'That would mean you're actually about twelve.'

He laughed. 'That's my – um – wife,' he said. 'So I will completely understand if you tell me to get lost, but, are you ever in London? I'd like to take you for lunch.'

Just the way that he said 'take you' made me feel like all the muscles in my thighs had been removed. But – wife? The gorgeous ones were always married. Still, at least he hadn't tried to pretend he was un-attached.

'And I suppose your wife doesn't understand you,' I said, swallowing my disappointment.

'Too well,' he replied, handing over the cash for the three drinks. 'She understands me only too well.'

Arrogant swine, I thought, as I watched his 'under-standing' wife fight her way back through the throng. She wore her matching gold handbag and high shoes like a protest: look at me. They were too old for her. She reminded me of a five-year-old dressing up in her mother's clothes. Except that no five-year-old could ever apply lip pencil with such precision.

'Darling, I was just telling Anna how good we thought she was,' he said, handing her one of the glasses of wine. Michelle regarded me with thinly veiled suspicion.

'Yes,' she said. 'You were very good.' Her American accent made her sound even more sarcastic than she intended, or so I believed. She was beautiful, with an immaculate blonde bob and cheekbones you could grate cheese on, but her wrinkle-free eyes were cold. I disliked her immediately. 'Thank you,' I said, nodding politely.

Ken reached into his jacket pocket and extracted a business card, which he handed to me. 'I don't usually get involved in this sort of thing,' he said, and for a second I wondered what he meant. 'But I'm working with a new singer who's about to make a video for his first single. It's kind of country-rock, only more hip: the guy's name is Dwight Unsworth. Baz Lurhmann is directing, as a favour. Anyway, I happen to know they're looking for an actress to play Dwight's girlfriend in the video. They've got a very specific look in mind, and I know you'd be perfect for it. Call me if you're interested, and I'll pass on your name to Baz. Nice to have met you.'

There was that lovely warm hand again, briefly squeezing mine, and he was gone. Michelle, eyes narrowed, glanced back at me as she moved away behind him. Her expression was, very clearly, 'Try anything with him and you're dead.'

I pushed my way back to Vicky, who had been trying to lipread the exchange.

'Married?'

'Oh yes. Also just asked me to lunch, and then if I'd like to star in a Baz Lurhmann rock video.'

Vicky snorted. 'Yeah, right! While his wife was standing there? The nerve!'

'No. He asked me to lunch before she got back. They clearly aren't happy together; it's written all over their faces.'

'You're never considering it!'

'I am. He's gorgeous. And Baz Lurhmann? I'd be mad not to follow it up, at least.'

She laughed, knocking back her vodka and tonic. Several people turned to see where the honk was coming from – Vicky's laugh had always been a source of embarrassment to the faint-hearted.

I remembered how beautiful she had looked then, her long curly brown hair falling over her shoulders as she tipped her head back. Her skin had been so pearly in those days, before she had children. It was much more crêpey now; desiccated, almost. Her laugh lines have taken up permanent residence as wrinkles, and all her features seem to have drooped. But in the bar of that theatre, I couldn't believe that it wasn't her whom Ken had gazed at and come on to. She had a much smaller part in the production than I did, but she'd really shone. She was so natural.

There are certain actors who should be phenomenally successful, and you just can't understand why they aren't. Vicky, in her day, had been more gorgeous than Gwyneth Paltrow and a better actor than Kate Winslet, but she'd never made it. She won a Laurence Olivier award for Most Promising Newcomer in 1992, and we all thought, Go girl, you're away, Hollywood beckons, but it had all been downhill from then on. She'd recently cut the top half off the blue sequinned dress she wore to the award ceremony, and given it to Crystal for her dressing-up box, which I thought was terribly sad.

None of us ever did make it: neither Vicky, nor I, nor any of the others on our course at Reading University. A few minor successes – mine being a starring role in a Dwight Unsworth video of a song which went to Number One (yes, Ken's offer was kosher, and yes, I got the part. And more) – but nothing to set Broadway alight. It could be a soul-destroying business, if you let it rule your life. Which was partly why I had always wanted children so badly, so that the acting wouldn't have to be the sole focus.

The traffic had advanced approximately half a mile. The children were still gurning at me, and I needed the toilet. A tourist board sign on the verge of the motorway said Carnegie Manor was half a mile away, confirming that it was the same place Ken had taken me to that time.

I remembered how I'd felt when he brought me there. We were in his company BMW, I had new underwear on, and an old joke rattling around my head:

'What's the difference between a BMW and a hedge-hog?', the answer being: 'With a BMW the pricks are on the inside.' I kept thinking of it, chortling to myself, opening my mouth to share it with Ken, then closing it again as I realized how he might not appreciate it. He probably thought I looked like an insane goldfish.

Still, it didn't prevent him undressing me with his teeth on the thick old-fashioned counterpane of a huge double bed in an attic suite, with a view over the beautifully manicured grounds – not that I saw much of *them*. We'd smoked sly joints out of the creaky casement windows, and hadn't left the room all day. Neither of us mentioned Michelle's name all weekend, although I did have one thing to say on the subject:

'If you ever cheat on *me*, I'll kill you.'

'It's a good thing I have no intention of doing so, then,' he murmured, and for some reason I believed it. I'd never stopped believing it, either – Michelle and he had just been wrong for each other, it was as simple as that. Ken and I were meant to be together. We would grow old and die together; I was sure we would. Hopefully with a few children around, but even without.

One other thing I remembered about that weekend at Carnegie Manor: we'd had our first argument there. Not, as I might have anticipated, about Michelle or his infidelity but, of all things, about meat. It came from nowhere, at the end of a blissful day. It was clearly a defence mechanism on my part, because it happened just when I was beginning to realize that this was the man I wanted to spend my life with.

It started with the steak. We went down for dinner, and I had almost retched to see the great hunk of rare beef on his plate. It seemed to be still practically quivering with life. I managed to hold my tongue and avert my eyes throughout the meal, trying to con-centrate on my delicious pumpkin ravioli, but felt sicker and sicker each time I inadvertently caught a glimpse of Ken's knife piercing the meat, and the blood running out, staining his dauphinoise potatoes a delicate pink. By the time we got back to our room, I couldn't bear to let him kiss me. I suddenly panicked, thinking that this was symptomatic of our relationship; that it was tainted, dead like meat on hooks in an abattoir before it had even had a chance to live. The row blew up out of nowhere, a small furious typhoon out of a clear blue sky.

'What's the matter?' he'd said when I pulled away from his embrace.

'Nothing,' I replied unconvincingly.

'What? Are you tired? Have I worn you out?'

I shook my head. 'It's not that.'

'What then? Don't tell me I've got B.O. Or does my breath smell?'

'That's getting closer to it.'

I still remembered the look of hurt on his face. He cupped his hands and huffed into his palms.

'It's not you, exactly. It's just . . . that steak.'

'The steak?'

'Yes. I should have told you earlier but I didn't want to spoil your dinner. I'm vegetarian.'

'So? I was eating it, not you.' I heard a tone of aggression spring into his voice.

'I know. I'm sorry, I just find it hard to cope when I see people eating raw meat.'

'It wasn't raw.'

'Well, near as dammit it was.'

He tsked, and headed for the bathroom. 'I'll clean my teeth then.'

I followed him in, watching as he unzipped his washbag and extracted his toothbrush and a tube of Colgate. I hated myself, but I couldn't stop: 'Colgate contains glycerine, you know. That's usually animal derived. And it's tested on them too.'

Ken glared at me. The mood was definitely gone. 'So what am I supposed to do? Clean my teeth with my finger?'

I smiled and handed him my own tube of Nature's Own toothpaste. 'Borrow this, if you like.'

'Are you always like this?' he growled.

'Like what?'

'So . . . sanctimonious!' He finished brushing his teeth. 'Ugh. That tastes like shit. But at least my teeth are clean. And here, look, I'll even squirt on some more of this stuff if you're that worried about the smell.' He sprayed a generous blast of his aftershave around his neck.

'Actually,' I'd said piously, 'a frequent ingredient of perfumes and aftershaves is castorium, which is the anal sex gland of a farmed beaver. And another ingredient you'll find often used as a fixative is ambergris, which is made from a whale.'

Now he was really annoyed. His neck turned dark red, as if reacting to the aftershave, and he swung around to face me. 'Are you *trying* to wind me up? If so, it's working. I'm going to bed.' And he marched out of the bathroom, slamming the door so hard that one of the round glass ceiling lights broke and came crashing down, raining splinters of glass on top of me, in my hair and clothes and around my stockinged feet.

I stood there, shocked and marooned, but somehow resigned. Yes, I had been trying to wind him up. At first I hadn't been able to think of any earthly reason why, after the blissful day we'd spent together. Then I realized: he was married. I was testing him, trying to make him cut his losses before we all got in too deep. More than likely, he'd never leave his wife, and the whole affair would be the sorry mess that Vicky had predicted. What had I been thinking?

After a few minutes, the bathroom door slowly creaked open again. Ken appeared, wearing a hotel bathrobe and his outdoor shoes. With his bare, hairy shins completing the picture, I couldn't help smiling at him. He crunched across the sea of glass shards towards me.

'Stand still,' he said, tenderly brushing glass out of my hair with his fingers.

'All gone?'

He nodded, and picked me up in his arms.

'I'm so sorry,' I said, burying my face in his towelling shoulder as he carried me out of the bathroom and laid me on the bed like a princess. 'I was being a total pain in the arse. I don't know what came over me. Must have been the drink.'

'I hope you aren't always like this when you're drunk,' he said softly, undoing my suspenders.

'No. I'm not, I swear. And for what it's worth, I really like that aftershave,' I mumbled, as his hand crept up my inner thigh.

'I'll tell you something, shall I?' he whispered back to me.

'What?'

'That delicious red wine we just drank two bottles of probably had gelatin in it – it's used as a clarifier in the wine-making process. And it may well have contained cochineal, too, which is—'

'Yeah, yeah, I know,' I said, shame-faced. 'It's crushed beetle. What can I say? I'm a sanctimonious preachy cow *and* a crap vegetarian. And I wear leather shoes. So could we please pretend that the last ten minutes never happened? I promise I'll never protest again when you want to eat steak.'

Two hours later, we were drifting off to sleep in each other's arms, warm and sated and comfortable once more. I was almost away when I felt Ken's finger tap my shoulder. 'Hnngh?' I mumbled.

'"The anal sex gland of a farmed beaver"? That was a joke, right?'

I laughed drowsily. 'No. 'S true.'

'Wow. I wonder how they discovered *that*?'

He didn't stop using aftershave, but from that day on he never again ordered steak in my presence.

8

The following Tuesday at the exact time prescribed by Pamela Wilkins, I dialled the number of the main switchboard of Gillingsbury College. It was engaged. I imagined Poor Wilf eating his sandwich and not bothering to answer the switchboard. I redialled. Still engaged. I took a deep breath. Hit redial again. Engaged again.

In front of me on my desk at home I had a post-it note with my stage name on it: Anna Valentine, and a made-up address: 27 Field End. I had looked at streetmap.co.uk and decided against selecting a real road from there, just in case it turned out to be close to Adam and Max's house. Gillingsbury wasn't a big enough town to take that risk. I made up a name and checked it against the index on the map, to make sure that I hadn't picked somewhere which was actually an industrial estate or a dual carriageway. I then decided that Field End could well be situated in a small village on the outskirts of Gillingsbury – there was a place called Wealton which looked as though it would do. I just hoped against hope that Adam didn't live there. Still, I had Plan B in mind – if questioned about the address, or if there was even the slightest murmuring of recognition of Wealton – 'my brother runs the pub there' – I'd decided to announce, smoothly, that it was

only temporary and I'd soon be moving to a new flat
. . . It didn't really occur to me until later that unless
Adam himself lived at 26 Field End, Wealton (unlikely,
since it was a fictional address), he probably wouldn't
shriek, 'No way! That's incredible! *I* live there!' In my
entire life, no teacher or professional person had ever,
when asking me my address, volunteered any kind of
personal information pertaining to the revelation of it.

Which in itself was another problem. Even if I
enrolled on his course, did I expect Adam suddenly
to start talking about his son, for heaven's sake? Of
course he wouldn't. I imagined him showing us how to
use tile-cutters, or what colour grout to apply to the
finished design (I'd once seen a demonstration of
mosaics at an art fair), and then casually announcing,
'My son Max's life was saved by a bone-marrow donor,
you know. Would you like to come and meet him?'
Yeah, right. What had I been thinking? The only way I
would ever get to know Max would be by forging some
kind of extra-curricular friendship with his father. And
I'd never even met his father.

The line was still busy. 'Come on, Wilf, you idle git,'
I muttered.

The whole thing was insane. Yet the more I thought
that, the more something in me – stubbornness,
probably; a desire to make such a ludicrous scheme
work; or maybe just a fatty streak of adventure – felt
compelled at least to attempt it. I reasoned with myself
that if Adam was eye-wateringly ugly then he'd be
grateful for my attentions, and if he was breathtakingly
gorgeous, it would be all the easier for me to flirt with
him.

All the while dialling, getting the engaged tone,
and redialling instantly, I pushed aside the nagging
persistent voice in my head reminding me that this
wasn't really very nice of me. I was content in my
relationship with Ken, despite everything we'd been
through, so there was absolutely no way I'd end up
letting Adam *seduce* me or anything – I'd just have to

use my acting talents judiciously and expertly to ensure he realized that I just wanted to befriend him . . . Actually, I hoped he was ugly. I wouldn't have wanted the temptation of flirting with some broad-shouldered crinkle-eyed love-god. It was a pity that he was unlikely to be gay, given the circumstances – I decided I could have done with a nice gay friend. It wasn't impossible – perhaps the shock of Max's mother leaving had sent him over to the Other Side. Or perhaps she'd left *because* he was gay! That would have been ideal.

Dial. Busy. Hang up. Redial. It had become automatic, a background sequence, its tinny percussive beat accompanying my daydreams. I realized that probably the only reason I was thinking all those thoughts about Adam was because the whole thing was so unreal. Despite his letter to me, and his name in the college prospectus, and Pamela's cow-eyed infatuation with him, Adam Ferris was a figment of my imagination. Or a 'fig leaf' of my imagination, as a girl at school had once said. I pictured Adam as Michelangelo's David, executed in turquoise mosaic on a panel in my garden, with said fig leaf of my imagination protecting his modesty. The fig leaf would be done in nice dull green chips of tile. Ken would ask what on earth it was doing next to the shed. 'It's my new hobby,' I'd tell him proudly . . .

The line was ringing. I was so distracted by my flight of fancy that I hardly noticed the change in tone, and had to stop myself from automatically continuing to hang up and redial.

'Gillingsbury Adult Education College. *Could* you hold the line, please,' said Poor Wilf, in the long-suffering tones of an overworked martyr. Before I got the chance to reply, something which approximated Mozart's Requiem performed on a stylophone filled my ear. I tutted impatiently. Adam would probably have gone home by the time I finally got through.

'How can I help you?' said Poor Wilf eventually. If

Pamela Wilkins was the Queen of Hearts, Poor Wilf was the froggy footman, I decided.

'I'd like to speak to Adam Ferris in the Art Department,' I said, as bravely as I could.

'Just a moment.' More classical music being tortured on an instrument with very small keys and an on/off switch.

'Art Department?'

My throat went dry. It felt more nerve-racking than the opening night of a theatre run. I decided that it must have been the deception of it. Despite being an actress, I rarely did anything under false pretences – mostly because I was too frightened of the consequences. 'Is that Adam Ferris?'

'Yes. What can I do for you?' He sounded lovely: cheerful without being overly hearty. I instantly pictured chunky knits and moccasins like Cornish pasties; and reminded myself that I was doing nothing wrong. Just a touch of deviousness, that was all.

'I'd like to enrol in your beginners' mosaic class,' I said boldly. 'But I wanted to make a tabletop out of bits of old plates—'

'*Pique assiette*,' Adam commented.

'Pardon?'

'*Pique assiette*. It's the name of the technique for making mosaics out of found objects, particularly broken crockery. It means stolen plate. Sorry. Do go on.'

'Right, well, anyway, your secretary thought I should talk to you about it first. She thought it might be too advanced for me.'

'Well,' said Adam, 'provided you weren't thinking of an eight-seater dining table with a design of Roman soldiers out hunting, executed in an exceptionally intricate pattern of micromosaic, I don't see why not, but . . .'

'Oh great,' I gushed, although even if he'd said, 'the beginners' project this term is mosaicking your grandmother', I'd have started mixing up grout on the spot. I felt so close to Max, even just by speaking to Adam. And I knew that Adam would turn out to be easy to befriend; he had one of those easy-listening mellow voices. Nobody bad could have a voice like that . . . For the first time, I hoped he wasn't upset by my lack of response to his letter.

'Unfortunately,' he said apologetically, 'there's a problem. I'm afraid all my beginners' classes are completely booked for next term. There's a waiting list for the daytime ones.'

I was floored. I hadn't anticipated that at all. 'What?' A poxy little adult education college, oversubscribed? Didn't the residents of Gillingsbury have better things to do than spend hours sticking bits of broken tile onto boards? Now how the hell was I going to meet Max?

I nearly gave up. I nearly decided, Oh well, if I wanted to meet him, all I had to do was to write back, officially, as Anna Sozi. It was simple. We'd meet. I'd even let the Anthony Nolan Trust take my photograph with him . . .

But it was the idea of that photograph that made my insides freeze up. The notion that, like Anthony Nolan himself, photographs might one day be all that was left of Max's childhood, and that my contribution would have turned out to be futile after all, like all the babies lost and their lives unrealized. I couldn't do it. I couldn't risk it.

It took every ounce of self-control I possessed not to sound desperate. Why hadn't the Queen of Hearts warned me that this was a possibility?

'*All* of them? No places on any of your courses? I mean, it doesn't have to be mosaic, I just want to do something creative. You do pottery, don't you?' The words began to slip away from me, out of control like wet clay whirling unchecked on a potter's wheel. *But I want to meet Max!* I fumed inside my head.

There was a brief silence at the end of the line, and I reined in my emotions with difficulty. Adam's nutter-radar was probably screeching at him, I thought. You always got nutters on adult education college courses. He was bound to think I was one.

'I'm sorry. Courses do get booked up very early, and the last few places on all my courses have just been taken.'

Perhaps it was not meant to be. Now there was a phrase I sorely overused, I thought hollowly. But Adam was saying something else.

'However, if you're interested in creating mosaics—'

'Yes, I am,' I interrupted eagerly. There was a beeping at my end of the line, puncturing Adam's words, breaking them up like coloured tiles. 'Sorry. My call waiting's going off. Could you hold on a minute please?'

'No problem.'

I quickly switched calls. 'Yes?'

'Who are you nattering on to, babes?' It was Ken.

'Oh. Ken. Listen, can I call you back. It's – um – Fenella.'

'OK. I'm about to go into a meeting but if you ring me—'

I switched back before he could finish. 'Sorry about that.'

'No, I was just saying, if you'd like to get involved in a mosaic project, I'm organizing a big community mural. It's to go in the underpass by the station, you know?'

'Oh, yes,' I lied.

'Well, anyone's welcome. We'll be doing it for the next few weeks, until term starts. Longer, if I can get a commission for three more panels, which, hopefully, I will. It's free, you just drop in. It's a great way to learn about the basics – tile-cutting, design, backgrounds, et cetera.'

'Brilliant,' I said, punching the air with my non-phone fist. 'Where?'

'Moose Hall on the Devizes Road.'

'Er, I think I know it.'

'Opposite the turning into Queens Drive.'

84

'I'll find it,' I said confidently. 'Thanks.' Something occurred to me. 'And – um – will you be there every day too?'

'Most days,' he said, sounding amused. 'What's your name? I'll look out for you.'

I cleared my throat. 'Annavalentine,' I gabbled, to try and prevent him even thinking Sozi.

'Right. Excellent. See you there, I hope. And I'm sorry about the college courses. Do you want to go on the waiting list? People do sometimes drop out.'

'No. No, it's all right, thanks. But I will come down and help with the mural though.'

After I'd hung up from him, I couldn't stop beaming. It was perfect. I screwed up the piece of paper with the fake address on it – no hassle with college registration, no risk of being checked up on. All I had to do was turn up and meet him. Plus, since it wasn't a formal class, there would probably be far more opportunity for chat. It would have sounded weird to ask the teacher about his family life in the middle of a lesson, but surely not at all odd to bring it up in a more social situation. And – be still, my beating heart – wasn't it still the school holidays? Max himself might quite likely be there!

I felt so excited and happy that I had to go and stand on my head for ten minutes, to try and calm myself down.

9

Getting pregnant had not been easy for me. That glib chat you sometimes heard: 'Blah blah, first night of our honeymoon, not even trying and, whoops! We conceived!' That was so not us. And that was why Holly had been such a miracle – she'd really lasted the distance, staking her claim in what I had come to believe was the inhospitable and – metaphorically – chilly expanses of my uterus. All the other potential babies –' or, as the doctors called them when they were about to hoover them out of me: 'the remaining products of conception' (a phrase which made 'embryo' and 'fetus' sound positively warm and unclinical) – had given up far more easily.

The first miscarriage was fine, because I hadn't even known I was pregnant. I just thought I was having a particularly heavy period, and it was only with the later ones that, in retrospect, I realized what had gone on. The second was bad: eight weeks, and I'd done the positive pregnancy test three weeks earlier. Ken and I had had three whole weeks of euphoric planning and celebrations, Ken revelling in his newly proved virility: 'I am All Man!'; me greedily and reverentially shopping: fingering great big stretchy trousers with huge elasticated panels in the front of them as if they were being displayed in some designerwear Mecca instead of

Mothercare, actually looking forward to the time when I'd legitimately be able to wear such monstrosities. Then came the bleeding, a little at first, just enough to worry but not panic. 'Some women bleed all through pregnancy,' said the doctor, and I thought, That must be nice for them. Not.

Two more days of polka-dot spotting, furtive and panicked late-night phone calls to NHS Direct so as not to worry Ken, an inconclusive scan, and then, *wham*, the mass evacuation. Fleeing for the emergency exits without stopping to collect possessions. Matter-of-fact but revolting talk by doctors of clots, and the reality, the even more revolting lump of what looked like grey shivery liver coming out of me like a deformation, an accusation.

Gross as it was, though, I wanted to keep it. I knew what it was: 'the remaining products of conception', and what would surely have become my child, a living breathing human being, had things been different. I wanted to put the lump in a matchbox and bury it in the garden, with a little cross made of ice-lolly sticks marking the place – anything would have been better than flushing it down the toilet with as much respect as you'd give a belly-up fairground goldfish. I made the mistake of telling Ken that I wished I could have done that, but he didn't understand. Didn't want to think about it, I suppose. Ken was the world's most squeamish man. Anything involving more than a bead of blood was enough to turn him green. He couldn't even watch medical dramas on television; so the knowledge of a medical drama in his own downstairs loo was just too much to bear. He was at work, anyway, when it all unfolded.

He'd been away at a conference when I had my third miscarriage. That was the worst one: eleven weeks, when we were just teetering on the cusp of believing that everything would be OK, that this one was tenacious, clinging on with its minuscule fingernails to the cliff face of my insides. We'd even begun to believe it was not only clinging on, but thriving, blooming like a desert rose. And then, out of the blue, there I was again, examining bits of toilet paper and crying over the tell-tale signs. The doctor saying, 'It's a bit sad . . .' his words tailing off into nothing as if he realized that the gross understatement of them could hardly be a comfort. The craven panic which threatened to overwhelm me when I even considered this happening again. I had to have hypnotherapy before I could face having sex – and that was *before* Holly.

Poor Ken took that third one really badly too. He kept saying how he couldn't forgive himself for not having been there for me, but really, what could he have done? In a way I was glad he'd been spared the ordeal – God knows he later went through enough with Holly. But it was around then that our sex life took such a dramatic nosedive that it was a miracle Holly managed to get herself conceived at all.

It was just before Holly's conception that I gave the bone-marrow donation. In retrospect I wondered if it was all part of a divine plan; if maybe that was why I had the third miscarriage. If I'd carried that baby to full term, then I wouldn't have been eligible to make the bone-marrow donation – pregnancy precluded one from donating. Then perhaps another donor wouldn't have been found for Max, and he would have died.

I couldn't help feeling that my would-be baby, the one before Holly, gave up his or her life for Max. It really had helped, to think that. But it also made the urge to meet him even stronger.

The actual bone-marrow harvest hadn't been too bad. Not what you'd call a pleasant experience, and my lower back had been stiff for weeks afterwards, but not agony or anything. In a weird sort of way it felt like an atonement, like I was saying to God, If I've done something wrong, and that's why my babies keep dying, then I'm sorry, and perhaps if I do this for a stranger, then please can I have a baby who'll stay?

I remembered coming round in the hospital after the

operation, lying on my stomach, pain coming in waves from the small of my back, but with enough drugs in me to be able to objectify the discomfort: regard it as something happening to a different person – the pain didn't go away, it just felt attached to me via a hazy umbilicus of unconcern. It was a strange sensation. Anyway, of all the various medical indignities I had been subjected to over the years, the bone-marrow harvest had definitely been among the most minor. It wasn't as bad as the d. and c. I had after miscarriage number three.

I had to confess that I didn't think much, at the time, of who my bone marrow would end up in. I hadn't even given much thought to the prospect of saving a life, apart from a brief swagger of pride when we'd first registered. It had just seemed the right thing to do. Vicky and I had both been on the Anthony Nolan Trust register of would-be donors for years, since we were at university. An aunt of Vicky's had died young from leukaemia, so Vicky and I had gone along to our local GP and given a blood sample to send to the Trust. I remembered sitting in the waiting room with her, giggling at the 'Beware of Sexually Transmitted Diseases' poster and flipping through old copies of *Cosmo*, waiting so long that we got bored and went to play with the train set on the floor in the corner, great hulking nineteen-year-old students crouching over the battered wooden carriages and mismatched pieces of track, earning us a ticking-off from the receptionist and much tutting and head-shaking from a coughing old lady in the corner. But we'd felt far too virtuous to care. Look at us, I'd felt like proclaiming. We're not here for our own benefit, you know, we could soon be saving someone's life! But it hadn't seemed real, then; more like a game.

Neither of us had heard from the Trust again – in fact, I'd almost forgotten that I was on the register until they had approached me two years back saying I was a potential donor for an anonymous leukaemia sufferer. Max could have been anyone, male or female, old or young, from any corner of the globe. It was another small miracle, I reflected, that he ended up living less than a hundred miles from me.

And that there I was, driving down on a hazy early August morning to that place to meet his father, and to help stick bits of broken tile onto a board. I wondered again if Max was going to be there too.

Part Two

10

Despite Adam's directions, Moose Hall was far more difficult to find than the college had been. Perhaps because I had expected a large impressive edifice, with at the very least a stuffed moose head trophy outside, I drove past it at least four times without seeing it.

Moose Hall – the name reminded me of a book from my childhood, some surreal story about minced moose-meat, or maybe moosed mincemeat? Odd how gruesome that sounded as an adult, when it had been just funny words to me as a child. A bit like Shock-headed Peter, I mused, as I drove like Miss Marple, nose an inch from the windscreen, peering at the houses along Devizes Road. *Struwwelpeter*, to give Shock-headed Peter its correct untranslated title, was full of hideously frightening tales of girls being burned to ashes after playing with matches, or boys having their thumbs cut off for sucking them. You'd have thought it would give a child nightmares. But perhaps a child didn't attach any significant meaning to the words. They were just words, and pictures. They had no resonance or impact on the things which really mattered to them: family, television, toys, sunshine.

I thought of Max, and how nightmarish much of his own short life must have been. I hoped he had just seen it like the words of a frightening story – something to take in his stride, to let wash over him. Perhaps he succeeded in making his own reality, of chemotherapy, needles, pain, exhaustion, no different to reading about minced-up mooses or thumbless and bleeding story-book children.

Hell, where *was* that bloody hall? For a brief moment I wondered if it had all just been a story too, a yarn Adam had spun to get rid of me, the madwoman on the telephone desperate to be creative . . . If so, I'd swallowed his fairytale as easily as a child would have done.

I pulled up next to an old man walking a toffee-nosed hairy little dog.

'Excuse me,' I said, through my open car window. 'Do you know where Moose Hall is, please?'

The man barely glanced at me, but instead gazed back in the direction I'd just driven from. 'Down there, on the right.'

I was puzzled. 'I just came from there.'

He shrugged. 'On the right. Down there.'

'Thanks,' I said, and pulled away. I must have been too busy thinking about minced moosemeat and chemotherapy to spot it. I did a three-point turn and drove at five miles an hour back the way I'd come, craning my neck at all the houses on the right-hand side of the street.

There it was, after all, in the middle of the terrace. I couldn't believe I'd missed it, although it wasn't at all what I'd been expecting. It was one of those tiny, neglected Victorian halls that every town seemed to possess, uncared for and tucked away. The grimy paintwork was flaking off the front in huge jagged strips, and the once-impressive portico over the door crumbling and dangerous. An easel with a large wrinkled sheet of paper pinned to it stood outside the front: 'Mosaic Workshop – Open to All', it said in faded crayoned letters.

I found a parking space and squeezed into it, and,

taking a deep breath, walked up to the heavy wooden door and pushed it open.

I registered the children first, four or five of them, racing around the hall in a blur of skinny legs in shorts, brandishing felt-tips at each other and fighting over a chocolate biscuit. My heart nearly stopped – which one was he? Which one was Max?

A woman yelled: 'Orlando and Spike, stop it! Millie, give Spike his biscuit back. And you, Petra, stop being such a troublemaker. If you can't all work quietly, you'll have to go home.'

No Maxes. In a way, I was relieved – I didn't think I could have handled meeting him with no preamble like that. The prospect of introducing myself to Adam was nerve-racking enough. I did another quick scan around the hall, to try to identify Adam. There were three men present: a rather good-looking black man in tiny denim shorts, an older, softer, balding man with a small beard, and a rake-thin hippy with three rings squeezed into one hole in the side of his very protuberant nose. He looked like a misplaced Dickens character, and had the faint air of surprise to go with it; as if Uriah Heep had been forced into a Little Feat T-shirt and couldn't figure out why. They were all wearing white stick-on name badges, but I was too far away to read what they said.

A trestle table in the centre of the room was covered with a large board, at which the men, plus four or five women, were working. Boxes and boxes of tiles lined the walls of the room, all shapes and sizes and colours, some already broken into pieces, most whole. Dust and chips of tile carpeted the worn floorboards, and the children's shouts mingled with the sharp crack of tile-cutters.

On another, smaller table near where I stood were plates of sandwiches with curled-up corners, a tin of Rich Tea biscuits broken like the tiles, and a bowl of sugar with several teaspoons left in it, staining the sugar brown with stirred tea. Beth Orton's plaintive, tremulous voice was wavering out of a boombox, and a kettle rattled and steamed on the floor nearby, warming my shins with its fresh boil. That's dangerous, I thought, with those children tearing about. I had to suppress an urge to move the kettle to a safer place.

The woman who had shouted at the kids detached herself from the group of adults and came over to greet me in the doorway. At first I thought something traumatic must just have happened to her, because her mouth was open in a pained sort of rictus as if she were walking into a particularly biting wind. But when she spoke, she seemed perfectly normal.

'Come to help?' she asked, far more cheerfully than her appearance suggested, and I nodded. She was younger than me, I saw, hippyish but not offensively so. She wore a lot of heavy amber jewellery, her long straight brown hair was shiny, and her teeth white. It was just that expression which made her look a bit unfortunate.

'I'm Serena,' she said. 'Let's get you signed in, and then I'll introduce you to the gang. What's your name?'

'Anna,' I said. 'Anna, um, Valentine.' I watched as she wrote ANNA on a sticky label, peeled it off, and handed it to me on her fingertip, where I duly stuck it above my left breast. I signed the clipboard she held out to me, adding my fake address, glad that I'd had the forethought to make one up, even if I hadn't thought I'd be needing it.

'Ooh, you live in Wealton?' said Serena, looking at me with what appeared to be respect. 'It's lovely out there, isn't it?'

I panicked, momentarily. 'Well, I haven't been there long but, yes, it certainly is lovely.' I supposed I ought to have been relieved that she hadn't looked puzzled and said something along the lines of, 'So, what's it like living right next to the nuclear power station/sewage plant/maximum security prison?'

Please don't ask me exactly where in Wealton, I

prayed silently. But she had already turned and was gesturing me to follow. 'Come and meet everybody else.'

When we got to the work table, one of the men had disappeared, and I saw from their name badges that neither of the other two was Adam.

'This is Ralph,' confirmed Serena, nodding towards the black guy. He waved and smiled at me, brandishing a pair of tile-cutters, before replacing the plastic goggles he'd pushed back on his head, and breaking a terracotta tile into quarters with two efficient cracks. 'And this is Paula, Mary, Margie and Mitch.'

I instantly mentally rechristened the last three Mary, Mungo and Midge. Midge – Mitch – was the hippy, and somewhat belatedly I realized that he was sticking out a dusty hand for me to shake. 'Hi,' I said, smiling brightly, taking it. 'I'm Anna.'

There was an awkward silence. Mitch really was almost disturbingly ugly. His hair was a pale gingery colour, long and wispy, and his nose dominated him as though it had been intended for a different and bigger man's face. His lips were so thin they were non-existent, and the rings in the side of his nostrils looked scummy at the edges.

Just then, a shaft of sunlight came through one of the dusty skylights, illuminating the partially completed mosaic.

'This is amazing,' I said, in Ralph's direction. 'Did you do this little girl skipping? You've captured her expression perfectly.'

Ralph looked pleased. 'Thanks. Adam and I did it together.'

'Adam's the man in charge, isn't he?' I fished. 'Is he here today?'

'Yes. He was here a minute ago. Where is he?'

So that had been Adam. The older, softer one. I felt a second's stab of disappointment, overtaken immediately by the thrill of having seen Max's dad.

One of the women – Paula – lifted up her head. She

was the only one wearing a protective mask, and when she spoke her voice was a little muffled.

'He's just popped out for some milk,' she said. 'It's his turn to make the tea.'

I noticed then that she was very pregnant, her belly huge and high and round inside baggy dungarees. My heart sank, and I dropped my gaze to study the panel of mosaic.

It was beautiful. Like a sort of flawed miracle, in fact. I was amazed at the way that the barest of sketches in charcoal on the baseboard just sprang to life in the finished coloured sections. A woman sitting on a bus, watching a girl skipping outside, fish in a pond, birds flying in a ceramic sky, the yolky whorls of a yellow sun. I couldn't believe that such detail had been created just from clumsy shards of broken tile. For the first time since I'd arrived I actually briefly forgot about Max, and was consumed with a desire to contribute towards this brilliantly coloured yet fractured world.

'It's fantastic,' I breathed. 'Are all of you experts at this? I've never done it before; I hope that won't be a problem.'

'Nor had I,' said Mary, who was a neat middle-aged woman in a stripy chef's apron. Her hair, although beautifully coiffed, was covered with a thin layer of dust. I thought what an extraordinarily disparate bunch of people they were.

'You get the hang of it really easily,' added Margie, who was younger, with a Dutch accent.

Serena handed me a pair of plastic goggles, which I self-consciously donned. 'I'll show you how to use the cutters,' she said, passing me a pair. 'You place them on the edge of your tile, at a ninety-degree angle to it, and just press. Don't put them too far over the tile or it'll shatter. Do it over a tray so we don't get bits of debris in the picture. And if you want to make a circle, just "nibble" around the edges, like this.' She demonstrated, and then gestured for me to try.

I picked up a red tile, applied the cutters, and

pressed. Nothing happened. I pressed harder, and it broke into about fifteen pieces in my hand. 'Never mind,' Serena said. 'That's the joy of it – we can always use different-sized pieces. Just put them in that box over there.'

'Who wants tea, then?' said a voice from the back of the hall.

I turned, and there he was. Max's father. Coming towards me holding a two-litre bottle of milk and with a broad smile on his face. 'Hello,' he said enthusiastically. 'A new recruit, excellent! I'm Adam.'

I felt inexplicably weak at the knees. 'Anna Valentine,' I managed. 'We talked on the phone.'

'Yes, of course, I remember. Great that you could make it.'

When I looked at him close up, I saw that he wasn't as old as I'd thought – late thirties, perhaps. It was just the fact that he was balding and very slightly paunchy that had given me that impression. He wasn't exactly good-looking, but his remaining hair was ebulliently curly, he was strong and broad-shouldered, his eyes were astonishingly blue, and his smile was one of those joyful ones to which you couldn't help but respond. It hurt my heart, knowing how much pain there must have been in there, but then I felt a little ashamed at my deception. I oughtn't to have been privy to that kind of information, not without announcing my identity. It was voyeurism, in a way. I was already watching Adam, without him knowing.

'Hello, Anna,' he said now, putting the milk down on a bare section of the mosaic board, next to a half-finished overalled builder leaning on a charcoal sketch of a shovel. 'Nice to meet you. Where did you say you lived?'

I looked him straight in the eye and pretended that he was my lead man and that we were on stage at the Crucible. 'I'm new to the area,' I said without flinching. 'I'm just renting a little place in Wealton.'

'Lovely,' Adam said, in the same slightly reverential

99

tone as Serena had. I thought, I must drive out there and have a look at the place. I appeared, inadvertently, to have chosen well.

'I trust Serena's shown you what to do?'

'Well, she's told me how to do it. Which bit should I start on?' It seemed presumptuous, to think that I'd ever be able to add anything creative to such a beautiful mural.

Adam pointed at an empty corner of the board, which had a rough sketched outline of a basket with what looked like a baguette sticking out of the top of it.

'Can you do that shopping basket? You'll need two different browns, and if you cut pieces about the same size, you can lay them in alternate colours to look like the weave.'

Where's Max? I longed to ask. But instead I nodded, and valiantly took up my tile-cutters.

Two hours later, my right thumb was aching and stiff from cracking tiles, and my hands scratchy and speckled with grey adhesive, but I had woven my very own brown tiled basket. I felt inordinately proud of it – it even *looked* like a basket! But it was made of bits of tile! I was surprised at how thrilling it was, watching it clumsily emerge within the smudgy black lines on the hardboard.

I didn't say much at first, just speaking when I was spoken to, but I listened intently to as much of Adam's conversation as I could. He was on the other side of the table putting the finishing touches to a pond with a beautiful rippled surface, so I didn't get much of a chance to talk to him directly and, unfortunately, Ralph and Mitch had rather unsubtly worked their way around towards me and were competing shamelessly for my attention.

I realized with hindsight that my over-enthusiastic smile had perhaps been a mistake. Mitch was gazing at me with undisguised lust and, at one point, when I glanced in his direction, he lost concentration and cut his finger on a shard of red tile intended for the side of the bus he was working on. At least that got him out of the way for a while, as Mary bore him off to find a big enough plaster to staunch the flow of blood.

I'd thought that this would be my chance to talk to Adam, but, seeing a window of opportunity, Ralph slid in instead. He was a very handsome man, but something about him rather disturbed me. His shorts were, frankly, unsettling enough – so brief that they resembled a pair of denim Speedos; but even more so was the intensity of his conversation. Within half an hour, I had learned that his wife had left him for another man; that he was having problems paying his mortgage; that his youngest child had glue ear and grommets and his oldest child thought the marital break-up was his fault (at that point I wondered if the shorts would be used against him in court as evidence); and that he played golf with a handicap of nineteen. All without drawing breath. My head was reeling with the effort of trying to nod at the appropriate junctures, whilst eavesdropping on Adam's murmured chat with the women on either side of him, and simultaneously trying to cut regular rectangles of beige and brown tile for my basket. It wasn't easy, what with the Beth Orton tape in the background and the children's intermittent piercing squeals as they squabbled over pens and biscuits.

Just when I was beginning to think there could be nothing left that I didn't know about Ralph, he excused himself. 'Just going for a jimmy,' he said.

'Where's he going?' asked Margie, puzzled. She had shown no interest in anything Ralph had said up to that point, so I was beginning to get the impression that the other women had all been through this compulsive-disclosure thing with him already. It was probably some rite of passage that everybody working on the mosaic had to endure.

'For a jimmy. A Jimmy Riddle. It means he's going to the toilet,' I explained, my voice feeling faintly rusty with the lack of use since Ralph had been banging on.

'I don't understand. Why does that mean he's going to the toilet?'

'It's cockney rhyming slang. Jimmy Riddle equals piddle. Pee.'

'Oh,' she said, looking none the wiser. 'I do not understand your English expressions. I would be terrible on *Who Wants to Be A Millionaire*, I think. I would not be able to answer the really easy questions. They had one the other day: "It is raining cats and – what?" I thought the answer was ducks. That was for one hundred pounds, and I would have been out.'

I started laughing, and when I looked up I saw that Adam was too. I thought how much more attractive he was when his face relaxed and his eyes creased at the corners.

'I knew somebody called Jimmy Riddle once,' I said, cracking some thinner pieces of tile for the basket handle. 'He didn't even call himself Jim or James. Just Jimmy. He was a plumber, too, so maybe he did it on purpose.'

Everybody laughed at that, even Paula, the haughty-looking pregnant one. I felt myself relax, and realized that I was enjoying myself.

'So what do you do, Anna?' Adam asked, just as Mitch, Mary and Ralph all arrived back at the table. Mitch had a bulky bandage around his finger and a tiny little boy sucking a dirty thumb trailing behind him, holding onto the edge of his Little Feat T-shirt.

I opened my mouth to tell Adam that I was an actress, when Mitch thrust his injured digit into the centre of attention. Blood was already beginning to seep through the white gauze, and I worried that it might drip on my basket. 'I'd better call it a day, guys,' he said mournfully. 'It won't stop bleeding. Think I might need a stitch or two. So me and Spike will head off. See you tomorrow, yeah?'

'Bye, Mitch, bye, Spike,' everybody chorused, trying to appear concerned.

Another child sidled up to the table, his small pointed face so dwarfed by the huge plastic safety goggles that he looked like the personification of a bug-eyed grasshopper. He pulled at Mary's sleeve. 'I'm hungry, Mum. C'n I have a sandwich?'

Mary looked at him with exasperation. 'Orlando, you had an enormous breakfast, and you had three biscuits less than an hour ago. You'll have to wait.'

'I'm hungry too,' added a chubbier dark-haired girl who appeared behind him. 'And we're bored doing colouring. Can we stick some tiles on?'

'Only if you wear the goggles, Petra, I'm afraid,' said Adam. 'We can't risk you getting a bit of tile in your eye.'

'Is she yours?' I ventured to Adam, trying to sound natural.

'No. She and Millie are mine,' Serena interrupted. 'Orlando's Mary's son.'

It felt too contrived to press on and ask Adam if he had any children. I hoped he'd volunteer the information so I could legitimately ask him about Max, but he didn't say anything further. I was just going to have to be patient.

But patience was not a virtue with which I'd ever been over-endowed. The next time there was a break in the conversation (some time later, when it was Ralph's turn to make the tea) I said to the general assembled company, 'So, are all your kids still on summer holiday?'

Paula laughed. 'I can tell you don't have children, then. There're weeks to survive before term starts!'

I can tell you don't have children.

For a moment I was almost felled by grief, cracked into a dozen sharp pieces. I couldn't reply. I couldn't even breathe. It always got me that way, out of the blue. Maybe she could tell. Maybe they could all tell that I was here under false pretences. It had nothing to do

103

with not being aware of term dates. It was to do with my fucked up Tefal-lined womb that nothing and no one would stick to. They could feel my failure like an airborne virus, leaching out and mingling with the dust in the air . . . No wonder Paula was standing over the other side of the table, I was probably subconsciously giving off Dr Death vibes that she could feel as a threat to the perfect child inside her, waiting contentedly, curled up and kicking. It was bound to be a beautiful healthy baby – after all, most women had that sort – and an almost murderous jealousy settled on me, taunting me with fingers of blame. It was the most basic, instinctive thing in the world. In fact, practically any woman could do it. You didn't have to be smart, beautiful or successful to give birth; just screw at the right time, sit around for nine months eating pastries, then open your legs and push. It was a doddle.

But *I* couldn't do it.

'Are you all right?' Adam asked, and the concern in his voice was almost the final straw. I felt my knees begin to buckle, and I dropped the tile-cutters onto the table, chipping an edge off Paula's tiled street lamp.

'Fine,' I managed. 'Sorry, I – er – I'll be back in a minute.'

I turned and, trying not to run, walked unsteadily towards a door by the stage with a sheet of A4 paper sellotaped to it, bearing the word 'TIOLET' written in a childish hand in different shades of felt-tip pen. Tiolet, like violet, I thought vaguely. A much more attractive word than toilet. I pushed open the door and found myself in a short corridor, with another, open door at the end leading to the aforementioned 'tiolet'. I squeezed in and sat down on the toilet seat, shaking. It was a shabby room with pipes running up the flaky maroon-painted walls. Marbled drops of red in the tiny cracked basin in the corner indicated that this was where Mitch's finger-bandaging operation had taken place.

The air in the little bathroom was infused with a

not-unpleasant scent that I hadn't smelled for nearly thirty years, but which came back to me immediately as soon as I breathed in, a welcome distraction from the pain in my head and heart: it was the exact smell of the cages I used to keep my hamsters in when I was a child. The memory felt like an unexpected gift; I remembered how much I'd loved those tiny light balls of fluff with their shiny eyes and caramel-coloured fur.

I put my head in my hands and thought of my dad giving me the hamsters for Christmas, remembering his glee at my reaction, and then I thought what a terrible shame it would be if Ken never became a father. Despite his excessive working hours (although, who knew, perhaps a baby might be reason enough for him to cut back on the work commitments), he'd be a fantastic dad.

Suddenly I wanted to go home. This was futile, ridiculous. Running the taps in the sink first, to rinse out Mitch's bloodstains, I washed the tile and cement dust off my hands, and splashed my face. Then, taking a deep breath, I walked back into the hall.

'Sure you're all right?' Adam asked again.

I pretended to look surprised. 'All right? Yes, of course, I'm fine.' I looked exaggeratedly at my watch. 'But I'm afraid I'm going to have to shoot off now – I didn't realize how much time had passed.'

'You will be back again soon, won't you?' asked Ralph plaintively, and I nodded.

'Yes, I've really enjoyed myself.' That much at least was true. I felt a very satisfying glow of having accomplished something for the community. OK, so it was only a tile basket, and it wasn't even my own community, but that didn't seem to matter. Secretly, I didn't think for a moment that I *would* be back, the preposterousness of the situation once more settling on my shoulders almost palpably, like a heavy snowfall, but no matter. Not really. I hadn't met Max but at least I knew that Adam was – unless I was an utterly terrible judge of character – a good man and a loving father.

There was nothing really to gain from meeting Max. He couldn't replace Holly or the others, and I really ought to have been looking forwards, not backwards.

I said my goodbyes to the group, and Adam came over to shake my hand. His own felt large, dusty, cracked and hard, and I thought, Those are the hands he hugs Max with. He looked me in the eye and said, like he knew there was more to it than a desire on my part to crack tiles: 'I'm sorry we didn't get a chance to talk properly. I do hope I'll see you again.'

I smiled until my cheeks ached and nodded enthusiastically, waving behind me when I got to the door and carolling more 'byees' to everyone; but as soon as I got outside the fake enthusiasm fell away from me like a discarded overcoat, my shoulders slumped, and I felt the corners of my mouth droop.

I wished I'd never gone there.

11

I wept most of the way home, steady tears dripping into my lap. The tears weren't just for Holly – it would have been Dad's birthday that day, a fact that I'd managed to push to the back of my mind in the earlier excitement of meeting Adam.

I tried to calculate how old he'd have been, bearing in mind that he died when I was eighteen, in 1986, aged fifty-two, but I couldn't make my brain do the maths. I couldn't bear to think of us all having a jolly birthday party round at Lil's, probably, with Olly and Russ, and a lavish birthday cake; Dad sucking at his pipe and grumbling mildly about his advancing old age, reading his cards and smiling. It hurt.

'You're a user, Anna,' I said out loud. 'It's your fault he's not alive.' A large bug crashed and exploded on my windscreen, and for a moment I wished myself into similar instant oblivion. I hadn't plunged a bread knife between Dad's ribs or anything, but I was haunted by the thought that I might just as well have done.

My father had died immediately after he found out that I was having an affair with his best friend Greg. He'd had a heart attack in the pub in Harpenden, the local that he and Greg always frequented. It was called the Fox and Goose, a dingy place with brown walls and sticky purple lino, which seemed to have Whitesnake perpetually on the jukebox. It wasn't that either Dad or Greg liked Whitesnake particularly – Greg was into Prog Rock, and Dad had been more of an Acker Bilk man – but they had been drinking there so long that they probably ceased to notice the dubious music years before.

Greg had taken Dad there that night to break the news that he was in love with me. They'd have been at the small table in the corner; Greg would have been smoking Silk Cut, squeezing his eyes shut, inhaling each drag deeply from the side of his mouth and drinking chasers with his pints; whilst Dad stuck to bitter and tinkered with his pipe, laying out all the pieces of pipe-smoking paraphernalia on the table in front of him, but rarely touching a match to the tiny bird's nest of tobacco in the cherrywood bowl.

I wish I could have stopped time right at that moment; rushed in and put my hands over Greg's mouth to hush him up, so that I could be driving home for Dad's sixty-whateverth birthday do now, instead of replaying the scene over and over in my mind as I'd done for the last sixteen years . . . I would so love to be celebrating Dad's birthday with him.

He would almost certainly have been wearing his habitual stay-press slacks with the knife-edge creases that day, either his mossy green ones, or the bilge brown: the uniform of most dads up and down the country until well into the eighties, before Gap began its rapid ascent to world sartorial domination. Greg would, doubtless, have been in his jeans. It was the fact that Greg bucked the trend and wore jeans which had made me fall in love with him in the first place. The jeans and the cigarettes had set him apart from all the other fathers, tricking me into believing that he was on my wavelength, blinding me to his coarse skin and the broken blood vessels in his cheeks, the hallmarks of a burgeoning forty-five-year-old lush. I mean, they were proper Lee jeans, without any sort of creases ironed into them.

It sounded so trivial, but one of the things I really missed about my dad was that he never lived to acquire a fashion sense. Mum at least lasted into her sixties, outliving him by ten years. Dad would have been such an attractive sexagenarian. He was rake slim and tall, with the easy smile of a model and floppy hair, like Jeremy Irons in *Brideshead Revisited*. But he was shy, too, and I think in a way he had looked up to the younger Greg. Admired his louche good looks, casual trendiness, and ability to drink vast quantities of alcohol and still chat up women with aplomb.

Although it had been a huge deal at the time, what Greg and I actually had was nothing very much, not when I thought back to it. A few fumbles on the kitchen floor late at night, after my parents had gone to bed, the white ceramic tiles freezing against the hot skin of my back. His hand inside my bra, his alcohol-scented promises in my ear, hours and hours of passionate, Silk Cut-flavoured kisses.

I'd wanted him, for years, and I systematically set about making him fall for me. After the squeaky-voiced, spotty teenage wimps from the boys' school, his masculinity was as overpowering as a strong after-shave, and by the time I was seventeen, I was obsessed with him. At every opportunity I sent him sly, flirtatious glances from under my eyelashes, making sure that my school shirt was artlessly untucked and the hem of my skirt sliding high up my thighs as I crossed my legs in front of him. I watched him shift in his seat and prickle with sweat, and my thrilling new-found power made me hug myself with excitement.

He and his wife Jeanette used to come round for drinks and dinner on a regular basis, and when they did, I made sure I was always available to hand round nibbles and top up Cinzanos. One night, when Dad had popped out to buy more wine and Mum was upstairs showing Jeanette the new bedroom curtains, Greg and I found ourselves alone, at last. We were both shaking – although it later occurred to me that Greg's unsteady hand as he pulled on his Silk Cut might have been attributable to mild delirium tremens.

'You're so grown up these days, Anna,' he said, leaning forward, his eyes glittering with lust.

'So when are you going to take me out to dinner, then?' I managed to reply, blushing furiously at the blatant come-on.

'Whenever you like. You tell me when you're free.' We were staring fixedly at each other, like frightened rabbits.

'I'm very busy,' I replied, trying desperately to affect insouciance. 'But I'll look in my diary – I'm sure I could fit you into a small space somewhere.' *Boom boom!* as Basil Brush would have said.

The double entendre hadn't been intentional, but it certainly hit the mark. Greg's pupils had instantly dilated even further, and his gaze shifted to my breasts. He later confirmed that it was the moment when he fell in love with me, as opposed to just lusting after me, which he claimed to have been doing for years prior to that.

'Freudian slip?' he'd murmured, moving closer. I could feel the heat blazing in my cheeks. I wanted to move away, but couldn't, paralysed by his glorious manly confidence. His lips were millimetres from mine, when we heard footsteps in the hall, and we sprang apart.

'Red or white?' Dad sang, coming back into the room with his pipe in one hand and an off-licence carrier bag in the other. 'Anna, go up and ask the girls which they'd like, would you?'

That had been eight months before Greg told Dad about us, during which time Greg and I had done everything we possibly could, sexually speaking, without penetration actually occurring. Poor Greg. I felt quite sorry for him. He had been, to put it crudely, gagging for it. For the first few weeks he'd relished the sexiness of our foreplay, but as time went on, he must have been thinking that he was just too old for heavy petting. But I had not let him go all the way. I thought that was probably why he convinced himself that he really was in love with me, enough to tell Dad, and to risk losing his wife.

On that horrific evening, Greg and I had engineered a hasty liaison behind the trolley train in the Asda car park, shortly before he'd been due to meet Daddy in the pub. Through plumes of Silk Cut he'd told me that he was going to leave Jeanette, and 'that was that'. I remembered him grinding out the cigarette stub under the sole of his Dunlop Green Flash trainers. Adults never wore trainers in those days, except for the performance of physical exercise. It was another thing which had impressed me about him.

'That was that', he'd said. If he hadn't said it, I'd have told him not to. I was in love with him, but I was now eighteen years old, and the gates of adulthood, with all the freedom and potential just visible through the bars, were beginning to swing open. I had finished my 'A' levels, and had a place at Reading University, starting that October, studying English and Drama. However much I adored his jeans and Green Flashes, his Silk Cuts and his hairy chest, I did not wish to start taking huge bagfuls of his dirty washing down to the launderette, or cook him steak and chips every night. Not to mention the grief I'd have got from my family about it – Jeanette was Mum's best friend.

But because he'd said it so firmly, all my rehearsed objections had dissolved on my tongue like sherbet. He seemed so convinced, so masterful, that I couldn't argue. I rationalized it by thinking that if he wanted to leave her all that much, it probably wasn't anything to do with me anyway. I could still go to college, I'd just come and visit him at weekends. Or he could move to Reading with me. And I felt ready to lose my virginity. When I told him so, he instantly looked at his watch.

'I won't be long,' he said. 'See you in the Feathers in half an hour. I'll tell your dad, meet you after for a quick debrief, then I'll get off home and break it to

Jeanette. Our new life starts here! And don't worry, it'll all be fine.'

That had been the last time I ever saw Greg alone. I'd sat at the bar in the Feathers, a pub round the corner from the Fox and Goose, for two hours after that, waiting for him, my trembling fingers nursing the dregs of a warm blackcurrant and soda, but he hadn't come. I'd even heard the wail of the ambulance siren going past the door, without knowing its destination. Eventually I'd gone home to find the hastily scribbled note from Mum telling me to meet them at the hospital, but by the time I got there, it had been too late.

Greg and Jeanette had been at the funeral, of course, but every time Greg had looked meaningfully across at me, I'd stared at the carpet, filled with horror and revulsion. The mere thought of his hairy chest – and what I'd encountered due south of it – made me want to vomit with guilt into the tepid vol-au-vents which Mum handed round back at ours after the service.

At least he hadn't decided to tell Jeanette first, I thought. That had been a small comfort.

12

'Vicky, please let me in. I'm outside your front door. I've been worried about you. I only want to see how you are.'

A small voice floated down the stairs: 'Mummy, do you think I'm adorable?'

There was no answer from Vicky, as far as I could tell, to either of us. I tried again. 'Vicky, come down, please. I'll keep phoning and knocking you until you do. Anyway, I promise I won't take up much of your time . . . Or I could take Crystal to the swings, if you like.'

'Mummy, am I?'

'I'll fill up your whole answering-machine tape. I know you're there, I can hear Crystal through the letterbox.'

I heard Vicky's voice then, somewhere upstairs. 'Yes, Crystal, you're adorable. Most of the time.'

A pause, an inhalation I could swear I heard too, then a howl of outrage: 'I WANT TO BE ADORABLE *ALL* THE TIME!'

Good grief, but that child was a drama queen. However, it seemed that she had succeeded where I was failing, to flush Vicky out of the undergrowth of her turmoil. Footsteps thumped down the stairs and the door swung abruptly open. Vicky stood in the doorway, a cross expression on her face and Pat riding on her left hip. She wore no make-up and her hair badly needed a wash. Her skin was a familiar greenish hue which would have left me in no doubt that she was pregnant, even if she hadn't suspected it herself.

'Sorry, Anna, I didn't hear you knocking.'

Remembering that I was meant to be here to offer moral support, I let the obvious lie slide. Instead, I leaned in and planted a kiss on her cheek, followed by another on Pat's plump smooth one. I had a sudden urge to take him out in the car just so that I could drive over a cattle-grid and watch his cheeks wobble. He was that sort of baby.

'Hello, you two. Any chance of a cup of tea? Give us a cuddle, Pat.'

Somewhat ungraciously, Vicky stood aside and admitted me, passing Pat into my outstretched arms. Her house was even more of a mess than ours was, but where our mess had a neglected air to it, a sort of chilly, damp mess, Vicky's was the messy chaos of small children, exhaustion and not enough hours in the day. Toys were strewn on all the floors, including the not-very-clean kitchen tiles, and the breakfast things were still on the table despite it being half past eleven.

'You sit down,' I said to her, 'and I'll make the tea. Where's Crystal?'

'In a strop upstairs, as per. Hiding in our wardrobe. Hopefully she won't find any mothballs and eat them. Oh, I can't wait for nursery to start.'

Vicky flopped down onto a pile of unironed baby clothes in a wicker armchair in the kitchen. I put Pat down and he immediately crawled away to play with the standard lamp in the corner, so I chased after him and picked him up again.

'Come on, Patch, you can help me make tea. You can pour out the boiling water.'

Vicky must have been in a bad way, because she didn't even look up to check that I was joking. She was

114

staring into space, chewing the skin around her thumb-nail. She looked utterly defeated.

I came over and crouched down in front of her, putting my hands on her knees, as Pat made another bid for freedom in the opposite direction. There was a rough, sticky pinkish patch on the front of the left leg of her jeans, which I hazarded a guess was yesterday's yogurt. 'So you are pregnant, then,' I said. She nodded, misery etched into the creases of her forehead.

'I don't know what to do,' she whispered.

I would never have suggested that she didn't need to do anything except take plenty of folic acid and let nature take its course, but I couldn't help thinking it.

'Have you told Peter yet?'

'No. He'll be thrilled,' she said glumly. 'If he was as stressed about it as I am, it would be so much easier. I wouldn't feel so alone.'

'You're not alone. You've got me.'

Vicky's eyes welled with tears and she looked away.

'I mean it, Vicky, of course I'll be there for you, whenever you need some extra help with the kids, or anything.'

'I don't think Ken'd be too happy if you were to move in here twenty-four hours a day, because that's what I need.'

Ken probably wouldn't even notice, I thought, remembering my mosaic-making experience of the day before with a sudden secret flash of glee, followed instantly by shame – why did I feel gleeful about having a secret? I rubbed the rough blistered skin on my right thumb, my badge of achievement. Despite the wobbly moment with Pregnant Paula's comment, and my subsequent hasty departure, I had already begun to see the mural project through rose-tinted glasses, and planned to go down to Gillingsbury again the following day. Perhaps this time Max might be there, I thought. I couldn't sit around moping about Holly and Dad for ever.

I had an urge to invite Vicky to come with me – maybe I could pretend that I'd just been aimlessly driving around and had spotted the sign and gone in? Or maybe not . . . The thought of Crystal in the car with us for over an hour, and then charging round Moose Hall with Spike and his cronies, was not a particularly enticing one. I felt guilty for thinking it, but sometimes I did wish that cuddly, pliant Pat was my godchild instead of bristly Crystal. Much as I really did love her, she was living up to her name at the moment: brittle and precious; nice to look at but not very practical. I hoped it was just a phase.

Besides, Vicky didn't do anything on an impromptu basis any more; the children had eradicated all her former spontaneity as briskly as a pulled clean Etch-a-Sketch. I missed the old Vicky, I thought, with a pang. I missed having a laugh with her. She was a brilliant mimic, and we used to conduct endless conversations in different accents, switching fluidly between Norwegian and Polish, Pakistani and Russian. But she never did her accents these days; or told me funny stories; or made up mad personas to try and fool drunk men in bars: pretending that she was a divorced millionairess looking for a new husband, or a former Miss World (a pretence she could pull off with no difficulty, back in the old days), or a lady mud-wrestler (although her arms were too spindly to get away with that one, even when she professed to be bantam-weight).

When had she got so serious? Still, I supposed, I was hardly a bundle of laughs myself any more. We'd grown up, that was all. But it still felt like a loss. And at least she had Crystal and Pat to show for all that seriousness, which was more than I had. I just wished she enjoyed them a bit more. I was *sure* that, however tough having kids was, I'd find so much joy in being a mother. It made me sad that Vicky found it such a struggle.

Now she'd have a third. Envy churned inside me like

the rumble and pinch of indigestion, and I had to swallow hard before I spoke again.

'I'm really pleased for you though, Vic. Didn't you always want a big family?'

She snorted. 'Yeah. That was *before* anyone told me how bloody difficult it was.'

I opened my mouth to gush forth platitudes: it would be fine, she'd manage, how lovely to have another child, it would all be worth it once they were all out of nappies, and so forth; but she shot me such a forbidding look of warning that I didn't say a word.

'I don't want another baby,' she said finally. 'I don't want to need a double buggy, and five seats if we ever went anywhere on an aeroplane, and another six years before I can even begin to get any time to myself. I don't want to get more stretch marks and cellulite and wrinkles.'

'You don't have stretch marks, not that I've ever seen. You look great in a bikini, and after two kids that's no mean feat.'

Vicky sighed irritably. 'The straw that broke the camel's back, that's what it'll be. And this camel's on its knees already.'

'Why don't you get a nanny?'

'Where would we put a nanny? We can hardly have all three children sleeping in the same room, can we?'

I shrugged. 'Why not? Lots of kids share rooms.'

'Not Crystal, though. She'd never stand for having Pat in her Barbie bedroom.'

'You don't have to have a live-in nanny, you could just get one during the day.'

'Anna, do you have any idea how much a nanny costs? You have to go through an agency, of course, and round here it's over a thousand pounds just to register! And then you have to give them sick pay and holidays and paid leave whenever your own kids are sick. Katriona has this woman three days a week, and it costs her thirteen hundred pounds a month! That's not much less than Peter earns.'

Secretly, I was pretty horrified at that – it did seem outrageously expensive – but I ploughed on: 'OK then, what about an au-pair? They're cheap, and don't they do the cleaning too?'

Vicky rolled her eyes. 'And where would she sleep? In the garden shed? Plus, I wouldn't leave a new baby, or Pat for that matter, with some non-English speaking Eastern European with a dodgy reference.'

It just wasn't worth trying to argue about the speciousness of that comment so I gave up, and instead rescued Pat from where he had wrapped himself in the floor-length dining-room curtains until he was almost completely cocooned, and wailing to be rescued.

'Shall we go and find your sister, Pat? Let's see where she's hiding,' I crooned in his tiny velvety ear, and was rewarded with a huge smile. Pat's two miniature front teeth were growing uncertainly down out of his soft gums as if they were worried they weren't supposed to be there yet. I clasped him to my chest, cradling his small sturdy back in my palm. When he was a baby his whole back had fitted in the curve of my hand. I thought again of Adam's hands shaping wet clay, and then of Ken's handshake.

I didn't know what else to say to Vicky. Of course she had every right not to be ecstatic about having another baby, but still, a life was a life, and even she admitted that she would be glad she'd had her children so close together, once they were more grown up. She was so bloody lucky even to have the choice.

I carried Pat up the stairs and called Crystal's name. Instantly I heard a squeal, and the metallic jangle and crash of coat-hangers being knocked off a rail, and Crystal scrambled out of her parents' bedroom looking red-faced and dishevelled.

'Auntie Anna! I didn't know you was here,' she said, grabbing my leg and hugging it.

'Hello darling,' I said, crouching down to kiss the top of her head, feeling her thick auburn hair against my lips. 'How are you?'

'Not too good, I'm afraid,' she replied gravely, taking my hand and pulling me towards her room. 'Come on, and I'll tell you all about it.'

I put Pat down on the carpet and gave him a Spot board book to chew, which Crystal immediately substituted for another, seemingly identical one. 'We don't give *that* book to Pat. Only *this* one,' she said authoritatively. Then she patted the duvet next to her. 'Sit,' she said, like a mini Margaret Thatcher.

'So, what's up, then?'

'*Well*,' she said. 'I fell over this morning and – look! – it really, really hurt.' I squinted at the teeny red spot on the back of her hand, barely visible to the naked eye.

'Hmm. Doesn't look too serious to me, Crystal. Did Mummy call the doctor?'

Wrong thing to say. Crystal's lower lip began to tremble. 'No, she didn't. I kept tolding her that she must, but she didn't, and I wasn't even allowed a plaster.' She paused for dramatic effect. 'I don't think Mummy LOVES me any more!'

She crumpled into my side like a bereaved soap opera character, her shoulders heaving although no actual tears were forthcoming. Still, I hugged her back.

'Of course Mummy loves you. She adores you! She's just not feeling very well at the moment so you must try to be extra nice and extra helpful, OK?'

'I'm always extra nice and extra helpful,' Crystal replied, the little Pollyanna.

'I'm sure you are. Now why don't we all go downstairs and tell Mummy how much we love her?'

I hefted Pat and the chewed book, took Crystal's hand, and our little caravan made its way back downstairs. Vicky had moved from the wicker chair, and when I looked around for her I spotted her lying flat out on the small sofa in their conservatory, fast asleep. She always had had an enviable ability to crash out with no notice whatsoever, something which, I thought, must surely help in her current sleep-deprived circumstances. Our first college production had been

Alice in Wonderland, and one of the parts she'd played was the Dormouse, so whenever I saw her asleep, it always reminded me of her in that furry brown mouse suit. I was about to try and distract Crystal by telling her about Mummy once being dunked in a big pretend teapot, but it was too late.

'I REALLY LOVE YOU, MUMMY,' she bellowed in Vicky's ear, shaking her vigorously by the left breast until she was awake again.

Very calmly, Vicky sat up and pushed Crystal gently to one side. She swung her legs down from the sofa onto the floor, and led me by the hand into the living room. Ignoring the protests of both children, she closed the door behind them and took a deep breath.

'I know you won't approve, but I'm not asking for your approval, just for your support.'

'You're not—'

She nodded. 'I am. I'm going to have an abortion. I can't cope.'

'But you can. You will!' I looked at the enlarged photograph of a seagull in soaring flight above Vicky and Peter's mantelpiece, the deep, free blue of the sky, the white liberation of its wings. I understood why Vicky liked it so much. I thought I was going to cry. '*Please* don't,' I said, still holding Vicky's hand, but thinking of Holly's tiny creased fingers.

Vicky snatched her hand away and turned her back on me, wheeling around so fast it was like a punch. 'No, *you* please don't!' she snapped. 'This is not about you, Anna. It's about me, and what's best for my family. I could have chosen not to tell you but I have. Don't let me down when I need you.'

I couldn't think of what to say, not when my overweening emotion was one of horror, bordering on – and I hated to admit it – disgust.

Crystal was hammering on the sitting-room door – it had a slippery round ceramic doorknob that she couldn't quite negotiate – and Pat was crying.

'Why don't I take the kids for a walk?' I said, not

meeting her eyes. 'I'll take them over to Lil's. She was saying the other day that she hasn't seen them for such a long time. You could go and have a bath or something.' And think about what you're proposing to do . . . I mentally added. She couldn't just get rid of her baby. She couldn't.

Vicky shrugged. 'Whatever.' Then she clutched my arm, too hard. 'But you are *not* to tell Lil about this, any of it. Do you promise, on your life?'

'Why not?'

The expression of anger on her face made me wonder, for a second, if she was going to hit me. 'Because I'm asking you, that's why not! It's my business, I don't want you two sitting there tutting about what an awful person I am. I wish I'd never bloody told you now.'

I hugged her, but my reluctance must have showed, because it felt awkward. 'Sorry. I promise I won't tell her.'

'Or anybody else. Ken. Peter.'

'*You aren't even going to tell Peter?*' This got worse and worse.

'Going to tell Daddy what?' yelled Crystal through the keyhole, frantically rattling the door handle until Vicky took pity on her – or, more likely, decided to end the conversation right there – and opened the door.

'Auntie Anna's taking you both out,' she said. 'Let's get ready.' She turned to me and hissed in my ear: 'Or anybody else. *Promise.*'

'I promise,' I hissed back, reluctantly. At that moment, for the first time in the sixteen years I'd known her, I thought I hated her. We'd had our ups and downs before, silly rows over sillier things: a few days' bad feeling the time she got a part in an Ayckbourn at the Wimbledon Theatre that I'd been after as well; or when she got in a strop with me because I couldn't think what to buy Crystal for her third birthday, and suggested giving Vicky money to get her something instead. But they'd always blown over. This was the first time that I thought possibly it might not have done.

With an atmosphere thick enough to slice, we managed between us to stuff the children's small arms in their cardigans, strap Pat into the pushchair and plonk Crystal onto the buggy board attached to the back of it. Vicky packed Pat's changing bag and hung it on one of the pushchair's handlebars, as if she didn't want to hand it to me directly.

The three of us set off, Crystal coasting on the board like a surfer dude catching a wave and Pat's finger in his mouth, in pre-nap mode. At the end of the garden path I turned to look back, but Vicky had already shut the door.

13

I was back on the M3 again the next morning, with a full tank of petrol, tapping my wedding ring percussively against the knob of the gear stick in time to Run-D.M.C.'s *Greatest Hits* on my car stereo. August rain slanted heavy splashes against the windscreen, and the frenetic thwack-thwack of the wipers helped distract me from the butterflies of anticipation dancing in my stomach. The rain was so heavy that I had to turn the volume of the CD up to eight.

It was all Lil's fault. I'd told her about my trip to Gillingsbury, and she'd encouraged me to go back there again, even after I told her that Max hadn't been around the first time. I'd just about managed not to blurt out what had happened at Vicky's not fifteen minutes before my arrival, but the effort had nearly killed me. So in order to keep off the subject I'd gone into tedious amounts of detail about my previous trip to Wiltshire, and how much I'd enjoyed participating in the mosaic project. After a while, even with Crystal and Pat present as reminders, I found myself managing to put some distance between me and the row with Vicky. Lil was such a good listener.

Having the chance actually to talk to her was an added bonus to our impromptu visit. Crystal had been as good as gold, and spent the whole time playing with a miniature cooking range that Lil produced from somewhere: a metal doll's-house Aga complete with inch-square gingham tea-towels and teeny little pots and pans. She was silent for at least half an hour, lying on her stomach on Lil's floral patterned carpet, engrossed in making dry raisin stew and baking slivers of digestive biscuit into loaves, occasionally muttering to herself about what time Barbie would be round for dinner. Vicky's obvious tension and stress must have been rubbing off on her, for she was noticeably calmer now that she was away from home.

'I don't want to have to lie to anybody,' I'd said, watching as Lil cradled the sleeping Pat in her arms.

'Why would you need to lie?' Lil replied, glancing up at me from where she'd been concentrating on stroking Pat's eyebrow (an old midwife's trick, apparently, to help babies go to sleep: stroke their eyebrows and they automatically close their eyes. Not that she'd needed to do it with Pat – he'd been sparko before we even arrived). 'Tell Ken, if you feel the need to tell him anything, that you're doing a mosaic project for the community.'

'What if he asks where?'

She put another biscuit into Crystal's outstretched hand, which Crystal neatly trimmed down to the size of a penny by nibbling around the edges before slotting it into her oven. 'Tell him it's a local community college project.'

'I don't know. It seems . . . underhand.'

'Well then, if it bothers you, tell him the truth. Tell him it's in Gillingsbury.'

I gave her a dark look. 'He'd think I'd finally lost the plot! Unless I then fed him some other cock and bull story about getting involved in it via some imaginary friend down there, whom he's never heard me mention. It's mad.'

I knew what she was going to say next, and jumped in before she'd even opened her mouth. 'No, I still don't want to tell him about Max.'

She shrugged, causing Pat to list a little on her bony lap. He flailed briefly, and lay still again. For a moment I closed my eyes and imagined that these two children were Lil's great-great-niece and -nephew, on their weekly visit to her. Poor Lil – she'd been so excited when I finally passed the supposed danger weeks of my pregnancy, and we announced it. Now it was looking increasingly unlikely that she'd *ever* have any great-great-nephews or -nieces, given that my brother Olly wouldn't touch a woman with a ten-foot bargepole.

'Well, I suppose you can't tell him that you were in Gillingsbury at all then,' Lil had said, contemplatively.

'No, I can't.'

'Really though, he's not all that likely to ask. You're not doing anything wrong. And you are going back there, aren't you, so you'd better get it straight in your own mind.'

I hadn't been sure if I *was* going back, up to that point. But Lil said it as a statement, which, coming from her, turned it into an endorsement. I instantly forgot about Vicky's pregnancy and even, briefly, my own childlessness, and began to look forward to it, as if her words were a licence to overlook the nascent deception already tiptoing out of my conscience. 'Yes. Tomorrow.'

Why not? I deserved a change of scene. And the sullen, closed-down expression on Vicky's face, when I'd delivered her children back home again, made the idea of putting a hundred miles between us even more appealing.

By the time I reached the outskirts of Gillingsbury, negotiating the complex one-way system with a great deal more aplomb than on my first visit, I was glad to have arrived. My back felt stiff from hunching over the wheel, my eyes ached from the blur and wash of water in front of them, and I was fed up with Run-D.M.C. Plus, I was hungry, and, for some reason, far more nervous than I'd been two days earlier. That last visit could have been a one-off, an experiment. This one was a conscious, premeditated decision.

However, the sign wasn't outside Moose Hall this time, and the door was closed. I panicked for a moment, and it struck me how disappointed I'd have been if the project had finished, or if nobody was there. But the paint-flaked door yielded when I turned its iron handle, and I walked in to find bright overhead lights illuminating the gloomy dusk inside the hall. The bad news, though, was that the place was empty, apart from Serena striding towards me, her footsteps echoing on the dusty boards.

'*Hello* again! I was just on my way out,' she said, but nerves had dried my mouth and tightened my throat, and I began to cough. Once I started, I couldn't stop, and within seconds I was doubled over, hacking.

'Perhaps you'd better wear a mask this time,' called Serena, walking back to a table with a large bottle of Evian and some plastic glasses. She poured me a cupful of water.

'Thanks,' I croaked, drinking it down in one draught. A different and barely begun section of mural now sat on the trestle table in the middle, so I was reassured that at least the project hadn't suddenly been completed. 'Where is everybody?'

'Not many showed up today. The rain puts them off, I think. Anyway, there were so few of us that we decided to go to the pub for lunch. I just stayed behind to finish my wheelbarrow' – she gesticulated vaguely towards the centre of the room – 'and I was about to lock up. Would you like to join us?'

'Is that OK?'

'Of course. Mitch will be delighted to see you again.'

My heart sank. Why Mitch? I contemplated finding an excuse to go and walk around the shops or something. The thought of being wedged into some red-velour pub-bench hell, as Mitch droned on to me for the next hour, was enough to bring me out in hives.

126

'So, who else is there?' I tried to sound casual.

'Only Margie, Ralph and Adam today. Very poor turnout.'

I took a deep breath. 'I'd love to come. Thanks.' I'd just have to be tough with Mitch. And hope that Ralph wasn't wearing his pornographic shorts.

The pub was just around the corner – luckily, since I hadn't brought a coat and the rain had intensified. It was a large and sprawling whitewashed building; a wonky sign above the porch announced 'The White Horse. Estab. 1595', before dripping water down my neck as I paused to hold the door open for Serena.

Inside, it had the chilly unwelcoming feel of a pub in summer daylight hours – like many old pubs, it was the sort of place shown to its best advantage by artificial light, a couple of roaring fires and lots of people rubbing shoulders at the bar. At lunchtime it just looked forlorn and neglected. I couldn't see anybody else in there at all, but Serena led me with authority around a corner, and there they were, sitting at a large table in an alcove, all four of them attacking gargantuan ploughman's lunches. Ralph – who, I was relieved to notice, was wearing long cotton trousers with un-fashionably elasticated ankles – and Margie had their heads close together, deep in conversation, but they stopped talking when they saw us.

'Sorry,' said Adam when he saw Serena. 'We were starving, so we went ahead. Oh, hello, Anna! How are you?'

'Fine, thanks,' I said, smiling back at him and wondering if Max had inherited those same startling eyes. 'I hope it's OK, me being here.'

'Of course!' they all chanted in unison. Mitch patted the seat next to him – it was indeed a red-velour bench – but thankfully, so did Adam, and the seat next to him was an empty chair right on the other side of the table. I practically elbowed Serena out of my way in my haste to get to it, and she said, rather pointedly, 'Who wants another drink?'

I felt slightly crushed, and stood up again. 'No, please, let me get these in.'

'No, it's fine, I'm halfway there. What would you like?'

I dithered, then sat down. 'Well, I'll get the next round. Could I have a pint of bitter shandy please?'

'Same for me' said Adam, holding out his empty glass.

'Snakebite, please, Serena,' said Mitch, wiping a few drops of liquid off his straggly moustache. I had to prevent myself rolling my eyes. Honestly, did people really still drink *snakebite*? I'd thought that had gone out with Iron Maiden and patchouli oil.

'Orange juice for me, thank you, Serena, and – another lager, Ralph?' added Margie. 'Hello, Anna, it's nice to see you again. So many people just show up once and never come back, even when they say they will.' Then she turned back to Ralph, and continued the conversation they'd clearly been engrossed in before our arrival.

'Aren't you going to eat?' asked Mitch, ripping off a huge, thick strip of ham, the sort of meat which made me quiver: purply and raw-looking, with a trimming of white fat and some suspicious-looking veiny bits running through it. 'This ham is delicious; here, try some.' He thrust a wobbling forkful of it across the table towards my mouth, and I recoiled. I could just about cope with watching people eat that pink, thin-sliced processed stuff, but this was all far too hard-core.

'No, thanks, I'm a vegetarian.'

Mitch rolled his eyes. 'Vegetarian, schmegetarian. You wait till you taste this. That'll get you off the veggie burgers for good.'

'*No*, thank you,' I said, a little more forcefully than I intended.

Adam looked up with interest. 'Mitch, my friend, I didn't notice you were eating meat. I thought you were a person of hippy principles?'

'McDonald's, man,' mumbled Mitch through a mouthful of ham. 'My downfall. I bloody love a Mackey D.'

'Do you eat meat?' I asked Adam. His ploughman's was a delicious-looking concoction of Brie, pickled onion and chutney, and my stomach rumbled audibly. 'Sorry,' I said. 'I'd better go and order some food in a minute, I'm starving.' Just in time, I refrained from adding, 'I had a long drive to get here.' Whoops, I thought. Better be careful. It also suddenly occurred to me that at all costs I had to avoid Adam catching sight of any of my credit cards, my driving licence or my chequebook, all of which bore the name Anna Sozi.

'Well, I'm not technically a veggie. More of a piscatarian who eats the odd bit of chicken.'

'Which odd bit – its bollocks?' said Mitch, throwing back his head and treating us all to a view of his scrawny, spotty neck as he barked with laughter at his own perceived hilarity. The man was a nightmare. And he had the longest hairs coming out of his nose that I'd ever seen on any creature that wasn't a horse. Or maybe a walrus.

'I never used to eat meat at all,' Adam continued, 'but I've got a little boy, and when he was younger he was . . . quite ill, and didn't eat much.'

I forgot my hunger in an instant. I also forgot to breathe, and bit my lip so hard that I nearly drew blood. Max! Adam casually mentioning him like that suddenly made him real to me, more so than he had been in Adam's letter, or in Pamela Wilkins's comments about him.

'But he really liked chicken, so I started cooking it for him because there were so few things that he *would* eat. And then I discovered that I quite liked it too. But neither of us eats red meat.'

So Max liked chicken. I wondered how much of an accurate picture I could build of him, what sort of wobbly tower of gleaned titbits I could create without actually having met him. OK, so at the base of the

129

tower we had the fact that his mother wasn't around, and that he liked chicken. It was a start.

'Is he all right now?' I asked, forcing my voice to sound normal.

Adam's face relaxed, his eyes crinkled, and I wanted to lean over, grab his cheeks between my two hands, and kiss him. 'He's *fine*,' he said, with such pride that tears jumped into my own eyes.

'That's great,' I said. 'Really great.' I stood up. 'Better go and order my lunch.'

'In fact,' Adam continued, looking at a point over my right shoulder, 'here he is, the man himself!'

I felt as if my body had suddenly turned into a woollen garment which somebody was unravelling from the bottom, yanking an end of yarn at my heels that was travelling up my calves, threatening to topple me. Turning slowly, I forced myself to start walking away from the table towards the bar. It would have looked odd, to sit back down again, and besides, I needed a minute to compose myself. I saw an elderly lady in an old-fashioned spotty rainhood holding a little boy by the hand, and the top of Max's head, thin brown hair, thin arms in an old yellow *Toy Story* T-shirt and trainers which flashed red when he walked. I couldn't bring myself to look at his face, not yet, because it was too overwhelming.

Adam called after me, 'Anna, would you mind ordering an Appeltise and a cheese sandwich for Max, while you're up there?'

I nodded and waved behind me, unable to turn back around, completely choked with my good fortune.

When I got back to the table the lady in the rainhat had gone. Max was sitting on a pulled-up stool, on the opposite side of Adam to my empty chair. He was leaning into Adam, who had one arm draped protectively around him, and the sight of them together made me panic all over again, not sure if I'd be able to go through with it . . . at least, not without appearing

130

very strange indeed. I hadn't really expected to be meeting him for weeks, if not months – and yet here he was, on my second trip to Gillingsbury. Come on, Anna, I thought fiercely. It's a meant-to-be. Focus.

So I focused on Max. As the adults talked across the top of him, his sleek caramel head was bent over a miniature racing car, the wheels of which he was spinning up and down his thin bare arm. His feet, looking big in the smart trainers, rested on the top rung of the stool. He had a vaguely pudding-bowl haircut, the sort that I'd seen quite a bit on small boys, and which seemed to be trendy again at the moment. His eyelashes were absurdly thick and black and, like Mitch's nose – only for different reasons – didn't quite seem to belong on his face. His expression was serious. He was utterly gorgeous.

I sat down, more nervous than on my opening night as Asa in *Peer Gynt* at Salisbury Playhouse. Walking on stage in front of a hushed and expectant full house was a doddle in comparison to this.

'They're bringing the food over in a minute. Here, this is for you,' I said, sliding the glass of Appeltise across the table to Max.

'Thank you,' he said, shyly, looking up at me with enormous blue eyes. He was like some tragic little poppet in a Hollywood movie. I half expected Lassie to materialize at his side. It took me three attempts to swallow the lump in my throat.

'This is my son, Max,' said Adam.

'Hello, Max. I'm Anna,' I managed. 'I came to help your dad with his mosaic project. Have you seen it?'

He nodded, flicking his eyes back down to the car. 'Brum, brum,' he said to himself. Then he parked the car on a beermat on the table and picked up his glass with an unsteady hand. The straw bobbed around in the bubbles of the drink, and it took him a couple of attempts to navigate it successfully into his mouth. He looked like a blind kitten nuzzling for milk, I thought sentimentally.

Get a grip, Anna.

'Two hands, Max,' said Adam, and he obeyed, finally negotiating the straw and taking a deep drink, the glass now firmly cupped in both palms.

'It's very fizzy,' he whispered to Adam, wrinkling his nose.

Adam smiled at him. 'Your sandwich'll be here in a minute, darling. Did you have a nice time at Mrs Evans's this morning?'

He nodded. 'Yeah. Only I don't like her dog, and that other boy what was there didn't want to play with me.'

'Cameron?'

Another nod.

'Oh, don't worry about Cameron. You know that Mrs Evans said he likes to play on his own sometimes.'

I followed this innocuous exchange with the sort of rapt attention I usually reserved for cliffhanger episodes of *EastEnders*. I couldn't believe I was really there, listening to their conversation. Or that Max was really there, when he might well not have been.

A rotund young woman in a huge pair of combat trousers and a too-tight T-shirt brought over my Cheddar ploughman's and Max's sandwich. A worried expression instantly settled on his face.

'Dad,' he whispered, poking at the few strands of cress which decorated the plate. 'I don't like this stuff.'

'Can I have it?' I asked. I waited for the grateful nod, then pincered it off his plate in one small scoop straight into my mouth. 'Yum. Cress,' I said, chewing its gritty stalks with enthusiasm, although actually I couldn't stand it. 'Did you know you can grow it from seed, on paper?'

I was going to say 'blotting paper', but then I thought that he might not know what that was. Or if, in fact, anyone ever used blotting paper these days. I was grateful to Crystal for providing some insight into the mind of the four-year-old, but it struck me how much I didn't know. Max was older, nearer to five, and any-way, boys were so different to girls. Crystal would probably have marched back up to the bar with the offending cress still on the plate, and said, 'What the bloody hell is this? I asked for a plain cheese sandwich, not one with *green shit* all over it.'

Then again, that might not have had anything to do with age or gender, but more to do with Crystal.

'We'll give it a go sometime, shall we, Max?' said Adam. 'I haven't grown cress since I was a kid. It was such a buzz, wasn't it' – he turned to me – 'watching the little seeds sprouting. You could practically see them grow.'

'Yes, and then you made an egg and cress sandwich, with your very own home-grown cress. It *was* a thrill.'

Max nibbled a corner of his sandwich and looked unimpressed.

I ripped open my hunk of French bread and put some cheese and pickle inside it, although by then my appetite had vanished again.

'So what do we need to do this afternoon?' I asked, replacing it untouched on my plate. 'Is there much left?'

'Well,' said Adam. 'The good news is that I've got the commission for two more panels – I was hoping for three, but I don't think we'll have the funding. So, yes, there's a lot still to do before term starts. Are you going to be able to come down again?'

I shrugged. 'I don't see why not.' Wild horses wouldn't have kept me away, I thought, gazing at Max.

'Excellent. Our numbers have diminished quite a bit in the last week, so it's great to have some fresh blood, as it were.' He took a swig of his shandy, and pinched a bite of Max's sandwich.

'Oi, Dad,' said Max, but he was smiling.

Over on the red-velour bench, I heard Mitch say to Serena, 'I'm having my damp seen to tomorrow.' When he didn't get a response he added, in case there was any doubt: 'Not my own *personal* damp, you understand.'

133

Serena, unsurprisingly, could not have looked less interested. Ralph and Margie were still conversing with such intensity that I wondered if I'd missed the fact that they were a couple. Odd that he seemed to have been flirting with me the other day.

'So, what do you do, Anna?' Adam suddenly said, looking intently at me.

'Um, I'm an actress,' I said, a little taken aback, although I'd already decided to be truthful, at least about my profession. 'But I'm, well – cliché I know – *resting* at the moment, which is why I've got time to help with your project.'

'Wow, that's so interesting. I've never met a real actress before. What have you been in?'

I hated this question. 'Oh, nothing too exciting. A few episodes of *The Bill*. I had the lead in a sitcom on BBC2 a few years ago, I don't know if you remember it. It was called *Butterfinger*.'

Blank faces all round, Mitch and Serena included; although I could tell that Mitch was excited by the knowledge that I'd been on telly. He had immediately stopped talking to Serena, and tuned into what I was saying.

'I've mostly done rep though, you know, touring the country. Plus a few West End musicals.'

'Awesome,' breathed Mitch. 'What, like *Chicago* and that, where you have to dress up in fishnets and stilettos, and do lots of them high kicks?'

Ugh. What *was* it with men and high heels? I wondered what Ken was up to; whether he was thinking of me as he sat in his office. Oh, it was Friday, wasn't it – no, he'd be coming back from Brussels. So he probably wasn't thinking of me, in or out of high heels. I made a mental note to try and remember to put the bins out when I got home.

'Well, I've never been in *Chicago*. I was in the chorus of *Les Mis*, though, but there certainly weren't any stilettos involved in that.'

Adam was the only one who laughed. 'I loved that

show. I wonder if you were in it when I saw it? It was a while back, though – ninety-five, maybe?'

'No, I was in it for a few months in ninety-nine.' The year before I gave the bone-marrow donation. *To your son*, I thought.

'Did you go with Mummy?'

Max's voice piped up at a moment when everyone else was silent, and his words hung in the air like out-of-season Christmas decorations. Glancing around, I noticed all the others nonchalantly looking up, waiting for Adam's answer. There was something going on here, I thought, and if they didn't know the details, they knew enough to be curious.

Not as bloody curious as I was, though.

Adam smiled, although he looked awkward and the smile didn't crease his eyes. 'Yes, I went with Mummy. It was a lovely evening. We had dinner first, at a Thai restaurant in Soho, and I tried to eat a banana leaf that turned out to be the wrapping for my dumplings, and not something you were meant to actually eat. It stuck in my throat and wouldn't go down until the waitresses were on the verge of calling an ambulance – it was very embarrassing. But the show afterwards was fantastic.'

'Where was I?' Max was staring greedily at his father, and I got the impression that Adam's wife wasn't talked about all that often in their household. Maybe she'd run off with somebody else – surely, if it was Adam who'd strayed, he wouldn't have sole custody of Max.

'You weren't even born yet, darling.' Adam ruffled Max's hair. 'Have another sandwich, won't you – you hardly had any breakfast.' For a brief second he looked crushed and lonely. It was obvious that something bad had happened.

Mitch leaned over the table, picked up my left hand, and examined the four silver rings I wore, one on each finger. My guess was that his mind was still chugging along on a train of speculation about Adam's marriage, for he suddenly said, 'You married then, Anna?'

I resisted the impulse to snatch away my hand, and

as I opened my mouth to say yes, my husband's called Ken, something unexpected happened. In retrospect, I suppose it was because I'd been awash with such overpowering pity for Adam at the very point Mitch asked me the question – not that it was any excuse, and I'd be haunted to my deathbed by my traitorous words – but they just popped out. Once they were out, I couldn't unsay them.

'No,' I said. 'I'm not.'

14

'So how was your day?' was Ken's first question to me when he arrived home that night. It was reassuring to be back in the world of the givens: the scrunch of Ken's key in the front door, the thud of his overnight bag hitting the hall floor, his footsteps seeking me out in my usual place at that time of the evening – socked feet up, in the corner of my beloved royal blue velvet sofa, watching television. A change might have been as good as a rest, but there was still a lot to be said for the comfort of routine. Even the sound of his mobile phone ringing – why did it always ring the second he stepped through the door? – was welcome. Not as welcome as the way he switched the call off without answering it, though.

'It was good, thanks. Yours?'

'Not bad. Want a drink?'

'Got one already.' I waved my hand towards the half-full glass of wine on the floor next to me, but unfortunately Ken chose the same moment to lean towards me to give me an I'm-home kiss, and I accidentally swatted him in the face.

'That's a nice greeting,' he said, backing off and rubbing his nose.

'Sorry, darling.' I laughed at his rueful expression. 'Come here.'

We kissed, and his arms encircled me, losing me in the scented remains of his day: the sweat of decisions, the recycled air of a plane's cabin.

'So what did you get up to today then? Been running?'

'Not today . . .' I took a deep breath. 'Actually, you won't believe it, but I've been helping make a mosaic mural!'

Ken raised his eyebrows. 'Really? Where? How come?'

I twirled a strand of hair around my fingers and fixed my eyes on the television, trying to sound nonchalant. 'It was a spur of the moment thing, really – I was just driving past this little hall and I saw a sign outside saying "Free Mosaic Workshop – No Experience Needed", and I just thought, Why not? You know I'm always banging on about wanting to do something creative. It turned out to be a community project, making a mural to go in an underpass by the station.'

Don't ask me which station, or which hall, I prayed, although I'd have been very surprised if he had. Ken had never really been a stickler for details.

'Wow,' was all he said, sliding his arms out of his jacket and unlacing his shoes. 'Did you enjoy it?'

I helped him pull off his shoes, and watched him unstick his socks from his feet. *My* socks never stuck to my feet when I took off my shoes; nor did they smell of Marmite, like Ken's did. Perhaps it was a guy thing, like the way his jeans always wore thin in exactly the same place: just inside and to the right of the crotch. I found it hugely endearing, knowing those secret inconsequential things about him that (I hoped) nobody else did. It was like having a priest hole in your house, or a den in the garden. 'Yeah. You know, I really did. I'm going to go back again. It was fun. I made a basket.'

'Great,' he said, kissing me again. 'It'll be good for you, getting involved with something like that. Can't wait to see the end result!'

Hmm, I thought. That might not be happening any

138

time soon, unless you find yourself driving past Gillingsbury station. And it was fairly unlikely that Planet Music would be holding their next conference at the Gillingsbury Travelodge.

'I'll get you a glass of wine,' I said, unfolding my legs and standing up, feeling better for having unburdened myself without actually having had recourse to a lie.

I picked up Ken's shoes and was about to turn towards the kitchen, when a trailer for a new series came on TV. A familiar face filled the screen.

'Bloody hell, I don't believe it.' I froze in my tracks, pointing at it with the toe of one shoe. 'It's Rosemary Gregson.'

'*A major ten-part drama based on the bestselling novel by Catherine Kirkbride*,' intoned the voiceover – funny how they never called them *minor* ten-part dramas. Nothing ever changed – I still only had to look at Rosemary Gregson to want to punch her in the face.

'Who's Rosemary Gregson?'

I shook my head with incredulity. 'She was in our class at Reading. Vicky and I privately voted her Least Likely to Succeed. I've never seen her in anything before so I thought we'd been proved right. To be honest, I thought she'd be a fat housewife with four kids by now. She's got the voice of a guinea pig. We were convinced she must have been sleeping with one of the tutors to get on the course in the first place.'

'The looks of a guinea pig too, in my opinion,' Ken said loyally, although in fact Rosemary was quite pretty. She still had that English bloom, and short curly brown hair in the style of a young Elizabeth Taylor. At Reading she'd had the obligatory blonde Sloaney highlights – trying to model herself on Princess Di, as Vicky used to sneer.

'I've got to ring Vicky,' I said, dashing for the phone, without taking my eyes off the television set. '*. . . starring Rosemary Gregson as the eponymous Annabel . . .*'

'Aaargh, not the starring role! Say it ain't so,' I

muttered, speed-dialling Vicky's number. She answered straight away.

'Vic, it's me. You'll never guess who I've just seen on—'

She stopped me mid-flow. 'I don't want to talk to you.'

'*What?*' It wasn't that I'd forgotten about our disagreement, but in all the excitement of meeting Max, it had downgraded itself in my head to an emotional hiccup, a mere misunderstanding. I had assumed the same would go for Vicky.

I vaulted onto the offensive immediately. 'Why, because you're going ahead with the—' Just in time, I realized that Ken was listening, and managed not to compound Vicky's disapproval of me.

'It's none of your business.'

'Oh come off it, Vicky. Don't be like that.' I made a face at Ken, left the room and took the phone upstairs, all rancorous thoughts about Rosemary Gregson having flown out of my head. 'I thought you said you needed me?'

'I did,' said Vicky, bitterly. 'I needed you to be supportive, not all judgemental and biased.'

I felt so hurt that I could barely breathe. There was a moment in time, an extended second which seemed to be flagged up like an arrow pointing to a crucial pause in a screenplay, where I could have smoothed things over, apologized – although for what, I thought angrily: for losing Holly, for the miscarriages, for my gut-wrenching desire not to see another human life wasted? – but that second hung heavily then dropped away, swinging down the phone line into infinity, and the balance of our friendship tipped.

'Well, I'm sorry if I'm bloody *biased*,' I hissed at her. 'What do you expect? If you're looking for me to sanction you killing your unborn child just because you're not getting your ten hours' sleep a night, then I'm afraid you're on your own.'

I instantly regretted saying it. True or not, they were

cruel words and she treated them with the contempt they deserved, cutting me off immediately. I was left listening to the static silence of terminated conversations all over the city, then I threw the phone onto the bed, with so much force that it bounced off the duvet and hit the wall on the other side.

Ken found me lying on the bed staring at the ceiling, some fifteen minutes later. 'What's the matter? You and Vicky had a row?'

'Oh Ken,' I said, unable to stop my voice cracking. 'I hate falling out with her.'

'What were you rowing about?' He sat down next to me, his weight on the mattress causing me to list slightly towards him. I leaned my head on his lap and he stroked my hair.

'Um . . . well, just the kids, really. She . . . moans about them so much.'

I was so tempted to tell him the real reason, but I knew if I did, and she found out, that really would have been the end of our friendship. The secrets were already beginning to stack up, I thought, a messy growing pile of them, like unshuffled cards.

'It's hard for her, Annie. She gets no help from Peter, does she?' Ken didn't like Peter much either. 'Crystal's a handful, and Pat doesn't sleep properly and is always ill with something or other. No wonder she's finding it a struggle.'

'Well, nobody ever says it's easy, do they? I mean, isn't that just part of the deal? You put up with the drudgery of the first five years because you've got two gorgeous children, and then you forget about all the hassle, just like you forget about the pain of childbirth?' I couldn't keep the envy out of my voice.

'That may well be true; but easier said than done though, isn't it?'

'Whose side are you *on*?' I demanded, moving my head away from his hand.

'Chill out, Anna, I'm not taking Vicky's side. I'm just

141

saying that you seem to be pretty down on her, when she's having a hard time.'

I rolled over, turning my back on him. You don't know the half of it, I thought. Downstairs, his mobile rang again. 'You told me you'd switched that off,' I said accusingly. He didn't reply. 'Go on, you'd better answer it.'

He walked out and thumped down the stairs, and I punched the residual dreams out of my pillow with anger and frustration. Everything in my life suddenly seemed bitter as lemons. Surely, on top of everything else, I wasn't going to lose my best friend too?

I met Vicky at the interview day for the Reading University drama degree. It was a few months before Dad died, and Greg and I were in the thick of our affair. When I first saw Vicky, she was leaning against the wall outside the Ladies' loo in the drama department, with a deliciously gorgeous boy apparently licking her tonsils. The boy was grinding his crotch into Vicky's, oblivious to the passers-by, as if they were alone in a forest clearing at midnight pressed against a tree, not in a college hallway in broad daylight. I'd gaped at them: at the boy's curly blond hair mingling with Vicky's purple spiked affair. She wore torn fishnets, a denim mini, and a battered leather jacket which, I later discovered, said 'The Circle Jerks' in wobbly white paint on the back.

I was glad then that I hadn't allowed my mother to force me into my interview suit, a heinously unstylish affair consisting of a long, A-line skirt and equally frumpy boxy jacket, in what looked like blue curtain material. I felt square enough as it was, in my tight black woollen tube skirt and neat white blouse. I could have been mistaken for a stray waitress, had it not been for my trusty Doc Martens. I'd told Mum that I wouldn't go to the interview unless I could wear them; and now I was unutterably relieved that I'd held out. Mine were only eight-hole black to Vicky's sixteen-hole burgundy, but at least they were Docs.

Vicky had come up for air and caught me staring. I blushed puce, for, as embarrassing as it was to admit it, watching them bumping and grinding right there in front of me was turning me on. I was mad about Greg, but suddenly I wished he was twenty years younger. *Greg* would never have snogged me in a public place. Even when we were alone, he spent most of his time looking nervously over his shoulder.

Lifting her right hand and forming a fist, Vicky made a triumphant gesture in my direction, beaming such a naughty, sweet smile at me that I couldn't help laughing. The boy heard, wheeled around, then glared first at me, then at her.

'What are you looking at?' he said. Vicky and I both stared shamelessly at the lump in his drainpipe jeans, and cracked up.

He covered his crotch with his hand. 'Catch you later. Maybe. Slag,' he said, and sloped off round the corner.

We fell about; my own laughter partly out of admiration for Vicky's chutzpah and blatant sauciness.

'Is that your boyfriend?' I asked.

She snorted again and wiped her eyes carefully, trying not to smudge the thick black Siouxsie Sioux kohl. 'I wish! Sexy, wasn't he? No, we just got chatting and I told him he could snog me if he wanted. Wasn't sure if he'd take me up on it, but he did. So that was a good start to the day. He's here for an interview for Chemical Engineering, but that's all I know about him. Have I got any lippie left on?'

I inspected the faint pink residue on her lips. 'No. I think he's probably wearing most of it.'

She unzipped one of the pockets of her jacket and extracted a stub of scarlet lipstick, which she impressed me further by applying impeccably without needing recourse to a mirror.

'Are you here for the drama interview?' I asked her, and to my delight she nodded.

'Yeah. You?'

'Yeah. Twelve o'clock, isn't it, that we've got to do our sketches?'

She nodded. 'Fancy coming for a coffee and a fag first?'

I beamed, and away we went.

We'd been told to prepare a three minute sketch, using a prop, about anything we liked – a brief which was terrifying in its scope – although for some reason I hadn't anticipated performing it in front of the assembled group of about thirty eighteen-year-olds. When I'd walked into the large rehearsal room, a couple of paces behind Vicky, my throat constricted at the sight of so many people, none of whom I had anything evident in common with, excepting age. I focused instead on the flaky white emulsion of the Circle Jerks logo on Vicky's back, allowing her to lead us to a space on the scratchy blue carpet tiles where we sat down. She hunched her shoulders and crossed her legs in front of her, apparently not caring that the gusset of her tights was in full view below the short denim mini. I'd wanted to sit cross-legged too, but when I attempted it, my tube skirt stretched out like a woollen roof between my knees, so I had to fold my legs awkwardly round to the side of me instead, which made my back hurt. Perhaps I wasn't cut out for a career on the stage after all, I'd thought miserably. My small triumphs in the local drama club seemed provincial and paltry in the shadow of what, I was sure, was the cornucopia of raw talent around me.

There was a girl to our right in full Sloane uniform: all the requisite items present and correct. Stripy shirt with collar turned up – check. Barbour – check. Thick navy velvet hairband in her shoulder-length wavy highlighted hair – check. Pearls – check. Navy pleated skirt – check. Pale pink lipstick – check. She knelt primly on the floor as if in the saddle, with a ramrod-straight back and an irritatingly expectant expression on her face. Even though nothing was happening, she had an open notebook on her lap and a Mont Blanc pen poised in her hand. Vicky and I took one look at her, rolled our eyes, and pointedly didn't engage her in conversation even though she had no one to talk to. We were a pair of bitches at that age.

Finally the interviews started. Vicky's surname then had been Attwood, so she had to go first; and she set the benchmark sky high. Her interview piece was everything I'd guessed it might be: hilarious, sharp, moving. It was about a girl who got pregnant and had the baby, and her struggle to adapt to the trials of teenage single motherhood, which she conveyed in three minutes, brilliantly, with just a baby's dummy as her prop.

By the end of it, tears stood in my eyes and I clapped until my palms were sore, and it was clear that the tutors were equally impressed. Simon Maltby, a short, bearded earnest man who was the spit of the man illustrated in *The Joy of Sex*, only with spectacles, looked close to tears himself, and he and the other tutor (the implausibly named Elton Casagrande) nodded at one another until I thought their heads would fall off.

The next few pieces were instantly forgettable, mostly because I was distracted by the Sloane. Immediately Simon and Elton had stood up to welcome us, she had begun to take notes in an ostentatiously scratchy scribble which continued non-stop throughout the introduction and through everyone's sketches. When the tutors called her name – it was Rosemary Gregson – Vicky had leaned over and offered to carry on writing notes for her while she did her sketch. It was a suggestion which Rosemary greeted with a glare of steely disdain, as if Vicky were a mongrel snapping round the heels of the thoroughbreds at the hunt. (Ironic, really, since we later discovered that Rosemary had grown up in a small terraced house in Ruislip, and had probably never been hunting in her life.)

Rosemary walked across to the stage area, smoothed

down her skirt, and delivered an extraordinary soliloquy to a dear departed family Labrador called Pickles. Her prop was Pickles's collar and lead, and whilst every cell in me sneered at the rank sentimentality and the melodramatic tears which Rosemary had no problem squeezing out, I had to admit that I was almost as moved as by Vicky's piece. I had to turn my head away so that Vicky couldn't see my face when Rosemary, in her rather squeaky voice, declaimed that the spot in the bluebell woods marked by a small wooden cross was where she went to remember her Pickles.

Vicky, meanwhile, was pretending to puke next to me. I blinked away the tears and sniggered with her, and we viciously slagged her off to each other later in the post-sketch debrief. However, the tutors had clearly disagreed with our diagnosis, because she ended up on the course with us.

I'd gone next. My piece, in contrast to the emotionally overwrought efforts beforehand, was a lame monologue by an overweight woman on the phone, telling her friend how well she was doing at Weight Watchers whilst simultaneously ingesting a bar of chocolate. As my props, I'd brought an ancient Bakelite telephone with a frayed fabric-covered cord, and a Mars Bar; only I hadn't really stopped to consider how difficult it was to cram chocolate into my mouth at the same time as enunciating with any clarity. Plus the Mars Bar made me feel sick. At the end, there was a smattering of applause (polite from everyone except Vicky, who really went for it). Simon Maltby steepled his fingers together and said, 'Interesting. Where did you get that from?'

'I brought it with me,' I said. 'I found it in our garage.'

He'd smiled condescendingly. 'No,' he said. 'I meant the idea, not the telephone.'

'Oh,' I said, looking at the floor. Later, Vicky pointed out to me that I had chocolate collecting at the corners of my mouth, and a thin strand of toffee stretching like cat dribble off my chin.

I couldn't believe it when I heard I'd got in too. I was almost more pleased that Vicky and I would be together for the next three years, than I was about the place.

15

I drove back and forwards from home to Gillingsbury every day for the following two lots of Monday to Friday, letting my car's wheels swallow more than miles: first accelerating over Vicky's hurt silence; and then, two days later, speeding past my disappointment at having got my period. Since Ken and I weren't having sex at all, it would've been the second Immaculate Conception had I actually been pregnant, but even so, I couldn't shake the usual crushing feeling of anticlimax I always got when my period arrived.

I tried to imagine how Ken and I would be feeling if I was late, if a test had shown positive. One thing was for sure – mingling with the anticipation would be something far darker: fear. We were both afraid of the horrific familiarity of the process; of hopes raised then dashed; of the weeks passing in terror watching my belly growing and every day wondering if this was going to be the day when I started to lose it?

In many ways it was easier not even to try; and Ken's body was confirming this by ensuring that he literally wilted whenever I went near him. Which wasn't often – he was spending so much more time at the office that I was beginning to wonder why he bothered to come home at all.

But if we didn't try, we'd never have a baby. It wasn't

fair. Every time I thought of Vicky, my teeth clenched with emotions I couldn't quite identify: rage or rancour, or maybe jealousy or defeat. Whatever they were, they weren't good feelings.

Every time I set out on the drive, I wondered if Max would be at the other end, sitting on a chair dangling his skinny legs and fiddling intently with a small toy. I saw him in my mind so often that I was always faintly surprised when I walked in and he wasn't there, as if the others had whisked him off behind a curtain for a joke when they saw me coming. But he never had been, not for a whole fortnight. Once, apparently, I'd just missed him. Then he went to his grandparents' for four days; and then Adam told me he was going to be with a childminder – Mrs Evans, the lady in the rainhat who'd brought him into the pub – until the mosaic project was completed. Adam didn't like Max spending too much time at Moose Hall with all the tile dust getting into everything (meaning, into his lungs). I was anxious enough myself about the state of his lungs for it to lessen the disappointment I felt at not seeing him.

Although then I realized that the school year was about to begin, and panicked. No more mural project. No possibility of seeing Max at all, once I no longer had an excuse to see Adam. I started to daydream about Max in school uniform, imagining long baggy grey shorts and a striped tie, and maybe a maroon blazer. He haunted my thoughts as if he were the object of my affections. I had a crush on a four-year-old boy! If that didn't make me certifiable . . . but I was desperate to see him again. On every drive back home from Gillingsbury, I tried to plot how I could engineer another meeting without overtly flirting with Adam, which, of course, would have been a deeply unfair thing to do. I didn't fancy Adam, I told myself sternly. Nice though he was, it wasn't Adam I wanted to be with, it was Max.

But it was impossible to get to Max except through Adam – what was I going to do, invite *Max* for a drink at the pub? Yeah, right. The bigger and more elaborate the mural panels became, the more they represented my chances slipping away. I wished Max had never been at the pub that time. If I hadn't met him at all, it might have been easier to let it go.

As far as I could tell, my options were as follows. First: to get myself on the reserve list for one of Adam's art classes and hope that a place came up. That was my least favourite course of action, since, assuming I even managed to enrol in something, it would have been even harder to 'socialize' with Adam in a class situation than it was at Moose Hall with Mitch breathing down my neck, and Max definitely wouldn't be around when Adam was formally teaching. Second: be proactive and invite Adam and Max out somewhere. But where? And, more to the point from Adam's perspective, why? Much as I liked Adam, it wasn't as if we'd really had a chance to bond. Even spending whole days together on the project hadn't created a deep and lasting friendship between us or anything. No, despite my best efforts, I got the distinct impression that although Adam liked me well enough, it wasn't as if I was his new best friend. I imagined his forehead creasing with confusion and polite surprise, were I suddenly to announce that I'd like to take him and Max to the cinema, or out bowling.

Third option: come clean and tell Adam who I really was. But I still wasn't able to do that. My original reasons for not wanting to reveal my identity seemed even more valid than ever now that I'd met Max, and I shuddered to imagine what Adam would think of me for *not* asking to see Max in the weeks since I'd known him. It would make me appear as a total freak.

That left option four: to hang around near their house and 'bump' into them . . . Good grief, that would be like being sixteen again. Surely I couldn't stoop to those depths?

But desperate times called for desperate measures – the project was practically finished, which was how I found myself in their street one sunny humid afternoon the following week, after Moose Hall had been locked up for the day and everybody had gone home, lightly frosted as usual with a greyish patina of tile dust. Adam had left early, saying he was going to collect Max from the childminder's, and I'd judged that it could take anything from twenty minutes to an hour for them to get back to their house (although I wasn't sure exactly how I figured that, since I didn't actually know where the childminder lived). I knew where Adam and Max's house was, though. I'd looked it up on BT online, which allowed me to print a handy street map of the location at the same time. I had the map folded up in my bag, and already knew the route from Moose Hall off by heart: take the Devizes road into town, cross two roundabouts, follow the one-way system until you got to Dean Street, then Hardcourt Road was the third on the right. They lived at number forty-three.

I also knew that Adam drove an old yellow Saab, of which there was no sign as I drove slowly down the road. Number forty-three was a shabby, unremarkable two-storey terraced house, with no garage, unless it was around the back. I added this somewhat spurious piece of information to my mental Max files: likes chicken, mother not around, Dad drives Saab, no garage.

Hardcourt Road wasn't in one of the better parts of Gillingsbury. There was a rusting hulk of a car on blocks a few doors down from Adam and Max's, and loud music from three different open windows clashed badly. On the corner, four teenage kids and their small hanger-on, a boy of about ten, were doing what kids did best: loitering, smoking, laughing meanly and looking disaffected. I parked nearby and sat in the car for a while, with the engine running so I could keep the air-conditioning on. I wasn't quite sure what to do next, so I flitted through the radio stations. On Radio Two, Steve Wright and his sycophantic posse were spouting spurious 'factoids': did you know that if your pillow is

151

over five years old, ten per cent of its volume has become comprised of bits of dead skin? Ugh, I thought, remembering how I'd punched mine after my row with Vicky.

I couldn't believe that Steve Wright was still going. He reminded me of a bygone era, of being seventeen and driving around after school in my friend Julia's bumblebee 2CV, aka the Yellow Peril, or, pretentiously, the Deux Chevaux. That car reminded me of trysts with Greg, of drinking Baileys out of paper cups in school lunch breaks, and of listening to Steve Wright in the Afternoon, circa 1984, on the ancient car radio. One of Steve's jingles at that time had been a woman's voice, protesting in a rising cadence, 'No, no, no . . .' then the brisk sound of a zipper, and then '. . . oooh *yes*.' We'd repeated it ad infinitum, often shouting it out of the flip-up windows of the 2CV at attractive men walking along as we whizzed around the town centre.

The memory made me smile, and I was away, lost in thoughts of my schooldays. Back when I was innocent, and my only worries were whether I'd get the lead part in the school play, and whether or not I ought to let Greg undo my bra and get his hands on my breasts.

I wondered what Julia and her Deux Chevaux were doing now. At least one of them would surely be on the scrapheap, and it was less likely to be the car. She'd been far too fond of those lunchtime Baileys, as I recalled. Her 'O' levels had passed her by in a sticky blur of coffee-flavoured liqueur, and she failed them all, which was when our paths had diverged.

A sharp rap on my own car window made me jump. One of the boys from the corner was standing in the road right next to me. He bent down and leered in at me as I lunged for the central-locking button, and his mates all creased up as if that was the most hilarious thing they'd ever seen. Their small sidekick was trying simultaneously to smoke and look cool, and failing on both counts: he took two or three shallow puffs of a cigarette, stubbed it out, and replaced it in his mouth with a baby's dummy – which disconcerted me almost as much as the slap on the window had.

Once I'd composed myself and checked that it wasn't just some innocent enquiry, I gazed straight ahead, refusing to meet any of their eyes, and waited, stock still, until they sauntered off, bored with making faces and rude gestures at me.

There were still no signs of life from number 43, or any yellow Saabs in sight, so rather than risk the youths coming back again, I decided to get out of the car. I walked up to a small parade of shops at the end of the street which I'd noticed when I'd driven past earlier.

One of the shops was a picture-framers, and as soon as I spotted it I knew I had my purported reason for being in the area – I could say I was just dropping something off to be framed. For the sake of authenticity I went into the shop, setting off a loud electronic two-tone beep when I trod on the doormat. It startled me, but didn't even seem to register with the elderly woman sitting reading behind the counter.

I perfunctorily inspected a rack of handmade birthday cards and a wall full of corners of picture frames stuck with velcro onto green baize. Eventually the woman looked up from her book, apparently surprised to have a customer. She gave me a vague smile before dropping her eyes back to the page again.

I didn't pay her much attention either, though. I was gazing at the right-angled corners in all their different colours and textures and wondering what I would frame, if I could have anything in the world. A signed photograph of Elvis Costello? That lovely ten by twelve of me as the lead in *All My Sons*? Max, beaming at the camera?

No, of course not, if this was *fantasy* photo-framing, it wouldn't even be Max. It would have to be a montage of my own children. Holly's school photo, gap-toothed and grinning, Louis's second birthday, perhaps, blowing out candles on a Thomas the Tank Engine cake, with Vicky's Pat contributing puff (with those cheeks, I had no doubt that he'd be expert at it). Gemma sitting on a garden-centre Santa's knee, looking as worried as she was ecstatic? A baby photo of Joe, in a tropical-fruit print swim nappy? (Yes, I didn't care that it was indulgent; we'd given them all names.) That was what I'd have framed, if I could have chosen anything at all.

I had to beep-beep my way out of the shop again. The woman was so engrossed in her book that I didn't think she'd notice if I broke down in tears there and then, but I didn't feel like risking it. I wandered along the pavement back towards the car, for a moment forgetting what I was doing there.

It was really hot, that muggy late-afternoon heat which seems to jump out at you and take refuge in your armpits and crotch. I delved in my bag for the car keys, thinking longingly of cranking up the air-conditioning in the car and driving home again – this having been a stupid idea, obviously – when suddenly the four troublemakers were surrounding me. They had slunk out of a narrow side alley that I hadn't even noticed until then. Oh no, I thought, that's all I bloody need. I surreptitiously dropped my car keys back into my bag, and clutched the bag more tightly to my shoulder.

'Yes?' I said, in my most schoolmistressy voice, trying to sound bored yet aggressive. 'Could you move, please, you're in my way.'

'*Could you move, please, you're in my way,*' mimicked the tallest one, pulling a po-face at his friends. He folded his arms and moved closer to me. I looked up and down the street but it was empty. I could still hear music, though. If I shouted loudly enough, surely people would appear at the windows? I contemplated a judo kick – I'd done a few years' martial arts at college – but decided it was too risky. I couldn't take on all four of them, however weedy they were. Poor Max, having to live near those losers.

Then I heard a click, and saw a flash of silver from the boy next to the face-pulling one, a shorter, spottier one. He was slyly brandishing a penknife with a three-inch blade. 'Give us your bag,' he said, conversationally.

I'd always considered myself a tough woman, brave and, despite my skinny frame, reasonably strong. Now, when the chips were down, I wasn't so sure. Regardless of the adrenalin whooshing around my body, I felt my knees weaken. I looked around again. Bloody marvellous – thirteen years of living in London, many nights walking home in the wee small hours without any sort of incident; and now, in a sleepy Wiltshire market town at five o'clock on a summer's afternoon, I was being mugged at knifepoint. Penknife-point, maybe, but I still felt scared.

Then – and it was just like one of my teenage fantasies – I was unceremoniously rescued.

'What the hell do you think you're doing, you little toerags? Get lost. NOW.' Adam had marched up behind me, pushing a terrified-looking Max behind him to keep him out of range. He pointed at the one with the knife. 'I'll be on to your mother about this.' I had to admit that he looked kind of sexy when he was angry.

'Yeah, I bet you will,' sniggered one of the other ones. 'A right motherfucker, ain't you?' They all joined in with the laughter, but it was half-hearted and slightly nervous. Then they turned as one and, without another word, sloped back off down the alley.

16

'Hello, Max,' I said, rather rudely not thanking his father for saving my Quorn bacon; but at that moment I couldn't cope with looking at Adam in case I burst into tears. I still felt as if someone had removed my kneecaps, and it was a relief to crouch down, under the pretext of talking to Max on his own level. Stupid, I thought, to be so frightened by some spotty kids with a penknife. 'Remember me? We met before. I'm Anna.'

But Max jerked his head away and hid his face in Adam's leg.

'What is it, mate?' asked Adam, tilting Max's chin up with a cupped palm.

'I don't like those boys,' Max whispered. 'They scared me.'

'You know what, Max?' I said, swallowing hard. 'They scared me, too. They weren't nice boys, were they? Lucky we had your dad to look after us.'

Adam tousled Max's hair. 'You're OK now, Max,' he said. Then he reached out and gave my bare arm a little reassuring squeeze too. His fingers felt sandpapery and solid, and I imagined them stroking the hair back from Max's forehead when he was sick.

'Are you OK?' he repeated to me. He jerked his head towards number forty-three. 'Listen, we live just over there. Why don't you come in for a cup of tea?'

I didn't need asking twice. My legs were like jelly, and I badly needed to sit down properly, so I wobbled off across the road behind Adam and Max.

Max insisted on turning the key in the lock, and I waited while Adam lifted him up so he could reach it. 'Sorry,' said Adam. 'Just one of our little rituals.' I couldn't help looking behind me, to make sure we weren't about to be ambushed, but the road was empty once again, apart from a large ginger cat who sat on the bonnet of a nearby car, licking its bottom and glaring at me over an outstretched back leg.

I'm going into Max's house! I thought. It was obviously a meant-to-be. And I hadn't even lost my handbag in the process. Suddenly I felt a bizarre wash of gratitude to the four teenagers who had inadvertently helped me achieve my aim.

Max eventually managed to get the door open, and Adam set him down over the threshold. 'Do come in,' he said, standing to one side to allow me through. I stepped into a narrow hallway, dingily painted but with a lurid orange and lime-green batik wall hanging. It wasn't to my taste, particularly, but it did have a kind of chaotic brightening charm. The same could have been said for the rest of the downstairs. The decor was most definitely a few steps up from hippy chic, with Indian throws over the two sofas in the front room, and a shabby but beautiful Gabbeh rug on the floor. Max's toys were strewn around the place, and newspaper was spread on a dining table to protect it from some kind of painting activity which hadn't yet been cleared away.

'Max and I were making pretend stained glass,' Adam said, gesturing towards some sheets of plastic daubed with splodges of paint. 'You have to let it dry for twenty-four hours, then it peels off and you can stick it on windows and things.'

'But mine didn't come out right,' Max contributed. It was the first time he'd volunteered anything to me in conversation, and his words were music to my ears.

'Why not?'

He actually took my hand and dragged me towards the table. 'Look. Dad did his OK but I couldn't make the pen get the paint out straight, it comed out in all blotches.' He stuck a finger into one of the creations, smudging it further. 'Not dry yet, Dad,' he called.

'I think that one's lovely,' I said, trying to work out what the blobs of red paint were meant to represent.

'It's a apple,' he said, shooting me a sideways look which told me he knew exactly what I'd been thinking. He was smart, I thought, with unwarranted pride.

I knew I'd go to sleep that night with the memory of that small hand in mine. The perfection of his fingers and the sticky touch of his skin made me happier than anything had for a long, long time.

'Cup of tea?' asked Adam. 'Or would you prefer something stronger, for the shock – a brandy? Or a glass of wine, if it's a bit early for the hard stuff? There's some white in the fridge.'

'Well,' I said, thinking about the drive back. But I didn't need to leave for a while – with luck, I wouldn't have to leave for a while – and I *was* still feeling pretty shaken. 'Wine would be nice, if you're having some too.'

'Oh, any excuse,' said Adam, going through to a narrow kitchen and opening the fridge. 'It's good to have company.' Then he seemed to remember the circumstances under which I'd come to be in his house. 'So, what happened out there? They didn't hurt you, did they? I'd always thought they were harmless enough until now. Bunch of little shits.'

'Da-ad!'

Adam clamped his hand over his mouth in mock shame. 'Sorry, Max. Anna, would you like to come through? Our back room's a little bit more civilized.'

Reluctantly leaving Max at the table, where he was switching on a computer, I followed Adam out to the kitchen. 'No, they didn't hurt me. The knife was all part of the act. I'm sure they wouldn't have used it. But

I probably would have ended up handing over my purse, just in case.' I got a steely chill in the pit of my stomach just thinking about the flash of that knife. 'I really am grateful to you,' I said, abruptly.

'It was nothing,' Adam replied. 'They know that I know where they live, so they wouldn't have dared try and get nasty with me. The tall one and that one with the tattoo are brothers. They live in a flat with their mother at the top of the road. I'm just wondering if I should tell her, or maybe we should go to the police instead? It might be simpler – the mother's a piece of work, really, and I'm not sure if I want the aggravation of trying to complain to her.'

I was horrified at the thought that I'd caused aggravation to Adam; not to mention the idea of the police interviewing me, possibly with Adam present. Lying to him about my name and address was one thing, but to the police was quite a different matter.

'Oh, don't, please. Honestly, it's fine. I'm fine. Nothing was taken. They were just trying it on. And I really don't want to go through all the palaver of involving the police, or for you to get a load of grief from this woman either.'

'They shouldn't be allowed to get away with it. I wish I'd given them a good kicking to make sure they never try it again.' Adam sounded quite vicious. I couldn't imagine him giving anyone a good kicking, although he was certainly strong enough to. It was distinctly at odds with the idea that I had of him as a superannuated hippy.

He poured two generous glasses of wine, recorked the bottle and put it back in the fridge. 'Cheers.'

'Cheers,' I replied, accepting one of the glasses and taking a large swig. 'Oh, that's better.'

'It's a shock, isn't it, being mugged. Happened to me once in India. These two men pulled a knife on me, too, but they meant business, so I just handed it all over: cash, passport, everything. Took me days to get it all sorted. But at least I wasn't hurt.'

Adam gestured for me to come through the kitchen and sit down with him at a small pine table in a conservatory tacked on the back of the house. It was tidier than the front part, but the table had more rings than Tiffany's, and when I rested my elbow on it, it came away astonishingly sticky. It was patronizing to say that the place lacked a woman's touch – better perhaps to say that it lacked a cleaner.

'It's a good thing you came along,' I said, trying discreetly to rub the stickiness off my arm with a moistened finger. 'I was about to do something that I heard you were meant to do when being attacked by a group – throw your bag as high in the air as you can, because it surprises them. They'll look up at the bag, thus giving you the opportunity to leg it. But I've never been quite convinced that it would work, so I'm kind of glad I didn't try it.'

I had a sudden, awful vision of the scenario had I actually done that. My handbag, looping skywards in slow-motion circles, raining all its contents down on Hardcourt Road: loose tampons, lipsticks, tissues, keys, face powder, old bendy sticks of chewing gum – and worse, the map with Adam's address on it, and my documents stating that my name was Anna Sozi. All of which would have been lying in the road for Adam to come along and find. And where would I have been? I'd have run off and hidden, safe, but with absolutely none of my personal belongings, and my cover well and truly blown.

'Actually, you know, the more I think about it, the more ridiculous that idea is. I mean, you might as well just *hand* the bag over to them, mightn't you? If you chucked it in the air and ran away, they'd have got what they wanted in the first place, wouldn't they – your credit cards, car keys and money.'

Adam laughed. He bent down and picked up half a wizened carrot from the floor under the table, and lobbed it with deadly accuracy from where we sat right through the archway to the kitchen and into the sink.

'True. Mind you, I think I've heard that theory myself. I think actually it's more of a strategy if they *aren't* muggers, but are threatening physical violence on you for other reasons. It's definitely got that element of surprise.'

'Rapists, you mean,' I said. 'But you don't often get gangs of rapists, do you?'

'No, you don't, thankfully.' He paused. 'Well, this is a cheery conversation, isn't it?'

I knew what was coming next, and concentrated on a close inspection of Max's drawings on the fridge door, which I could see through the archway. They all featured people with arms coming straight out of the sides of their heads, and vertical lines at the bottoms of their legs which I thought at first represented grass stalks, but then realized must have been toes. Four separate lines, not joined to anything else, and then a large round circle for the big toe. Still, they were better than Crystal's efforts. At least you could tell they were meant to be people.

'So, what brings you to these parts, anyway? You live in Wealton, don't you?'

'I was just enquiring about getting something framed,' I said, as nonchalantly as I could.

'Yes, they're great, those framers. I've used them myself, quite a bit.' Luckily Adam didn't ask what I was having framed. *Oh, just imaginary photos of my unborn children . . .*

'I'll miss the project, when it's finished,' I said, to change the subject again.

'I know. It's been really successful,' he replied with pride. 'The contractor who's redoing the underpass by the station is coming to collect the panels on Friday. I'm organizing a night out for everyone who's been involved, to celebrate. A pizza or something. I hope you'll consider coming?'

'Of course, I'd love to,' I said, although I couldn't see much to celebrate. Just when I had a chance of getting to know Max, it would all be over.

'Daddy, I'm hungry,' said Max from the archway. He smiled at me, and I wanted to stay there for ever.

Adam leaped up. 'Sorry, honey, aren't I a terrible father? Sitting here drinking wine when it's your tea-time. Fish fingers and spaghetti hoops sound OK?'

'Fine,' said Max, putting his thumb in his mouth and leaning against the wall. He looked tired, and I instantly began to worry. Was he all right? Were those violet circles under his eyes normal, or signs of something sinister? Adam, however, seemed unperturbed.

'Excuse me while I put some tea on for this poor child,' he said, extracting a blackened, greasy grill pan from the oven and fishing a box out of a freezer compartment in dire need of defrosting. The box was covered with such a thick layer of snowy ice crystals that it was impossible to tell what was inside, but Adam seemed to know. He upended the box on the kitchen counter, and one fish finger plus a lot of orange crumbs fell out.

'Damn, only one left. We live on fish fingers. I'm not much of a chef,' he confessed. I was horrified: Max couldn't live on fish fingers! He needed wholesome, home-cooked food, free from salt and preservatives, bursting with vitamins. I had to bite my tongue to stop myself interrogating Adam as to whether Max got enough fresh vegetables.

'Not that he'd eat anything else if I did cook it,' he continued. 'He only likes pizza, eggs, sausages, chicken nuggets, and chips, of course, don't you, mate?'

'And cheese. And bread. And yogurt. And biscuits. And apples, and pasta,' Max added.

Almost identical to Crystal's diet, then, I thought. Still, Max didn't look undernourished.

'Do you like pasta with tomato sauce?' I asked, an idea forming. Crystal ate yards of spaghetti, but only with butter and cheese on it, 'nothing runny'.

Max nodded.

I stood up. 'Well, it just so happens that I make a pretty mean home-made pasta sauce,' I said casually.

162

'Shall I cook it for you – both of you, if you like? Seeing as there's only one fish finger left. It could be my way of thanking you for saving me back there.'

'Well . . .' said Adam, stroking his beard and gazing at a spot on the ceiling.

Both Max and I held our breath. 'Oh please, Daddy, let Anna stay and make my supper.' Max plucked his father's arm and I could have floated up to the ceiling on wings of delight.

'Wow, he really is tired of your cooking,' I said, laughing, although I came back down to earth with a bump when I became aware of Adam's real hesitation. Perhaps I'd misjudged the situation – what if he had a girlfriend coming over later? Hardly ideal for her to find another woman in the kitchen.

'I'm afraid we probably don't even have the ingredients,' he said eventually.

'You could go to the shop, Daddy!' Bless him, I thought, what a star. But that only made Adam seem even more uncomfortable.

'No, honey, we've just got in.' He turned to me. 'It's a lovely idea, but I don't really want to drag Max out again.'

Belatedly, I got it. He didn't want to take Max, but he wanted even less to leave him in the house with me, when he didn't really know me from, well, Adam. I'd got carried away with myself. All the hours of daydreaming about getting to know them had given me a false sense of intimacy with them both when, in reality, I'd only met Max once before and just spent a few hours making a mosaic with his father. For all Adam knew, I could be planning to abduct Max, or worse.

Or perhaps he really just didn't want me to stay to dinner . . . ? I felt torn. If that was the real reason, then my offering to go to the shop wouldn't make Adam feel any better about it. But if I *didn't*, then that was it anyway. I decided that I had nothing to lose except my pride. I'd offer, and if he still turned me down, that would be the end of it.

'I'm happy to nip out to the shops,' I said, cringing at how desperate I sounded. 'If you'd like me to cook, that is.'

'Well, if you're sure,' he replied. 'I really don't want to impose on you.'

'It would be my pleasure, honestly,' I said, looking into his eyes but wishing I was looking into Max's. Might as well go for it, I thought, it's my last chance. 'I mean, I'd love to get to know you both a bit better. There never seems to be a chance to chat properly at the hall, does there?'

I waited, every muscle tensed. The pause seemed to last an eternity.

Eventually Adam smiled. 'So, we have nothing in the fridge except a couple of onions and a bit of old garlic. I'm afraid you'll have to get everything else. My big shopping day is tomorrow.'

'No problem,' I said, imagining myself floating back up to the ceiling like an escaped helium balloon, my head bumping against the beaded lampshade. 'Where's the nearest food shop?'

'Tesco Metro on Shaftesbury Road.'

Oh no. Would Shaftesbury Road be on my map? Was it a walk, or a drive? I grimaced. Did Adam think it strange that I had to ask where the nearest shop was? 'Sorry, Adam, remind me – I'm quite new round here. Shaftesbury Road?'

'End of the street, right, and right again. The main high street. It's a five-minute walk, but I'd take the car if I were you. Just to be certain you, er, aren't hassled again.'

The thugs. I'd forgotten about them. 'Oh. Yes.'

'Shall I walk you out to your car? Max, you stay here, I'll be back in a second.'

So Adam escorted me across the road again, and I drove off to buy supper for him and Max, as if it was something I did every day. When I looked in the rear-view mirror, Adam was standing in the middle of the road, waving cheerfully at me.

As I wandered around the fresh-bread-scented Tesco's, I couldn't shake a strange dreamlike feeling that they *were* my family, and that after I'd made pasta sauce for them, I'd be tucking Max into bed and settling down in front of the TV with Adam. Bloody hell, I thought euphorically, that's too weird.

In the car park, once I'd dumped the bag of groceries on the front seat of the car, I dialled Ken's number. His office phone went straight to voicemail.

'Hi darling. Listen, someone from the mosaic workshop's just asked me if I could take care of their little boy this evening, so it looks like I won't be back until quite late. I know you're out, but just thought I'd keep you posted anyway. See you back at home. Love you. Bye.'

Then I switched off my phone and dropped it to the bottom of my handbag.

17

'Dad.'

'Yes?'

'Know what I saw on TV today?'

We were sitting at the table in the conservatory, which I'd wiped down with a frail, crispy J-cloth I found under the sink, and served up penne with my special tomato sauce. Outside, a row of six huge dying sunflowers drooped along the edge of a small, unmowed lawn, their once-bright heads brown and defeated, like slain giants. Adam and I had our wine, Max had a plastic beaker full of watery Ribena. I felt as if I were in heaven.

Max was using his knife to scrape sauce off his penne. I tried not to look disappointed as he speared the cleaned pasta tube with his fork and raised it gingerly to his mouth. He'd eaten all the mangetouts I'd steamed to go with it, but hardly any of the pasta.

'What did you see on TV, love?' Thankfully, Adam was managing a lot better. He'd nearly finished his plateful. A small blob of sauce had dropped onto his T-shirt, but he hadn't noticed and it seemed a little too personal to point it out.

'I saw how lamp-posts is made. *Green* lamp-posts is made from leaf oil heated up, little bits of cloud, and metal.'

Adam grinned at me. 'Really? Who'd have thought? Anna, did you know that's what green lamp-posts were made of?'

'Hmm, actually I didn't have any idea, until Max told me. That's amazing.'

Max nodded with a self-satisfied air. He managed to find two more pasta tubes which were fairly unsullied by the sauce, but then ground to a halt. 'I'm full,' he announced, uncertainly. 'Please may I get down?'

'You haven't eaten much, are you sure you're full?'

Max nodded.

'So you won't want any pudding?'

A disconsolate shake of the head.

Adam looked at his watch. 'Oh well. Say thank you to Anna, then you can play on the computer for ten minutes while we finish our supper, then it's bedtime. You can have a bath in the morning.'

'Brilliant! On school nights I always have to have a bath,' he said to me, as an aside. I immediately wondered if Max's postponed bathtime had anything to do with my presence. If so, then that was a good sign – if Adam had wanted me to leave, he could have used bathtime as a good excuse.

'Are you looking forward to going back to school, Max?'

'Yes! I'm not going to be in Nursery any more. I'm going to be in Reception, and I won't have to play with Aaron White in the home corner any more.'

'Well, I think Aaron will still be in your class, Max,' said Adam. 'We must get your new winter uniform tomorrow. All those name tapes to sew in!' He made a face at me, and it took every ounce of restraint I possessed not to offer to sew Max's name tapes in myself.

'Thanks for cooking dinner, Anna, it was absolutely delicious. We don't get many meals like that outside of restaurants.'

Max turned to me then, casually resting his hand on my leg. I wanted to clamp my own hand over the top of

167

his, press it down and iron it to me, to make his skin into my skin.

'You're very welcome,' I replied faintly, the combination of Max's touch and Adam's words leaving me feeling that I had never enjoyed a simple compliment more. Max wandered off into the next room and we heard the electronic crescendo of the computer being switched on. I drained the dregs of my wine glass, and Adam held out the bottle to me.

'Better not. I've got to drive home.'

'Not yet, I hope. And you could always get a cab.'

I laughed, then stopped abruptly, worried that he'd think I was laughing at the ridiculousness of the idea of staying longer. I wondered what he'd think if I told him that a cab back to my real house would cost a hundred pounds at least. How was I going to get out of this one?

'Well, maybe just a drop more.' I'd only had one glass. I'd be fine to drive. If there had ever been a time I needed a drink, it was then.

'Is there any more pasta?' Adam asked, finishing up his last mouthful.

'Yes, in the pan.' I wanted to laugh again at the strangeness of the situation. We were like an old married couple having a weekday supper together, as natural as breathing, our child playing in the background – and yet we'd only just met.

Nonetheless, I was loving it. It was the scene I'd dreamed of for years: the quiet pull of domesticity, the chattering of a child, the astonishingly potent comfort of gratitude, of being needed. Even if it was the wrong man, the wrong house and the wrong family, I still wanted to relish it, and make it last as long as possible. If Ken hadn't always been travelling or out, or if he were perhaps less obviously the provider, then maybe I'd have felt closer to the idyll with him, even in the stillness of a child-free home. But I had never felt like this with him. Love didn't come into it; it wasn't about love.

Still, I was relieved that I'd labelled the situation the

way I had: wrong man, wrong house and wrong family. It would have been worse if I'd thought that all those things were right, and it was *Ken* who was out of place.

It wasn't the wrong child, though. Max was, somehow, the right child.

I wished I knew why Adam had let me stay and cook dinner. Had he felt sorry for me? Was he too embarrassed to say no? Or was he attracted to me, and saw it as some kind of come-on? I hoped not. It was tricky. I was genuinely glad I liked him so much – it would have been so much harder to bond with Max had I not – but it was of paramount importance that Adam didn't think this was the start of a courtship. The last thing I wanted was for anybody to get hurt in this little charade of mine.

I was about to open my mouth and splurge out some lies along the lines of thinking about getting back, because my partner would be home soon, when I thought, No, how can I say that? He already thought I wasn't married, but marriage wasn't the issue. It was how weird it would sound, for me in effect to announce: Well, I'm off home to cook another supper for another man. Or woman. Would it have made things easier if I pretended to be a lesbian? At least that way he would know that I wasn't coming on to him.

All of a sudden I realized that cooking supper for another man was really a very intimate gesture, unless that other man was a very old friend, or a family member. It was categorically not what one did when one was meant to be in a relationship with someone else. The bait of Max, wriggling right in front of my eyes on the line, had confused me and I'd risen to meet him, eyes shut, mouth open. I wouldn't have dreamed of cooking for another man under any other circumstances. No wonder Adam had initially been hesitant.

And now – oh God, what was I getting into? – Adam was looking at me with, unless I was very much mistaken, a faintly dreamy warm expression, his eyes smiling and his mouth curving upwards. He might as well have had a speech bubble coming out of his mouth containing the words 'I really like you, Anna'. I may have been out of practice, but I still knew a smitten look when I saw one.

'You will stay a bit longer, won't you, Anna? I need to get Max to bed soon, but it would be lovely to have more of a chat after that.'

A chat. A chat. He didn't mean just a chat, did he? Look at those eyes, I thought frantically. He fancies me, and because I've cooked supper, he thinks it's mutual. Once Max had gone to bed we'd be drinking more wine, he'd put on a mellow CD, and before I knew it we'd be rolling around together mussing up the Indian throw on the sofa and waiting to see who'd make the first tentative queries about birth control. Then, whoops, I'd be having an affair that I didn't want, with a person I hardly knew, who lived a hundred miles away and whom I didn't even really fancy. Aargh.

If I left now, though, just when I was getting to know Max, how would I be able to come back, having burned my bridges with his father? And I had an urge, almost physical in its intensity, to read Max a bedtime story. It might be my only chance to, I thought. I had to risk it. I could handle Adam; head him off at the pass. For heaven's sake, I'd just tell him that I only wanted to be friends. Simple.

Strange electronic noises filtered through from the other room, reminding me of Ken and his BlackBerry. 'What's Max playing?' I asked abruptly.

'Pinball, probably. He's not very good at it yet, but give him a few more weeks and he'll be expert.'

'Pinball? How do you play pinball on a computer?'

'Go and have a look, if you like. It's really good.'

I didn't need asking twice. Scraping back my chair in haste, I shot through the kitchen into the living room as if I were the silver ball in the pinball machine, kicked into action by a coiled spring. Max was sitting at the table clicking away, accompanied by a soundtrack of what sounded like digital stomach gurgles.

'Yes! Wormhole!' he crowed, after a particularly jubilant gurgle.

'May I see?' I asked, pulling up a chair next to him. He nodded, without taking his eyes off the screen.

The pinball was identical to the machines I'd played many times in pubs over the years, and I marvelled at the way a complex three-dimensional game was rendered one-dimensional, whilst retaining a faithful impression of the clacking handles, ramps, and those three mushroom-like structures at the top between which the ball noisily ricocheted. Max was controlling the two flapping gates at the bottom with deft pressure on two of the keys on his computer keyboard – a Z and a slash, as far as I could see – and it was the space-bar which pulled back the spring to release the ball, but apart from that, everything was the same as on the real thing. The ball careered erratically around, and I had to remind myself that it wasn't even a real ball.

How was it possible, I thought, that somebody could design a computer program as complicated as virtual pinball, and yet no one, from the vast field of medical research, had discovered how to prevent a miscarriage? Not all miscarriages were due to birth defects in the fetus, they knew that much. It wasn't even something as complicated as preventing the common cold or curing cancer. It made me angry to think of computer nerds spending years developing a way of getting one stupid imaginary silver ball to behave like a real ball in a pub machine when there were so many other, important discoveries to be made.

The machine gave a low, disappointed gurgle. 'Game over. Terrible score,' said Max. 'Only six numbers.'

I squinted at the screen. 'No, Max, your score was one hundred and four thousand, four hundred and ninety-two – that's brilliant, isn't it?'

'Is that less than six million?'

'Well, yes.'

He frowned. 'That's no good then. Dad can do six million. Do you want a go?'

171

'Um . . . OK, I'll give it a shot. Although I'm sure your score will be higher than mine.'

'Can I sit on your knee?'

My breath caught in my throat. 'Of course.'

Max slid onto my lap, all gangly arms and legs, his bony bottom so different to Crystal's solidity. I wanted to gather up his limbs and keep them together; keep him literally in one piece, for ever. He smelled of sawdust and shampoo, tomato sauce and pencil lead. I pressed my lips together in an effort to stop myself kissing his hair. His presence made it more difficult to see the screen – he didn't seem to realize that his head was blocking my view – but I didn't care.

My first attempt at pinball was a disaster. The ball just about limped to the top of the screen, flicked itself half-heartedly against the mushrooms, and plummeted down in the gap between the two flappy gates which I was trying to control. Score: fifteen thousand.

'If you press them both together, it makes a bigger space for the ball to go through, so it's better not to,' said my coach earnestly.

'Hmm,' I said. 'So I see.'

I tried again, and did slightly better, although this time I was distracted by Adam putting on a CD: Van Morrison, *Astral Weeks*. It wasn't Marvin Gaye's *Sexual Healing* or anything, but all the same, undeniably mood-setting and borderline smoochy. As my virtual ball disappeared into a hole, prompting a cacophony of whoops from the machine and a 'Yay, Anna!' from Max, I found myself trying to remember what sort of underwear I had on. Even though I had absolutely *no* intention of allowing myself to be seduced. It was an oddly Pavlovian reaction, I thought. If he opens another bottle of wine, or, heaven forbid, lights any candles, then I'll know I'm in trouble. A rogue part of me felt a small thrill of anticipation, which I tried to crush immediately. What the hell was wrong with me? Flirty thirties, that's what Vicky called them. Maybe I was just experiencing an attack of the flirty thirties;

wanting to know that, even though I was happily married, I was still attractive to other men.

I sneaked a peek over my shoulder to see what Adam was doing. He was bending down, collecting up some Happy Family cards which had lain scattered on the floor. I couldn't help but notice that his bottom in its faded Levis was rather appealing. Very appealing, in fact.

Not that that had anything to do with anything.

I was losing it. I really ought to leave now, I thought. But the warmth and weight of Max on my lap pinned me there, a happy captive. Just go with the flow, said the devil on my shoulder. Worry about the complexities of it all later.

'Right, bedtime, Max,' called Adam. He came over to us, holding a mug of milk.

'Awww, Dad,' said Max, but he slid off my lap immediately, taking his father's hand. I was very impressed. Where were the tantrums, the pleading and bargaining, the histrionics which always accompanied that same announcement in Vicky's house?

Vicky. Was she still pregnant, or not? Vicky and her problems seemed a million miles away from this shabby warm terraced house, and I felt grateful for it. Being with Adam and Max was like an escape: I was exempt from real life when I was here; immune to everything except the immediate experience. It was as good as a holiday. I hadn't realized how much I'd wanted a break from my life.

'Say goodnight to Anna.' Then he turned to me. 'I'll be about ten minutes, so do make yourself at home. Watch TV if you like – the remote's on the armchair.'

'Goodnight, Anna,' Max said dutifully, hovering at his father's side. Then he let go of Adam's hand, skipped forward and gave me a spontaneous and warm hug around my middle which left me dizzy with emotion. I hugged him back, unable to reply, thus losing my chance to ask to read him a bedtime story. There was just going to have to be a next time, that was all, I thought, waving at him as he and Adam turned to walk up the stairs. My vision was so blurred with tears that they looked as if they were floating away from me.

Once they were out of sight, though, the spell was suddenly broken. I was alone in this strange narrow house with fingerprints on the wallpaper and greying skirting boards, Van Morrison in the background and the glare of a computer screen accusing me of thinking about infidelity. It was nice to have felt that I belonged here, but I didn't.

But if I left now, I agonized, when would I be allowed back? Max might ask after me for a time, then pretty soon he'd forget me, once he was back in a termtime routine of packed lunches and skinned knees, friends to play with and friends to fall out with. Adam might say: Remember that nice lady Anna who cooked us supper that time? Max's brow would furrow. No-oo, he'd reply. I don't remember.

I paced up and down the front room in a state of mind which, if not quite a panic, was a definite funk. Decisiveness never had been my strong point – my dad used to call me Little Miss Ditherer – but I really couldn't decide what to do. Then I began to worry that Adam would hear me wearing tracks through his carpet, so I made myself stand still, and distracted myself by having a good nose around the room instead.

Photographs of Max, some with Adam, some on his own, dotted the built-in shelves on either side of a drab tiled fireplace. There was a small snap of a much younger Max, bald, and looking heartbreakingly un-well, with the stick limbs and translucent skin of the child invalid. He lay, half smiling, in the arms of a woman whom I assumed was the absentee mother. Her beaming face seemed at odds with Max's obvious frailty. She was quite pretty, despite being slightly moonfaced and soft under the jaw – one of those women who knew that their smile was their best asset. I could hear Adam's voice in my head, besotted with

174

her when they first met: 'You have such a beautiful smile.'

'You ain't all that,' I muttered at her photograph. 'And where the hell are you now? Don't you think your son needs you?'

Still, I thought, her absence was what made my presence possible, so I ought to have been thankful to her.

I tilted my head to one side to read the spines of the books on the lower shelves. They were an eclectic mixture of titles, the vast majority of which made me feel ill-educated and inferior: Wittgenstein, Heidegger, Goethe, Kundera. I searched in vain for something to identify with, a Marian Keyes or a Stephen King, but the closest Adam came to contemporary fiction was a copy of Joseph O'Connor's *Inishowen*. I was impressed. There were a lot of spiritual-sounding books too, confirming my suspicions about Adam's hippy origins: Thomas Moore's *Care of the Soul*; Rudoph Steiner's *Understanding Angels*, Parkers' Astrology. What with Van banging on in the background, I realized that the house reminded me overwhelmingly of a step up from a student room in a hall of residence in the late seventies: the batik hangings and tie-dye cushions, tatty philosophy and unhoovered carpet, potted cactuses, Van Morrison and – I checked – other hippy staples such as the Doobie Brothers, Little Feat and the Byrds on the CD shelf.

I was slightly ashamed that my reaction was so snobbish, a sort of 'so this is how the other half lives'. Wealth had crept up on Ken and me, measured by his regular bonuses and promotions, and a percentage of royalty points on a pop album which had gone several times platinum two years previously. Our houses, although we hadn't done much with them, had become larger and larger, in better and better areas; when we socialized, we did so with people of our own social status or higher. I'd sort of forgotten that not everybody had such a comfortable lifestyle: two cars, a cab

175

account, thinking nothing of spending over ninety pounds on a dinner for two, or five grand on a fortnight in the Caribbean. Although the chance would be a fine thing, I thought wistfully. We had the wherewithal for a lounger by a turquoise pool somewhere tropical, but Ken never seemed able to take enough time off to make it worth the effort of going. He just proudly showed me his payslips instead, and talked about his bonuses as fondly as if they were his offspring, as if that ought to make up for it.

It struck me suddenly that I would have swapped my life and all its material trappings in a heartbeat, for this scruffy little house with Max in it. Money couldn't buy what I wanted most.

Upstairs a toilet flushed, Max giggled, and footsteps pounded along a hallway and into a room over my head. I heard the squeak of bedsprings; the sound of curtains being drawn; Adam's voice, soothing but firm, then quiet. I strained to hear more, but could make out nothing other than the low hum of reading.

To distract me from the envy I felt that I wasn't reading to Max, I delved into my bag and extracted my mobile. Switching it on, I saw that there was a text message from Ken: 'HOPE YOU WON'T BE TOO LATE. WILL BE HOME WHEN YOU GET IN COS I'VE GOT A SURPRISE FOR YOU! LOVE YOU XXX'

Guilt washed over me, bathing me in its sickly green light until I felt like I was drowning. The message made up my mind for me: I had to go. I had to get home to my husband before things got out of hand, Max or no Max. I shoved the phone back in my bag, and looked around for something to write a note to Adam on. If I saw him, I wouldn't be able to leave.

At that moment, I heard a tread on the stairs.

'Sorry, Anna, to put this on you, but do you think you could pop up here for a minute? Max wants to show you something.'

My head blocked out Adam's voice. My head made for the door, took out my car keys and left without another word. My head knew it was for the best. My head was on the road home – before it realized that my body had bounded two by two up the stairs and was squeezing past Adam in the hallway to end up standing by Max's bed.

'Guess what I can do, Anna? I forgot to show you earlier. Listen.' Max was lying with his head on the pillow, in Bob the Builder pyjamas, looking utterly angelic. He put his finger into his mouth, inflated his cheek, and made several enthusiastic 'pop goes the weasel' sounds by yanking the finger out again.

'That's brilliant. I couldn't do that until I was much older than you are.'

'And listen, I can do this too.' He clicked his fingers as if summoning a waiter. Then he popped his mouth again.

I laughed. 'Fantastic. Thank you for showing me. And now I think you'd better go to sleep. Shall I turn out the light for you?'

'Yes please. But leave the door open cos I'm afraid of the dark.'

'OK. Goodnight, Max.'

'Goodnight.' He rolled over onto his side, clutching a stuffed tiger under his armpit, and twiddling a strand of hair between his fingers. I was itching to stroke his head, but made myself stand my ground. I shouldn't even have gone up there. I took one last long look at him and his bedroom – he had a dragon and a castle appliqued on his duvet cover, with a prince and princess on the pillowcase – and wished him fairytale dreams. I couldn't resist folding his clothes and placing them in a pile on top of the nearest available surface, which was the keyboard of a small brightly-coloured kiddy synthesizer, and then I lined his scattered shoes up in a pair, before treading heavy-hearted out of the clouds and down the stairs.

Back towards my boring, childless, meaningless life.

18

Adam had gone down ahead of me. As I'd suspected he might, he had hastily turned off the overhead lights and opened another bottle of wine. He'd also lit some twisty beeswax candles, which were spitting quietly but audibly over the sound of the music (Lowell George now, instead of Van). He'd placed the wine on a coffee table in front of the sofa where he sat, trying to look casual. I imagined him running around like a maniac in the two minutes before I'd followed him downstairs, trying to set the scene and yet look calm and cool when I arrived. It didn't fool me for a moment, and my heart went out to him.

He *had* seen my offer to cook supper as a come-on, and because we'd got on so well, it would have been only natural to snuggle into the candlelit sofa, not touching but chatting more intimately, on a first date all the more exciting for its spontaneity. I realized how much I missed that first-date thing. I knew it was wrong, and unspeakably dangerous, but I wanted it to feel like a first date.

'I love this song,' I said when 'Twenty Million Things' came on. 'It's Lowell George, isn't it? I don't have this record but always wanted to get it, just for this track.'

Adam beamed. 'I'm very impressed you recognized

it. Little Feat are my all-time favourite band.' He hesitated. 'Would you like another glass of wine?' He held the bottle poised over my empty glass, as if demonstrating the heavy air of suspense in the room.

I wanted to stay so badly. The heady combination of being rescued, cooking for Max, and two glasses of wine had given the evening a rose-coloured hue, and Adam's obvious attraction to me was in turn attracting me to him. There was something so inviting about him: his warmth and openness, unthreatening bulk and soft edges. And he'd smelled so damn nice, too, when I passed him on the way into Max's room. He was growing on me, like honeysuckle.

'OK. Thanks. I'd love another glass,' I said. 'But just a small one, I don't want to be over the limit, and I mustn't get a cab home, I'm going to need the car tomorrow morning.'

I sat down, bracing myself for the inevitable questions that I knew would come once we really got talking. It was fair enough, I thought: I'd thus far steered conversation away from any mention of my personal life, and it would begin to seem as if I was being deliberately evasive if I continued to avoid Adam's enquiries. Which of course I was . . . but on balance it seemed better to tell a few mild lies than to come over like some sort of International Woman of Mystery. I didn't want him to start suspecting that I was on the FBI's Most Wanted list, or anything.

'So you aren't working at the moment?'

I took a sip of the good, cold wine. Must remember to drink a lot of water before I left, I told myself.

'No. I haven't done for a while, actually – a combination of wanting some time off, and not getting the right job. I'm kind of over rep – all that travelling – so I've been holding out for a TV gig. Actually, I'm waiting to hear about an audition I had for a West Country cable soap. I'm hoping I get it.' Well, I *had* been hoping, until I heard that I hadn't got it . . . never mind. Adam didn't need to know that.

179

'And what brings you to Gillingsbury?'

I hesitated. 'Oh, you know, no particular reason. I've always really liked the countryside round here. I just wanted to get out of London and live somewhere a bit more rural.'

He nodded. 'You . . . live on your own over in Wealton?'

Since it was an imaginary house, I felt justified in filling it with as few or many imaginary inhabitants as I liked. I toyed with the idea of saying that I did have a partner, but the naked vulnerability in Adam's eyes stopped me. I might never see Max again if Adam thought I was already in a relationship.

'Yes. Young, free and single, that's me.' Oh, this was terrible. I wasn't sure what I felt worse about: lying; raising Adam's hopes; or being there with him when I ought to have been at home with Ken. I tried to temper the statement, but it came out laboured and unconvincing: 'I just wanted a bit of a break from relationships, really. You know, time out and all that. I think everyone should be single for a while, after a long relationship.'

I made a long-suffering 'please don't ask me anything more, it's too painful' face, and it seemed to do the trick. Adam, looking somewhat crestfallen, didn't pursue it.

'So, tell me about your family. Are your parents still alive?' he said instead. That was an easier one, I thought, relieved.

'No. My dad died when I was eighteen. Heart attack . . .' I had to swallow the memory, hard, like a sharp corner of a nut that wouldn't go down. 'And Mum died when I was older. Cancer,' I rushed on, not wanting his condolences. I wanted to carry on talking about them, because I was on much less shaky ground. Those facts were immutable; a non-flexible history which couldn't be rewritten like I'd been rewriting my own.

'I've got one brother, Olly. He works at John Lewis, but is taking some time off to travel. We get on fine, but I don't see much of him.'

'And how did you get into acting?'

I relaxed. Another easy one. 'I caught the acting bug from my mother, I suppose; she was a leading light in the Harpenden Am-Dram society. My parents met there, actually. Dad couldn't act or sing, but he said he just joined to meet girls. He always got the very minor second-spear-carrier-type parts. He used to admire Mum from the back of the stage – she'd be up there, giving her all to whatever role it was. She loved it.' I sighed. It seemed like such a lifetime ago. 'She wasn't all that keen on *me* going into the theatre though. Said it would be far better as a hobby, and that I'd spend most of my time out of work.'

'And do you?'

'Yes,' I said sheepishly, and we laughed.

At the time, though, I'd been a lot less acquiescent.

'How do you know? I might be really famous,' I'd replied defiantly, Mum's resistance merely strengthening my own resolve. She had been funny like that – one minute building me up and praising me, the next, dooming all my ventures to failure, constantly changing her mind and blowing hot and cold. She'd done the same with Olly. When he first came out as gay, the year before she died, she'd been speechless with horror for a week; but after that had flirted madly with Olly's first boyfriend (or rather, the first one we'd been allowed to meet), and had begun to boast about it to her Am-Dram friends. None of *their* children were anything nearly as exotic as being homosexual. The most glamorous thing that had ever happened to any of their dreary offspring had been when Harold and Minty Handy's daughter Joy got a job on the Estée Lauder counter at Debenhams.

'Poor Mum. I still miss her,' I said. It was true; although I'd never missed her as much as I missed the steady constant presence of my father, with his quiet humour and warm hugs.

'She used to be quite disparaging to Dad really, putting him down for what were his strengths:

traditional family values, stoicism, hard work – but she was devastated when he died. Olly and I had her down for husband number two within three years, but she never married again. She had lots of dates, though, and enjoyed telling us about them afterwards. You know' – I waved my wine glass in the air and affected a very luvvie voice – '"Oh darlings, he was simply ghastly! Said he liked theatre but didn't know his Ibsen from his elbow! And he let his tie go in the soup!"'

Adam laughed, but there was sympathy on his face.

'She lost the spark in her eyes after Daddy died,' I finished, feeling suddenly sad. 'Sorry, I'm really banging on, aren't I? You're a very good listener.'

'You're a very good talker.'

'I'll take that as a compliment, shall I?'

'Do . . . So how old were you when she died?'

'Twenty-seven. Olly was twenty-four. There was only a month between when she was diagnosed and when she died. She just hadn't been able to accept it. Didn't have time to, I suppose.'

She'd died in a fury of disbelief, railing against everyone: God, us, herself, the doctors, the NHS . . . It had been terrible, but Lil gathered all three of us up in her thin strong arms and got us through it, moving into Mum's house and taking care of her and us. Mum never had any idea of how much Lil had done for her.

'She just did not want to go. Not that anybody ever does, I suppose . . . Anyway, tell me something about you instead.'

As Adam opened his mouth, I realized exactly how comfortable I felt in his house – more comfortable, somehow, than I did in my own home. Guilt pricked at the back of my neck as I visualized Ken already back from work, fixing himself a drink and calling the office in LA whilst watching *EastEnders* with the volume muted. He'd be peeling his socks away from his feet, probably at this very moment, and thinking about what to cook. I ought to give him a call on the way back to tell him that I'd already eaten. I thought of his text message and wondered what the surprise was that he had waiting for me.

'Before I forget,' Adam said, 'are you up for this end-of-project dinner I'm planning? Nothing too fancy, probably just a few beers and a curry at the Raj. Or maybe a pizza. Haven't decided yet.'

'When is it?' I smiled back at him. Although I had to admit the prospect of dinner with Mitch and Ralph present wasn't exactly riveting – I wasn't sure that there could be anything left in Ralph's life that he hadn't already told me about, while Mitch would probably get drunk on snakebite – it represented another definite meeting with Adam, and might in turn lead to the next encounter with Max which, I reminded myself, was the main incentive.

'A week on Saturday. Will we see you at the project again before then – there're just the finishing touches to do – or shall I just take your phone number and give you a call about it nearer the time?'

'Oh, I really want to see it to the bitter end! Although it sort of depends on whether I hear about this job or not. I might have to go up to London for another interview. Would you mind if I take your number and give you a ring?'

He didn't seem to mind that I had declined to give him my number, and wrote his own down with one of Max's felt tips on a corner of a page of the previous weekend's *Observer* magazine, which he ripped off and handed to me. I tucked it into the side pocket of my combat trousers, and we sank companionably against the back of the sofa again.

'Max is really, really wonderful,' I said, gazing across at the photos of him.

Adam rubbed his chin and looked pleased. 'Thank you. Yes, he's a fantastic kid. I don't know how he manages to be so cheerful all the time, after everything he's been through. Still, kids don't know anything else, do they? He just does seem to be naturally sunny.'

'He is,' I agreed. 'But I'm sure that's all credit to you.

You should see my goddaughter, Crystal. She's only a few months younger than Max, but, boy, she hardly opens her mouth except to complain about something. She's like a four-year-old version of Johnny Vegas, only not intentionally funny. I do love her, though. I just don't think she gets enough attention.'

'I worry that Max gets too much. I mean, we all had to put our lives on hold for him when he was ill, and if he said "Jump" we'd all say "How high, Max?" Not that I begrudge it; I love spending time with him. But I do sometimes worry that he ought to be a little more independent.'

'I think you do an amazing job, taking care of him,' I said with feeling. 'He's clearly very content and stable.' My eyes were drawn to the photo of him with his mother, and I was dying to ask – but I couldn't. Instead I said: 'It must have been terrible when he was ill.'

I saw Adam's shoulders instantly tense up. He didn't say anything for a moment, and then when he did speak, he was staring at a spot on the ceiling.

'It was the worst time of my whole life. Pretty much every morning for two years, I thought, I can't bear it. I don't want to get out of bed, because I can't bear seeing my son so sick; with all the needles and tubes and machines. Being so thin, and losing his hair, and not being able to keep anything down. He couldn't play, or run around – or, for a while, even walk or talk. He was too wiped out. It was just terrible . . . But we had to let the doctors do what they had to do, because the only thing worse than watching him suffer was the thought that he might die. And, in a weird sort of way, however terrible it was, we got used to it. I got so used to not being able to bear it, that I bore it. If you see what I mean.'

I was so horrified to see tears swimming in Adam's eyes that I didn't even notice the one rolling down my own cheek. I swallowed hard, but he saw, and when he put his hand on mine and squeezed it, I didn't move away. In fact, it seemed the most natural thing in the world for me to turn my palm up and let our fingers intertwine.

'I'm sorry to bring it up and upset you like that,' I said. 'He is – he's OK now though, you said, isn't he?' I wanted to hear Adam say it again.

Adam nodded and smiled, still holding my hand. 'Yes. He's OK now. And I'm sorry I got all heavy on you. I don't think I'll ever be able to remember it without getting upset, as long as I live.'

'That's fine.'

He turned and looked in my face, and I felt such a surge of connection that I just stared mutely back at him. I had a sudden flash of fear: people say that you know when you meet your soulmate. I'd thought I had when I met Ken – but what if I'd been wrong?

Then I remembered Ken at home, waiting, and his angular, kind, tired face, and I knew that however much I identified with Adam, had even begun to fancy him, it was Ken whom I loved.

'I'm really glad to get to know you a bit better, Anna,' said Adam, still holding my gaze, and my hand.

'Me you too,' I said awkwardly, feeling like a teenager. 'It's been a lovely evening, and thanks again for rescuing me.' I made a big show of looking at my watch, which involved extricating my hand. I was genuinely shocked to discover that it was past eight o'clock. 'Oh crikey, I must go. I'm, um, expecting a call this evening.'

I stood up, and Adam followed suit. We were standing, slightly hemmed in by the coffee table bearing our unfinished glasses of wine. He was much taller than me, and of course broader, but when he tentatively leaned forward and hugged me, we seemed to fit together. I hugged him back equally tentatively at first, and then with more conviction – his chest was warm and solid, so different to Ken's narrow torso. Ken was the one I loved, but it didn't stop the hug from feeling great. Adam smelled musty and sweet. I didn't dare raise my cheek from where it was pressed against his collarbone, because if I had, I knew I'd have been tempted to see if his lips were as soft as I was guiltily imagining they were . . .

Maybe it was the novelty of being hugged by somebody other than my husband, or maybe I did just genuinely feel I'd bonded with this man, but my body was responding in spontaneous ways; ways which it hadn't done with Ken in quite some time. I had to pull away from Adam in case he felt my nipples harden against his chest.

I felt awful: awful, and tremendously aroused at the same time. It wasn't a comfortable feeling.

'Right, well, thanks again,' I gabbled, grabbing my bag from the sofa and checking that I had my phone.

'Ring me about the curry, or pizza or whatever. I should know what we're doing next week. Good luck with the soap job in the meantime,' said Adam, grinning at me and rubbing the side of my arm affectionately. There was something extremely endearing about his easy familiarity with me. 'And maybe we could get together ourselves, soon?' he added.

I tried to convince myself that the only reason I was agreeing was because of Max. 'Definitely. Perhaps we could take Max for a picnic or something?'

'Great. Let's arrange it at the group dinner, or give me a call. I might not be around at Moose Hall that much tomorrow or Friday – I've got to start planning my courses for this term. I've left Serena in charge.'

'OK. Well, see you at the dinner then.'

'Yes. Look forward to it.'

I ran across the road and got swiftly into my car, relieved that my tyres hadn't been slashed or my paintwork scarred. Adam was waving from the doorway, but I still looked nervously around me to make sure there were no slouching figures emerging from alleys. The memory of the incident had already faded, though, after the joy of spending the evening with Max and Adam. I'd seen Max's bedroom! He liked me!

Adam liked me! . . . Although that probably wasn't something to be quite so jubilant about. I felt worried for a while, and then as I accelerated round the roundabout towards the London Road, I cheered up again. I could handle Adam. It was actually great that we liked one another so much. It would be easy to damp down the mutual attraction into friendship; I was sure it would. I'd just have to plan my words carefully, and make sure I didn't lead him on. So, no more hugs then. Which was a shame. He'd been lovely to hug.

In fact, I convinced myself as I sped along the Roman road out of the town, it was probably all in my mind anyway. Our evening could just as easily have been construed as a developing friendship as a burgeoning relationship. More than likely it was just my own vanity, assuming that he fancied me.

The light was fading, and the hedgerows at the roadside began to blur into bosky shapes only occasionally illuminated by the lights of oncoming vehicles. I couldn't see the beautiful patchwork of fields on the hillsides beyond those hedges, but knowing that they were there was comforting. Gradually learning the topography of the landscape seemed to help validate my claim on Gillingsbury, and on Adam and Max. Along with the feel of Adam's warm hand, and the closeness of our hug.

My guilt evaporated. However weird and screwed up it all was, it was also somehow *right*. It had been a lovely evening; Adam was a lovely man, and Max was even lovelier. I had made two new friends, and however logistically tricky it was going to be to juggle them with my life at home with Ken, I just knew it would be worth it. I would make it work.

19

'I'm home!' I called as soon as I got in the front door. My shoulders felt stiff and my eyes tired from driving nearly a hundred miles too fast in failing light, and my bladder was seriously overburdened, but I was happy to be back. I hobbled towards the downstairs bathroom, waiting to hear Ken's welcoming voice, but there was no answer.

When I emerged, feeling several gallons lighter, the house was still and gloomy, no nice cooking smells or welcoming hum and flicker of television to greet me as I wandered about. My heart missed a beat when I saw a note, scribbled on the back of one of Ken's chart printouts, propped up against a vase containing some freesias well past their prime. My guilty conscience reared up again, assuming that he'd somehow discovered I had been out cooking dinner for another man and not babysitting at all. I told myself to get a grip – there was no way he'd be cruel enough to text message saying he had a nice surprise for me, and that he loved me, if he'd been about to leave me. Besides, hadn't I already decided that I had nothing to feel guilty about? Nothing had happened at Adam's. Hugging was what friends did, wasn't it?

I unfolded the note with trepidation, but all it said was: 'Tried to ring to see what time you'd be back.'

Damn, I'd forgotten to call him en route. Although that was probably just as well. It would have been hard to call from the motorway and pretend I was actually sitting watching TV in a living room somewhere. 'Decided to get a quick game of tennis in. Back at 9.30. Look in the breadbin!'

The breadbin? Maybe his surprise was that he'd baked me some cookies. That would indeed have been a surprise – Ken was a superb cook, but in that exclusively male way: all for effect rather than for provision's sake. He could knock up an astonishingly good skate wing on a base of Puy lentils, but I'd never known him to bake anything as mundane as a muffin or a flapjack.

I lifted the lid of the breadbin. Inside was a British Airways cardboard envelope. Oooh, I thought with a rush of pleasure, hadn't I just been dreaming about how nice it would be to get away for a holiday? I had visions of Barbados at Christmas, or perhaps sooner, maybe a nice quiet Tuscan villa in September, when it was still warm but not too hot there. I'd need a new bikini – if I did a gazillion sit-ups every day between now and—

I got the first shock – *next week*? He'd booked us two tickets to Ibiza, departing next Saturday! I squinted at the itinerary. But what about the night out in Gillingsbury? I was so flummoxed that I didn't hear Ken come in behind me.

'What do you think?' he said, the pride in his voice unmistakable even as I was jumping out of my skin with fright.

'You startled me,' I said, leaping up, still holding the tickets. 'Hi, darling.'

I kissed him, but couldn't meet his eyes. He was still in his tennis gear, the dark hair on his chest showing through the damp white shirt sticking to his skin.

'Good match?'

He nodded, wiping his forehead on the hem of the shirt, then frowned. 'Yeah, but Simon thrashed me:

six–three, six–two. Forget that, though. What about the holiday?'

I opened my mouth, but it was a good few seconds before any words formed.

'I don't know what to say.'

'I know, I know, I bet you thought I'd never be able to get two weeks off. I managed to get hold of Olly – don't ask me how, it was a nightmare – and he says he knows a hotel that's not too full of girls in white stilettos, and he's been working in this great club—'

'I'm not sure that I can come,' I interrupted, wincing at the shocked expression on Ken's face. He was unaccustomed to having people not fitting in with his plans.

'What do you mean? How many times in the last six months have you said you were desperate to get away for a bit, and how often have you said how much you missed your brother? I thought you'd be delighted.'

I thought of Max, fast asleep under his castle duvet. 'Things have changed.'

'What things?'

I looked around our kitchen. Nothing in *here* had changed. There were no fingerpainted masterpieces stuck to the fridge door, no primary-coloured plastic beakers upended on the draining boards, no splodges of dried cereal spackling the counters. How could I tell Ken without hurting him?

But there was no way I was going to miss the night out with Adam, not just when we were beginning to get closer. I had to see him, so we could firm up the next outing with Max.

'*What* things have changed?' Ken repeated, through a clenched jaw. 'I went to a lot of trouble to organize this, you know. I mean, it's not like booking a bloody package holiday: I had to write to your brother care of that PO Box number he put on his postcard – perish the thought that he might have a mobile that works – and then wait for him to ring me at the office, then make

190

sure he knew somewhere decent for us to stay, then book the flights . . .'

I was only half listening. Of course, I had to go to Ibiza; see Olly, chill out with Ken. I was sure I could come up with some excuse to placate Adam. He wasn't going to ban me from ever seeing Max again just because I couldn't make one night out with the mosaic team, was he? It was so sweet of Ken to go to all that trouble.

Ken had turned away from me and was pouring himself a glass of apple juice from the fridge. I could see from the set of his shoulders that he was furious with me.

'Ken—' I began, touching his damp back tentatively. 'I'm sorry.' As I stared at the black hairs on his neck, where the ends of his short haircut tapered down into stubble, I realized that if I went to Ibiza, I wouldn't see Max for over a fortnight. By the time I got back, it would be September; he'd have started his new term, and opportunities to spend time with him would be curtailed even further. I felt an almost physical longing to be with him, to feast my eyes on his thin, delicate limbs and to bask in his smile. It felt like an addiction. Now I'd spent time with him, I wanted to spend *more* time. And with Adam, too . . . I remembered that hug, and goosebumps broke out down the backs of my arms and legs.

'I can't come,' I blurted, surprising myself almost as much as I was about to surprise Ken, 'because I got that job on the cable soap. Remember that audition I had?'

Ken wheeled around, slamming his glass on the counter and grabbing the sides of my arms. 'You got the job?' he said incredulously, his entire face lighting up. 'You really got it? I thought Fenella hadn't been in touch, so I assumed that you were out of the running. Why didn't you tell me you'd been called back? I suppose you were worried that it might be tempting fate, I know you – isn't that right?'

I nodded, thinking that maybe it was less of a lie if it

191

wasn't spoken aloud, and tried to look as pleased as he did.

'You'll be working again! Oh, babe, that's such wonderful news. And it starts filming that soon?' His face clouded. 'So you'll be away for – how many days a week?'

'I'm not sure yet,' I said, staring at the floor. I'd never lied to Ken before, and it was making me feel nauseous, especially in the light of having so recently denied I was even married to him. 'Maybe three or four. But it won't make that much difference to us, will it? I mean, most nights I'm in bed before you even get home. And we'll just have to make more of our weekends.' I felt terrible, sure that he'd be able to tell I was lying.

He nodded and hugged me, whirling me around the kitchen. He was sweaty and slightly odorous, but I had never minded the smell of Ken's sweat. 'Oh, you're such a dark horse. I'm so proud of you.'

'I'm sorry about the holiday.'

'Don't worry. I booked the tickets on Air Miles, so we haven't lost any money. I'm sure there's time to cancel the hotel without having to pay the whole cost. Your brother'll be disappointed, but I'm sure he'll understand when you tell him the reason. We'll go later in the year, shall we – Olly says he and Russ will be staying for several months, they're having such a good time – when you've been on the show long enough to ask for some leave. Maybe you can get Fenella to write two weeks' holiday before Christmas into your contract. Darling, I'm so pleased for you!'

'Thank you. I don't deserve you,' I said with feeling, giving him a hug, sweat and all. He kissed the top of my head.

'It's just what you needed – and it might be the start of big things happening for your career, don't you think?'

'Well,' I said modestly, thinking: In for a penny . . . 'They've got this really hot director on board. He's the one who did that brilliant TV ad for John Lewis, remember? Fenella said that everyone's raving about him.'

'So will I be able to watch you on cable then?'

If I pretended I was playing a role, the lying did become easier. Slightly easier. I couldn't go back now.

'I don't think so, no. I'm pretty sure it's just regional. Anyway, hot director or no hot director, it'll probably be lame as hell. You know what cable soaps are like: all shaky walls and no budget. And it goes out early afternoons.'

'Good salary?'

'Not too bad – about five hundred a week.' No worries there – all my acting earnings (though they'd barely crawled into five figures for the past ten years) went into my own account. All I'd have to do is to intercept the bank statements, which was easy when Ken was never home at the same time as the postman's deliveries.

'Fantastic! That'll boost our savings. You know, you should buy yourself a new car. It's about time we upgraded that old banger of yours.'

I nodded and gulped, feeling as if I were digging a hole in the sand for myself. At the moment it was fine, cool and damp on my hot skin, but I knew that sooner or later the hole would feel oppressive, cold and wet; I'd want to get out, but the walls would start crumbling . . .

Then I thought of Max, and felt a shift to pure joy, because I'd just granted myself an unconditional licence to spend as much time with him as Adam would permit. All I'd need to do was to tell Adam the same lie, and then neither Adam nor Ken would question my extended absences. Lying was a state of mind, like confidence, I decided. You just had to brazen it out, and not show any lack of conviction.

There was absolutely no point in worrying about the consequences until – unless – I had to. As long as I kept things chaste with Adam, then even if I did have to come clean to Ken one day, I was sure Ken would understand. Maybe we would end up buying a second home in Gillingsbury for real. By that time, I'd be good enough friends with Adam that he'd have ceased to see me as a potential girlfriend. Adam and Ken could become friends. Maybe Adam would let us take Max on holiday . . .

'Have you told Vicky yet?'

Vicky. I wondered how she was. Perhaps it was a good thing we weren't currently speaking. Of all the people to fool, Vicky would be the hardest. Ken didn't *expect* me to lie to him, Adam didn't know me well enough to be able to tell, but Vicky would know instantly.

'No. We've fallen out, remember?'

'You should make up. She'll be so pleased for you.'

I sighed. 'I don't think she will be. She's so hating being stuck at home with the kids, I think that me telling her I'd landed a big role in a soap, even a crappy cable one, will only make her feel worse.'

'Well, it's up to you, of course. But life's too short for you two not to be friends.'

Ken disengaged himself from me and dashed over to the wine rack in the dining room. 'This calls for a celebration!' he said, brandishing a dusty bottle of champagne. 'Stick this in the freezer for twenty minutes while I go and have a quick bath, then we'll crack it, shall we? It's that one we've been saving for a special occasion.'

He thrust it at me and disappeared, bouncing up the stairs with more enthusiasm than I'd seen in him for months.

I felt horrible – and then I looked at the label on the champagne. It was vintage Moët, the bottle we'd been given when we got married, that we always said we'd save for a *really* special occasion. Birthdays, anniversaries and Christmases had all passed, but nothing had seemed important enough. At least not until I'd been in my fifth month of pregnancy, when we finally began to relax and believe that we were in the clear; that this one was a keeper. At nine months, I'd waddled over to the wine rack, retrieved the bottle and put it in the fridge to chill. While the hired birthing pool was being filled in the front room, I remembered like a snapshot Ken carefully setting out two champagne flutes on a tray, all ready for us to celebrate.

What I couldn't recall was who had taken the bottle out of the fridge again, put it back unopened at the bottom of the wine rack, and returned the glasses to the cupboard. Somebody must have done it. Maybe it had even been me.

I slumped down on the stool in the kitchen, still cradling the bottle to my chest. Perhaps it was my sweat-soaked guilty fingertips, or perhaps it was the memory of that terrible day, but before I knew it, the champagne had slipped from my grasp and crashed onto the terracotta tiled floor, smashing dramatically. It frothed uncontrollably at my feet, bubbling in and out of the shards of glass on the floor, while I continued to sit there, frozen with horror that I'd been reduced to telling such a whopping lie to my husband. When Ken rushed back into the kitchen to see what was going on, he assumed that the tears on my face were sorrow at the loss of our precious bottle.

20

In the midst of all the confusion of broken glass and a kitchen floor suddenly alive with the tiny hiss of popping bubbles, we heard a knock at the front door.

'Now what?' said Ken, tipping a dustpan full of shards of green glass into the bin, as I mopped my tears and the champagne off the floor. 'It's bloody nearly ten at night,' he muttered, swiping a hand through his damp hair and making it stand up in spikes as he stomped towards the door.

'Oh, hello,' I heard him say, hardly more enthusiastically, to the visitor. 'We've had a bit of a disaster in the kitchen, but do come in.'

I hastily checked my reflection in the door of the microwave, to make sure I didn't have mascara all down my face.

'It's Peter,' Ken announced from the kitchen doorway, failing to sound even vaguely pleased.

'Peter? Hello. Come in. Is everything . . . all right?'

Peter sidled over to a dry section of kitchen floor, looking even sweatier than Ken did, although he wasn't dressed for any kind of sport, and, indeed, to my knowledge the only exercise he ever took was raising a pint glass to his mouth. Vicky used to refer proudly to him as her 'bit of rough', and he certainly did have that big-muscled, square-jawed thing going on, which, in combination with his thick midriff and bushy red hair made him, in my opinion, look weird and menacing. On the odd occasion I'd seen him cradling Pat, he'd looked like a bouncer ejecting a small troublemaker from a toddlers' disco.

Physical appearance aside, though, I knew that he loved Vicky, and that was what was important. I just wished I could find a polite way to tell him that the best way to express his love for her would be to go to the pub less, and get up in the night with Pat more. But the pub was his priority. Especially when they were showing the footie on Sky in there.

Vicky and I had hooted with laughter when she'd first related the story to me of a conversation they'd once had in the pub, in the early days of their courtship. Peter had been totally besotted with Vicky, unable to believe his good fortune – to the extent that he'd even voluntarily sat with his back to the big screen during the match.

'I can't think about *anything* other than you,' he'd declaimed dramatically, and then, with precision comedic timing, had leaped out of his seat, wheeled around, punched the air, and, along with the other thirty males in the pub, screamed '*GOAL!*'

I uncapped him a bottle of Becks and handed it to him without asking. It was strange seeing him without Vicky.

'Thanks,' he said, eyeing me and the wet floor with considerable suspicion. 'What happened here?'

'Anna's got a new job!' Ken said, squeezing me round the waist. 'We were about to celebrate, only the champagne went for a burton. Let's open some wine instead, Annie, shall we?' He reached two large wine glasses down from the cupboard and uncorked a bottle of white which had been resident in the fridge door.

'Congratulations,' said Peter, not asking what the job was. 'You don't seem very happy about it.' He leaned against the kitchen counter and I got an uncomfortable feeling in my throat.

'So, how's Vicky?' I asked, as heartily as I could.

'That's why I'm here.'

'Really?'

Ken made a face at me from behind Peter's back, crossing his eyes and pretending to strangle himself. 'I've just run a bath, so if you'll excuse me for a few minutes, I'll go and jump in it,' he said to Peter. 'I've been playing tennis, and I'm heinously sweaty.' He was out of the room and up the stairs, carrying his wine glass, before either of us could reply. For somebody who dealt with enormous crises every day at work, he was astonishingly adept at running away from them at home.

'You'd better come through and sit down,' I said reluctantly, dropping a dry tea-towel on the floor to soak up the rest of the mess. The champagne was already beginning to smell sour, and when I stopped for a second to think about what was represented by the broken glass and pale amber liquid, tears prickled at the back of my eyes again. However reluctant I was to talk to Shock-headed Peter about Vicky, it was at least a welcome diversion from the pain of that shattered bottle and its smashed dreams. Not to mention all the lies.

I led him into the living room, where he sat down self-consciously in the centre of the sofa, feet together, as if I were about to interview him for a job. I felt suddenly sorry for him. He had a brow-beaten, defeated look; I wasn't surprised – I knew from past experience what Vicky was like when she was depressed.

'So, how is Vicky?' I repeated, more tentatively.

Peter just gazed at me and shrugged helplessly. 'Not good.'

'Is she ill?'

'Well. No. Well, maybe. I mean, she's going to bed really early, and she doesn't look all that bright, but, you know, that could just be because she's so miserable.'

I felt like slapping him around the head. For heaven's sake, I thought, this was Vicky's third pregnancy, you'd have thought he'd be able to recognize the signs by now. How could he be so dense? *Ken* could predict when my period was due within three days of arrival, and I'd have bet that Adam would have been able to do the same with his moon-faced wife, before she left him . . .

'So, what I came to say is that, you know, Vicky's got a lot on her plate at the moment, looking after the kids, and you know that Pat was in hospital with a urinary tract infection—'

'*Was* he? For how long? Is he all right now?' I sat bolt upright, my fingers twitching to ring Vicky and see if she was OK. It wasn't the first time Pat had been hospitalized – he'd had suspected pneumonia when he was about seven months old – and Vicky and I had both cried ourselves weak, seeing him lying on that great high penned-in bed under a frieze of primary-coloured balloons and teddies, struggling for breath. It had been awful.

'He's fine now. They only kept him in for a day. The antibiotics cleared it up. But you know, it was tough. I mean, I had to close up the workshop early and everything.'

'So what can I do?'

Peter drained his beer, as if the infusion of it into his system gave him the courage to speak his mind. 'You could apologize.' His voice was cold.

'What? What for?'

'For whatever it was you said to her that made her so miserable.'

I paused, stunned, trying to work out how best to react. A noise came from inside the chimney, startling us both, followed by a shower of soot and small stones. An echoey, panicked cooing followed.

'Pigeon,' I said. 'Stuck in there.'

'Light a fire,' said Peter conversationally. 'Smoke the bugger out.'

Yes, thanks, Shock-headed Pete, I thought. That's constructive. Perish the thought that he might think about the *pigeon's* feelings, wedged in that dark, choking place, not knowing which way was up. In my mind, the pigeon assumed Vicky's face, and the pathetic scritching of its sinewy feet moved me unbearably.

'I have tried to apologize,' I said abruptly. 'Not that the row was my fault – there are two sides to every argument, you know, and I don't think anybody was specifically to blame in ours. But she wouldn't listen. There's nothing I can do if she won't talk to me.'

Peter gave me a look that said, 'Well, grovel, then'; and the pigeon cried in the chimney.

'I'll try talking to her again,' I said. 'But to be quite honest, Peter, I think it's you that she really needs to speak to.'

'Me?' He looked utterly astonished. 'What have I got to do with it?'

I made myself move across from the armchair to sit next to him on the sofa, but failed to bring myself to touch his arm, as I'd intended. It was funny, I thought, how it had been so difficult to tear myself away from Adam earlier, who was a similar build and age, and whom I knew even less well than I knew Peter. Attraction was a strange, unpredictable beast. I wondered what Vicky would think of Adam when – if – she met him; whether he'd elicit in her the same kind of unfavourable response that Peter did in me.

'Listen,' I said. 'I hope you don't mind me saying this, but I assume you're here because you think I can help?'

Peter looked as though he wanted to pretend he hadn't heard, but was forced to acknowledge this truism. He gave a curt nod.

'I honestly don't think that Vicky's and my row is the main reason she's unhappy at the moment. Admittedly, it probably hasn't helped, but I'm sure there's more to it than that.'

'What is it, then? She's not ill, is she?'

The words 'She's pregnant, you meathead' danced delicately on the tip of my tongue, as fizzy as sherbet, and I had to clamp my lips together to stop them bubbling out at him. If I'd told Peter then, that would have been the end of it for me and Vicky. She really would never have spoken to me again.

But perhaps I *ought* to tell him, I thought in sudden panic, flailing around like the pigeon for the right words. Perhaps our friendship would have to be sacrificed, if it would save a life. There was no way that Peter would allow Vicky to have an abortion, if she hadn't already had one. If I told him, then that would be the end of the debate. Vicky and Peter would have three children, and in ten years' time when Crystal had got over her tantrums, and Pat his weediness, and the new baby would be nine and thriving – she'd thank me for it. 'I can't imagine life without them all,' she'd say fondly, gazing at her brood.

Although, on the other hand, in ten years' time, Crystal might be living up to her name and smoking crystal methylate, shacked up with some undesirable teenage loser. Pat's health might get worse, not better; and maybe the new baby would turn out to be twins, or triplets, or disabled, and Vicky's life would be ruined entirely. Or maybe she'd already had the abortion, and Peter would divorce her for doing it without telling him, and then her life would be even more ruined . . .

Oh, this was not fair. It was a crushing responsibility. I felt damned if I did, and damned if I didn't.

'Anna?'

'No, she's not ill, not as far as I know,' I said at last. 'But she's finding everything really tough at the moment.'

Peter sniffed and wiped his nose, dragging his palm upwards, flattening his nostrils. 'Kids are tough. Especially our little shits. I mean, love 'em to bits and all, but they don't half drive you mad.'

'It's really hard for Vicky, to be stuck inside with them all the time. She misses working.'

'Crystal's at nursery every day,' he said defensively.

'Yes, but only during termtime, and still only in the mornings. She doesn't go to school till after Christmas,

201

does she? And then she's tired when she comes home, and won't sleep in the afternoon.'

'Well, that's just the way things are, isn't it? I mean, what does she expect me to do: give up my job so she can go back to work?'

'No, I'm sure she doesn't expect anything like that. It just might be good if . . .' Oh hell, how was I going to say this? '. . . if maybe there was some way that she could have a bit more help with the kids. A bit of time to herself every now and then, maybe a couple of days a week? Or a couple of nights a week when you could get up with Pat instead? I know what Vicky's like when she doesn't get enough sleep, and she's always needed loads, hasn't she? I'm sure even two nights' unbroken sleep a week would make a huge difference.'

'So what do you want me to do? Grow tits and feed Pat myself?'

I struggled to remain composed, thanking my lucky stars that I had the good fortune to be married to a sensitive, considerate man like Ken.

'No. But you could encourage her to wean him – and once he's weaned he may well sleep better anyway.'

Peter was pulling feathers out of the sofa cushions, dropping them and watching them float down onto the rug. At first he had just been worrying at their scratchy ends, gradually working them out, but now he positively yanked at them. Before, I'd felt a vague but politely suppressed antipathy towards him. Now I decided that I actually really disliked him. The feeling was clearly mutual, judging by the look he was giving me.

I ploughed on. 'Or how about getting some childcare, maybe two or three days a week? Someone who could take Pat, and collect Crystal from nursery, just to let Vicky have some time completely on her own.'

'Can't afford it,' said Peter.

'It would be worth it,' I said gently. 'Honestly, I really think she needs it.'

'I – Can't – Afford – It. I'm a self-employed carpenter, not a merchant banker.' He stood up, leaving a bottom-shaped impression in the sofa cushion. 'Anyway, I'd better go. I thought that if you two made up, then Vicky would be happy again. But if you're not willing to do that . . .'

I sprang up too. Honestly, enough was enough. 'Peter, I told you I've tried to make up, but she isn't having any of it! I also told you that I'll try again, but that's all I can do. I hate seeing her like this too, you know, and I'm just as worried as you are.'

He nodded at me, and, with a muttered, 'Well, thanks then, see you around, I'll let myself out', was gone.

I picked up the nearest sofa cushion and whacked it against the wall with a strangled scream of frustration. More white feathers flew out, and in the chimney the pigeon gave a hopeful flutter, evidently thinking that help was at hand. But it was wrong – there was nothing I could do for it, either.

21

Lifting the corner of the voile curtain, I watched Peter walk away in the dusk. He was one of those men who, although already broad in the beam, thought for some reason it was a good idea to keep his wallet in the back pocket of his trousers, making his bottom seem misshapen as well as oversized. As I watched him go, I felt a commingling of relief that I was married to Ken, and renewed guilt that, after the unexpected hiatus of Peter's house call, I was going to have to resume deceiving the man I loved.

I had to lean my forehead against the hall wall before I went upstairs, telling myself that I could do it, I could lie to Ken because I didn't have nefarious or adulterous motives. I wasn't trying to deceive him over anything which would actually hurt him – I mean, why would he mind that I was visiting a little boy whose life I'd saved?

Then tell him the truth, my conscience retorted.

But I couldn't do that either, because he'd be furious that I was blowing out the holiday he'd so painstakingly organized, and that I'd lied to him. Plus, I had to admit that it would be convenient to have Ken believing that I was working. He might not understand were he to know that I was – I hoped – spending large amounts of time with another man.

It wasn't as if Ken never told *me* fibs, I thought defensively. He often fudged the issue of what he did when he was working late. My idea of his working late consisting of him being chained to his desk, weary in shirtsleeves and alone in the office, bar a slope-shouldered cleaner lethargically pushing a carpet-sweeper around. In reality, upon my asking why he stank of cigarette smoke, or was back so late, it had often transpired that 'working late' meant supper in a restaurant with several female colleagues. Which I now construed as potentially meaning: with one attractive female colleague.

I groaned involuntarily, still propped up by the shabby magnolia wall. My very own Wailing Wall. I wondered whether, if I scribbled a prayer and shoved it under the carpet – the closest I'd get to putting it in between the ancient bricks of the real thing in Jerusalem – the pressure in my head would be relieved, a kind of articulated trepanning. But what would I have prayed for: the courage not to lie, or the conviction to carry off the lies?

'What *are* you doing?' Ken appeared at the top of the stairs, a towel round his waist, the hairs on his legs still wet and slicked down in patterns like crop circles.

I jumped, accidentally headbutting the wall. 'Ouch. Nothing. Banging my head against a brick wall: Peter's a nightmare. I don't know how Vicky stays married to him. He hasn't even realized that she's—'

I stopped myself just in time. Hell, I was going to have to be more disciplined than that. Vicky's pregnancy should have been the easiest of all my secrets to conceal.

'Never mind,' I said. 'I'm sure you aren't interested in the ins and outs of their marital problems.'

'Correct,' Ken replied. 'We've got more important things to talk about.' He padded down the stairs to wrap his arms around me, and I relished the scent of his warm damp chest.

'Have we?' I asked cagily. He was so sinewy, compared to Adam. I shook the image of Adam out of my head crossly. So what? Why did I have to keep comparing them all: Adam to Ken, Peter to Adam, Ken to Adam, as if Adam was some great benchmark of manhood against which every other male must be measured. What did Adam have to do with anything, anyway, except as Max's dad?

'Yes. Like, if we're not going to be able to meet your brother in Ibiza, then when shall we go on holiday? And where? To be honest, though, the news about your new job has kind of got me out of a hole. I booked the holiday, then Christian announced he was arranging a meeting in South-East Asia, and of course wanted me to speak at it. I said no, and he wasn't best pleased, but now . . .'

'Well. That worked out then.'

He gently pushed me away, so he could look at my face to see if I was being sarcastic or not. Satisfied that I wasn't, he hugged me again. 'Sorry I'm away so much.'

'Sorry I'm going to be away so much too,' I said with feeling. 'Although maybe it'll make it easier for both of us. You won't need to feel guilty about your travelling, knowing that I'm not even here. We'll just have to have extra good quality time when we are together, that's all. And I expect there might be places other than Ibiza that you'd prefer to go to on holiday.

'And speaking of quality time . . .' I added, reaching up to kiss him. He pushed the fringe away from my forehead, and kissed my eyes, cupping his hands around my face. I tried to pull him down with me onto the stairs, but he resisted, laughing self-consciously.

'Oh, come on, baby,' I wheedled, slipping my hand under his towel. I'd always loved the sight and feel of a man in nothing but a towel; and the stairs used to be one of our favourite venues for sex – great angles.

But Ken twisted deftly away from me, yawning exaggeratedly. 'Better not, sweetheart, I'm wrecked.

I've got a mental day tomorrow, and it's getting late.'

'Never mind,' I said, making an effort to kiss him tenderly on the lips before grabbing a banister and hauling myself up. I retreated into the living room and turned on the television: *Sex in the City* was on; that would have to do instead.

Ken had gone to work by the time I awoke the next day. It was a balmy summer's morning, and the pull of birdsong and dappled light on tree branches led me out into the garden, still in my pyjamas, with a bowl of cereal in one hand and the telephone, ready to ring Vicky, in the other. I didn't feel strong enough to do it on an empty stomach, so I sat on the step leading down to the overgrown lawn and ate first, the clink of my spoon against the china lending a percussion accompaniment to the chirping of a blackbird in the hedge nearby. A squirrel sat on its haunches on the far edge of the lawn, eyeing my Shreddies with envy.

If I had a job, I thought, I probably wouldn't have time to do this. If I'd really got that job on the soap, I'd have been waking up in some gruesome digs, nylon sheets and air freshener, with a landlady who checked up on me and grumbled when I forgot to lock the back gate. I'd be frantically cramming lines – I'd never found learning lines easy – and worrying that every biscuit I ate would add another ten pounds on camera.

Far nicer to have an imaginary job, really. All the biscuits I wanted, and all the time in the world. I told myself that I was so fortunate that I didn't have to work. Still, I realised, I'd better start thinking as if I really was going to be working. I'd need to figure out how I was meant to be learning scripts, and what to tell people about the soap. It was going to require quite a lot of planning.

I tipped my head back and let the sun warm my face for a few minutes, pulsing orange behind my eyelids, pretending that I was solar-powered. I'd worry about the fake part later, I decided. For the moment I just needed the strength to say the right thing to my oldest friend.

Finally, trying to excavate shreds of cereal from my back teeth with my tongue, I plucked up courage to dial Vicky's number. Vicky picked up after two rings, and I had to rearrange my tongue into the correct position before I could speak.

'It's me. Don't hang up, please.'

'What do you want?'

I sighed. She wasn't going to make it easy for me then. 'Just to see how you are.'

'Whether I'm still pregnant, you mean?'

'Amongst other things. More to see if you're still not speaking to me, I suppose.'

'Well, I'm not.'

My heart flipped in my chest and each blade of grass zoomed into sharp focus. I must have jumped, because the squirrel shot up a tree out of sight. She'd really had an abortion! 'You – aren't?'

'Speaking to you, I mean. I am still pregnant.'

The relief was intense. Somewhat to my surprise, I started to cry. The solar-energy infusion hadn't worked then.

'Why are you crying?' She sounded harsh, but I could tell she was concerned. 'Has something happened?'

I couldn't talk. I tried to hold my breath, but it burst out of me in jerks. 'I miss you, Vicky, that's all, and I'm worried about you. Please, can't we put this behind us? It's your life. You have to do what's best for you. I'm sorry if I interfered.'

There was a long, long silence. In the background I could hear Pat chuntering away to himself, and the theme tune to *The Tweenies*.

'I miss you too, Anna. And it's not that I don't understand why you feel so strongly about it.'

'Peter was round here last night,' I said, even more relieved, but feeling as if I was treading softly through a minefield.

'What did he want?' she asked in a panicked rush.

'He's worried about you.'

'*You didn't tell him?*'

'Of course I didn't. Although I can't believe he hasn't guessed. How many weeks are you now?'

'Eight and a half. Maybe nine. So what did you tell him?'

I swallowed my envy of the casual way she didn't even know exactly how many weeks gone she was. With all of my pregnancies, I'd counted towards the so-called 'safe' twelve weeks, day by day, practically hour by hour. Never achieved it, though, apart from with Holly.

'He thought that the reason you're so down is because of our row. I told him that it was probably more because you're so tired and stressed, looking after the kids. I suggested he got you some help. Or helped you a bit more himself.'

'Oh. Right. Thanks. I expect that went down like a lead balloon.'

'You're welcome. And no, I don't believe I am your husband's favourite person . . . So you've decided to keep the baby, then?' I couldn't hold the question in any longer.

Vicky tutted, loudly. 'I didn't say that, did I?'

'Sorry. But you're still pregnant.'

'Yes. Mainly because I don't get the opportunity to put my make-up on every day, let alone arrange a major surgical procedure without the knowledge of my husband.'

I bit my lip so hard that it bled. As much as I disliked Peter, he had a right to know, but I couldn't risk pointing it out to Vicky. Thankfully she decided to change the subject.

'So what have you been up to in the last couple of weeks?'

Suddenly the enormity of what I'd done began to sink in. It was insane: I, who had spent years regaling Vicky with the minutiae of my life and emotions, right down to the most tedious little details, was now faced with the choice either of having a total change of character, becoming monosyllabic, secretive and unforthcoming – which she would assume was me sulking over her pregnancy; or else having to spin an elaborate web of deceit, dropping imaginary names of cast and crew members, having to elucidate on the finer points of my soap alter ego's misadventures, describing my life down in – where the hell was I meant to be filming? Oh yes: Bristol.

I'd have to come clean and tell her. Ken, bizarrely, would be easier to fool because he neither watched soaps nor was particularly interested in the specifics of my days. He was very much a 'right here right now' type of person, and never really thought about anything which didn't directly involve him. It made him sound selfish, but he wasn't; just focused. He couldn't bear people telling him their dreams, for example; so the notion of him remotely giving a damn about the plot of a cable soap opera – even one starring his wife – was risible.

But I didn't feel back on a strong enough footing with Vicky to explain about my deception, and about Max. Not yet, I thought. And I couldn't tell her the lie either, because if she believed I had a job it would make her even more dissatisfied with her life as a reluctant stay-at-home mother. I had to trust that Peter was fairly unlikely to mention it to her – I very much doubted that I was a topic of idle conversation in their household.

'Not much,' I said vaguely. 'The usual. Oh, I got involved in a community mosaic project, which was kind of fun. Got me out of the house, anyway. And' – I rushed on, lest she were about to ask for details – 'I'm seeing Lil later today. Things are fine with us now. Haven't seen a lot of Ken, though, as per usual. We're . . . trying to organize a holiday, but it's proving difficult to get a clear space for it.'

'Right,' said Vicky. 'Crystal! Don't bash the remote, you'll break it. *Crystal!*'

'Well, I'll let you go, then,' I said uncertainly. 'Can we meet up soon? Why don't we organize dinner later this week, just you and me. Get Peter to babysit, and we can have a proper chat over a bottle of – oh no, you can't drink, can you?'

That's torn it, I thought, regretting the words immediately. I hadn't meant to sound censorious, and I'd actually been thinking about the fact that she was still breast-feeding, rather than that she was pregnant, although I knew right away that she'd see it as another veiled criticism. Sure enough, I heard the heave of a long-suffering sigh.

'Yes, Anna, actually I *can* drink if I bloody well feel like it. I have few enough pleasures as it is.'

'Sorry, sorry, sorry, I didn't mean anything by it.'

'Listen, I'll call you if Peter's got a free night next week, OK?'

'OK. Take care. Let me know if I can do anything to help in the meantime.'

'Bye, Anna.'

Bet she doesn't ring me, I thought disconsolately. When I turned back round, I saw next door's cat, a huge ginger beast with mean eyes, just finish licking out my cereal bowl, and it made me unaccountably furious. 'Get lost!' I shouted at it, throwing a little clod of earth at it. It bolted away with a yowl, and I gathered up the bowl and phone and trailed back inside.

I had said I'd visit Lil, although what I really wanted to do with my day was to go to Gillingsbury. But I thought I'd better wait until the dinner on Saturday week. I couldn't just lurk around Max's house, and now the mosaic project was finishing, I didn't have any other excuse to be there.

Or did I? A surge of energy flooded into me as I realized that, since the previous night's conversation with Ken, the groundwork for my life away from home four days a week was now laid. And it would only be convincing if I actually *was* away from home for four days a week. Wow. I'd really done it. I'd been focusing so much on the pain of lying that I hadn't considered the freedom that the lies represented. I knew I had some money in a savings account, a few thousand pounds that my grandmother left me in her will, that Ken was not aware of. I could rent a place in Gillingsbury! Maybe not the house in Wealton I'd concocted – too expensive, probably – but what about a studio flat there? Do some art courses during the week, or force myself to take up tennis so that I could get good enough to play against Ken, or just do a lot of jogging around country lanes. No responsibilities, other than watching some minor daytime soap and assigning myself a character from it, so that I'd be able to talk about my 'part' with authority when called upon to do so. Somehow it seemed a life more purposeful than if I'd done the same thing at home.

Living in this house, I realized, had not been conducive to moving forwards. How could it have been, when everything was subtly focused on regret and disappointment? It infused the air, tinging all Ken's and my conversations and putting pressure on both of us: him, in the bedroom, and in the sheepish turn of his key in the door after yet another sixteen-hour working day; me, in trying to fight the emptiness that nothing seemed able to fill.

It could be my fresh start. It would be like separating from Ken to 'find myself', without Ken ever even knowing! What he didn't know, he couldn't be hurt by – and in the process, I'd be near Max. I would reinvent myself as a successful, strong, single woman, living the life I wanted, on my own terms. Have a few adventures. Make some new friends; not just Adam, either, maybe some new girlfriends.

My new resolve made me feel happier, more so than I'd felt for months, and I bounded up the stairs two by two to get dressed and head out. Maybe there'd be time for a quick coffee with Lil, I thought, before I headed off to Gillingsbury to start registering with estate agents.

22

I'd driven down to Gillingsbury and visited every estate agency I could find. I'd come away with sheafs of property details which I'd pored over during the weekend. At the beginning of the following week I'd gone to view three properties: a flat above a bookies' (too seedy); a studio in a converted church (too small); and a place actually in Wealton, a first-floor flat overlooking the duck pond (a definite possibility). It was a start.

When I got home again, I rehid all the property details under the mattress, and rang Adam, on the spurious pretext that I was checking to see if the group dinner was still happening that Saturday. I'd felt irrationally disappointed that I hadn't bumped into him or Max as I'd trailed round after Josh the agent in his too-big grey suit and bumfluff. At first, an answerphone message clicked on, and my throat tightened to hear Max's little voice on the tape: *'I'm too busy playing to come to the phone. Leave us a message instead'* – but before I could speak, Max was cut off and Adam's voice interrupted with a brusque 'Hello?'

'Hi. It's Anna.'

I paused, testing him, waiting for his own pause, for the furrowed brow that could be sensed through a phone line. But he didn't fail me; he jumped right in without hesitation, and it gave me a wriggling sensation of pleasure in my belly.

'Anna! How are you? Lovely to hear from you.' It was in his voice, that certain tone that you only heard when someone fancied you; a smiling warmth that screamed, 'I REALLY LIKE YOU.' I realized, with something approaching horror, that the same tone was in my own voice. I also realized that it had been a long time since Ken had spoken to me like that.

'Great. I'm fine. Thanks. How's Max?'

'Oh, full of beans. Back to school this week.'

Then, something happened: we started talking. From a tiny acorn of small talk I suddenly felt as if I were standing beneath the great leafy branches of an oak tree of real conversation. In twenty minutes we'd encompassed Max; the vagaries of infant-school library-book selection; Mitch's unenviable personal habits; the mosaic panels; the state of art education in the country as a whole; the state of the British theatre; my 'new job' on the cable soap and Adam's impressed congratulations. Each new branch grew seamlessly from the trunk of the call.

Without noticing, I'd taken the phone through to the living room and was lying sprawled out on the sofa, my leg hooked over the back of it, utterly at ease. I heard the unfamiliar sound of myself laughing, and imagined in my nostrils the sweet earthy smell of Adam's hug from the other night. Uh-oh, I thought. I'm in trouble here. I could have talked to him all day. Part of me started to worry that I was keeping him from something more important, while another part of me started to worry about how much I wanted another of those hugs.

'Right. Well, I suppose I'd better let you go. I was just ringing about—'

'Anna, I know I'll see you at the weekend, but we might not have much of a chance to chat at the dinner, so I wondered . . . would you like to go out for a Chinese, just the two of us, some other night? Next week, maybe?'

'Yes please,' I gabbled instantly, as if I was playing Snap and had to speak really fast or else I'd lose my stack of farmyard animals. I was blushing, and forced myself to uncurl my toes inside my shoes.

'That would be lovely,' I said more slowly. I'd have to tell him that I only wanted to be friends, but that was fine. I was very out of practice at reading the signs – perhaps this was all Adam wanted too.

Then I remembered our hug again, and the way he'd looked at me, and thought, Yeah, right, pigs might fly, right off the back of the Snap cards . . .

What I should have said was: 'It was kind of you to ask, and I've really enjoyed our chat, but I'm involved with someone.' 'When and where, then?' I found myself saying instead.

'How about the Chinese in Crane Street. A Taste Of the Orient, it's called. I could book us a table for next Monday, at eight o'clock?'

'Great. Well, I'll see you on Saturday anyway, but I'll look forward to Monday too. Thanks for the chat.'

'Don't mention it,' he replied formally, but still with the smile in his voice. 'Thank *you*.'

And I *was* grateful for the chat, I realized. I couldn't remember the last time I'd enjoyed talking to anyone as much. About real subjects, too, not just about what was going on in *Coronation Street*, or what Ken was doing at work. I hung up feeling more cheerful than I'd felt in ages, and wondered if I'd be able to get an appointment to have my hair trimmed and blow-dried before the big night.

Just as I was lifting the receiver to call my hairdresser, the phone rang again. It was Josh, the baby-faced estate agent.

'I wondered if you'd made any decisions yet,' he mewed. 'Only there's another party very interested in the flat in Wealton you liked so much.'

I didn't believe him for a moment: he sounded so piteously needy and unconvincing. But I thought again of the flat, with its bright windows overlooking the village green, and the duckpond reflecting the quiet blue expanse of open sky.

'Why not?' I said, as much to myself as to him. 'It's available right away, isn't it? I'll call in first thing tomorrow to sign the contract and sort out the deposit.'

23

The mosaic project dinner in Gillingsbury that Saturday night was a first for me, on many levels. My first social engagement as Anna Valentine, tenant of a small chintzy one-bedroom flat next to Wealton's absurdly picturesque duck pond. My first few days away from home; my putative first week on my new job. It had all been much easier than I could have anticipated, too. The trials of my current existence which I'd so bitterly bemoaned – the row with Vicky, Ken's work-related travelling, my inability to find an acting job – all transformed themselves from negatives to positives, turning themselves inside out and giving me a surprisingly glorious feeling of liberation. I'd really done it! And it was going to be fine. If Ken ever found out, I decided I could explain it away as a deep desire for change in my life, which I hadn't wanted to undertake at the expense of any inconvenience or worry to him. Heaven knows he worried about me enough as it was.

I had 'moved in' on the Thursday, a day after Ken flew to Singapore. He knew he could reach me on the mobile, so he hadn't even asked for my new address, although I'd told him that I'd found digs on the outskirts of Bristol. Easy. The flat was furnished, thankfully unoffensively, so I didn't need to take much, and I didn't take anything which Ken would have missed: just some old crockery and cutlery, spare bed-linen, towels, toiletries, and a suitcase of my clothes.

The only thing which marred my enjoyment of the process was not having anybody with whom to share it. Lil had been the obvious candidate, since Vicky was clearly unavailable, but, although I'd seen her (Lil) the day I first looked at flats, and wanted to tell her the truth then, I had instead trotted out my cable soap story. In the end I'd decided that it was better if absolutely nobody knew. It was the only way I could be sure that the secret remained under my control, and besides, I had an uncomfortable feeling that she wouldn't have condoned such a deep level of subterfuge.

By Saturday morning, I felt really at home. I drove the two miles into Gillingsbury and went to the market, where I was entranced by bargains such as ten large waxy oranges for a pound, a bunch of astonishingly fragrant pink roses for four pounds, and a whole slew of cleaning materials for less than a fiver. I made conversation with at least six Gillingsbury residents, all wearing – despite the warm early-September morning – anoraks of varying decrepitude and sludgy nylon colours, and who all said: 'Oooh, Wealton? It's lovely out there,' or: 'An actress? Have you been on the telly?'

Finally I treated myself to a cut and blow dry in the local hairdresser's, since my regular London hair-dresser hadn't been able to fit me in at such short notice. The stylist, Denise, somehow managed to give me a bit of a beehive, but it was nothing that putting my hair up in a ponytail for the rest of the afternoon hadn't remedied.

Then I drove home again, arranged the oranges in a fruit bowl, the roses in a vase in the window, and made myself a large avocado and tomato sandwich from the still-warm bread I'd purchased. I felt very pleased with myself. So pleased, in fact, that I kept laughing out loud at the sheer outrageousness of what I was doing. My downstairs neighbour met me as I was coming in chuckling to myself, and clearly thought I was somewhat deranged. She was an elderly lady called Dora, with a tiny head perched on a large ungainly frame, and she walked with her neck stretched forwards all the time which, in combination with her permanent smile, reminded me of the Bear in the Big Blue House, a benign grizzly character off one of Pat's favourite TV shows.

Still, I later realized, *she* had been in no position to say anything about anti-social behaviour. Her two huge dogs barked and howled like the hound of the Baskervilles every morning until she took them out – it was probably why my rent had been so reasonable. It shattered the calm of the village green for ten minutes a day and scared the ducks rigid, but I found that I didn't really mind. Ten minutes wasn't the end of the world, and I wasn't there all the time anyway.

By Saturday afternoon, I'd had a call on my mobile from Ken, who promised to send me a postcard from the Raffles Hotel if he got the chance to go there, and grunted that he had no idea whether Singapore was nice or not since he'd spent the entire time in a conference room. Oh, apart from one afternoon on the golf course. He had asked how rehearsals were going, and seemed perfectly satisfied when I replied that it was all fine; the digs were great; my landlady was called Dora and had two large smelly dogs which barked a lot; the cast were lovely except one frosty old battleaxe called . . . Valerie (I fished the name out of nowhere), who thought she had the lead role even though she only had a bit part as my character's senile grandmother.

Whilst Ken and I had been talking, I ripped the cellophane off a packet of index cards I'd bought in the Gillingsbury W H Smiths, and wrote on the top one: 'DORA – BIG DOGS – LANDLADY'; and on the one underneath: 'VALERIE – FROSTY – BATTLEAXE – THINKS SHE'S THE DOG'S BOLLOCKS, PLAYS MY GRANDMA'. I loved index cards. Sometimes I wished my whole life could have been mapped out by terse commands on index cards; they just seemed so authoritative. The modern equivalent of injunctions carved on stone tablets . . . or perhaps not. But I did find them reassuring.

Ken hadn't quizzed me further, other than to ask if I had a lot of lines, and did it feel good to be working again – both questions which were easily dealt with. Largely because I got the impression that he wasn't really even listening to the answers.

Still, it had made a refreshing change from when he usually rang me from business trips. For once I hadn't experienced that crushing sense of envy and stale frustration, because he'd been calling me from Sydney Harbour/a pyramid in Mexico/a golf course in Buenos Aires, whilst I was usually still in my pyjamas at home sitting on an unmade bed with my finger up my nose (metaphorically speaking, of course). I felt positively gleeful after he'd hung up, and far less guilty than I'd been up to that point.

At four o'clock I rang Adam to double-check the arrangements for that evening. It had taken a colossal effort on my part not to call him sooner, but I'd been determined to get myself settled before I did so. And, although it felt strange to admit and I didn't understand precisely why, I was playing hard to get. I wanted him to be really pleased to hear from me again.

He had been *really* pleased to hear from me. Touchingly pleased, but in such an utterly disingenuous way that, actually, my heart kind of skipped when I heard his voice. 'Anna! Brilliant to hear from you, I was wondering what you were up to. How's the job going?'

'Fine, thanks,' I said with my fingers crossed. 'I've done my first read-throughs – I was in Bristol the last couple of days.' Unsurprisingly, lying to Adam was a lot easier than it had been to Ken. In a way that was good, I thought, because I could tell things to Adam first, as a sort of rehearsal before I told Ken.

'Wow, congratulations. I can't believe that I know a

real TV star. Max will be so impressed. When will we see you on television? Soon?'

''Fraid not,' I said, thrilled at his (misplaced) pride. 'It's only on cable, in Devon and Cornwall, I think, and maybe parts of Wales.'

'Oh, well, we'll have to wait until next summer. Max and I usually go down to Devon to stay with a friend of mine for a couple of weeks. I'll make sure we catch it then!'

Shit. I tried to take a deep breath, feeling my face heating up, but it appeared that a large brick had lodged itself in my windpipe. Keep calm, Anna, I thought. It's not an insurmountable problem. You just have to find the name of a real West Country cable soap, then whenever anyone says they saw it but didn't spot you, you pretend that you weren't in it that month; you were on holiday or something.

Besides, who knew what would be going on by the following summer. I could always pretend that the series had been axed, or else that my character had been killed off in a freak tree-pruning accident. I decided that it was best not to think too much about possible ways to trip up, or it would start to worry me to the point of not being able to keep the charade going at all.

'Anyway, I just rang to check that we're still on for tonight,' I said, changing the subject.

'Definitely,' he replied. 'You're still coming, aren't you? Fantastic. We're meeting at seven-thirty in the restaurant — it's Emandels in Bridge Street, near the clock tower. Do you know it?'

'I can find it. Who's going to be there?'

I heard paper flapping. 'Here's my list . . . Let's see: Serena, Mitch, Margie, Ralph, possibly Pamela, maybe Mary if she can get a babysitter for Orlando, you, and me, of course.'

I'd been hoping that Ralph and Mitch would be washing their hair that night, but no such luck. 'Is Pamela the pregnant lady?' I asked.

221

'No. That was Paula. She isn't coming, her baby's due at any minute. She said she can't get out of her armchair without a winch, and her ankles are the size of salamis.'

Lucky Paula, I thought with such vehement envy that I felt queasy. 'I don't remember Pamela,' was all I said though. 'She wasn't one of the regulars, was she?'

'No, Pamela didn't work on the project. She's the art department administrator at the college – you probably spoke to her on the phone. She babysits for me too sometimes.'

Of course! Love-struck broad-beamed Pamela. How could I have forgotten? 'Oh yes. I met her, when I came to try and enrol.'

'Are you still interested in joining a class, by the way? People always drop out after the first few weeks, so it's worth putting your name on the reserve list if you are.'

'Oh, right. Yes, you know, I might. I'll have another look at the prospectus and see what I fancy. What would you recommend?'

'Totally depends on what you like to do. I teach life drawing, and that's usually a good group. But wasn't it you who wanted to make a mosaic tabletop?'

Oh yes, so it had been. I'd forgotten about that. 'Definitely. Maybe I'll sign up for both, and see which I get a place on first.'

'Well, I'd better go. Max is round at a friend's, and I need to go and collect him in a minute.'

'How is he?'

'Fine, thanks. He's great. He's been asking about you, actually.'

'He has?' I hoped that my voice didn't betray the joy which oozed out of me, coating me with sticky euphoria.

'Mm. You made quite an impression.'

'So did he. I'd love to see him again.'

'Well, we must arrange to get together. Maybe next weekend?'

I liked the fact that Adam always seemed one date ahead – making plans for something else before we'd done the last thing. We still had our Chinese *à deux* to come. But I needed to see Ken the following weekend. 'I'm working, unfortunately. More script readthroughs. How about one day after school, if he's not too tired?'

'Yes, perhaps. Although he gets quite booked up, going to mates' houses, football, that sort of thing.'

It felt like a knockback, but I tried to put a brave face on it. 'And if you ever need a babysitter, I'd be happy to help out, when I'm not working myself, obviously.'

Then I thought how needy that sounded and, it seemed, so did Adam. 'I think we're all right in that department, with Pamela. But thanks anyway.'

In one fell swoop all my confidence and ebullience melted away. I felt like a teenager who'd plucked up courage to ask out her crush, only to be told that he didn't fancy her. After his initial pleasure on hearing from me, Adam had seemed much cooler than in our last phone conversation. Perhaps he'd decided it was time to Play It Cool – the complicated dance of courtship felt so unfamiliar to me, like a foxtrot or a two-step for which everyone except me knew the moves. Of course it didn't entirely make sense that Adam would have known either, since he too was – technically – married, but I just got the feeling that while I was fiddling with fans and dance cards and tripping over my feet, he was elegantly waltzing around the room, swooping forwards and backing off in time to the music . . . Perhaps he'd dated lots of women since his wife left. He was certainly attractive enough, once you got to know him.

There was a commotion outside my window, and I looked down to see one of Dora's dogs running full pelt into the pond, causing the ducks to flap away in abject panic, with the dog crashing through the shallow water after them. Dora herself stood on the bank, restraining the other one which, although practically throttled by her tight grip on his leash, was still managing to bark itself hysterical in high, strangulated tones.

'So, see you later,' said Adam with finality. 'I really must go, or Max will think I've forgotten about him.'

'Right. See you later,' I said, and hung up, too flummoxed even to think about running outside to try and offer Dora some assistance. Instead I just watched as a middle-aged bald man in a Barbour jacket obligingly ran along the bank after the duck-chasing dog, until he got close enough to grab the lead. A small crowd of assorted dog-walkers, ramblers and mothers with toddlers had gathered on the little ornamental bridge straddling the pond, and were watching with fingers pointed and mouths agape – not just the children, either. That was country life for you, I supposed, where the biggest excitement of your day was a dog splashing after some panic-struck ducks.

I wondered what on earth they'd all think about me, if they'd known. It would probably have kept them in gossip for days. And why did I feel so despondent about a man I didn't want, and couldn't have anyway?

I was surprised at how hurt I felt at Adam's apparent unwillingness to let me babysit. It tainted the euphoria of my day, affecting all my subsequent decisions. As I balanced on the bed in order to check my appearance in the flat's one small mirror on the bedroom wall, I realized that I had chosen a totally different outfit to the one I'd vaguely been planning. I'd replaced the intended smart black wide-leg trousers and silk button-up Agnès B shirt with my short denim miniskirt and my lowest plunge-necked contour-hugging top: Ann Widdecombe to Divine Brown in three easy stages. How had that happened? And how had a simple lack of enthusiasm for my offer to babysit led to me doubting my own attractiveness? I suddenly felt as if I were seventeen again: anguished and insecure about whether the object of my affections liked me, or whether it was merely wishful thinking.

For the first time I confronted the thought which had, prior to that point, merely been skirting around the periphery of my mind. I had a devastatingly handsome, hugely successful and – reasonably – devoted husband; a good man whom I respected and loved and wanted to grow old with. Yet, for some unfathomable reason – and I was pretty sure it wasn't *just* to do with Max – I had developed a stonking great crush on a paunchy balding ceramics teacher.

It was true, I realized, as I stood on the bed still twisting my torso around to try and look at my bottom. I hadn't allowed myself to indulge the notion before, but ever since I'd cooked them dinner, I had found myself thinking about them both constantly – and thinking about Adam very differently to the way I thought about Max. Thinking about how Adam's blue eyes were so honest, and his smile so open. About his broad shoulders – despite the slight paunch, he was a powerful, well-built man – and strong legs. Seeing him over and over in my mind, bending down to pick up Max's toys. The way that almost everything he said had either made me laugh, or feel good, or feel admiration for him. The rough skin on his large hands, which had given me a rasping thrill when they'd held mine in welcome and farewell. That hug . . .

I tried to analyse it. Maybe it was solely because he was so different to Ken. Since we'd been married, I hadn't really spent any amount of time with any other males. It was only a temporary infatuation, I told myself; a reaction to the strange situation I'd found myself in. I'd get over it.

Of course it had nothing to do with sex. But why, then, was I having mini-fantasies about getting down and dirty with a pottery teacher? Imagining that I got a place in Adam's life-drawing class, and that his hand would guide the charcoal stick in my own, as we gazed on the flawless body of a model (even in my fantasy I couldn't work out which sex to make the model. If male, it would be sexier for me; if female, perhaps Adam would mentally put my head on her body). Our eyes would meet over my easel, and he'd praise my work with an expression which would tell me that it wasn't just my drawing he was impressed by.

And why could I not seem to stop trying to picture what his body looked like beneath his loose jeans? I remembered with shame the way that, on one of our last days together on the mosaic project, he'd brushed my hand as he showed me the finer points of grouting, and I had blushed like a schoolgirl. So it had started back then, and I'd been in denial, despite the fact that I had even taken to fits of inane giggling whenever he said something funny – which was often – the like of which I had never heard coming from my own throat before. It was pathetic.

I sat abruptly back down on the bed. My hands were shaking, and I felt damp and hot between my legs. Then I lay back and closed my eyes, giving myself leave to imagine him pressing me up against the wall of the dingy hamster-cage Ladies toilet in Moose Hall, pinning my arms above my head. Even just thinking about it evoked that scent of sawdust and Dettol again, and there Adam would be, whispering, 'Shhh, Anna, we must be quiet,' (because, even in my erotic day-dream, Ralph would be hovering outside the door of the Ladies, waiting for me to emerge so that he could continue to bore me about his bunion operation or his fencing skills).

'Shhh, Anna,' Adam would say, and with that irresistibly appealing cheeky grin he would lean forward until his broad chest touched my breasts and I would be able to feel his breath on my lips, and he'd inch closer and closer until his bulk would be squashing me, in a nice way, of course, and then as the lower part of his trunk came closer, there it would be, the lump in the front of his jeans which would collide with me just as he began to part my lips with his tongue, and he'd exude that divine smell of his, a faint

226

but musky trace of aftershave mixed with bluebells in the forest, blocking out the hamster-cage smell, and then we'd kiss, slowly at first and then—

—but it wasn't about sex.

Not at *all*. He was just a lovely person, that was all. Surely it was natural to want to get close to such a lovely person. There was nothing unusual or worrying about being attracted to another man. It was what you did about it that would get you into trouble. And I had absolutely no intention of ever acting out my daydreams. Lucky too, I supposed, that Adam clearly didn't feel the same way about me. He was so obviously one of those easy-going men whom most women liked, I thought, and far too much of a gentleman ever to try anything on.

I'd never even considered having an affair and I certainly didn't want one – but there had just been something about the way Adam had looked at me, especially when I'd been at his house that time. With something almost approaching depression, I realized that if he did, as I suspected, find me attractive, and if he made a play for me, I'd find it quite difficult to resist.

Oh, see sense, Anna, I told myself. The last thing I needed was to have an affair. It would probably finish Ken off altogether. He'd been devastated about Holly too, and it would be a big enough mindfuck if he ever found out that I'd lied about the acting job. I couldn't have an affair. I couldn't do that to him, on top of everything else.

I'd read in a women's magazine at the dentist's that it was healthy for an adult woman to have crushes, just as long as they didn't make her miserable. A good crush could improve the circulation and boost the immune system, it said, not to mention the excitement of letting one's imagination run riot. So I granted myself a small, temporary licence to enjoy such new and strange feelings. It was OK to find Adam attractive, because he was an attractive person, inside and out. An attractive person who listened to me, who laughed at my inane jokes and looked genuinely interested in my throwaway comments.

And anyway, he probably didn't *really* fancy me. He was probably just lonely.

24

By the time I eventually pushed open the door of the restaurant, I was confused and wrung out with doubts and trepidation. It made me feel exhausted, actually, to think that this was only the beginning. No going back, not for now; not when I had a real chance to be in Max's life, and I'd paid a three-month deposit on the flat in Wealton.

'Anna! Hi! Come and sit down.' Mitch patted the seat of an empty chair next to him, so I pretended I hadn't heard, and headed in the opposite direction towards Adam.

It had not escaped my notice, the way my head swam at the sight of Adam in a clean white shirt, smiling at me, but I tried to ignore it. Unfortunately, since my minicab had been ten minutes late, the seats on either side of him were already occupied by his fan club, Pamela and Serena. They were practically hanging off his arms like groupies, vying for his attention in what I thought was a most unsubtle manner. I had to slide into a space in between Pamela and Ralph, although it wasn't an ideal position. Ralph and Dutch Margie were holding hands and gazing into each other's eyes, and Pamela of course only had eyes for Adam, and so both were leaning away from me as if I had some kind of dire personal hygiene problem. Everybody said hello to me, of course, and Adam did slide me a sly little resigned look, as if to say, 'Sorry I'm a bit trapped here, but I'll be with you when I can,' but I still felt awkward. I occupied myself by studying the menu and, when they weren't looking, my fellow diners.

There were eight of us present: myself, Adam, Mitch, Serena, Pamela, Margie, Ralph, and Orlando's mum – I couldn't remember her name. All the women were far more dressy than I was, sporting chokers and beaded garments, fake flower clips in their hair (Margie and Serena), and I could smell the hairspray which crystallized Pamela's large coiffure, as well as the perfume from behind her equally large ears. I was glad I'd had my own hair done that day but, as Mitch gazed shamelessly into my cleavage, I fervently wished I'd stuck to the black trousers and sober shirt combo.

We were a mismatched party. Mitch had brushed his long straggly hair, but still wore the grubby tie-dye T-shirt I'd first seen him in, and he looked distinctly at odds next to Orlando's mum – oh, Mary, that was her name – in her pearls and floral blouse. She was clearly not happy to be seated next to him, and was leaning across the table talking to Serena. I wondered what the other people in the restaurant made of us. They probably thought we were the local branch of Alcoholics Anonymous – at least until the waiter brought over a bottle of red and one of white, plonking them already opened in the centre of the table without offering anybody the chance to taste them first.

To try and cover up my discomfort, I took charge. 'Red or white?' I asked Pamela, gripping both bottles by their necks and waving them towards her.

'Red please,' said Pamela, looking at me with the sort of curiosity usually evinced by small boys discovering molluscs in the compost heap. 'Sorry, I recognize your face, but I don't recall your name. I'm Pamela.'

'Anna,' I said. 'We met at the college a few weeks ago. I was trying to get on an art course but they were all booked. You put me in touch with Adam and he got me down to the mosaic project. Which is why I'm here.'

I liked saying Adam's name out loud. I didn't get much chance to use it, and it felt familiar and comforting – 'mentionitis' was what Bridget Jones would have diagnosed it as.

Pamela nodded, but once I'd filled up her glass she turned back to Adam without further ado. I got up and went around the table dispensing wine, leaning away from Mitch when I came to him so that he couldn't look down my top. It didn't stop him grabbing my wrist, however, to pull me in so he could give me a large wet kiss on the cheek. I was pretty sure he'd been aiming for my lips, but I turned my head at the last minute. His breath smelled of stale hash, and his skin was clammy. I sloshed white wine into his glass as hastily as I could, and moved on.

Margie and Ralph were still in a huddle together, but when I got to them they were both frowning, and as I poured their wine I noticed Margie deliberately untwining her fingers from his, one at a time, and placing her hands firmly in her lap. Ralph rolled his eyes and looked away. Oh terrific, I thought. A domestic. I just couldn't understand what Margie saw in him. He was admittedly pretty good-looking in that strong, relaxed Jamaican way, but he was a bit of a bore, and quite possibly a lech. I liked Margie, and felt like telling her she could do better.

When the waiter had finally reappeared and been summoned by Adam to take our order – he seemed on a mission to give us as little service as was humanly possible – Serena delved into her shoulder bag and took out a packet of photographs.

'Listen, everyone,' she commanded, tossing her hair back over her shoulders. She was smiling, but still managing to retain her strange, bitter caught-in-a-wind-tunnel expression. 'I've got something to show you. Paula's had her baby: a little girl! Isn't that wonderful!'

There was a half-hearted smattering of applause from

around the table, and 'aahs' from the women. Adam picked up his glass. 'Let's have a toast to her and the baby, shall we? To Paula and . . .'

'Jasmine. Jazzy, she's going to call her,' Serena supplied.

'To Paula and Jazzy,' chorused everybody, chinking their glasses. My heart sank as my glass raised. Not baby photos, please, I prayed. Don't show me the baby photographs.

But it was inescapable. Round they came, a series of almost identical shots, the only difference being how close up the baby's face was, and whether her eyes were open or closed. There were a couple with Paula too, looking shattered and green in a towelling dressing gown, her hair straggly and her eyes bloodshot. She was unrecognizable from the perky pregnant woman I'd seen at Moose Hall.

I thought of Vicky then, and felt a wave of compassion for her. I wished she could have been there with me, laughing at Mitch's hideousness and Ralph's dress sense, buoying me up with her good humour and sense of adventure. I wondered if I'd ever have it back again.

'Look at this one,' crowed Pamela, talking directly to me for the first time. 'Isn't she just adorable!' She jabbed me in the ribs with her elbow, forcing me to accept the next photograph in the seemingly unending display. I glanced reluctantly at it, and bit my lip. The baby was gazing at the camera with such clear blue eyes and the sweetest expression of surprise: kind of, *Wow, what is this place? Give me a little while to get used to it, and I think I might like it!*

Holly had worn that exact same expression for the last ten of her twenty-seven minutes of life, once her face had unsquinched from the bumpy ride, and the creases began to smooth themselves out. It was so unfair. Just when she'd started to relax and look around her, it had been time to leave again.

'Isn't she gorgeous?' persisted Pamela. I managed a

nod before shoving the photograph into Ralph's hands. If anything, he was even less happy than I'd been about seeing the baby pics. He and Margie were hissing at one another under their breath, and he passed the photograph straight on to her, upside down. She didn't look at it either, handing it wordlessly to Mitch on her right.

I downed the remainder of my wine and poured myself another glass. There was no white left, so I switched to red, although I rarely drank red wine. Adam was still being batted like a conversational tennis ball between Serena and Pamela, who were discussing yoga positions. Nobody was talking to me at all. At least the photos had stopped coming round, which was a relief.

I put my elbows on the table and entertained myself by gazing at the ceiling. Dozens of empty wine bottles, the Mediterranean sort with their own wicker half-baskets woven to their bottoms, were strung from faux fishing nets on the ceiling. I imagined them breaking loose and crashing down on the heads of the diners, like so many lethal glass bombs. If I could have aimed them – I saw myself huddled in the doorway with a little remote detonator – I'd have taken out Mitch and Pamela for starters. Then everyone else, one by one, until it was just Adam and me left, when we could finally be alone to talk about Max and gaze into one another's eyes . . .

'What do *you* do to relax, Anna?' Adam was speaking to me. I jerked into an upright position and leaned back in my chair to reply, because Pamela wasn't moving a muscle to allow Adam to talk around her. Adam leaned back too, and we exchanged what I construed as another secretive smile. I willed him to wink at me, so I could be sure that we were complicit in understanding the grimness of the evening thus far, but there was just the smile, too ambivalent for me to be certain.

'I suppose it depends. I like to run. I find that very

relaxing. I don't do yoga any more, although sometimes I stand on my head, and that helps too. Or else the usual, you know: TV, a good book, a bubble bath. Why? What about you?'

Adam considered. 'Play my guitar, usually. Listen to music. And reading to Max is very relaxing.'

'How is he?' Max's name was an automatic trigger for me to ask how he was – I was pretty sure I'd done it on many occasions.

'Fine, thanks.'

Pamela deliberately leaned her broad shoulders back in her chair, blocking Adam's view of me. We both moved forwards, but she wasn't having that either. She leaned forwards too, turning her back on me. I noticed the way her polyester dress stretched tight across her torso. She looked like a ready meal cooked under plastic film when it comes out of the microwave with steam straining taut against the plastic. I imagined taking my fork and popping the polyester, to see if she'd subside with a puff and a whine. She was talking about Max too, in that proprietorial manner she'd used on me that time at the college.

'Oh Adam, he's ever so well at the moment, isn't he, bless him? Little poppet! That day I looked after him he had so much energy; racing around the art room, he was. I let him use the potter's wheel and, gracious, wasn't he covered in clay when I brought him home! I did so enjoy giving him a bath. He had me playing all sorts of games with him: I had to be the teacher, teaching my class to be mermaids and mermen by pouring special magic water onto their feet, so we had to fill up that tupperware pot and pour it on his feet. Wasn't it funny, Adam?'

Jealousy wrapped clingy green tentacles around my throat, and for a second I wondered if she and Adam could be an item. No, I decided, surely not. I was pretty sure that what I was witnessing was merely a show of defiance for my benefit, as the interloper who'd gate-crashed her cosy scene. After all, if it was that obvious to me that Adam liked me, it was probably obvious to Pamela too.

But I couldn't stop wondering if *I'd* ever get the chance to play mermaids in the bath with Max. I could think of nothing I'd like more.

We fought our way through a mountain of tepid linguine each, apart from Mitch, who had a steak. The pasta had been the recommended special, but there'd been nothing very special about it, other than the quantity and the astonishing stodginess of the dill sauce in which it was smothered. After four more bottles of wine, the dynamic at the table changed.

Ralph had clearly done something to make Margie seriously unhappy, because she was now sitting with her back to him, flirting with Mitch, much to Mitch's delight. Ralph was attempting to retaliate by gazing deep into my eyes and telling me all about his replacement windows and his ex-wife's ingrowing toenails. Fascinating. Thankfully for me, Margie soon had enough of Mitch, and decided that she wished to make Ralph suffer a little more, so she tapped him on the shoulder – more of a vicious poke, really – and I was only too happy to relinquish him back to the clutches of their domestic.

Adam had extricated himself from the Serena/Pamela brackets, and was occupying the empty chair next to Mitch. Crikey, I thought with pleasure, he must have been desperate to escape the harpies if he'd prefer to sit with Mitch. I couldn't hear what they were talking about, but I deduced that it was probably something to do with the mosaic panel, from the way in which both men were painting enthusiastic shapes in the air with their hands.

Pamela and Serena were talking to one another through gritted teeth about Adam, dropping his name so often that it was black and blue. Two more bad cases of mentionitis, I decided. I'd forgotten that Pamela was one of those women who adhered to the principle 'why just say it once when you could repeat it six times?' and was telling Serena, ad infinitum, how highly praised Adam's still-life class of the previous year had been.

'Oh, it was ever so good. Everyone said he's so good at explaining things. "My flowers were so lifelike," they said. They all thought it was really good. Really good. Everyone in the class thought it was ever so good.'

I turned back in the direction of Ralph and Margie, figuring that, even though Ralph was a bore, at least he only said things once. But they had their heads together, like two fighting rams, and were embroiled in their dispute.

After another brief, heated exchange, Ralph pushed his chair back and strode across the restaurant towards the toilets, his face like thunder. Margie wore a 'don't talk to me' expression, so I gazed across the table at Adam, watching him as he was deep in conversation. I wondered exactly what it was about him that women seemed to find so attractive. Some people just had that.

Dad's friend Greg had been like that too, only more louche. Despite the twenty-five-year age gap, all my schoolfriends had been jealous as hell that he and I were an item. Not that I'd confided in many of them, though, what with Greg being married. But it was hard not to boast about the gorgeous blond man who looked like David Soul, and who bought me expensive presents: real perfume and genuine silver jewellery. Hard not to be flattered when he ran his hands over my bottom and actually moaned out loud. I remembered the time he'd come to wait for me outside the school grounds – I'd told him to meet me by the fence at the back of the playing field, along which ran a lane next to some allotments. I didn't recall telling him that I had hockey as my final lesson that day, but maybe I had, because he turned up early. When I'd jogged over to him in my short-sleeved Aertex shirt and pleated mini games skirt, the look on his face was one of pure unadulterated pain. Nobody has ever looked at me with such lust, neither before nor since. I saw the bulge in his Lees from fifty paces. He'd had to turn and walk briskly away – not easy, in his condition – before the PE teacher called the police and had him arrested for loitering.

'What are you smiling at, Anna?' called Mitch, and he and Adam both looked expectantly across the table at me.

'Um. Oh, well, nothing really. Just remembering my PE lessons at school, for some reason. And yes, Mitch, before you ask, we did wear short skirts. Ours were bottle green, with hideous thick matching PE knickers. They bore more resemblance to nappy wrappers than lingerie.'

I'd only mentioned the knickers because the image it created in my head was so unappealing that I thought it would cut Mitch off in his burgeoning fantasy – but I was being naïve. The look on his face wasn't far off the one on Greg's that I'd just been recalling.

'Bet you looked really tasty,' he said dreamily, stroking his chin.

'No,' I replied shortly. 'I didn't. Is anyone having dessert? I see they do tiramisu.' *Make it stop*, I begged silently to the heavens.

Adam looked at his watch. 'I've got a feeling there's going to be some live music in here later. Might be worth hanging on for.'

Somehow I doubted it. I was getting itchy with boredom. I'd hardly spoken to Adam at all, and I felt a pang of loss that I'd turned down a holiday in Ibiza for this very average meal with a bunch of people with whom I had nothing in common. I'd thrown away the chance of some rare quality time with my husband, not to mention the chance of catching up with my brother, whom I hadn't seen for months. I could have waited, I thought. Max would still have been there when I got back.

I quelled the urge to admit defeat and go back to the flat. Whatever else I might have been, I was determined. There was no way I was going to go through all this and not end up as bosom buddies with that child, I thought. No way, and especially not after giving up my holiday with Ken for it. The thought of Max asleep under his castle duvet in the flickering pink light of the magic lantern in his room filled me with renewed resolve. If I could just get Adam to invite me back for a coffee, I'd be able to nip upstairs under the pretext of using the loo, and feast my eyes on Max. Kids were amazing when they were asleep: other-worldly and flawless. Even Crystal looked like an angel, snoring away on her princess pillow.

Margie had stopped looking quite so aggressive, and the corners of her mouth had drooped as she lit a cigarette, without asking if anyone minded.

'Are you all right, Margie?' I asked, topping up her glass and moving my head away to avoid her exhaled smoke.

She turned, and I saw that her eyes were brimming with tears.

'What's up? Is it Ralph? He's been a long time in the loo, hasn't he?'

'That bastard,' she managed, from between clenched teeth. 'He's not coming back. And he's left me to pay his share of the bill.'

'What were you rowing about? If it's not too nosy of me to ask?'

'Actually I don't mind if you do. We were fighting because of his wife.'

'His ex-wife?'

'That's what I thought – his ex-wife.'

And her ingrowing toenails, I thought. 'You don't mean they're still together?'

She crumpled. 'We have been seeing each other for two months now, and all the time he says, I just live in the spare room because I can't afford to move out. We are getting divorced. We don't love each other any more.'

'And?'

'They do love each other!' She actually thumped the

table with her fist. By now, the rest of the table had abandoned their dessert menus, and were looking on with great interest.

'I'm really sorry – poor you. But how do you know? Did he tell you?'

'He told me that he does love me but that he loves her too, and he can't leave her because she'd be too upset. They don't have sex any more, you see. I think that is why he loves me.'

'But that's awful.' I felt utterly indignant. What a low-life, to use poor Margie like that! And what about Ralph's unfortunate wife? I was tempted to blurt out that Ralph's shorts were repugnant, and that he was a misogynistic two-timing bore they'd both be much better off without.

'I think I will go home too,' Margie said eventually, in her precise Dutch accent. 'I am tired. Maybe I will feel better in the morning.'

'I expect so,' I said sympathetically. 'I hope it all works out for you.'

She handed fifty pounds across the table to Adam. 'I hope that will be enough for us both. Let me know if it isn't.'

'Sure. Thanks, Margie. Take care. How are you getting home?'

'I walk. I live close to here, it's no problem. Five minutes.'

'Would you like me to see you home safely?' Adam asked.

'Thank you, Adam, but it's not necessary. I will be fine.'

When Margie had left, I said to Serena, 'So, are your kids with a babysitter tonight, or is your husband looking after them?'

She gave me a hard stare, presumably for bringing up her husband in front of Adam. As if she was trying to pretend to him that she didn't have one, I thought with hilarity – until I remembered my own, far more radical deception.

'My husband is.'

'Oh. And is he expecting you back at any particular time?' I fished.

'He does allow me to have a social life, you know,' she said, pretending to be joking, but with a knife-edge of steel in her voice.

'Gosh, it's actually quite late, isn't it?' I said, looking at my watch. 'What about you, Adam – who's looking after Max tonight?'

Adam looked at his watch, faintly puzzled. 'It's not that late. It's only ten-thirty. I've got a neighbour's teenage daughter in, and because it's not a school night she doesn't mind what time I get home, within reason, of course. It's all the more money for her, and she only lives four doors away.'

'Oh look,' said Mitch, pointing towards the restaurant door. 'This must be the entertainment.'

A tall, skinny woman with a crooked blonde curly wig on had entered, carrying a battered amp, a boombox, and a microphone stand, which she set up in the corner near the restaurant's fireplace. She removed her beige mac to reveal a tight bodice and checked dirndl skirt, and straightened her wig. She looked like a man in drag.

'Testing, testing, one-two-three,' she shouted into the mike, tapping it vigorously. 'Good evening, ladies and gentlemen, y'all! I'm Wiltshire's Own Dolly! Let's have a *yee-hah*, shall we?'

She was greeted with a perplexed silence in the restaurant, and we all looked at each other, puzzled, until she pushed PLAY on the boombox and began to sing 'D-I-V-O-R-C-E' along to a backing track, at which point we all, including the dour Pamela, collapsed into less-than-discreet gales of laughter.

'She's meant to be Dolly Parton?'

'Surely not. She looks nothing like her!'

'Look, her bra's more stuffed on one side than the other!' This came from Mitch, who apparently made it his business to examine every female bust with which

240

he came into eye-contact. But he was right. The chest of Wiltshire's Own Dolly was clearly as flat as the tundra: she resembled a string bean with tissues in its bra. I had never seen anybody less like Dolly Parton in my entire life.

Still, her hearty (if flat) singing did liven up the evening. With the exit of Margie and Ralph, and the ingestion of more bottles of wine, our table became more sociable too, and I began to enjoy myself. Several times, as I regaled everybody with funny acting stories or jokes (I have the undesirable habit of telling terrible jokes when I've had a few drinks), I caught Adam looking at me and smiling; and every time I made him laugh, I felt a deep flush of pleasure.

When Dolly finished her set, and we finished our desserts – watery tiramisu for me, Pamela and Adam, and great doorstop wedges of chocolate brownie for the others – there was a moment's lull as we sat back in our chairs, full of carbohydrates and alcohol. A siren wailed, and blue lights flashed briefly through the window as the police car sped past.

'A typical Saturday night in Gillingsbury, chucking-out time at the pubs,' said Adam reflectively. 'Max has got a total phobia about police cars at the moment. He'll either grow up to be a model citizen, or he'll be in Borstal by the time he's fourteen.'

'Why?' I asked, elbows on the table, immediately fascinated.

'Oh, I'm sure it won't last. It's my fault – I must have said at some point that if he didn't behave then the police would come and get him, although I don't even remember it. But he and his friend Christopher got into a fight at school last week – on his first day back! It seems that some older boys egged them on to start punching each other, and they all got told off by the teacher. He came home crying, saying that the police were going to arrest him and put him in prison. He was in a terrible state. He wouldn't let me answer the phone in case it was the police, and he turned white every time he heard a siren outside.'

'Oh poor Max,' chorused Serena, Pamela and I. Pamela added 'poor, poor Max,' at least three times for emphasis.

Somebody's mobile phone rang. 'That's mine,' Serena said reluctantly, delving into the cavernous handbag hanging off the back of her chair. 'Hello? Oh. Right. Bother. What, everywhere? Has she got a temperature? All right then. I won't be long. Bye.' She flung the phone back in the bag, looking extremely annoyed. 'It's Petra, my youngest. She's been sick all over her bed, apparently. I'm going to have to go home. Perish the thought that Leo might clean up a bit of vomit without dragging me home to do it, but still, that's men for you.'

'Yeah, man, I think I'm gonna call it a night too,' said Mitch. 'I've got some sensi to smoke. If anyone would care to join me back at mine, I'm happy to share the pipe.'

'No thanks, Mitch,' we chanted, as one. Great, I thought. That's everyone sorted, except Pamela the Limpet. Mitch and Serena fiddled with banknotes and change, and after an excessive amount of fussing from Serena, eventually left. Serena kissed Adam with great enthusiasm on both cheeks, and merely nodded at me. It was true to say that I hadn't cemented any new friendships that night – unless things with Adam picked up.

'Did you know,' said Pamela, once they were gone, 'that your nose and your ears never stop growing? I read it in a magazine. They never stop growing. Your nose and ears. They keep growing—'

'Really?' said Adam, sounding inordinately interested and rubbing his own earlobes. But when Pamela turned away to try and summon someone to bring us our bill, he winked at me. I blushed with pleasure, that small gesture sending my hopes and spirits soaring higher than they'd been all day. The split-second's movement of Adam's eyelid told me there was no way there was anything going on between him and Pamela, besides Pamela's infatuation. It told me to hang on, he wanted to get the chance to talk to me alone, and we were nearly there. It told me that he did find me attractive, and that he was sorry we hadn't spoken all evening.

'Where do you live, Anna?' Pamela asked. It was the first direct question she'd put to me.

'Wealton,' I said, knowing what was coming.

'And you're clearly not driving,' she said, staring pointedly at my empty wine glass. 'Taxis get awfully booked up on a Saturday night. If you're not driving, you'll want to order a taxi now, otherwise you'll be waiting for ages. They get very booked up.'

'How are you getting home, Pamela?' asked Adam, taking the bill from the waiter's outstretched hand.

'I've got the car outside. I'd offer you a lift, Anna, but I live in the opposite direction. I could drop you off on my way home though, Adam.' Game, set and match to Pamela, I thought. Adam was too nice to turn her down. Then she'd try and finagle a coffee from him, and then before you knew it she'd be up there, tucking Max in and cooing over him, while I'd have to sit here on my own enduring Wiltshire's Own Dolly and her Kleenex-stuffed front. I wondered how long Pamela had been in love with Adam. And whether he knew. And whether anything had ever happened between them. Surely not. It was more likely that *Serena* and Adam had engaged in a spot of extra-curricular tessellation. She might have been annoying, but she was at least attractive. And perhaps I only found her annoying because she liked Adam.

'Thanks, Pamela, that would be great,' he said, and my heart plummeted. What a waste of an evening. What a waste of a holiday! And I was no nearer to Max.

'Can I suggest that you drop Anna off at mine, if she's going to have to wait ages for a cab? I don't like to think of her waiting here, or at a cab rank.'

I shot him a grateful look, hopes raised again.

'Of course,' said Pamela through gritted teeth.

Adam studied the bill and then announced the amount we owed. Pamela pointed out that she'd only had one glass of wine and so shouldn't pay as much. So I put in an extra ten pounds, because I had been drinking. Even so, I noticed that the money everybody else had left was hopelessly insufficient, and that Adam ended up paying at least fifty pounds extra to cover the shortfall. I hoped he was going to let the others know later that there had been a deficit, but somehow I knew he wouldn't.

Wiltshire's Own Dolly, who'd been sitting at the bar knocking back fluorescent cocktails during her break, took the stage for her second set. 'Hello again, Gillingsbury!' she said, with considerably more vigour than before. Her wig had slipped slightly, and her lipstick was smudged. 'This is one y'all should know!' She fiddled with her boombox, and the opening chords of 'Nine to Five' resounded around the almost-empty restaurant.

'I believe that's our cue to leave,' said Adam, pushing back his chair. We trooped past the makeshift stage, to the obvious displeasure of Dolly, and out of the door. It was a relief to be out in the cooled-down night air. I noticed that the fresh air in Gillingsbury was much fresher than at home, where London loomed on the horizon in a yellowy halogen fug of emissions and city breath. I could tell I was in the country here. When I looked up, all I could see were constellations in velvety blackness.

The three of us set off towards Pamela's car, when running footsteps came up behind us. We turned in surprise to see a tall figure in a wonky blonde wig teetering towards us, still singing into a cordless microphone. Her voice, a cappella, (she was out of range of the backing track) sounded horrendous, like nails down a blackboard. 'These folks are leaving already?' she said into the mike, mid-verse. 'You can't go, honey'

– she stroked Adam's cheek and even he, the politest man I knew, recoiled – 'you're far too cute. Why don't y'all stay? A girl needs an audience . . . "Nine to five, what a way to make a livin' . . ."'

Unable, quite, to believe that we were being pursued along the pavement by a six-foot singing Dolly Parton impersonator, all three of us – even the rotund Pamela – looked incredulously at one another and then, without a word, made a run for it, leaving Dolly to shimmy with bravado back to the uninterested waiters and tired barman.

25

Pamela's car was a superannuated beige Beetle whose floor was littered with petrol receipts and sweet wrappers. She pulled into Adam's road, switched off the engine, and for a moment we all seemed to sit and gaze out at his house. It looked quite different at night, a sleepy stillness papering over its daytime shabbiness, and I felt a wave of gratitude that I was back there again. Perhaps Max would wake up, and I could give him hot milk and read him a story? I wondered how much noise I'd have to make downstairs before he'd stir, and had a fleetingly amusing mental picture of myself stomping around as hard as I could, talking at the top of my voice and dropping things – although then Adam would be more likely to turf me out than invite me to settle his son back to sleep.

'Thank you so much, Pamela. See you at college on Monday,' Adam said, opening the passenger door. A windscreen scraper fell out, although it must have been at least eight months since frost had caramelized any swirls on Pamela's car windows.

'You're welcome,' replied Pamela, in such a flat, depressed voice that I felt sorry for her. Unrequited love was a killer. Perhaps she too had thought that tonight would be the night. I looked over the front seat at the back of her dark lank head and thought how lonely it must be to be a middle-aged spinster.

'Yes, thanks, Pamela. I really appreciate the lift,' I said, trying to make sure there were no notes of triumph in my voice. 'Have a lovely weekend – what's left of it. I'll be in touch about getting my name on the reserve list for an art class.'

'Goodnight,' she said, not even turning her head to acknowledge my departure. Adam picked the ice-scraper out of the gutter, replaced it on the back seat, and leaned over to kiss Pamela gently on the cheek. The slam of our two doors resounded around the quiet street, and she drove off. I saw her peer suspiciously at us in the rear-view mirror. Poor Pamela.

'Is Wilf single?' I said as we crossed the road, having made a mental connection between Poor Pamela and Poor Wilf.

'Who?'

'Wilf. The receptionist at your college.'

'Oh, Wilf, of course. Um. I think so, yes.'

'You should do some matchmaking, then. He and Pamela would be ideal for each other, don't you think?'

Adam laughed, fishing for his key in the front pocket of his jeans. 'Well, perhaps. Although I think they're both pretty set in their ways.'

'How long has Pamela been in love with you?'

He opened the door, and there was a delicious sense of anticipation as we stood close together in the small dark hallway. Then Adam clicked on the light switch, and a smash of yellow destroyed the moment. He looked suddenly grave, as though he'd turned off his laugh as the light went on. 'Is it that obvious?'

I nodded. He opened the door into the living room, and mouthed at me, *I'll tell you about it later.*

A teenage boy slouched at one end of the sofa, and a girl sat bolt upright at the other. The Indian throw between them had been hastily smoothed out, and they appeared to be watching with avid interest a Party Political Broadcast on television. The girl was very

247

pretty, with long straight blonde hair and skinny legs in tight jeans, and the boy looked sullen and spotty, a typical teenager, swamped in a Slipknot sweatshirt.

'Hello, Mr Ferris!' gabbled the girl, pretending to look surprised. 'I didn't hear you come in. This is, um, Chris, he's been keeping me company, I hope that's OK. Max has been fine, not a peep out of him, did you have a nice evening?'

Adam frowned for a second, and then grinned. 'Hello, Chris. Yes, thanks, Stephanie. We had a very nice evening, didn't we, Anna?'

'Mm,' I said. 'Very interesting, anyway.'

Adam handed the girl fifteen pounds, and in ten seconds flat the pair of them were gone, Stephanie with a series of 'bye thank-you byes' and Chris without a word.

'She clearly likes the strong silent type,' I said, after they'd shut the front door.

'Lord alone knows what they were getting up to in here,' said Adam, surveying the room for signs of debauchery. 'But I suppose that bringing your boy-friend round is one of the perks of babysitting. And they didn't look too *déshabillés*, did they?'

'If I knew what that meant, I might be able to tell you,' I said, flopping down into an armchair. 'Is it rude?'

'It means "undressed".'

'Oh, right. No, they didn't.' For some reason, the way he said 'undressed' sent a shiver through my abdomen. 'So, tell me about Pamela.'

'Want a drink first?'

'Crikey, that bad, is it?'

'No, not at all. I'm just being a good host, that's all. Glass of white, or how about a little Scotch?'

'Ooh, Scotch, please.'

He headed for the kitchen and I followed him.

'It's a bit tragic, really,' he said, contemplating a bottle of Jim Beam he'd reached down from the top of a cabinet. 'Most of the time we don't mention it, but every now and again it flares up, usually at Christmas parties and so on. She'd had a bit of a crush on me for ages, baking me cakes and things. That had gone on since I started at the college, before Max was born. Seven or eight years ago. The baking used to drive my wife crazy – she felt it was like a criticism of her because she never cooked.'

'Your wife never cooked?' I was fascinated, and appalled. Poor Max.

'Well, that's beside the point, but no, rarely. Anyway, Pamela was brilliant when Max . . . when Max was ill. She came to visit him a lot, and helped me out massively. They're still close. But I sort of felt . . .' he paused.

'What?'

'That she was only doing it as a way of getting closer to me. And as much as I appreciated her help, it pissed my wife off no end and, to be honest, it annoyed me too, that somebody could be using my son like that.'

I gulped, and felt my face flush. He must never find out, I thought. What I'd done was even worse: used *him* to get close to Max.

'Anyway, then Marilyn left, and I think Pamela thought it was her chance to muscle in and fill the space. More than fill the space,' he said with a grimace, and I couldn't help smiling.

'It was awful. I had to sit her down and explain that although I really liked her, it would never work. I wasn't looking for anyone new. I didn't know if Marilyn was coming back or not. I said everything I could possibly say without actually coming out with the words, "I wouldn't fancy you if you were the last woman alive." But I think she's still hoping.'

I remembered the envy in her small, hollow eyes – but I was more interested in discovering that Adam's wife was called Marilyn. The name suited her, I thought, visualizing her in the photo on the shelf. I opened my mouth to ask where she was now, what had happened, whether he still didn't know if she was coming back; but decided that discretion was the better part of valour. All in good time, I thought.

'You're very easy to talk to,' I blurted out instead. We were standing in the galley kitchen, leaning against the counters. When I turned to pick up my cold tumbler of whisky, I caught sight of our reflections in the curved chrome surface of the kettle, an arched tableau of total completeness: Adam and I contained at the epicentre of our own silver and spotlit universe. I had the oddest feeling of contentment, that here was a place I was needed; where I belonged. Perhaps it was wishful thinking, but I amazed myself by seemingly managing to erase all traces of my old life as Anna: Ken, Lil, Vicky, the babies – hers and mine. At that moment I felt that all that I was, and wanted to be, was reflected before me in that kettle, and borne through the rooms of that little terraced house on the breath of the sleeping boy upstairs.

'So are you,' replied Adam, and he put his hand on my shoulder. His touch was so gentle – not hesitant, just tender – but nonetheless I nearly jumped out of my skin. He was looking into my eyes and in an instant all my comfortable feelings of the moment before vanished, and my knees started to tremble. I had to put both my palms flat on the kitchen counter behind me to hold me up, and I couldn't meet his gaze. Blushing like a schoolgirl, I stared at the floor. My heart was pounding and I suddenly became aware of the linguine sitting like a breeze block in my stomach. Adam moved closer to me. I didn't notice that I'd stopped breathing until I heard myself gasping unromantically, like a fish out of water. I also realized that I was absolutely, knuckle-whiteningly *terrified*. It had been seven years since anyone other than Ken had looked at me like that.

'You're so gorgeous,' he whispered, and I felt his breath tickle the side of my face. Unbidden by my conscious mind, my arms slipped themselves around his waist and pulled him even nearer until we were hugging. He nestled his head into the crook of my neck, and the smell of him was both familiar and like a distant memory: a Chinese whisper of remembered scents.

'Anna,' he sighed. Then he looked up and tucked a strand of hair behind my ear. We were finally eye to eye, and the air between our parted lips seemed to crackle and fizz with anticipation as we moved closer together. Just as his mouth had found mine, and our lips touched with a crackle that throbbed deep within me, a small, disconsolate voice floated down the stairs in an interruption of such immaculate comedy timing that we both jumped apart, red-faced and laughing.

'Daddy! Daddy! I want you!'

'That's my boy,' said Adam sardonically. 'Sorry, Anna, I'll just go and see what he wants. He's probably had a bad dream.'

Let *me* go to him, I begged silently, even though I knew it wouldn't have been appropriate. I hadn't got to that stage – yet. As I checked my tousled reflection in the kettle, I thought it wouldn't be long, though, before I was, and the thought made my heart soar. Then I wondered, idly, what Ken was up to while I was kissing another man, although I found that I didn't even feel guilty. He would never know. I'd found something to make me feel contentment, for the first time since Holly died; and I was buggered if I was going to let anything stand in the way of it. In the long run it might even benefit Ken and me, I thought, for me just to feel needed again.

Adam came down the stairs, grabbed a beaker and began running the cold tap to fill it up. 'He just wants a drink,' he said. 'Don't move – No, on second thoughts, why don't you go and sit down in there? I won't be a moment,' and he raced off again.

I wandered through to the living room, my ears straining to hear Max's sleepy querulous voice again. I heard a few murmurs, but nothing I could distinguish as words. I sat down on the still-rumpled sofa, feeling every nerve ending tingling with anticipation and worry. How should I sit? Like the babysitter, bolt upright with feigned innocence? Or perhaps I ought to have conceded to the moment and arranged myself seductively, one leg bent up, or both, maybe, in a full-length sultry lounge? After some considerable dithering, I settled for a faux-relaxed sort of flop against the back of the sofa, slipping off my sandals first to give an impression of extreme casualness. Then I changed my mind, and pulled my legs up so that my feet were flat on the sofa cushion and I was hugging my knees. I scratched a few stray brushstrokes of nail varnish away from the edges of my toes, and waited.

I still wasn't a hundred per cent sure that I'd have gone through with it, if Adam had come down wanting to carry on where it looked as if we had been heading. As much as I wanted to be there with him and Max, and as little guilt as I seemed to be feeling, I still loathed the thought of being unfaithful to Ken. I'd always had such secret scorn for friends or colleagues who breathily gushed about their sordid affairs – actors in rep had plenty of opportunities for infidelity, and often availed themselves of said opportunities. To me, though, wedding vows were sacred, let alone the colossal betrayal being perpetrated on the innocent partner. It was the lowest of the low, a cheap trick arising from boredom or frustration, or the depressing thought that they were obliged to have sex with nobody other than their spouse for the rest of their natural lives . . . But if that really was such a depressing thought for them, then I had no sympathy. It had been their choice. Nobody had forced them to get married, and if they hadn't wanted to stay faithful, why bother getting hitched in the first place?

That was what I'd always thought. I truly believed I wanted to grow old with Ken, and to have his children – although that was easier said than done. But this – and I could scarcely believe I was qualifying it – was different. This was about Max, at the end of the day.

'You look miles away,' said Adam, who, I noticed, had also taken his shoes and socks off. He was standing at the foot of the stairs, smiling at me, with the empty red beaker in his hand. His feet were compact and chunky, with toes in a perfectly neat curve from big to little. Ken's were the opposite: toes all different shapes and sizes, ungainly bony chaos. 'What are you thinking?'

I grinned back at him, swallowing my turmoil like medicine. 'I was actually just thinking that I can't stand it when people say "at the end of the day".'

'Really? I don't mind that one too much. It's "you know what I mean" that drives me nuts. There's a caretaker at the college who can't say a single sentence without finishing it with "know what I mean?"' He padded silently into the kitchen, left the beaker on the counter, collected his whisky glass, and returned to join me.

'Has Max gone back to sleep?'

'Probably, by now. Even when he shouts downstairs, he's never fully awake. He just wants to know I'm still there, I think.'

He turned to face me, sitting sideways on the sofa next to me as if he was about to propose. 'So, Anna,' he said. 'I'm not very good at all this stuff, and I don't want you to think I'm bombarding you – I know we're already going out on Monday night – but I wondered if you'd like to come swimming with Max and me tomorrow as well? I mean, obviously, say no if you're busy . . .'

Ken jumped into my mind then, in his tennis whites, on court. I was watching him serve, for some reason, admiring the way his shirt rode up to expose his sinewy midriff as he lifted his arm high, and the resounding thwack of the ball as it sped in a green blur across the net. Ken looked incredibly sexy when he served.

But I made him jump out again, just as fast. I couldn't let myself think about Ken. It had nothing to do with Ken, and anyway, he was probably in a karaoke bar in Tokyo by now, chucking back the sake and being flirty with blonde English hostesses on their gap year. A chance to be with Max – that was what I'd been angling for all along.

'I'd love to,' I said.

Adam kissed me again, more decisively. That's it, I thought. Whatever else happened, I would never be able to undo that moment. I could never again say that I'd been completely faithful to my husband. My legs were shaking so much that I was glad I was sitting down, and I felt as if I'd never been kissed before in my entire life. I'd almost hoped that he would be a terrible kisser: one of those who shove great fat tongues into your mouth and leave them there, as if it was your job to do something with it; or with terrible breath – but no. His kiss was so tender, and somehow bespoke, as if I couldn't have ordered a better fit. The longer it went on, the more my fear and guilt evaporated, and I began to melt into it. He pushed me gently back against the arm of the sofa, and I felt his welcome weight pin me down and hold me there, and the twitch and swell of him through his jeans against my thigh. Another man's penis. I wondered what it looked like.

'You smell lovely,' I muttered, when we came up for air.

'You taste lovely,' he replied, stroking my face.

I didn't want to sleep with him, though. Ken had once said that he would probably forgive me a drunken snog – most likely because he would want me to say the same for him – but that if I ever slept with another man, that would be us finished. So I mentally classified what Adam and I had just been doing as your common-or-garden drunken snog. Despite the fact that Adam seemed utterly sober, and the five glasses of wine I'd consumed had had little effect on me other than to stain my tongue and lips a bluish purple colour.

'Do you often go swimming?' I asked, just for something to say, as Adam pulled my legs across his lap and began to caress my bare feet. It felt wonderful. My mother was the only person who'd ever stroked my feet, and in the strong rasp of Adam's fingers across my instep I thought I sensed an echo of my mother's soft hands, like the satiny sheen of a conker inside its spiky case.

'When I can,' said Adam. 'When it's not too cold. The forecast's not so great for tomorrow, but he'll be disappointed if we can't go.' I clearly had so much longing in my eyes that he laughed. 'And I can see that you'll be, too.'

'I'm really looking forward to it,' I said, blushing.

Adam squeezed my toes. 'So am I. And so will Max be.'

It had been worth giving up my holiday for, after all.

26

I eventually left Adam's house at around two in the morning, my chin sore with stubble rash and my eyes stinging with tiredness. As I slumped in the back of the cab, trying to process the night's events, I realized I must have been drunker than I'd thought, since I couldn't shake the conviction that I was returning home to Ken, and not to a small, bare flat next to a village pond. I still didn't feel guilty – not exactly, although perhaps a true realization of infidelity took its time to sink in, like an unabsorbent cloth trying to mop up a viscous spillage. I was just sad to think of our big, empty house, its windows dark and air undisturbed. If Holly had been alive, there'd have been life in that house. If Holly had been alive, everything would have been different.

I fell asleep as soon as I got into the bed, and didn't open my eyes again until ten o'clock the next day, when I awoke with a shaft of sunlight dazzling me, and unfamiliar yellow flowery curtains flapping in the morning breeze at the open window. I'd been dreaming about our wedding: the best day of my life. The dream rekindled the joy I'd felt that day, and a residue of it remained with me, like sleep in my eyes, bringing a lump to my throat at the knowledge that such pure emotion felt lost to me now; for ever, it seemed.

It had been a genuine, almost out-of-control joy. Like fearless and exhilarating trampolining. I had no flowing or complete memory of the event, not in any narrative sense, but instead a choppy stack of thin recollections as though the day had been sliced up into a myriad cross-sectioned moments, any one of which could be pulled out and examined at random. It was a macabre comparison, but it reminded me of the executed convict who'd donated his body to medical science to be sawn up into thousands of paper-thin rings, which were then photographed and entered into a computer to obtain a 3-D picture of a human body, inside and out.

Sometimes, when I tried to remember my marriage service, all I could summon up was the feel of the heinously uncomfortable underwear I'd rashly allowed the dress designer to recommend. I'd have been much happier in a G-string, but she'd persuaded me into what were, essentially, just a very expensive pair of Big Pants, which cut into my waist and squeezed the cheeks of my bottom. But there were memories of other feelings, too – the tenderness I'd felt at the sight of the two rings nestled in the plum velvet box proffered by the best man: one ring chunky, like a sturdy first-born twin; the other one delicate, its ailing sibling. I'd forgotten the words of the ceremony, but not the muffled clearing of throats, the coughing of the congregation, or the trendy liberal vicar, who'd agreed to marry us in church despite the fact that Ken was already divorced. He'd had a habit of earnestly removing his glasses every two minutes to emphasize his words, and then putting them back on again.

Ken had said he felt hypnotized that day; that his sense of self had been lost, swallowed up by the moment. His marriage to Michelle had been a register office do, so he professed that it felt like the first time for him too. The last one hadn't counted, he said loyally. He said he knew all our friends and family were there, looking at us as we walked up and down the aisle, but none of the beaming faces even registered. I was the opposite: I'd carefully scanned all of them, analysing where they had all chosen to sit, what they wore, how genuine their delight was. Checking that Michelle wasn't bursting through the doors at the back, objecting in her high, brittle voice – even though she'd moved home to America and had herself remarried, it had still played at the back of my mind as a small, awful possibility.

The newness of everything had been so joyful to me in such an ancient church. The fresh film in the photographer's camera; the budding lilies; the gloss of our rings; the ushers' dazzling white shirts; Ken's freshly washed hair. It had all shouted 'NEW START' to me, new leaf, new life together. A new kind of pure joy. Mum had still been alive then, and both our mothers cried during the service. It had made me want to cry too when I thought about Dad, and how it ought to have been him walking me up the aisle, not my brother. Ken said he never noticed the weeping mums; nor the persistently whispering choirboy. Nor the moment when I signalled to the best man to bring us a hymn sheet, and he offered me a Polo mint instead.

Although neither of us recalled a single word of the vicar's sermon, we'd both remembered his pre-marriage advice: always back each other up, never put the other one down in front of anyone else. Present a united front to the world. We did that for the first time as we walked triumphantly back down the aisle and out of the church, man and wife. Me almost feeling like a mother already, picturing myself in a maternity smock before I was even out of the wedding dress. I knew we were going to make fantastic parents.

Later that day, at the party, I had got rather drunk and so forgot all the conversations that people had with me, like an infant who exists in the sensation of the moment, and forgets every joyous instance as soon as a new one comes along. I'd hardly even spoken to Ken, although I kept my eye on him, only needing to see him to feel that joy.

I'd just felt delight in everything. In the mullioned windows of the reception venue, soaking through the diamonds of old glass until I thought they would pop out from the pressure, jubilation hissing unseen through a vent at the unpicturesque rear of the building where the kitchen staff put out the rubbish. I wondered what the other guests had been thinking, whether they'd felt it too or were more cynical: 'Ken's got married again, then.' But it had felt so strong to me, as though my every action were imbued with exhilaration. I felt it as we plunged the thick steel knife through the hard icing and soft yielding fruit cake; flowing out in the lost words of the speeches; even the triumphant victory of my pee when I'd hitched up my dress and rested my flushed forehead against the cool white wall of the Ladies' toilet.

Afterwards we had both agreed that the whole event had been a victory of some kind. As if we'd managed to pull off something extraordinary and unlikely. Real life, real emotion, I'd thought. I still thought.

27

I was getting used to my small flat. After just a few days I'd begun to wonder how Ken and I filled the space inside our big Victorian semi; why we'd thought we needed all those rooms full of things we didn't use: CDs we never listened to, bar a dozen or so favourites; DVDs still in their shrinkwrap; books we'd never read; kitchen cupboards full of unopened jars of things like capers and fruit in syrup. At least half of the clothes in our wardrobes were never worn, so why did we keep them? It was as though we'd stocked our house for another, imaginary couple, perhaps the people we wished we could be. Parents, who cooked, listened to music, and needed racks of clothes to accommodate the variety of a day's activities with children. The more I thought about it, the more unwitting artifice our relationship contained. Our home was like the set of a drama series about middle-class thirtysomethings – we had all the requisite objects in the correct places: wellies, rollerblades and scooters in the garage; wine in the cellar; suitcases in the attic; garden tools in the shed – but the house itself was dead. I had a sudden urge to ring home and leave a message on the answerphone, just to animate, briefly, the hollow emptiness of the place.

I liked my new, small rooms. It was much easier to

take two steps across the room to the bathroom, instead of having to walk down half a flight of stairs and along a long corridor; and to carry my tea from the kitchen to the living room was a matter of a mere five paces. It was a place small enough to contain my emotions, I realized, whereas at home they roamed unchecked and ghostly along the hallways and up the three flights of stairs, my misery drifting cobwebby off lampshades and picture rails. I briefly wondered if I could persuade Ken to move house, somewhere smaller and more rural – and then I laughed out loud. Ken couldn't get around to changing the salt in the dishwasher, let alone moving house. And if we'd moved into the country, he'd have been gone for another two hours a day, commuting.

As I sat curled up in the flat's one armchair, gazing out of the window at the ducks squabbling over some pretty indigestible-looking crusts being hurled at them by a toddler, I thought about Adam. I oughtn't to let him kiss me again, I thought. It wasn't fair on him, or Ken; although I felt more guilty about using Adam to get to Max than I did about cheating on Ken. It wasn't really cheating, I told myself. I wasn't planning to have an affair . . .

But then I remembered that kiss, and how Adam's eyes had held mine, unwavering and clear blue, and the heat of his body pressing against me, and how his solidity had made me want to cling to him as if to a life-raft. He had something for me, I knew that, and I suspected it was more than just Max. But did I dare to try and find out what it was?

No, I mustn't, I decided. I would apologize, say how much I liked him, but that I just wanted to be friends and it couldn't happen again. I loved Ken. And I really liked Adam, too much to hurt him.

A loud beeping from the direction of my handbag made me jump. I uncurled myself from the armchair and retrieved my mobile, accidentally kicking over my quarter-full mug of tepid tea, which spilled in a grey puddle on the cream carpet. I mopped it up with a dishcloth in one hand, thinking how I'd done a lot of mopping up of late, and simultaneously opened my text message with the other hand.

'MORNING MY DARLING,' it said. 'WILL RING YOU LATER. HOPE THE READ-THROUGHS ARE GOING WELL. IT'S V. HOT HERE. LOVE U, KEN XXX'

Read-throughs. I needed to get my act together a bit, I realized. People would soon start asking me about my part in the soap, and I didn't even know what it was called. It was easy enough to be vague – all soap plotlines were basically the same, featuring, at regular intervals, affairs, double-crossings, life-support machines and illegitimate babies – but I needed to be clear about certain basic facts in order to keep my story straight. And I still had to tell Vicky and Lil. A prickle of discomfort went up my spine at the prospect of lying to all those closest to me – but then I thought, So what? I'm going swimming with Max later! I stopped worrying about the lies, and wondered instead whether I needed to shave my legs before meeting Adam and Max at the pool that afternoon. I glanced out of the window at the lowering grey clouds, hoping that the change in the weather wouldn't mean our trip was off.

Lobbing the wet cloth into the sink – easy, from where I stood by the living-room window – I picked up my notepad and pen. My hands now smelled like stale dishcloth; the scent of lies, I thought, deciding not to wash them. It was a smell I'd have to get used to, since it was going to be with me permanently. Better to think of it as something external.

What was a good name for a soap opera? I decided it would be less risky to invent one, then at least I'd have full poetic licence to make up my own storylines without fear of discovery. I didn't recall telling anybody the title of the one I'd been for the real interview with: *Merryvale*. I ran through a mental list of suggestions, every one of which bore too much resemblance to existing series: I thought *Avondale* was good, until deciding it was too similar to *Emmerdale*. *Brewster Street* I liked, and *Walcot Square*, but I couldn't use Street or Square, too reminiscent of Coronation and Albert. Crikey, this wasn't easy. In the end, I settled for the real one, *Merryvale*. It was very unlikely that anyone I knew would see it, and if they did, I'd just say I got sacked early on and had been too embarrassed to admit it.

My mobile rang, and I was relieved to have the distraction from my burgeoning subterfuge.

'Hello?'

'Hi, darling, it's me.' The line was crackly, and for a confused second I thought it was Adam. 'Did you get my text?'

'Oh, hi, baby. Yes, I did, thanks.'

'Can you talk? You're not in rehearsals are you?'

'No, we don't work on Sundays. I'm just hanging out in my room. There's a duck pond outside and my landlady's dog keeps running into it and scaring the ducks.'

'So you must be quite far out of Bristol, then. It sounds villagey.'

'Um. No, not really. I suppose it must have been a village at one time. It's just a suburb now. So what have you been up to?'

'The usual. Meeting rooms. Dinners. Too many drinks too late in the hotel bar.'

'Who with?' I checked myself; I had no right to speak with such a tone of suspicion in my voice.

'Marcus Brittan, mostly. Tour manager for the Cherries.' Ken laughed to himself.

'What?'

'Oh, nothing. Marcus has got some brilliant stories, that's all. He used to work at the Mudd Club, you know, in New York in the early eighties: they had all these road maps under perspex on the bar, and they used to snort lines of charlie along the freeways. Apparently, newcomers used to be given LA to San Diego, which isn't very far, but the regulars could go all the way from Denver to Chicago! I thought that was hilarious.'

'Mmm,' I said, wondering why my phone conversations with Ken were always like this. Why couldn't we have talked about anything that mattered? Then it occurred to me that if the Cherries' tour manager was there, it also meant that the band themselves must have been around, plus that scraggy manager woman. I imagined them all in the hotel bar at three in the morning, knocking back tequilas and roaring with laughter at the idea of chopping out lines of coke along major North American highways. Could Ken resist the late-night pull of creamy brown skin, and a choice of three young girls who just wanted to be famous? I wasn't sure that I could have done, in his shoes. Hell, I couldn't even resist a portly bearded ceramics teacher with calluses on his hands.

'So have you done your read-throughs yet?'

'Yup. We did them yesterday. It went fine. I've got quite a few lines, so I need to get my head down today. Rehearsals start tomorrow.'

'What's your character like?'

'Bit of a bimbo. I have to wear a red wig and high heels all the time, so I'm bound to trip over and sprain my ankle sooner or later.'

'Nice cast?'

'Yeah. I think so. A few luvvies, couple of old school guys who think they're better than everyone else. Some precocious kids. The director's OK though; very talented, I think.'

'Not too fanciable, I hope.'

'Gay. Naturally. Don't worry, darling,' I said with my fingers crossed. All of a sudden I missed him. I wished I'd gone to Ibiza with him after all. All we lacked was the chance to have fun together, I thought ruefully; but he had all his fun in hotel bars and fancy restaurants with other people.

'Have you heard from Vicky?'

'No.' At least that much was true.

'Going to call her?'

'No.'

'So when will you be home?'

'Not till Thursday. But then I'm off till the following Tuesday. You're around at the weekend, aren't you?'

Ken hesitated. 'Most of it. Don't forget I've got that tennis tournament on the Saturday though, and a dinner afterwards.'

'Can I come?'

Another, far too long, pause. 'Sure.'

Well, sod you, I thought. Suddenly I felt totally alone, fallen between two stools, belonging nowhere. 'Whatever.'

'Don't be like that. I said you could come.'

'You don't exactly sound thrilled at the prospect.'

'Come on, Anna, let's not argue. I know it's hard, me being away. Tell you what, we'll go out for dinner on the Friday night, shall we? And on Sunday let's go to a film, and maybe lunch at the River Café.'

'OK. I'm sorry. I miss you, that's all.'

'You too. Look, I've got to go – there's someone at the door of my room.'

I wondered who. 'Right then. Bye, darling, call me tomorrow.'

'Bye, honey.'

28

It was a shame that it was the first day for weeks when the sun hadn't shone, but I didn't care. I felt happy under grey skies, sitting on a threadbare stripy towel of Adam's, on a grassy bank near the lustreless water of an outdoor baby pool.

Adam was wading around in it, with long checked shorts swirling around his legs, and his hand supporting Max's tummy. Max kicked and wobbled tentatively across the pool, buoyed by armbands and a chewed-looking float. He was a pale streak of flesh in the water, so insubstantial-looking that the white spray he churned up with his feet seemed more solid than he was. His swimming trunks were so minuscule that they were barely visible, just a blink of dark blue nylon. Even though Adam was there holding him, my heart jumped into my mouth each time Max's sleek head dipped underwater, and goosebumps speckled my bare skin.

'Coming in yet, Anna?' Adam called across to me, waving and smiling.

I grimaced jokingly and pointed at the thick clouds, bulging with unfallen rain. But I stood up anyway, adjusting my bikini top, and walked over to join them. It was muggy, not cold, but it still seemed odd not to see the sun.

'It's quite warm in here, Anna,' chirped Max. 'Look what I can do!' He held his nose, squeezed his eyes shut, and bobbed under the surface of the water, his hair streaming flat out on either side of a perfect natural parting like a zip across his head. He came up again immediately, panting, water streaming over his closed eyes and down his face.

I clapped. 'Very good, Max. Bet I can't do that!' I walked in, feeling the tepid water caress my thighs. The pool was almost empty, save for two three-year-old girls pretending to make soup in a bucket at one end of the pool, and a very pregnant woman sitting on the broad steps, playing pat-a-cake with a toddler in a swim nappy. I averted my eyes from the woman's bulging stomach and, as I did so, caught Adam in the act of clocking my nipples. They had sprung to life through my purple bikini top; and he quickly looked away when he saw that I'd noticed. But I wasn't offended. It was more as if he'd been inspecting them out of curiosity than in any sort of lecherous way.

He had been as friendly as ever when we'd met up at their place before coming to the pool, but hadn't tried to kiss me, beyond a polite peck on the cheek, or be in any way over-familiar with me, even after the events of the previous night. Perhaps I'd been too stand-offish, I thought; or perhaps he regretted it too. If that was the case, it would have made my life an awful lot easier.

I held my nose and knelt in the water in front of Max, pretending that I couldn't bring myself to get my face wet. 'You're much braver than me,' I said, up to my neck and at eye level with him. He gazed at me levelly then put his small wet hand on top of my head, like a benediction.

'I'll help you,' he said earnestly, and tried to push me under.

I allowed him to press my head down, then broke free and swam underwater around behind him, tickling the backs of his knees. Above the water's surface, I heard a muffled squeal and felt the commotion around me as he tried to run away. I chased him, still underwater, flipping my body over and around like a seal. I didn't go swimming enough, I thought. There was nothing quite like the sense of freedom that moving through water gave you, even when the water was only two feet deep.

Max hid behind Adam's back, squealing 'Homey! Daddy's homey!' That's what it was about Adam, I thought; he was 'homey'. A safe retreat from anything and everything unpleasant or threatening. He was a very special person. He deserved better than to have me trying to worm my way into his life, a two-timing, conniving married woman who lied every time she opened her mouth.

I felt ashamed of myself. At the same time, something sinuous and wet snaked down against my shoulderblades, and things began to feel loose around my breasts, as if my bikini top was so disgusted at my behaviour that it was trying to escape.

'Oh,' I said, and, 'Help. My bikini's come undone.' I reached round in a panic to try and do it up, with visions of me being frogmarched by the lifeguards off the premises for indecent exposure in front of children.

'Allow me,' said Adam, wading around behind me and tying the two straps of my halter top into a bow at the nape of my neck. His hands were so gentle, and they brushed against the highest of my vertebrae as if he were blowing warm air on my spine. I felt that he was examining me, inspecting my neck and back and bottom in a slow, obvious appraisal, but I didn't mind. I liked it.

The long-threatened rain suddenly began to come down, plopping around us, delighting Max and making me shiver even more. I can't stop now, I thought. I wanted Adam, even more than I had the night before. I couldn't confess, or back off. Standing thigh-deep in the chlorinated water, I wanted Adam more than I'd ever wanted another human being. Max was nearby, trying to catch raindrops on his tongue, and he was part of it too. I wanted to be like the rain, falling all around them, covering them; and at that moment I decided that I had to make a conscious decision not to feel guilty about lying to both Ken and Adam. Life took people in strange directions, and who knew what the outcome would be, if Adam and I did start a real relationship. We might be fed up with one another within a fortnight. I'd gone too far to back away now. I needed to know.

Adam must have seen something of my thoughts in my eyes, for he reached out and took one hand of Max's, and one of mine, as if it were the most natural thing in the world. We made a dash for it then, out of the water, to gather up towels and backpacks and clothes and escape to the dry café area. Max was grumbling that he wasn't ready to get out yet, and even though I was loving holding Adam's hand, I offered to go back in with Max for a little longer. But a low growl of thunder caused the lifeguard to blow his whistle and clear both the adult and baby pools.

'You can't get back in, Max, because you might get struck by lightning,' I told him.

'Would it hurt?'

'Yes, it would. The lightning would go into the water and electrify you to a frazzle. Never mind, maybe we can come again soon?'

'Is lightning worse than injections?' he said, making a face, as we rescattered our possessions on chairs around an empty vinyl-topped table in the café.

I nodded.

'Bet it's not worse than chemotherapy though,' he said, flopping down on a free plastic chair. His towel dragged on the floor, the corner of it soaking up someone else's spilled Coke. I noticed Adam's shocked face and felt so sorry for them both that I couldn't think how to reply, so I just leaned forward and picked up the sodden towel.

'Does anyone want a drink?' I asked.

'Apple juice please!' Max said enthusiastically. 'And some crisps? Daddy, can I?'

'It's OK with me,' said Adam. 'Thanks, Anna, a coffee would be great.'

While I was up at the counter ordering drinks and crisps, I heard my mobile ringing in my bag. Dashing back to get it, I reached it just before it switched to voicemail.

'Anna, it's me, Vicky. Where are you?'

'Oh – Vicky? Is everything all right?'

I felt the need to sit down hastily, taken aback by having to deal with the two separate compartments of my life simultaneously. The plastic chair stuck to the backs of my chilled bare thighs, and Max sidled up beside me, resting his cold hand casually on my leg in the same way he'd done that time I cooked them supper. I put my own hand over his, and squeezed it, once more feeling that inexplicable soaring of joy amid the tension of deception. So much emotion was exhausting, and now Vicky, on top of it all. I hoped she hadn't rung up to give me a hard time; the conversation we'd had when I'd been in the garden the other morning had indicated that we were still far from being back in each other's good books.

Holding the phone in one hand, I managed to wrap my sarong around my breasts, which soaked up the majority of the water, but my bottom was uncomfortably damp in the wet bikini.

'This is the third time I've rung your mobile, and I've left two messages at your house. We talked about having a day out, and I'm just trying to arrange it. That's all.'

'Sorry. I haven't heard my phone. I'm . . . at a swimming pool.'

You don't sound much like you're gagging for a day out with me, I thought, but I supposed that conciliation always had been an effort for her. Her voice wasn't friendly, exactly, but at least it lacked the barbed edge of our previous few conversations. I glanced across at

Adam, who was briskly stripping Max out of his wet trunks and into shorts and a sweatshirt. He looked across at me, raising his eyebrows. *It's a friend of mine*, I mouthed at him, and he nodded back.

'Hold on a minute, Vicky,' I said, putting one hand over the phone's mouthpiece, extracting my purse from my bag with the other, and beckoning Max over.

'Max, can you be really grown up and pay for the drinks and things? Daddy'll have to help you carry them, but you can pay.' I handed him a five-pound note and his eyes lit up with joy at the vast responsibility bestowed on him. I felt such pride for him as he marched barefooted up to the counter that I almost forgot Vicky was still on the phone.

'Sorry, Vicky.' It was amazing how a little physical distance between us had helped me detach from our argument. I thought she was going to tell me that she'd had an abortion; and, at that moment, watching Max pass the fiver gingerly to a matronly lady in a checked pinny, and hold his hand out for the change, I really didn't even care. It seemed as if Vicky and her children were a million miles away, not a hundred. This was where I wanted to be.

I watched Adam carrying the coffees and juice back, and Max rattling his bag of crisps. Adam had the stripy towel around his waist, but his shorts were still dripping all over the floor. I was about to put Vicky on hold again and volunteer to keep an eye on Max while Adam went to get dressed, but Vicky was getting fed up with my lack of attentiveness.

'Anna, please listen, I really want to talk to you.'

'Now isn't a great time,' I said, still so detached from her that I had to remind myself that this was Vicky, my bridesmaid; Vicky, putative godmother of Holly; Vicky, best friend since the age of eighteen. We'd shared everything from perfume and tampons to tragedies that neither of us could mention without crying. And yet people grew out of their friendships. It happened all the time.

'When is, then?'

The edge was back in her voice, and it sharpened me up a little. The least I could do was to give her my full attention. 'No. I'm sorry, Vicky, now is fine. I don't have much charge left in my phone, that's all, so it might suddenly cut out. Are you all right?'

I took a slurp of the synthetic, machine-produced cappuccino which Adam had handed to me, and it scalded my tongue, making my eyes water. Max put the change from my five pounds on the table in front of me, with a satisfied beam, and I gave him a thumbs-up sign.

The rain was coming down harder now, and a cold breeze blew through the covered café area. I thought longingly of my dry clothes.

'I'm keeping the baby,' Vicky blurted.

'But that's great,' I said cautiously. I didn't want to sound jubilant lest any 'I told you so' charges be levelled at me. 'And how do you feel about it?'

A beat. In the old, pre-children days, that pause would have meant that Vicky was taking a drag of her cigarette, but not any more. 'Depressed. But excited, sometimes, too – more so now that I'm getting used to the idea. Dreading the thought that it might be twins. But most of all I'm sorry for having fallen out with you about it. Oh Anna, no wonder you had a go at me for even thinking about an abortion. Forgive me?'

'Of course I do. And I'm sorry, too, for getting on my high horse.'

Adam was rubbing his shins with the towel, obviously pretending not to listen. Max was singing: 'Who let the dogs out? Woof, woof woof . . .' as he stuffed crisps into his mouth, his childish voice deliberately gruff. He repeated it in the same way, swallowed his mouthful of crisps, and then, to the tune of 'Polly Put the Kettle On', continued, 'Who-oo put them back again, who-oo put them back again, who-oo put them back again, we'll – all – have – tea.' Adam and

I both snorted with laughter, and I tried to turn my snort into a cough before Vicky hung up on me.

'I've missed you, Anna. So what about this day at a health spa – do you still fancy it? I'll get Peter to babysit. How about Tuesday? I mean, I could only go for a day, not away for the night or anything, but I'd really love to.'

'Um, yeah, definitely. It would be great. But the thing is, I've got a job.'

Another ghost of an inhalation. 'Really? In what?'

Be careful, I thought. I had to get my story straight – what I told Vicky had to be the opposite of what I told Adam. When I was in Gillingsbury, I was meant to be in Bristol, only Adam believed that when I was at home with Ken, I was actually in Bristol . . . aargh. My head was whirling, and I stood up. 'Back in a minute,' I whispered to Adam, and walked a little way away from them, going to stand under a canvas awning which ran along the edge of the big pool. Rain hammered noisily down on it, making it necessary for me to raise my voice; but when I turned uneasily to check that I couldn't be overheard, I saw that Adam had gone into the men's changing room, taking Max with him.

'On a cable soap. Based in Bristol. Remember, I had that audition? They took ages getting back to me about it. I've rented a flat down there. Down here, I mean. I'm here now. Just came for a quick swim and now I've got to go back and learn my lines for next week.'

I thought if I kept talking she wouldn't be able to interrupt with any awkward questions. 'It's a good part. Not one of the main characters, but she's got some decent storylines. And the rest of the cast seem nice. Didn't Peter tell you I had a job? Ken told him when he came over that night; you remember I told you he came over, and we were just celebrating only I dropped the champagne, and then Peter turned up . . .' I ran out of steam.

'Wow. Congratulations, Anna,' Vicky said, but

whether it was because of the rain or the slightly crackly line, I just couldn't quite interpret her tone.

'So, I'll be back on Wednesday. Let's try for a day the following week for the spa, shall we, when Peter can babysit?' At least if we went to a health spa, I wouldn't be able to drink, I thought. Going to a bar would have been a disaster – Vicky sitting there with her one pregnancy-permitted glass of wine, whilst I tipped back the rest of the bottle and got utterly tangled up in my own web of deceit. She'd have worked the secrets out of me in half an hour, with the ease of a masseuse easing knots from a shoulder blade.

'That should be fine. We could go to that posh place up the road, the Ivy Spa. And I look forward to hearing all about the job then,' she said, in that same blank tone.

We said our goodbyes, and as I put the phone away in my bag I turned to see Adam and Max standing expectantly by the exit turnstile. I walked towards them, and they both beamed at me.

'I've got your stuff,' said Adam. 'Why don't you go and get changed, and then we'll go home, shall we?'

When I emerged from the changing room, they were there, waiting for me, as if it had never been any other way.

29

I pushed open the door of A Taste Of the Orient at five past eight the following evening, shoulders back, a beam on my face, and my hair in a pleasing shiny curtain. Ken was still in Singapore. I felt free.

Adam was sitting expectantly at a small table by the window, watching me arrive. He had shaved and trimmed his beard even shorter, I noticed, and wore a freshly ironed button-down shirt, black jeans, and a broad smile. I was glad he wasn't smartly dressed as, after my rather OTT outfit of Saturday night, I'd decided to go casual too: my favourite Replay jeans, wedge-soled sandals, and a pink T-shirt with a sequinned logo across my breasts.

He stood up as I approached, held out his arms and hugged me gently, kissing my cheek. I felt the sequins snag slightly on the buttons of his shirt. He was the first bearded man that I'd ever found attractive – apart from George Clooney, obviously – and I felt an un-bidden stab of lust as I wondered what it would be like to feel his facial hair rub against the tender hidden parts of my naked body . . . Get a grip, Anna, I told myself, horrified. I supposed it was natural to be thinking about sex so much, since it had been such a long time since Ken had been able to face it – but surely I shouldn't have been thinking about it with Adam!

There was no way that I could have Adam. Although that was probably why I thought I wanted him so much.

A surprisingly lanky Chinese waiter popped up beside me. 'Can oi get you a drink, zir, madam?' he said, in the broadest of Wiltshire accents, pen poised over his pad.

Adam's lips twitched, but he looked the waiter in the eye. 'I'll have a Singha beer, please.'

'Zorry, zir, no Zingha. Only *Carrrrl*sberg.'

'That'll be fine.'

'Same for me,' I added. 'And some prawn crackers, please.'

The waiter vanished again. Adam and I grinned at each other in the restaurant's dim light, a tiny nightlight on our table just about illuminating our faces – owing to the heavy wooden shutters at the windows, the room was extremely gloomy. I hadn't even realized that there were several other couples dining with us – the place was as quiet as it was dark.

'This place has weird acoustics,' I whispered. 'Listen . . .'

We both cocked our ears, and giggled at the sound of magnified chewing noises, like cattle grazing. Not one of the other diners was talking, as if there had been some sort of mass quarrel taking place right before we'd walked in. I noticed through the gloom that our nearest neighbour had a plate of noodles sporting a shiny fried egg on top of it. There was something very surreal about the place.

'Have you been here before?' I asked, curious, and couldn't help feeling relieved when Adam shook his head.

'Pamela recommended it,' he said, somewhat sheepishly. 'Although who she came here with, I can't imagine. Her mum, probably. She takes her out for lunch every now and again. But the food doesn't exactly look spectacular, does it?' We gazed at our neighbour's egg-topped noodles, floating in an alarming puddle of grease.

The gangly waiter returned with our beers and crackers, and we ordered, studiously avoiding any mention of noodles. Then, since the heavy quiet in the restaurant was so unconducive to flowing conversation, we fell silent, gazing instead into one another's eyes in a rather shameless way.

'You've got beautiful eyes,' said Adam shyly over the prawn crackers. 'Really blue.'

'They're green, actually,' I said. '*Yours* are blue. Yours are lovely.' I glanced sideways at the couple on the next table, half expecting them to make gagging noises at our soppy observations. But the man had begun a sonorous, dish by dish monologue on the best meals he'd ever had; his wife nodding earnest assent throughout. The other diners eventually began to chat hesitantly too, as if someone had given them permission.

'You're very easy to talk to,' Adam continued. 'But you don't talk about yourself much, do you? I feel like I know you so well already, without actually knowing anything about you . . . it's strange.'

'Well,' I said, breaking the last prawn cracker in half and bracing myself, 'what do you want to know?'

Adam broke the remaining half of cracker into another half, which he left in the basket for me.

'Is there some kind of unwritten code of conduct in all Thai and Chinese restaurants, do you think, to the effect that it's extremely bad form to be the one to finish the prawn crackers?' I added, in an effort to postpone any interrogation. 'People always do it, don't they – keep taking bits of the last one, rather than just being the one to stuff it in whole.'

'Polite people, anyway,' Adam said, offering me the now-minuscule piece, barely more than a crumb, in the bottom of the basket. I laughed, and popped it in my mouth.

'Thanks.'

'So, tell me about yourself. Have you ever been married?'

Somehow him asking me outright made it feel more natural to answer truthfully. Kind of truthfully.

'Yes. To a man called Ken. For six years.' *Please don't ask me when we split up.*

But Adam just gazed at me expectantly. 'What happened?'

'Well. I don't know. I suppose we just grew apart – the old story. He travels – travelled – a lot. Works for a big record company, and when he isn't – wasn't – working, he was playing tennis. He's a tennis fanatic.'

'No kids, I assume?'

I swallowed hard, as the fragments of prawn cracker seemed to have reconstituted themselves into a viscous mass in my throat. The wallpaper in the restaurant was the obligatory flock, with green and silver raised patterns as thick as Fuzzy Felt farmyard animals. In my mind's eye, I saw Holly at about eight months, rubbing her fat cheeks across those soft shapes and chuckling with delight.

'No. That was part of the problem, really, I suppose. We – er – I mean, I had a few miscarriages, and then we lost a baby at birth. Holly.'

It was the first time I'd ever been able just to say it out loud, and although it sent ants marching up the back of my kidneys and made my breath shallow, I'd said it.

'I'm so sorry,' said Adam.

I took a swig of beer, but it didn't stop my bottom lip vibrating against the edge of my glass as if I'd been trying to produce a tune. 'Thanks. It was . . . a lot for a marriage to survive.'

He reached across the table and took my hand, interlacing our fingers as he had done the other night, rubbing his thumb into my palm, and then twisting each of my rings around until he came to the one on my fourth finger. 'You still wear your wedding ring,' he said, and I felt the roots of a blush begin to spread across my face. 'But then, I still wear mine.' He chinked his gently against mine, and it felt as if the ghosts of

278

our partners stood at our shoulders then, disapproving. Two rings, four people, and one very guilty conscience.

There didn't seem to be anything else to say, and for the first time our silence had a tinge of awkwardness about it. Our neighbour said: 'Well, of course there was that Harvester in Altrincham. Lovely prawn cocktail, they did, and very reasonable too . . .'

I stared at a Chinese dragon hanging on the wall near our table. It had a lurid gold snarl, exaggerated cheeks and fangs, and spray-painted ears which were peeling like an old front door in the sun.

'What's the situation with Max's mum, then?' I asked eventually. 'Although just say if you don't want to talk about it; it's not a problem.'

Adam grimaced and studied the dragon too, and I thought he was going to take me up on my offer. But he started to speak. He didn't meet my eyes, although his fingers remained clasped in mine.

'We were basically fine together for quite a long time, you know, rubbing along; until Max got ill, I suppose. There were a lot of tensions along the way, though, even back then – money worries, mainly. My job doesn't pay well, and Marilyn worked as a legal secretary. It was a struggle, meeting the mortgage and buying all the baby stuff Max needed. So when Max was diagnosed, we decided that she ought to be the one to carry on working as much as she could, because she had the full-time job. I took unpaid leave from the college and basically just moved into the hospital to be with him. I slept there – lived there during the week – for months and months. Marilyn visited all the time, of course, and used to stay there instead of me at weekends, to give me a break. But the consequence was that we rarely spent any time together. If we tried to go out on a date, all we'd talk about was Max's latest treatment and how he was responding. It completely took over our lives.'

'Yes. I can see how it would,' I said, my thumb meeting his in a swirly little dance. Our food arrived, but after giving it a perfunctory once-over to make sure fried eggs weren't involved, we ignored it.

'Then I realized that Marilyn was drinking quite heavily. I can't blame her – the stress was horrendous – but it was just another reason she shut herself off from me. In the end we were barely talking. I started to get angry with her for losing the plot when Max so badly needed us to be strong. Which didn't help, obviously. Finally, Max had the bone-marrow transplant' – a thrill, almost sexual in its electrifying jolt, crackled up my back – 'and eventually got the all-clear. A week later, Marilyn packed her bags and left. I couldn't believe it.'

'You must have missed her terribly,' I said sympathetically.

'No, it wasn't that. In fact I didn't miss her at all. I meant that I couldn't believe she'd walk out on him, after everything he'd been through. I was furious.'

'How did Max take it?'

'Pretty much as you'd think – he was devastated. But after the previous two years, I suppose he was used to pain and setbacks. He cried every night for a couple of weeks, and then gradually stopped asking for her. Now – it's weird – he hardly ever mentions her.'

'Where did she go?'

'All over the place. She went travelling, said she needed to get her head together.' He snorted bitterly. 'We got postcards from various far-flung places, which I used to hide from Max because they only reminded him that she wasn't there; and now apparently she's back living near her mother in Leeds. The last thing I heard from her was that she missed Max like mad, but didn't want to upset him by coming to see him after so long. I told her mum that she should come anyway, but that was about three months ago, and I haven't heard anything since.'

'That *is* weird,' I said. 'I absolutely cannot understand how anyone could abandon their child. Especially one as gorgeous as Max.'

Adam rewarded that with a faint smile. 'So that's my sorry tale,' he said. 'Now let's eat, before this goes completely cold. I hate lukewarm sweet and sour, you can really taste the MSG.'

'We've both got sorry tales, then, haven't we?'

Adam's smile got broader. 'Maybe we should stick together, in that case,' he said.

'Like the noodles.'

'Yes.'

I hadn't noticed at what point he'd unlinked fingers with me, but once more he took my hand, knitting our fingers back together like carefully-darned socks.

'You're so gorgeous,' he said abruptly. 'I could look at you all day. I'm so glad we met.'

Tears flooded my eyes, blurring my plate of food. 'Me too,' I said, and I suddenly realized that I hadn't been thinking about Max at all.

30

'Fancy a walk on the beach?'

I squinted at Adam, puzzled. Geography had never been my strong point but, the last time I looked, Gillingsbury was not on the coast.

'It's not far from here to the sea, about a twenty-minute drive,' he said. 'I've only had two pints, and I don't need to pick Max up from Mum's until the morning. What do you think? I love hearing the sea. I'm sure I'll live on the coast one day.'

I had a foolish vision of us buying a cosy cliffside cottage together, with thatch and a huge fireplace, like the one in Ireland in which Ken and I had once stayed. It had been right on the main National Trust path up the cliff, and we'd had to be careful to draw the curtains whenever we made love, because hikers with flapping cagoules and dishevelled hair would peer in through the cottage windows as they passed, listing forwards at forty-five degree angles to the wind. I liked the idea that the only passing traffic would be on foot. Much better for Max's frail lungs, all that sea air . . .

'I'd love to go,' I said.

True to Adam's word, we were there within twenty minutes. He parked in an empty wind-blown clifftop car park.

'There's a path down there,' he said, pointing towards the beach. 'Lucky the moon is so big and it's such a clear night – we'll be able to see where we're going.'

I got out of the car, and my hair was instantly whipped into a vertical frenzy, as if someone had connected me to a Van de Graaff generator. Sand scudded and eddied around the car park, haunting the edges of the parking bays. Pools of weak but eerie amber light from three lamp-posts illuminated the sand, turning it spun gold. The lamp-posts made me think of Max and his analysis of their composition: metal, leaf-oil and something else . . . I'd forgotten what, but it made me smile. Something to do with clouds.

'What's so funny?' asked Adam, locking the car doors.

'I was just remembering Max's description of how lamp-posts are made,' I said, and he grinned back.

'Yes. I don't know where he gets these strange ideas from. There's a big hole in our road at the moment, and he's convinced that it was created by a mole who'd been digging there, who then exploded, as Max said, "with a very small pop", thus creating said hole . . .'

I could have listened to him talk about Max all day. 'Surreal,' I said. 'It must be like living with Vic Reeves and Bob Mortimer. You know: "It's about this time of night that I like to slip a Caramac underneath a squirrel."'

We both laughed, and set off down the dark path. Adam reached over and took my hand, and we carried on in silence, the moon lighting our way. There was nobody around, although it was only ten o'clock. I released Adam's hand briefly to zip up my thin jacket, then picked it up again.

'Why are your hands so lovely and warm?' I asked, as he gently chafed my icy fingers. 'It's freezing out here.'

He looked concerned. 'Are you OK? If you get too cold, let me know and we'll go back.'

I smiled at him. 'No, I'm fine. The moon's incredible, isn't it? And so many stars. It's not like that in London.'

We fell into step, taking long strides down to cover the path's steep incline. It felt odd, being out with him like that – somehow more like a date than the meal had been. I thought of the muddy sky over our house in Hampton, of standing in the garden barefoot with Ken's arms wrapped around me. What I thought were stars up there usually turned out to be planes, circling the night sky like predators.

'Do you miss London?' Adam asked, and I could truthfully shake my head and say, No, I didn't. Omitting, of course, to add that I still lived there.

The tide was out, and we could only hear a faint swoosh and suck of waves on the shore. 'Shame the waves aren't bigger,' said Adam. 'But at least we'll be able to walk on the beach better than if the tide was high.'

'Is it too dark to skim stones? I love skimming stones. It's one of my favourite things.'

'Mine too,' he said. 'Let's see when we get down there.'

As soon as our feet hit sand, I felt that long-forgotten frisson of pleasure I always got when first setting foot on a beach. I imagined the sand pouring into the sides of my shoes and contemplated going barefoot; but it really was cold. Besides, the sand was soon replaced by a thick band of large pebbles instead, easier to crunch across. I thought of Ken again; how it annoyed me when he came back from tennis and took off his trainers, permitting little red stones from the courts to cascade over our bedroom carpet until it began to resemble a very small gravel-pit.

But Ken seemed a long way away, and kind of abstract, almost like someone I'd invented. The world that night belonged solely to Adam and I. We were its only inhabitants, and I dismissed my husband with an ease which, all the same, made me uncomfortable.

'It's like the whole sky is there just for us,' I said – not meaning to be sentimental; it really felt like that – and Adam stopped walking, put his hands on my arms, and kissed me, so unexpectedly that I swallowed my chewing gum. His lips were warm and dry and, over the salty tang of the air, I breathed in his glorious bluebell smell. I put my arms around him, and moved closer, opening my mouth to the kiss. His tongue caressed me, slowly and deliberately, much deeper than the way he'd kissed me after the group dinner. It felt as if he were already making love to me, and I moaned, the sound carrying away from me, lost in the wind. I felt lost.

'Oh Anna,' he said, sadly, as if he somehow knew I couldn't be his. 'You are so gorgeous.'

'So are you,' I replied, realizing that I was shaking. 'You're amazing.'

He kissed me again, and the stones under my feet shifted slightly, causing me to stumble backwards. He grabbed my arms tighter and hauled me in, like a fish on a line. His broad back made an excellent windbreak – although, thankfully, it was a lot more sheltered on the beach than it had been up on the cliff path – and I felt the skin of my face begin to heat up slightly in proximity to his own warmth.

'I can't tell you how nice you are to kiss,' he said, smiling at me, dropping dozens more little kisses on my cheek. 'I'm feeling flipping randy, actually.'

I laughed. *Flipping randy*. The anachronistic turn of phrase was so quaint. From anyone else, I'd have found it faintly ridiculous, but from Adam it aroused me. Since I'd known him, he'd come out with a selection of appealingly outmoded words that were a complete turn-on: *randy, tummy, whoops-a-daisy* . . . there was something blithe and disingenuous about the way he'd used them. It made me melt. Ken would have said *fucking, horny, stomach*: harder, more businesslike words.

'I could kiss you all night,' he continued. 'I've been dying to kiss you again.'

We kissed, and kissed, and kissed, until I forgot about my cold hands, and slipped them under Adam's jumper where the touch of them on his warm back made him jump and nearly lose his balance. In revenge, he took his own hands and slid them down inside the waistband of my jeans, until they cupped my bottom, but his were still warm.

'Not fair,' he murmured. 'Your bum's as cold as my hands.'

We kissed again, and I forgot about Ken. I forgot that I was married. I stopped feeling lost, and began to feel found instead.

When I came up for air, a movement startled me. I looked over his shoulder, half expecting to see a gang of giggling teenagers pointing at us, or a disgusted-looking dog-walker, but we were still alone. The movement had been the tide coming in, weaving a gleaming silent path towards us along ribbons of beach: tributaries swelling the sand like the blood pumping in my veins and swelling the neglected parts of me.

'Better make sure we don't get caught by the sea. I don't want my feet to get as cold as my backside is,' I said.

Adam led me further up the beach, back onto the big pebbles. 'Shall we lie down for a minute?' he said, a little slyly.

I looked doubtfully at the stones, but at least they were dry, so I allowed him to push me gently down until we were lying side by side in the moonlight. I felt like Deborah Kerr in *From Here to Eternity* – after I'd removed the remains of a washed-up plastic cup from by my head, and hoped that I hadn't lain in any small oil slicks. I was unbelievably turned on by his gentle assertiveness. Despite the freezing temperatures and the uncomfortable rocks, I felt itchy with lust and full of a strange, nervous thrill.

Adam slipped his hand inside my jeans again, this time down the front of them. Then he undid the button, and the zip, and I felt his fingers find the hot centre of me. I was a little taken aback by that, but had no wish to object. Despite us acting like a couple of horny teenagers, his tenderness and disingenuous passion moved me, and it was remarkably easy to block out the cold air and the bumpy stones which were our impromptu mattress, lost in long-forgotten feelings of pure pleasure. I hadn't even thought of objecting when he undid his own trousers and placed my hand on him, although afterwards I was surprised. His language might have been old-fashioned, but his courtship certainly wasn't. I'd thought I was far too old even to think about alfresco foreplay, let alone on a cold, stony English beach. But it was so liberating, just to be wrapped up in fooling around for pure pleasure, rather than obsessing about making and losing babies every time I started thinking about sex.

When we returned to the car, wind-blown and – in my case – slightly dazed, I pulled down the sun visor and inspected myself in the mirror behind it. I remembered the satiny feel of his penis, and thought how, when I touched it, it had turned me into a different woman. An adulteress. In France or Spain no one would have batted an eyelid; in Nigeria I could have been buried up to my neck in a pit, and stoned to death with rocks like the ones we had just been rolling around on. Different on the inside, and a total state on the outside: red-nosed, white-cheeked, hair a mad tangle, eyeliner smudged, and all my sparkly lipstick completely vanished. Someone who would never again be able to claim that she had been faithful to her husband. We hadn't gone all the way, but that was academic. And now I wanted Adam even more.

I looked across at him, at his calm blue eyes; and he smiled at me as if I were the most beautiful woman in the world. In the dim light of the car, his cheeks and mouth and jaw were illuminated with the tiny sparkles from my lipstick, like far-away constellations. I'd left my mark on him, just as I had in his son.

Four days later, I was sitting in another Chinese restaurant, in another town, with another man. I still had a bruise on the side of my hip from a sharp pebble, although the stubble rash had faded from my chin, but somehow – call it denial, or disbelief – I didn't feel that I'd been unfaithful; not *really*. Non-penetrative sex on a cold beach at ten o'clock at night just seemed like something which could not possibly have happened to me, Anna Sozi. Perhaps it had happened to Anna Valentine, though, who smiled when she remembered the feel of Adam rubbing against her, and the blue of his eyes as he'd gasped with pleasure.

This other man, Anna's husband, had linked fingers with me too. Why had he done that? He'd never used to be a finger-linker. His fingers were longer, darker and thinner: Cadbury's Fingers to Adam's Sponge, and I couldn't help thinking they didn't fit with mine so well. We were having noodles; noodles which were lighter, warmer, and twice the price of the ones our food-obsessed neighbour had ordered in the Taste of the Orient. The wine was a beautifully chilled Chablis which we were drinking from elegant glasses, instead of the fizzy *Carrrl*sberg of Monday; the waiter's accent was Beijing not bumpkin; the dessert menu most definitely did not feature lurid colour photographs of its choices; and I got the feeling that the head chef would rather have disembowelled himself with his meat cleaver than ever serve a dish with a fried egg on top.

Yet I couldn't shake the spooky feeling of displacement, of having been happier at the other place with its paper tablecloths and flock walls. Even when Ken looked in my eyes and said, 'You're so beautiful,' it had felt more . . . real . . . when Adam had said it. Which frightened me. It frightened me that I'd immediately thought of Adam, and wished I'd been sitting opposite him instead. It frightened me that I didn't feel guilty for thinking that. And it frightened me that all of a sudden everything upon which I'd built my married life – the trust of marriage vows, the stability of a nice home and a loving husband – it all seemed to be sweeping away down a hill in a relentless landslide of change, at the bottom of which stood Adam and Max, waiting for me.

'So, how's your first stint on the job been?'

We were down to the last two prawn crackers – dry crunchy speckled brown crackers instead of the greasy thin MSG-flavoured white ones, of course, presented in a china bowl instead of a flimsy wicker basket – but I couldn't face going through that little ritual again. I handed him one, and took the other myself. 'On the job' – made me sound like a prostitute. Which I was no worse than, in fact.

'It's great,' I said, imagining it all with a pang of regret: the new faces, the exciting sets, the cable-like jumble of unfamiliar names of crew and cast, real and fictional. Cameras, wardrobe, catering. I wished I had got the job. 'I think I did OK. I know I did much better than my screen husband. He's crap – he fluffed his lines so often that the director threw his clipboard on the floor.'

'What's his name?'

'Who – my husband? Adam. His character's called Adam, and the actor is a guy called . . . Len Smith. I so hope I don't have to snog him, he's heinous. Beardy and piggy-eyed. The director's name is Sebastian. We're supposed to be a new family who've moved into the street; me and Adam, and our twin babies.'

'Real babies?'

'Of course.'

Ken paused and looked away, and I felt the depth of his sadness. I decided to spare him from his unspoken queasy concern. 'It's fine. I'm dealing with it fine. Sebastian says . . .'

What? What had Sebastian said? And was that even the name I'd assigned him? Suddenly I wasn't sure if I'd said the director was called Sebastian, even though I *thought* I had, not one minute earlier. Before that too, I recalled telling Ken he was a hot new director who'd done some great ads, but couldn't remember if I'd given him a name then or not. I felt hot with guilt and the cumbersome weight of deception. It slithered around beneath me, yielding like the rocks on the beach had at the beginning of the week with Adam. Bringing Holly into it, albeit indirectly via the mention of babies, had all at once brought it home to me how hugely I was lying to my husband. Massive great lies, like giant belches in his face.

It felt way too enormous for me to confront. I'd gone too far to go back. I pushed the horror to the back of my mind and gritted my teeth: I was just going to have to be a good enough liar not to be caught out; it was as simple as that. For the time being.

At least I didn't have to be overly worried about being caught out on details – Ken had no memory for such trivia. Just in case Adam did, though, I excused myself and went out to the loo, where I found a petrol receipt in my purse and wrote on the back of it: 'HUSBAND: ADAM. ACTOR: LEN SMITH. BEARDY, PIGGY-EYED. DIRECTOR: SEBASTIAN.' I'd transcribe them onto my index cards when I got back to Wealton, and keep my story straight that way.

When I got back to the table, I'd hoped that the subject would have been forgotten, but Ken was clearly in one of his rare 'must be more interested in Anna's life' moods. (Although, in fairness to him, my supposed new job was the first thing he'd really had to *be* interested in, since a voiceover for a brand of cheese triangles I'd done, almost eighteen months ago, and that had only been good for a two-minute conversation over a G & T by the river one sunny afternoon.)

'Have you got many lines?'

'Quite a few,' I said, fiddling with the pepper pot. 'It's weird, having to learn lines again.'

'If you ever want me to test you, just shout,' he said, deftly shovelling rice and snow peas into his mouth with chopsticks, without dropping a single grain. Adam and I had used forks. Much simpler.

'Oh . . . thanks. But don't worry. I'm better just locking myself away and doing it while you're out at work.'

'That sounds distinctly dodgy.' Ken grinned. 'Wouldn't want to hear that sentence taken out of context!'

To my annoyance, I blushed. Then I began to stress about scripts. Surely Ken would expect to see them lying about the place at home? How could I be learning lines with nothing to learn them from?

'On second thoughts,' I said slowly, 'Lil offered to let me use her house if I ever wanted some space to learn my words. You know how lovely her living room is, overlooking the garden. I might take her up on it. I think it'll be good for her and me to spend more time together, even if I'm just sitting reading. And in a way I'd prefer not to bring my scripts home with me. If I leave them all at her place, I won't be tempted to walk around at home with my nose stuck in them the whole time.'

'Good idea,' Ken said. 'I don't want to be a script widower.' I felt like asking how he'd even notice, since he was never there, but I desisted.

'Here, have you tried this salmon?' I asked instead. 'It's lovely.'

A mental picture of Adam and me kissing on the rocks on Monday sprang unbidden into my mind, and I shuddered with guilty pleasure.

'What's the matter? Ghost walk over your grave?' said Ken, stuffing a large chunk of salmon into his mouth.

I nodded, still thinking of Adam's hands on my freezing backside. And wondering how soon I could see him and Max again.

Part Three

32

'I can't do any of the things I wanted to,' moaned Vicky. We were standing in the foyer of the Ivy Beauty Spa, perusing the list of treatments which a white-coated receptionist had handed us. It was almost two months since the grey day by the pool with Max and Adam, when Vicky had rung me to arrange the spa trip, but in the end it had taken that long to settle on a date and get it booked. I'd pretended it was hard to fit it in around my filming schedule, but really I hadn't wanted to tear myself away from Adam and Max for a single day more than I had to. Adam and I were a couple, I thought with wonderment, in what, to all intents and purposes, was a 'real' relationship, and I missed Max and him badly whenever I had to come home to Ken.

'It's not fair. I can just about put up with not drinking or smoking, but when I can't even do healthy things like have sunbeds and detoxing body wraps . . . well, I mean, what's the point?'

I thought I'd better not tell her what the point of being pregnant was, not if she didn't already know. 'Sunbeds aren't exactly healthy,' I replied instead.

'They are,' she said. 'They make you feel good, and look good; therefore they're healthy.'

'They make you feel sweaty and claustrophobic, and give you skin cancer,' I said.

Vicky sniffed. 'Spoilsport.'

'I was trying to make you feel better about not having one.'

'Whatever. So what are you going to do?'

I hadn't much fancied the detoxing seaweed body wrap which Vicky had proposed we both have, before she'd been informed that her pregnancy precluded her from it; but her attitude annoyed me. Yes, I wanted to build bridges with her, but I wasn't going to let her trample all over me all day with her hard-done-by attitude. However she felt about it, she was carrying a small miracle inside her, and if all she could do was whinge about it, I wasn't sure that I could stomach it.

'I think I'll do the seaweed thing anyway. You don't mind going for a swim or something while I do that, do you?'

Vicky rolled her eyes and looked sulky. 'Suppose not.'

In the end she plumped for an eyelash tint and a manicure and pedicure, while I went for the body wrap and an Indian head massage. We were handed fat white robes, tied into soft square parcels with their own belts, and sent off to get changed.

As we undressed, I glanced at her body. I hadn't seen her without her clothes on for ages, probably not since before Pat was born. She'd always been so slim – not skinny, like me, but with gentle firm curves I'd coveted. Now her curves had softened into upholstery, and her bottom had taken on a distinct shelf-like appearance. Although her pregnancy was showing, her belly was not yet taut again. It was at that stage where it could have been mistaken for over-indulgence, or weak abs.

She caught me peeking at her. 'Don't look at my horrible body,' she said, yanking on the towelling gown and tying the belt briskly round her middle.

'It's not horrible,' I replied, pulling on my own gown.

'It is. It's revolting, and I hate every inch of it. I've even got fat on my back now, under my bra strap.'

'Honestly, Vicky, you've got a lovely body. You're just pregnant, that's all.'

She snorted. 'Just think what sort of state it'll be in after this one pops out.'

After this one pops out. She had no idea how I envied her confidence in the reproductive process.

'Well, I'd still rather have your body than mine. At least it's feminine. I still look like a boy. No wonder I always have to play the principal male lead in panto.'

'So? That's good, isn't it? I'll only be good for the back end of the horse after this.'

I turned away from her and dropped a pound coin into a locker, feeling my heart sink into my spa-issue white slippers. If the day was going to consist of Vicky bemoaning her lot, I thought miserably, I was going to wish I'd never bothered. I could have been in Gillingsbury, helping Max's class make rice krispie cakes at their weekly cooking morning.

But she perked up once we'd had our complimentary half-hour massage and were lying side by side in an octagonal room full of sun loungers, with a plastic cup of lemon-flavoured water to sip from, and cold wet cotton-wool pads on our eyelids. A motherly white-uniformed lady had tucked thick striped duvets over us, and left us with piles of *Hello* and *OK!* to read. Which was somewhat problematic, with the cotton-wool pads in place.

'Mmm. I could get used to this,' said Vicky.

'Weird, though, isn't it, being tucked up in bed by a woman in a white coat. When were you last tucked in by anyone?'

'Shhhh,' said the only other occupant of the room. Vicky and I removed an eyepad each and glared at her, an elderly lady with a perm so stiff that the curls didn't appear to be flattened by her lying on her back. But she had her own pads on, and didn't notice.

'It's not a bleedin' library,' said Vicky loudly.

I giggled, and the lady tutted. Fortunately the door

297

opened and the attendant called, 'Mrs Turner? Time for your next treatment.'

'Good thing too,' said Mrs Turner sniffily. 'It's not exactly *relaxing* in here with all this noise.'

She bustled out, like Margaret Thatcher in a bathrobe. Before the door had quite closed behind her Vicky called, 'Yeah, bye then, Mrs Turnip. Hope your next treatment's a colonic irrigation, you old battleaxe.'

We collapsed into childish laughter, and I thought, No, this was a good idea after all. All Vicky needed was to get away from her life for a while; to have a chance to lighten up.

I supposed that was what I'd been doing too, with Adam and Max. Yet I was getting so used to it, it was beginning to feel as if my life in London with Ken was my non-routine life, and not the other way around . . .

'Vicky,' I said, sitting up and discarding the cotton-wool pads. They had lost their chill, and felt soft and compact, moulded to the curve of my eyelids. 'I've got something to tell you.'

She sat up too, alarmed by my tone. Her pads fell off, scales from her eyes; although I wasn't sure that I wanted her to have a Damascean level of revelation, at least not about my life.

'What?'

But I wasn't able to do it. I'd left it too long. The secret was stuck inside me, like a clogged-up pipe; or it could simply have been that I couldn't face her outrage at not having been told sooner. I bottled out.

'I'm . . . I'm . . . not very happy with Ken at the moment,' I blurted out. It was true, I thought; it must be true, otherwise I'd never have allowed myself to get into this situation with Adam.

'Any particular reason?'

I lay back on the paper-draped pillow and stared at the fake ivy wreathed around the pillar in the centre of the room.

'The usual. Him playing too much tennis, working too hard, never talking about anything other than work.

Even our social life, such as it is, is work-related – you know, dinners with artists or managers, gigs, show-cases.'

'But it would be worse if he was unemployed. At least he earns a really good salary. And you always used to like all that socializing with bands and stuff.'

'I know. I just . . . well . . . things change. I don't want to spend my whole life being a useful executive wife.'

'Why don't you take up tennis?'

I snorted. 'Oh, for heaven's sake, Vicky, that's the sort of thing my mother would have said. It would take me years to get up to Ken's standard. Besides, I hate it. I hate playing with Ken, because he looks bored after about two minutes, and then starts sighing whenever I hit the ball out of the court – which is all the time.'

'Are you trying for another baby?'

Vicky hadn't looked at me when she said that. She'd been flipping through *Hello*, pages turning in a blur of fake tans, bleached teeth and ostentatious interior design; too fast for her to take any of it in. Which was how I knew she was paying attention to my answer.

'No. We aren't even sleeping together.'

'What – not at all?'

'We haven't done, for months. He leaves so early and gets in so late. Plays tennis all weekend. Even if we wanted to, we don't get the chance. In fact, he's not even—'

I was going to say 'able to', but then I thought how mortified Ken would be if he knew I was discussing his sexual problems with my girlfriends. '— that bothered about it,' I said instead.

'But don't you want to get pregnant?'

Vicky discarded the magazine and rolled onto her side. I turned onto mine, too, so we were facing one another, eye to eye, under our duvets like third-formers at boarding school, whispering after lights out.

'No. Yes. Yes. But it's complicated. I'm . . . I'm afraid to. And so's Ken.'

Vicky reached out and took my hand. It felt so good to confide in her again. 'Of course you're scared, who wouldn't be? Is there someone you could talk to about it? A counsellor, I mean? What about that woman you saw before?'

I shook my head. I didn't want to talk to anyone about it, because there was no one to whom I could tell the whole truth. I suddenly felt entirely alone.

'At least talk to Ken,' said Vicky. 'He'd make time for you if you needed to, I'm sure he would. He adores you.'

Tears welled in my eyes. I thought of Max playing in the garden on his climbing frame, hanging upside down by his knees from the top bar, his manic laugh shrill in the air as he swayed back and forth. Beneath him, the lawn was patchy and scuffed from too much running around on, too many games of football. The grass in Ken's and my back garden was thick and lush, threaded with weeds, untouched.

Then I thought of Adam the night before, making love to me with such tenderness that I could have just died with pleasure. His weight on top of me, the way he spread my legs with his knees, looking into my eyes the whole time with his unwavering blue gaze. Adam adored me, too.

'I think it might be too late for Ken and me,' I said, vocalizing for the first time the small thought which had been curled up, dormant, in my brain for some weeks.

The door opened, and our 'nurse' appeared. 'Mrs Sozi, it's time for your next treatment.'

'Don't say things like that, please,' Vicky whispered as I pulled back my duvet and stood up, dazed at what I'd just admitted. 'You and Ken are made for each other. I'm sure you can sort it out . . . Listen, we'll talk more later, OK? Come and find me when you've finished your wrap.'

I smiled at her, taking comfort from our friendship; from the fact that the circle had turned and she was now trying to help me. Even if I wasn't sure that she was right, at least it felt good to begin to unburden myself.

'See you later then,' I said, allowing myself to be guided out of the room, down a corridor, and into a smaller treatment room, where I was greeted by another pert employee. There was something vaguely akin to *One Flew Over the Cuckoo's Nest* about this place, I thought: all the Nurse Ratchetts leading us about, as submissive as sheep in our woolly white gowns, stripping off – for that was what I'd just been told to do – lying down, getting up, resting, stretching . . . I thought I might need a day's rest to recover from the experience. Still, at least Vicky and I were talking.

Talking about the fact that Ken and I were falling apart.

'Pop these on for me,' said my latest tormentor, handing me a very small, very ugly pair of bunchy paper knickers. Her nametag read 'Marie-Rose', and she was far too young to be bossing me around. 'I'm just going to measure you up, so we can see how many inches you've lost at the end of it.'

I hadn't thought I needed to lose inches, but as I stood there facing a full-length mirror, in extremely unattractive disposable underwear, with a twelve-year-old beauty therapist drawing lines on me in black marker pen – biceps, waist, thighs, hips, knees; measuring me with a tape measure at the site of the black lines, then recording her 'findings' in a notepad – I did think, Well, maybe I could do with tightening up. I'd never quite lost the saggy skin on my stomach. When I bent over, it concertinaed into fussy little creases which never used to be there. I felt like a side of beef waiting to be carved.

It was easier to focus on my body than to think about the future. At that moment I wouldn't have cared if my entire body had been as creased up and baggy as a shihtzu puppy, if only someone could have told me what to do; how it would all sort itself out without anyone getting hurt.

Marie-Rose walked over to a bucket in which several rolls of bandages floated in a brown scummy liquid.

'Right, now I'm going to bandage you with these, which have been soaked in a special Dead Sea mud. It's full of minerals and vitamins, which draw out the toxins and any excess fluid, although I'm afraid it doesn't smell particularly nice, does it? We leave it on for an hour. It'll make your skin lovely and soft, and when we measure you up again at the end, you'll find that you have lost quite a few inches, once we add them all up.'

She didn't look old enough to be *able* to add up. However, she managed to mummify me in the warm brown malodorous bandages, tongue in the corner of her mouth, frowning, like a preschooler putting papier mâché on a balloon.

'There!' she said eventually, standing back to admire her efforts. She handed me some flimsy nylon garments and a pair of plastic sandals. 'Pop these on for me, and go and relax. I'll let you know when it's time to get it all rinsed off.'

The nylon garments turned out to be some kind of gross approximation of a shell suit, which I pulled on over the rapidly-cooling bandages. I looked utterly disgusting.

'What, you mean I've got to go out like this?'

She nodded, a hint of a smirk at the corners of her taut young mouth. 'I'll come and find you in an hour or so.'

I had an urge to ask her if she knew that she had the same name as prawn cocktail sauce, that cheap mixture of ketchup and mayonnaise; but I said nothing, and waddled back out to the main chilling-out area. Mud from the bandages was running down my legs and into the plastic sandals, making me squelch as I walked. Beautiful women in pristine bathrobes sniggered at me and wrinkled their noses as I passed them. I felt like some hideous creature fresh out of the swamp; and I smelled like one, too.

I found Vicky reclining glamorously on a lounger, reading the newspaper and sipping camomile tea, her fingers splayed outwards to protect her still-drying vermilion nails, and foam separators wedged between her toes. She roared with laughter when she saw me, muddy and glum, resembling Waynetta Slob's less attractive sister.

'Nice shell suit,' she commented.

'Piss off,' I said grumpily.

'Beautifully accessorized by matching jelly sandals.'

'Not funny.'

'Oh it is, Anna, it really is. Specially since you only had that treatment to annoy me, didn't you?'

I sat wetly down on the lounger next to her, a small brown puddle spreading at my feet. 'Yes, well, that's karma for you, isn't it? I'm certainly regretting it now. I look like nothing on earth, and this mud is absolutely freezing. It had better be worth it. Not to mention the humiliation – I mean, I have one thing to say to you: *paper knickers*.'

'Oh dear,' Vicky said, her shoulders heaving. 'I'm sorry, Anna.' Her expression sobered, and she put down her newspaper. 'And going back to what we were talking about before – I'm sorry you're feeling so bad about Ken, too.'

Part of me had hoped we'd finished that conversation, but another part of me wanted it too. Wanted to confide in someone, even if I couldn't tell the whole truth.

'I don't know what to do about it, Vicky.'

'You have to talk to him!'

'I don't want to.'

'Why?'

'Because . . . because . . . there's no point.'

'Of course there's a point. If you aren't happy, you have to let him know.'

303

'He'd only get defensive and clam up.'

'But surely it's better to get it out in the open.'

I sighed. 'Thing is, Vicky, I don't even know what I'd tell him, if I did talk to him.' I shivered involuntarily. 'This is torture. I'm freezing here!'

Vicky passed me her cup of tea. 'Hold this, it'll warm you up. Mind my nails, though.'

I cradled the delicate china between my palms, allowing its heat to penetrate my cold skin, like that night on the beach when Adam's hands had warmed my chilled body. I wanted to tell Vicky about Adam and Max, but I couldn't.

'When things aren't going well between you and Peter,' I said cautiously, 'do you ever, you know, think about other men?'

Vicky looked as guarded as I did. 'What do you mean? Old boyfriends?'

'Well, whoever. I mean, do you think about fancying other men? About the fact that you can never kiss anybody else as long as you live?'

'Yes. Doesn't everybody? But then you just think about what you do have in a marriage: the security, the kids . . . um, I mean, sorry . . .'

'That's OK.'

'. . . not having to take your clothes off in front of a stranger.'

'I just did that ten minutes ago.' I'd been trying to make a joke, but it didn't sound very funny.

'Yes, but that was different, unless you're planning to turn lesbian and have sex with your beauty therapist.'

I shuddered. 'No thanks.'

'So, have you met someone you fancy or something?'

'No. No, of course not. It was just a general observation. I'm just feeling depressed that I don't fancy Ken any more, but he's all I have in the way of options.'

'I'm sure it'll pass. Sometimes I can't stand Peter touching me. Other times I can't get enough of him.'

I persevered with my so-called hypothetical line of questioning. 'But what if you did meet someone you were really attracted to? Haven't you ever wondered what it would be like to sleep with someone else?'

'Of course. But I wouldn't.'

'Not even if you'd had six cocktails, and Peter was away on a stag weekend, and your mother was looking after the kids?'

'No! Why, would you?'

I looked at her sheepishly. 'I'm worried that I might, yes.'

'Oh, Anna, you wouldn't. I know you too well. You'd be tempted, but at the end of the day you'd never betray Ken.' I winced at her use of my least-favourite cliché. 'I mean, he's incredibly handsome, rich, successful, and he worships you – why would you want anybody else?'

I was both impressed and depressed with her misguided confidence in me. We lapsed into silence, lulled into a soporific state by the trickle of water from various chi-chi little fountains and waterfalls, and the murmured voices of ladies of a certain age out for a day's relaxation, discussing conservatories, feckless husbands, Botox. Vicky fell asleep shortly afterwards, mouth open, fingers still splayed. I felt too cold and uncomfortable to drop off – I was just counting the minutes before Marie-Rose Ratchett came back to hose me off so I could get warm again.

She eventually rescued me, and led me, still squelching, back to her torture chamber. I was shivering uncontrollably by the time she'd unwrapped the last bandage, and past caring that, in order to reach the ones down around my ankles, she practically had her face in my crotch. It was only after the last trace of mud had been showered off that I finally began to warm up again, although I was still required to stand, naked, while Marie-Rose conducted the final measure, declaring with triumph that I'd lost four inches.

'That's better,' I said to Vicky, back in the comfort of my fluffy bathrobe. 'I can feel my extremities again. Can I just tell you – that was really, really unpleasant.'

'Don't you feel great now, though?'

'My skin does feel nice and soft, I suppose. And apparently I lost four inches; although that's much less impressive than it sounds, since it was half an inch off my waist, a quarter of an inch off each arm, and so on. Bit of a con, if you ask me.'

'You'll sleep well tonight, I bet.'

'Did you have a nice snooze while I was gone?'

Vicky stretched, like a cat. 'Mmm, it was divine. Just to be able to drop off without Crystal or Pat jumping on my head after five minutes. That alone was worth the cost of this place.'

'We should do it more often.'

'Couldn't afford to do it that often, Anna. It's not cheap, is it?'

I felt guilty, and thought how we each had topics of conversation that we instantly regretted bringing up in front of the other: for her, it was anything to do with babies; for me, it was mentioning money, even indirectly. I was about to change the subject when she did it for me.

'So, I'm dying to hear all about the job. You haven't even mentioned it! Honestly, don't worry about upsetting me. I'm really happy for you that you're in work again, and I want to know every detail.'

'Oh Vicky, it's no biggie. Just a crappy cable soap. I couldn't even find it in the regional listings when I looked.'

'Don't put yourself down! A job's a job, and some of those cable things pay quite well, don't they?'

'This one doesn't,' I said, wincing. Back to money again.

'So what's it called?'

There was nothing for it but to look her in the eye and brazen it out. Any sign of weakness and she'd have me pinned down like a terrier with a rat, worrying the truth out of me with her razor sharp teeth.

'Merryvale. It's called Merryvale, which is the name of the village. I play the wife of a new family who've moved into the village to run the post office.'

Once I'd started, it got easier. I seemed to have spent much of my adult life relaying the plots of various episodes of soap operas to Vicky – we'd always filled one another in, when one of us had missed *EastEnders* or *Coronation Street*. I just pretended that I was doing the same thing now. Vicky listened avidly, only pausing to say, 'Babies?' in exactly the same hesitant tone that Ken had used when I'd mentioned the twins to him.

'Oh, you're so lucky,' she sighed, after I'd given her a precis of what I remembered from the real *Merryvale* storylines, with a few made-up anecdotes about my imaginary colleagues thrown in for good measure.

'I don't think I'll do it for long,' I said. 'My contract's only for six months, and if the viewers – either of them – don't like the family, we'll get the axe. Can't say it'll bother me all that much. It's such a hassle being away for half the week . . . When do you think you'll try and get back to work?' I asked, desperate to distract her from *Merryvale* before the truth tripped me up.

'God knows. I suppose not until the kids are all at school. Including this one,' she said, patting her stomach disconsolately. 'So, at least five and a half years. Deep joy.'

'You could go back sooner. If you had an au-pair.'

'Anna, we've had this conversation before, and there's no point in having it again,' she snapped.

I supposed it was my own fault, for bringing it up. 'Sorry,' I said humbly. 'Shall we go and have a swim?'

The rest of the afternoon passed in an uneventful haze of pampering and general lying around. We ate beansprout salad for lunch, and I spilled carrot juice down the front of my robe, which left a lurid orange stain. One of the Ratchetts brought me a clean one, lest I sullied the pristine appearance of the clientele (although I feared I'd already done that, by leaking liquid mud out of the legs of my shell suit). Vicky had three more snoozes, and I went swimming twice, and by five o'clock we were both exhausted and feeling very clean.

It had been a good day. I hadn't breathed a word about Adam and Max, but despite all the lies about the job I'd just spewed out to her, I felt that Vicky and I were closer again.

Lying, I'd discovered, was a scarily easy thing to do, once you put your mind to it.

33

Cheating.

It was just a verb, after all, a subjective semantic interpretation of a word which could equally mean taking a peek at an opponent's hand at poker, or copying the answers of GCSE questions from an illegally procured paper prior to the exam. And every time I woke up in Adam's bed to find his warm, solid body wrapped around mine, it somehow became easier to disassociate the word 'cheating' with what I was actually doing. It felt that what I was doing, for the first time in years, was living. Perhaps the sensation was heightened by the necessity for constant vigilance: ensuring that nothing slipped out; that I left no clues. It sharpened my senses and, I thought, gave Adam's and my lovemaking another dimension. But the longer it went on the more I enjoyed it, in a perverse kind of a way. I got a kick out of the secret itself, and out of the small rituals I'd developed to cover my tracks, like never carrying any identification when I was in Gillingsbury, and only using cash for purchases when I was out with Adam so he couldn't see my real name on any credit card. I worried about what this said about me and my scruples, but not enough to change anything. I'd decided I must be far less moral than I'd always given myself credit for – but if no one was getting hurt, it was my own funeral.

Unbelievably, six whole months had passed like that, but Ken still seemed to suspect nothing. (I'd even managed to spend Christmas Day with Max and Adam, by ringing Ken to say that I'd contracted a virulent stomach bug on Christmas Eve, the last day of shooting before the break. He and I were both meant to be having Christmas dinner with Ken's mum, and I knew he wouldn't let her down, once he'd promised to go. So I told him I was hanging over the toilet bowl in my flat in 'Bristol'; he went to his mum's on his own; and then I told Adam I had to be at Auntie Lil's for lunch on Boxing Day – true – and no-one was any the wiser.)

Ken's very lack of interest in my 'other' life acted as a validation to me that I could continue with it. Plus, I thought it quite likely that he had secrets of his own; that it behoved him not to enquire too closely about mine, in case I started pumping him for reciprocal information. I'd had a nasty moment on Valentine's Day, though, when he had asked his secretary to send roses to my digs, and she rang my mobile for my address. I'd had to give her the imaginary one I'd taken the precaution of making up some months previously, with a Bristol postcode, and then called Ken the next day to thank him profusely for the gorgeous flowers. As I'd feared, he sounded puzzled.

'Weird. Alex's just come in and told me that the florist said they couldn't deliver them, that the address didn't exist.'

I had been prepared for this, and laughed nonchalantly, thanking my lucky stars that I happened to be an actress and not a bank clerk. 'They must have got the orders muddled up. I got them all right, I'm sitting here looking at them. They're beautiful, thank you so much, honey.'

It was true that I was indeed sitting there gazing at flowers, only they weren't the flamboyant bouquet Ken would have sent. They were instead a small, rather drooping bunch of primroses Max had picked out of a hedgerow for me a few days before.

Ken hadn't once suggested taking a day off work and coming down to visit me, or expressed any interest in meeting my 'friends' from the soap. He had asked to see a VHS of one of the shows, but hadn't pushed it, and didn't seem bothered at my frequent forehead-slapping assertions that I kept forgetting, or that the production secretary had promised me one that hadn't yet materialized. He was travelling more than ever, and often we went for three weeks at a time without seeing one another (Needless to say, he had been too busy to get time off for the holiday he'd originally proposed we took before Christmas). I began to wonder if he'd even notice if I moved out altogether. After the conversation about the flowers, I had hung up, feeling aggrieved. My life with Ken had become more of a charade than my life with Adam and Max – after all, the only part Ken had played in my Valentine's gift had been to whip out his credit card at the appropriate juncture and hand it to his secretary – it had been she who'd arranged the whole thing. I thought of her tight, lithe body in its cropped tops and miniskirts, and wondered idly if she might have been the reason Ken wasn't enquiring too closely about my own domestic arrangements.

'Morning, darling,' Adam murmured into my ear, on the frosty March sunrise of the day that I decided to leave Ken.

I loved the way Adam woke up with me, limb by limb, as if he wanted to stretch my own body at the same time he stretched his. Not for Adam the immediate dash to the bathroom, the hasty dressing; out the front door before his half of the bed was even cool. Thanks to Max, who obligingly didn't wake up until after eight o'clock, Adam never climbed out of bed for at least half an hour after first opening his eyes. Usually we made love first, languorous but passionate and intense – he'd flip me over and curve his body

311

behind my back, wrapping his arms around me and pushing into me from behind.

After we'd finished and were lying in a post-coital doze, the sound of tuneless singing would announce Max's new morning. Shortly afterwards the door would slide open, catching on the carpet in a wheezy breath, and then the bed would be full of Max, his skinny arms and legs everywhere, giggling and rolling on top of me to squeeze into the coveted middle space.

The first time he came in after we'd made love, he'd made a face. 'Whewee, what's that smell?' We'd blushed as we smelled what he did: the warm, yeasty, loamy scent of semen and sweat, but somehow I liked that he'd said it. It was part and parcel of the intimacy which made up a family.

Most mornings he told us a joke – the same joke. It had been funny the first three or four times, but over the weeks his daily recitation of it became what made us laugh, which encouraged him still further.

'What do you get if you play country music backwards?'

'We don't know, Max, what do you get if you play country music backwards?' we'd recite, like a mantra.

I always started giggling before he answered, and by the time he'd finished, I was in fits. 'Your lover comes back, your dog don't die, your car don't break down and . . .' (Pause for dramatic effect, final punchline delivered in appalling American accent accompanied by wagging finger.) '. . . *it don't rain no more!*'

That morning in March, though, he didn't tell his joke. He hadn't woken up singing, either, but just padded in silently and burrowed into his usual spot.

'How are you, mate?' said Adam, concerned.

'My throat hurts. And my eyes hurt.'

I felt Max's head. 'He's a bit warm.'

Adam laid his own palm against Max's forehead. 'Yes, but he's just woken up.'

'He wasn't feeling great last night, though, was he?' I

persisted. 'And tons of his class have had this little fluey bug thing.'

'I don't want to go to school today,' Max said in a feeble voice, relishing the fuss. 'It's PE, and I really don't want to do PE.'

Adam sighed. 'It would be today. I've got that one-day course over in Marlborough, and I can't get out of it. I've got twenty students coming. Anna, I don't suppose . . . ?'

'Yeah, of course I could. I was only going to learn lines today anyway, but I'm pretty much up to speed for the next episode.' I beamed with delight at the prospect of a whole day alone with Max, fetching him cold drinks and playing board games with him. He clearly wasn't very ill; nothing that administering Calpol wouldn't fix. And whilst I had decided to leave Ken, there was nothing I could have done about it at that precise moment, not while he was away in LA.

'You're a star,' Adam said with relief, kissing my hair. 'All right, mate,' he added to Max, 'you can have a day at home. But no *Tweenies*, mind, and no more than two videos all the way through, OK?'

'Don't worry,' I told him. 'We won't have time to watch TV, will we, Max? We'll be too busy having fun.'

'I love you, Anna,' Max said, cuddling up to me in bed and twining his arms around my neck. I breathed in his sleepy warm skin and felt, as I always did when he told me he loved me, that I knew perfect happiness.

'Max is supposed to be sick, remember,' said Adam with a mock-stern expression.

'Got to keep his spirits up though, haven't we?' I called after him as he retreated into the bathroom. Max gave me another long, warm snuggly hug, and I thanked God for the two of them.

Later, after Adam had driven off issuing injunctions and instructions, Max and I retired to the kitchen table, with the blank canvas of the day laid out in front of us. Max was attired in the Spiderman dressing gown and slippers I'd bought him for Christmas, his hair was sticking up in spikes, and his eyes were huge in his pale face. He started idly doodling on the back of a letter to Adam from the college. He seemed a little bit spaced out and quiet, but I wasn't overly concerned.

'Want some cereal, sweetie?'

He shook his head.

'Grapes?'

Another shake.

'Banana?'

'I'm not hungry, Anna,' he said.

'What are you drawing?' I came and sat next to him, gazing at the wobbly shape which undulated over the page, punctuated every now and again by a thick dot.

'It's a nap.'

'A . . . ?'

'A nap. Of the world. Look, here's the North Pole.' He pointed to a dot at the top of the page. Taking another biro, I carefully wrote 'NORTH POLE' in small neat capitals next to the dot. He rewarded me with a faint beam.

'What's that one?'

'That's our house.' I wrote 'OUR HOUSE', just south of the North Pole. Warming to the task, he pointed again. 'That's Daddy's work. That one's where the people die. That one's where the horseys live. And that' – jabbing his pen at the southernmost point of the map – 'that's really, really, really, actually Heaven.' I duly transcribed 'REALLY REALLY REALLY ACTUALLY HEAVEN' next to it. My favourite spot was in the middle of the country, and it was a place called 'PICNIC? IF SUNNY'. It was near the train station, bordering 'AN ORCHARD WHERE APPLES ARE MADE', and backing on to 'WHERE 3 GOOD LITTLE PIGGIES LIVE'.

'This is a fantastic map!' I said ten minutes later, utterly lost in our task. 'Daddy will love it. What's this dot?'

'The South-East Pole,' Max said, but his voice had dropped to a whisper, and when I looked at him, my heart jumped with fear. Two bright red spots, like places on his imaginary 'nap', had sprung from nowhere into his white cheeks, and his eyes did not seem to be focusing. He pushed the map away. 'I don't feel very well,' he said, and leaned into me.

I picked him up and carried him through to the sitting room, laying him on the sofa. 'Stay there, darling,' I said. 'I'll get your duvet, and the thermometer. Do you want a drink of water?'

He didn't seem to hear me, just muttered, 'We didn't put Mummy's house on the nap.'

I ran up the stairs, feathery wings of panic beginning to sprout at my heels, my breath coming in fast gulps. Once on the landing, I had to lean against the wall to try and compose myself. 'Keep calm, keep calm, keep calm,' I chanted. 'It's just a bug, it's just a bug. He'll be fine. Calpol. Doctor? Maybe. Calpol first.'

I grabbed his duvet from his bed and charged into the bathroom where I located the Calpol and the digital thermometer. As an afterthought I ran a face-cloth under the cold tap, hastily squeezed it out, and cantered back downstairs with my arms full.

Max was moaning slightly, his hands moving in front of his face, clutching at fistfuls of air as if he were trying to bat away some invisible irritant. His pupils were enormous, and his skin had turned a livid pink. Meningitis, I thought, my throat almost completely closing with fright. What if he's got meningitis, or that this means his leukaemia's come back? He might die, oh God, no, please no . . .

I peeled the dressing gown away from his sweating body, and lifted up his pyjama top, looking for a rash. There was none, just his skin, pale and swampy and humid, but unblemished. With shaking hands, I managed to insert the thermometer into his ear and click the green button to read his temperature. One hundred and three. It sounded bad, high, but was it dangerous? I had no idea.

I grabbed my mobile from my bag and rang Vicky. No answer. When it switched onto voicemail, I ran into the kitchen and dialled Max's doctor's number off the cork pinboard on the wall. It was busy. I tried again. Still busy. I dialled Lil's number instead.

'Hello?'

'Auntie Lil, please help me, it's an emergency, I don't know what to do.'

As I said the words, I recognized them as the ones she'd used on me that time when she'd seen me running past her window, to lure me back into her life. I remembered how scared I'd been then, but it seemed like a lifetime ago. And this was a whole different league of fear.

'Anna? What's the matter, darling?'

'It's – I'm – I'm looking after a little boy. Max. His temperature just suddenly shot up to a hundred and three. The doctor's number's engaged. Should I dial nine nine nine? I don't know what to do!'

I heard Lil inhale. Exhale. That brief pause of hers both infuriated and comforted me. 'Stay calm, Anna. You have to stay calm. I'm sure he'll be OK. How old is he?'

'Five.'

'Their temperatures often go up and down at that age. You have to cool him.'

I remembered the wet facecloth which I'd left lying on top of the duvet, which were both now dumped on the sitting-room floor. 'I've got a facecloth,' I gasped, dashing in and peeling it off the quilt, where it had left an accusatory dark wet stain. Berating myself for not putting it on him earlier, I spread it across his forehead. He moaned again, still clawing the air.

'What's he wearing?'

'Pyjamas. Should I take them off? He's going all floppy!'

'Sponge him down. Sponge his head and his chest.'

I pressed the cloth against Max's narrow ribcage. Even after just seconds in contact with his skin, the chill had been removed from the cloth. He made a strange sound in his throat, half rolled over, retched, and vomited across me, a thin spray of yellowish liquid.

'He's being sick!' The panic in my voice was rising steeply. I heard it – shrill, unfamiliar.

'Anna! Listen to me!' Lil's own voice was sharp now. 'It's *vital* that you keep calm. Do as I say. Get a towel, clean him up as best you can, then take his temperature again. It's probably just a bug. He'll be fine.'

Max looked blearily up at me, and the trust in his eyes broke my heart. 'That really wasn't very healthy, was it?' he mumbled briefly, before sinking back down into the stained sofa cushions, turning his head away from me as if to indicate that it was his last word on the subject. He reminded me agonizingly of Adam.

'No, darling, it wasn't. But don't worry, we'll soon have you feeling better,' I said, stroking back the wet hair from his forehead. In almost as much of a daze as Max, I found a tea-towel in the kitchen, brought it back into the living room and wiped up the worst of the sick, cleaning Max's face and body first. Then I took his temperature again.

'Nearly a hundred and four,' I whispered into the phone, unable to believe this could really be happening. Not again, Lord, please, I begged. Not my Max.

'Very well. Try the doctor once more, and if you can't get through, then I think you ought to call an ambulance. Bearing in mind his medical history . . . just to be on the safe side. It's him, isn't it? The little boy you gave the bone-marrow transplant to?'

I was in no fit state to laugh at her perspicacity, but I managed a noise which was half-sob, half-sigh. She'd known all along. 'Yes.'

'Go on then. Ring me back later and let me know what's happening. Promise?'

'Yes. Bye, Lil.'

I managed to get through to the surgery on my next try. Getting the words out in the right order to the receptionist was somewhat more problematic, but I just

317

about succeeded. She put me on hold for what seemed like several hours, then returned with a brisk answer: 'Dr Lark will come right round. She knows Max.'

By the time the doctor rang the doorbell, I was nearly hysterical, weak-kneed with fear and practically gasping with the effort of not letting Max see my panic. I was convinced he was going to die, and all I could think was: How am I going to tell Adam?

'Is he any better?' the doctor asked. She was younger than I'd expected, about my own age, with a smart suit and sharp haircut which made her look more like a stockbroker than a doctor.

I shook my head, unable to speak at all. I pointed in the direction of the sofa.

'Hello, Max,' she said in a voice that managed to be both soothing and businesslike. 'It's me, Dr Lark. Feeling poorly, are we? What a shame . . . Let's have a little look at you now, shall we?'

She propped him up and examined him, limp as a rag doll in her arms, seeming not to notice the stench of vomit-wet duvet. The sight of the sweaty imprint of Max's feverish body in the sofa cushions made me cry harder, and I had to turn away, although Max was too out of it to register. He was crying too, weak mews of pain and confusion that made me want to crumple, boneless with grief.

'Spesh,' he whispered. 'I want Spesh.' I turned back, and he looked at me then, his eyes moving around me, as if he was watching me dance even though I stood still.

'I'll get him for you, darling.' I ran upstairs, grabbed the toy tiger from the floor at the side of Max's bed, and thundered back down, handing him over to Max. His fingers closed briefly around Spesh's front paw, but then he let him drop out of his grasp, forgotten again.

It seemed as if only two minutes earlier we'd been lying in bed looking forward to our day together, and now life had turned on the spin of a coin and come crashing down on me all over again, just when I thought I was happy; when I thought that even if things would be messy with Ken, I was where I wanted to be, and everything would be OK.

'If you haven't yet called his father, then I think you should,' said Dr Lark, replacing the thermometer in her bag. 'He's not a well little boy.'

My head was whirling with disbelief and nausea and terror, and I felt so much as I had after Holly died that I kept looking down at my stomach, expecting to see it still distended and flabby in maternity trousers, recently emptied and redundant like an accusation of failure. Please God, I prayed, not again.

34

Nine hours later, the crisis – at least for Max – was over. He was sleeping peacefully upstairs in his bed, in clean pyjamas, under a fresh duvet cover, with Spesh tucked up next to him. He was still pale, coughed occasionally, but his temperature was normal and he hadn't been sick since Adam got home shortly after lunch.

'It's just a virus,' Dr Lark had confirmed, after having scared the living daylights out of me by telling me to ring Adam. 'Nothing more sinister. He needs rest, plenty of liquids, and Calpol, and he'll be right as rain in a couple of days.'

I wasn't sure that the same could be said for me, though. I was an emotional wreck, and felt as if those nine hours had aged me at least nine years. I'd phoned Adam, pleading with the secretary at the place he was teaching that it was an emergency, and to go and interrupt him in his classroom. She'd hauled him out to talk to me; and the terror in my voice had caused the poor man to abandon his class then and there, leaving a lot of old ladies struggling alone with their gouache and watercolour washes, grumbling about course refunds and let-downs. He had got home within the hour – although before then I was able to ring him on his mobile and tell him that Max was going to be fine, that it was nothing to worry about after all.

Nothing . . . well, that didn't quite describe what I went through that day. I'd thought Max was dying. I'd thought that, after everything they'd already endured, Adam was going to arrive too late, and I'd have to tell him that Max was gone and it had all been my fault. Daddy, Holly, and then Max – I couldn't have handled it. I pictured myself handing Spesh over to Adam in a sorrowful gesture; pictured Adam's kindly face crumpling and him turning away from me. It had all been so real in my head that I had almost begun imagining Max's funeral, and what type of tranquillizer I'd need to be on in order to endure it.

Adam was talking to me. When I looked at him, I could see his mouth moving and that he was making eye contact with me, but I didn't seem able to work out what he was saying.

'What?'

He crossed the room and put his arms around me. 'Oh baby, you've really been through it today, haven't you?'

My last reserves of strength deserted me. I'd just about managed to hold it together since Adam got home, for both their sakes, but Adam's solicitous cuddle was my breaking point. My knees buckled and I collapsed against him.

'Adam . . . I thought he was going to die.'

'Ssh, baby, it's OK. He's fine. He's fine. You did the right thing. I'd have done the same. Don't worry.'

Even through my gut-twisting sobs, I realized that Adam thought I was apologizing for overreacting, for having Adam hauled out of his class and making him panic like that, when all Max had needed was Calpol and a snooze.

'No, you don't understand. I thought he was dying!'

'I know, I know. You gave me a nasty moment. But he's fine.'

Suddenly I was infuriated. I wanted to shake Adam. He was stroking my head, but I jerked away, causing him to get strands of my hair caught between his fingers, snaring us together in a cat's cradle of complicated connections and tangled knots.

'That's not the point! That's not why I'm upset!' Why are you always so bloody *calm*? I thought, beginning to feel the plot slip away from me. I wanted to tell him then, tell him everything, tell him how stupid he was that he had been going out with me for six months and hadn't realized that he'd never seen my credit cards or my driving licence; that, like Ken, he'd never gone on-line and discovered that I wasn't mentioned on any soap opera website, because some other actress, and not me, was playing the part of Trina in *Merryvale*.

Suddenly I stopped feeling touched that men were so trusting, that they didn't question anything when they were in love. Instead I experienced a wave of rage that they could be so stupid, so gullible – or, in Ken's case, care so little about me and my life that they didn't even *try* and express an interest. A woman would never have stood for such a huge part of their partner's life to be such an unknown quantity. In the (admittedly unlikely) event that either Adam or Ken had ever claimed to have a job in a soap opera, I'd have badgered them for visits to the set, invited cast members round for dinner, scanned the cable listings in the TV guides for mentions of it. I'd have wanted to know every twist of plot and cliffhanger, every costume change and edit.

How could neither of them have noticed I was living a lie? That it was Max who'd lured me here? Regardless of my strength of feeling for Adam now, I wouldn't have had an affair were it not for Max.

'Anna? What is it, darling? Please calm down.'

But I was in full-on meltdown. I couldn't speak for hiccuping and snorting – I never had been a ladylike crier. The artifice my life had become came hammering home to me, like a tide swirling over a painstakingly constructed sandcastle, crumbling it back into smooth oblivion from the moat upwards.

'It's Max,' I sobbed, hunched on the sofa with my face in my hands. 'He's the reason I'm here.'

'What do you mean?'

I was overcome with self-loathing. How pathetic and selfish I was, that instead of trying to sort my problems out with Ken, I'd merely run away and latched on to Max and Adam. Max wasn't my child. Yes, I'd helped save his life, but only in the happenstance collision of compatible blood-groups and bone-marrow.

Adam crouched down beside me, in full sympathetic social-worker mode. I heard his knees crack in chunky stereo, sickeningly loudly. 'Please, talk to me.'

'My name isn't Anna Valentine,' I mumbled, my face in the arm of a sofa, my body curled up in a fetal question mark, the disgraced child. 'It's Anna Sozi. I'm the woman who gave the bone-marrow donation to Max.'

The room was silent except for the sound, drifting through from the kitchen, of Max's baseball cap knocking around inside the tumble-drier.

'What do you mean?' Adam asked eventually. 'Why didn't you . . . ?' His voice trailed away to nothing. 'I'll get us some brandy,' he said, treading gingerly into the kitchen as if my revelation were live ammunition, landmines peppering the carpet. But before he could return, the doorbell rang.

'Ignore it,' he called through, somewhat needlessly, since I had absolutely no intention of opening the front door in my current state. But whoever it was rang again. 'Oh, get lost,' I heard him mutter. There was a hard edge to his voice that I didn't like. *Why* had I told him like that? Even amid my hysteria, the worm of uncertainty in the pit of my stomach told me that it had been the wrong way to do it: the wrong way, and the wrong time.

There was a pause. Adam got two tumblers out of the cupboard, and I managed to stop crying. My nose was stuffed up, my temples were pounding, and my eyelids felt like two inflatable bath pillows. I desperately wanted the brandy, could feel its fire in my throat already, warming me and calming me down.

'I think they've—' It rang again, cutting Adam off. 'Oh hell, I'll have to get it. Whoever it is will wake Max up if they carry on like that.' He wouldn't look me in the eye.

I heard his body brush up against the rack of coats in the narrow hallway. Heard the door squeak open. Then silence. At first I thought the visitor must have given up and walked off, and that Adam was peering after them trying to decide whether to call out. But then a woman's voice said, 'Mum called me straight after you rang her . . . How is he? . . . Aren't you going to invite me in?'

My heart sank. Not bloody Pamela. Why on earth had Adam rung her mother? I presumed he'd tried to get hold of Pamela herself, and then called her mother when he couldn't find her. I hadn't realized he felt so close to her, and it really annoyed me. Now she'd come beetling round, and we were probably stuck with her for the evening. I leaped up from the sofa – there was no way I was prepared to let her see me like that – and scurried upstairs to the bathroom, trusting Adam to stall her until I was in some way presentable.

I splashed cold water on my face, powdered my nose, and combed my hair, noticing the first silvery threads streaking through it. My eyes were bloodshot and droopy-looking, and my skin blotchy. I pulled at the bag under my left eye, and it took its time returning, settling into small puffy creases which never used to be there.

I'm getting old, I thought, in heavy despair. I may never have a baby of my own. It'll get harder and harder every month, and in a few years' time it'll be too late. I imagined my few remaining eggs rolling one at a time dispiritedly along my fallopian tube, like badly hefted bowling balls which stood no chance of knocking down any pins.

When I came out of the bathroom, I tiptoed into

Max's room. He slept more peacefully now, far under, lost in his dreams. I stroked his hair and pulled his quilt so it covered him more evenly. He stirred when I kissed his warm cheek, and made a soft guttural groaning sound, almost a creak. I remembered that semi-conscious sensation from my own childhood, the gentle kiss in the night which brought me swimming up to the surface, just long enough to feel the emotion of the parent kissing me, before rolling over back into the deep, safe in the knowledge that I was loved.

I had to remind myself that I wasn't Max's parent, though; and as I half closed the door so that Pamela's penetrating voice wouldn't wake him, I was fighting hard against a bleak, depressed feeling, and the dread that I had messed everything up.

I'd been so sure that it had been Pamela at the door that when I came downstairs and didn't recognize her, I thought it was because she'd been on a diet and dyed her hair. Then I noticed that she was at least six inches taller than the last time I'd seen her. And surely Pamela would never have worn jeans? Then I looked at her face and saw with shock that it wasn't Pamela at all. Her voice had sounded similar, but this woman was younger and more attractive. She had round, soft features, like a cloud with a face. She reminded me of someone, but I couldn't think who.

'Anna,' said Adam, holding out his hand to me – but still not looking into my face. I went across and stood next to him, shoulder to shoulder, in an unconscious show of possessiveness.

'This is Marilyn, my . . . um – Max's mother. Marilyn, this is my girlfriend Anna.'

We both gawped at one another. She seemed as nonplussed to see me as I was her, but then she raised her chin and lowered her eyelids, giving me a defensive sort of nod.

'Hello,' she said, her cloud-face freezing into icicles instead, losing its soft edges.

I nodded back at her, aware of the heat which flooded my own face and swept down through my body. I felt at such a disadvantage, tear-stained and ravaged; but more than that, I felt guilty, found out, exposed.

'You've decorated,' she said, although she wasn't examining the walls. She was staring at the picture of Max and herself on the bookshelf.

'Yes. We did it, what, three months ago?' Adam glanced at me for confirmation and I felt nothing but shame.

'It's quite nice,' she pronounced. Then she turned to me. 'Adam's explained that Max just had a virus,' she said, her voice loaded with the censure that I felt myself.

I still couldn't speak. Adam hugged me, and I was grateful for his kindness. 'Poor Anna's had a day of it. He really wasn't well, and you know how frightening that is to see.' In one fell swoop, he'd bracketed himself and her – the experienced Max-carers – against me, the overdramatic leg-end who got everyone in a flat spin just for a bit of fever.

Adam must have stage-managed it, although I wasn't aware how and when; but presently the three of us were sitting down drinking the long-awaited brandies. I hadn't even noticed him go into the kitchen, but my tumbler had two ice-cubes in it which cracked like Adam's knees and chilled my hand through the glass.

I wondered if Marilyn had been speaking to me whilst Adam had been getting the drinks, and decided that she couldn't have done. She started talking, though, after Adam put the drink in her hand. She was talking to him as though I wasn't even in the room. I waited, desperately hoping for a kind word, or the reassuring pressure of Adam's palm pressing on my knee, but none came. I could have assumed myself to be invisible.

I forced myself, through the post-weeping fug and an ever-encroaching headache, to dip in and out of what she was saying. Her voice was simultaneously defensive and vulnerable, and she kept staring at me meaningfully, in a 'must we really have this conversation with *her* here?' sort of way.

'. . . know it's been months . . . Sorry I didn't write, I honestly thought it would be better for Max to hear nothing than to get letters and calls from me . . . out of sight, out of mind . . . needed to clear my head . . .'

I know that feeling, I thought, blinking hard to try and sharpen up my vision, which was more blurry than it ought to have been. Adam sat motionless beside me, gazing intently at his wife. I had never felt further away from him.

She's not even his ex-wife, I thought. He's as married as I am. Strange how I'd never really considered that before. I leaned against the back of the sofa and fought a growing urge to close my eyes. I felt as if someone had dropped an anvil on my skull.

Marilyn stood up and walked over to the bookcase, picking up the photo of her and Max. She left a fug of perfume behind her; it was something floral and cloying that masked the faint smell of sick in the room, but which made my head hurt even more.

'I can't wait to see him,' she said. 'My baby. I've missed him so much.'

I vaguely noticed that although her legs were long, she had a big bottom, droopy in the unflattering jeans. I tried to imagine her and Adam in bed, but – thankfully – couldn't. Instead, I saw them together at Max's birth: her, puce and panting; him holding her legs and crying 'I can see the head!'; and them beaming at one another when Max emerged, limbs like red tentacles, his mouth a little red 'o' of surprise. They were his parents.

'Mummy?' Suddenly Max was there, at the top of the stairs, with exactly the same expression on his face as I'd just imagined on him at birth: bleary amazement and wonder and delight. 'Mummy! You came back! My *mummy*!'

Marilyn hurtled towards the stairs, Max started sliding unsteadily down, and they met in the middle in a giant confused cuddle, arms and legs everywhere, Marilyn sobbing loudly and Max half laughing, half crying as he patted and hugged, hugged and patted his mother. When I turned to look at Adam, I saw that there were tears on his cheeks.

'Adam,' I whispered, feeling that it would be an imposition to wipe away the tears, that it wasn't my job any more. 'I think I should go home.'

He dashed them away himself. 'OK, Anna.'

'No, really,' I went on, as if he'd tried to stop me instead of agreeing. 'You and Marilyn have things to talk about. And to be honest, I'm not feeling too hot. I've got a terrible headache. Will you call me a cab?'

'Of course.' He got up, too quickly, picked up the telephone and speed-dialled the cab company, although his eyes never left the figures of his wife and child hugging on the stairs.

'. . . yes, to Wealton. As soon as possible please,' he said on the phone, and I felt wretched. Marilyn was now sitting on the middle stair with Max on her lap, stroking his hair and holding him encircled in her arms. He glanced over at me through the banisters, but didn't return my smile. He looked utterly blissed out, as if my kiss in his dreams had caused him to wake into this strange new world where he suddenly had his heart's desire.

'It'll only be a couple of minutes,' said Adam.

'Right,' I replied stiffly.

Adam was the only one who said goodbye to me when I left, but his farewell peck was perfunctory. 'We'll talk about . . . we'll talk another time,' he said with finality. The front door closed behind me, and I was alone on the pavement.

35

The cab ride back to Wealton was a blur of dark trees and too-bright street lights hurting my eyes, and the voice of the cabbie swelling in and out of my consciousness. He was trying in vain to engage me in conversation, and it felt as if someone was sticking a pin in my leg to get a reaction. He appeared to be talking about his missing forefinger, in which he showed inordinate pride: 'Oi expect you're wonderin' wha' 'appened,' he'd said, in a broad Wiltshire accent. 'Larst 'Arvest, it was. Helping muy brother bring in the wheat. Larst 'Arvest.' For one confused moment I'd thought his brother was a Norwegian named Lars Tarvest, but I didn't even bother to respond, and when the driver looked in his rear-view mirror and saw the tears dripping silently down my face, he finally desisted.

I wondered where Marilyn was going to sleep that night. Adam didn't have a spare room. He'd probably offer his – our – bed to her, and sleep on the sofa. Or maybe she'd bunk in with Max, I thought, jealousy penetrating my befogged brain. The mental picture of Max in his low narrow bed curled around her like a question mark, drawing his thin limbs along her generous outlines was, oddly, more painful than the picture of her and Adam back in the marital bed –

which was the other possible scenario.

Then I wondered if Adam had told her who I was yet, and if so, *how* he'd told her: in amazement and gratitude, or with disgust and hurt at my subterfuge and ulterior motives? Thankfully I felt too unwell really to dwell on it. Especially since there was so much more he didn't even yet know.

When I opened the front door of my flat, the smell of rented accommodation filled my nostrils. I'd been living there for six months, and yet it still wasn't my home. At first I'd felt free; now I felt as if I had no home at all. I kicked off my shoes and rolled into bed, fully clothed, aching from head to foot. I was shivering, and my head was pounding. I wanted to get up to find some painkillers, but it had got so bad that I knew if I moved, I would throw up. I lay still for some time, thinking about Marilyn and Adam, about Vicky and Peter, and about my Ken – if he could be described as mine any more. Relationships were fragile, tenuous webs, spun with filigree threads of trust to keep them aloft, so thin that a puff of wind could break them – and yet we blundered through them with a reckless lack of care, and then seemed surprised when we destroyed them.

Ken had trusted me. That was why he hadn't been asking questions about my other life, my job – because it had never occurred to him that I was lying. My earlier scorn of him and Adam and their blind, misguided faith in me dissipated, to be replaced by a deep, throbbing shame. If I'd only resisted Adam when we'd first hugged. A hug was nothing; but now look at us. Practically living together. It had just seemed so easy at the time, though, so right: to allow him to hold me in his arms, to feel the strength of his shoulders and the strangeness of his scent, the welcome touch of unfamiliar hands gently reaching under my cardigan and stroking my skin. In one second, it had been as if I hadn't had any other ties at all. The entire cobweb of my life with Ken had been swept away, no longer even existing for me at that moment in time. Instant gratification, I supposed. Or was it something deeper; the first real knowledge of love? How would I ever know which?

I must have lain in bed, shivering, for a couple of hours, and then I was suddenly boiling, my clothes sticking to my body. I couldn't stop thinking about Ken. I wanted him. Either that, or I wanted not to hurt him. I didn't want him sexually, but for the old comforting routines – I wanted him to bring me a bowl to throw up in (for I could tell that was on the cards), to stroke my hair and offer me cold glasses of water to sip from, as he had after my miscarriages. But he wasn't there, and I was on my own.

Eventually I fell asleep, still fully clothed, almost grateful that I felt too ill to dwell on how miserable I was.

I was woken the next day, not by the usual alarm call of dog bark, duck squawk and sharp squares of sunlight, but by my phone. As I reached for it, woozy and still feeling sick, I realized that I couldn't decide whose voice I most wanted to hear on the end of the line, Ken's or Adam's. Half and half. If either of them had ever decided to look in the Call History file of my phone, the game would have been up: under both Incoming and Outgoing calls the roll read KEN, ADAM, KEN, ADAM, ADAM, KEN, documented evidence to them both of the Other Man.

But it was neither of them. 'Anna, darling, it's Auntie Lil.'

Her voice sounded to me like the lavender wool of her suit and the yeasty scent of her towel cupboard. 'I'm just telephoning to see how the little boy is. You were going to ring me and let me know . . .'

I burst into weak, grateful tears, because there was someone who cared about me there, to listen. To make it better. To help me sort out the mess.

'Anna? What's happened?'

'No. No, sorry, Lil, he's fine – Max is fine. The doctor came and said it was just a nasty bug.'

'Then what's the matter?'

'Oh Lil,' I wailed. 'Everything is such a disaster.'

'Talk to me, my darling. Tell me all about it.'

'I can't tell you over the phone,' I said feebly. 'I've caught the same virus Max had, I think. I'm in bed, and I feel awful. But I really want to see you.'

'Then come and see me. As soon as you feel well enough. Promise me you will, Anna.'

'I promise,' I said, feeling marginally better. 'I'll come home as soon as I'm fit to drive.'

It was a few more days, however, before I felt well enough to get back to see Lil, and by then everything had changed. I had a different story to tell her.

My flu symptoms subsided, but I couldn't seem to shake the gastric part of the bug that Max had – I vomited so often that my voice was reduced to a painful raw croak, and I had a constant gnawing nausea in my gut. I began to wonder if it might not just be a belated sense of guilt kicking in.

Ken had just flown off on a long trip to Australasia and the Far East, and rang me often on my mobile, full of concern, and as my mouth spewed out lies in the same way it spewed out solids – 'Two days off filming'/ 'good chance to learn lines'/'director sent flowers' – I thought how it served me right. I imagined Ken in the shadow of the Sydney Opera House, under blue Antipodean skies, making criminally expensive mobile-to-mobile phone calls (because I'd told him I had no phone in my flat), to be fed a load more lies . . . it was horrible. I felt horrible.

Then came the call I'd been waiting for; the one I'd been too cowardly to make myself – Adam, ringing to say that we needed to talk. It was *Adam* I wanted, I realized, as soon as he spoke my name. Not Ken, after all. My feelings for Ken were complicated, marred by guilt, duty, obligation, habit. Adam was the one I loved.

'I know we do,' I said, feeling nauseous again. 'When?'

We arranged to meet the following day, down by the canal.

'So,' said Adam politely, staring straight ahead of him. 'Let me get this straight. You engineered a meeting with me, giving a false name, because you felt too responsible for Max to let us know that you were really the woman who gave him the bone-marrow donation. Because in case he died, you'd blame yourself.'

Put like that, it sounded utterly selfish and preposterous.

'Well . . . yes. Kind of. Although it's not as simple as that. And "Valentine" is my stage name,' I said in despair, thinking of Holly's tiny white coffin, and then of the clammy vol-au-vents after Dad's funeral.

We were walking slowly along a canalside path, overhung with droopy willow branches and flanked by huge bushy stinging nettles. I pictured Max with us, swiping at them with a big stick, his thin bare shins at risk from their bite. If Adam and I had any chance at all of continuing our relationship – and I didn't hold out much hope, not with Marilyn back on the scene – I knew I'd have to come clean and tell him about Ken too. And the fake job. There could be no more secrets.

'Could you slow down a little bit? I'm still not feeling great . . .' I tried not to sound aggressive, but wasn't sure if I'd been entirely successful. I felt awful, actually, as if the blood in my legs had been drained out and replaced with sawdust. A duck landed on the water's surface, splayed feet braking, listing like a light aircraft in a stiff breeze. I wanted the comfort of holding Adam's hands, but they were out of my reach, shoved deep into his jeans' pockets.

He stopped and faced me. Part of me really hoped he'd say, 'And what other secrets have you been hiding from me?' so that I could take a deep breath and begin

333

to list them all. Alphabetically or chronologically, I hadn't yet decided. There were so many.

'You know I love you, Anna,' he said, and for a second I wondered if we had more than a chance, if I'd got it wrong and he was going to propose instead.

I nodded. I had always nodded when he told me he loved me. Although I loved him too, I'd somehow never been able to bring myself to say those three words back to him – it was just one betrayal too far. Once or twice I'd muttered, 'You too,' but, despite his hurt blue eyes, I'd never volunteered the information.

'These last six months have been incredible for me,' he continued, and again I wondered. 'You're so beautiful. We're so compatible in so many ways – sexually, spiritually, practically. We fit together, don't you think? And we've had some fantastic times.'

Wedding bells or the death knell of our relationship, I couldn't let him continue. I had to tell him.

'Stop,' I said. 'It's not even the whole story, that I got to know you under false pretences. There's more. Please listen.'

We sat down on a bench, not touching or looking at each other. My head was spinning but I forced myself to talk calmly.

'Before I tell you the rest,' I said, reaching out to touch his knee, 'I want you to know that I'm only telling you because I want us to continue, not to split up. I know that you have obligations to Marilyn, but it didn't work with her before and if it doesn't again, I'll . . .'

But what could I say: 'I'll be waiting?' Waiting at home with Ken? Oh shit, I was going to have to come clean with Ken too. I was going to end up a lonely old woman, and it served me right.

Adam squeezed my fingers briefly, then withdrew his hand.

'Do you remember the last time we walked down this towpath?' I asked, half smiling, half wincing, putting off the evil moment to indulge in an extremely nice memory. It had been shortly after the beach episode, and I'd discovered that Adam had a bit of a thing about alfresco sex: one pitch-black night, not far from where we were now sitting, he'd led me along the path until we came to a convenient willow tree. He'd pushed me up against its rough bark, lifted my skirt around my waist and, pulling down my knickers, slid first his fingers, then his tongue inside and around me, kneeling before me with his hands on my buttocks and his face pressed against me. I remembered the feel of his tongue, hot against my skin in the cool night air, and the thrilled dread of being caught out by the rapidly approaching flicker of a bike's headlamp along the dark path, or the footsteps of two other lovers with the same idea.

'How could I forget? said Adam. But he still wasn't smiling. 'So, tell me the rest, then.'

It was the hardest thing I've ever had to do, in my whole life.

'Well . . .' I stopped. 'I can't.' I looked at him, beseechingly.

'That bad?'

I nodded.

He sighed, and bile rose in my throat. 'Excuse me,' I said, rushing round to the back of the bench and vomiting into the stinging nettles.

Adam followed me round and rubbed my back, and I was grateful for his touch. I accepted the scrunched-up tissue he offered me, wiped my mouth, and found a bendy stick of chewing gum in the pocket of my denim jacket which went some way towards taking the taste away.

'This bloody bug,' I said. 'I know just how Max felt.'

'Please tell me,' said Adam. 'I can't stand it. Just tell me.'

I began again. 'Well. What I said was true, about getting your letter and being desperate to meet Max, but too scared to let you know who I was.' I grasped his arm. 'I never set out to use you, or hurt you, Adam, I promise I didn't. I certainly didn't intend to seduce you or anything . . . I just fell for you. And yes, I admit that Max was a huge incentive to develop the relationship, but only because I loved him so much too. The thing is . . . I so wanted to be part of a family. And I liked you both so much that I couldn't bear to give you up. When I should have given you up.'

At last Adam looked at me. Two cyclists, in full day-glo skintight cycling gear, swept obliviously past us, the stinging nettles swishing in their wake.

'Why should you have given me up?'

I fiddled with my wedding ring, twisting it round and round, watching with something approaching detachment as my tears dropped onto it. Then I saw the horrible realization dawn on Adam.

'*Please* don't tell me you're still married.'

'I'm so sorry,' I whispered through gritted teeth.

He leaned back on the bench. 'Let me guess. When I thought you were working, you were with your husband.'

My shamed silence confirmed it.

Adam rubbed his beard. 'So, how did you find the time to do any work, in between your husband and your lover?'

'There was no work,' I said in a very small voice. 'The job doesn't exist.'

Adam's lip trembled and I thought he was going to cry. I did this, I thought. I've caused him this much pain, after everything else he's already been through with Max and Marilyn. The thought of having to go and confess to Ken too made me want to die. I had to grip the sides of the bench to prevent myself standing up and walking off the edge of the path into the dark slow water of the canal, making sure I stayed under until it was too late and I didn't have to feel like this any longer.

'I love you,' I said for the first time ever. 'I really, really love you, Adam. It's over between me and my husband. It's been over for months. I was just too cowardly to tell him. It's you that I want. Please believe me. I wouldn't be telling you all this if I didn't want to be with you properly. Honestly. I'll go home tonight and tell him, I promise, if only you say we've got a chance . . .'

'Don't bother,' he replied in a hard, unfamiliar voice. 'Save yourself a confession – spare the poor guy. I wouldn't wish this on my worst enemy – I'm sure your *husband*, whoever he is, doesn't deserve it either.'

He jumped up, and grabbed hold of a tree branch, trying to snap it off, but the pliant willow was resilient, merely bending against the onslaught. In the end he tore the leaves off instead, throwing them on the path. It would have been comic, were it not for the expression on his face.

'I can't quite believe how spectacularly you've blown it, Anna,' he said, almost conversationally.

'Nor can I,' I sobbed. 'I'd give anything not to have done.'

A big brown and white dog galloped along the path, his owner, an elderly man, puffing along behind him. The man half stopped, as if to engage us in some pleasantries, but hastily decided against it.

'Please, Adam . . .' I said.

'Marilyn wants us to try and make a go of it,' he said. 'So perhaps this is all just as well. I didn't want to break up with you but, now I see that you weren't ever mine in the first place, I've got no reason not to.'

'You won't be happy with her,' I ventured, still crying, and he rounded on me. It was the first time he'd ever raised his voice to me.

'How *dare* you say that! After what you've just told me? Who are you to tell me what makes me happy – and who am I to know?' His face crumpled. 'I thought I'd found the person to make me happy. What a total, gullible idiot I am. All you are is a liar and a cheat, and I wish you didn't exist. No, I don't, because of Max. I just wish I'd never met you.'

He was right; I should never have said that about

Marilyn. But it hurt, so much, to hear him say he wished he'd never met me.

'It all makes sense now,' he said softly, ripping up one of the willow leaves in his fingers. 'You were so loving, and brilliant with Max, and I think we had real passion for each other – but whenever I tried to talk about the future, you just switched off, or changed the subject . . . At first I thought you were just cautious, afraid of being hurt; but then I did start to think that this relationship was more one-sided than I'd originally believed. I started to think that you didn't love me.'

But I do, I wanted to say. I wanted to scare the ducks off the river by shouting it out; I wanted to rattle the windows of Max's classroom with it. I wanted Max to know that his dad had changed my life, made me happy, made me love myself, helped me look to the future again. But it was too late, and Adam wouldn't have believed me any more. I couldn't blame him.

Instead I looked away, to a row of tall but unidentifiable trees wavering on the horizon. It was depressing how nobody except the older generation seemed to be able to identify trees or birds any more, other than the most obvious ones, I thought. Max and Crystal knew who Kylie Minogue and Britney Spears were, but wouldn't have had a clue about the difference between an oak and a sycamore, or between a wren and a sparrow . . . *Lil* could have recognized a mistle-thrush in an elm tree at a hundred paces.

It was easier to think about Lil and trees, than to think about Adam holding Marilyn instead of me.

'I'm sorry,' I said, wiping the tears off my face with the palms of my hands. 'I didn't mean it. I really hope you are happy with Marilyn . . .'

'Thank you. I think we will be. She's changed, anyway. She's stopped drinking, she's doing an Open University degree. She said that she was coming back, even before I rang her mum when we thought Max was ill. She really wants to make a go of it with me. For Max. She can't do enough for him. And he's so happy to have her back . . .'

'Of course,' I said, equally politely, feeling steel shutters clanging down all around me, sealing me into a prison of my own making. 'I will still be able to see Max though, won't I?' My throat seized up with fear that Adam wouldn't let me.

'I don't know.'

'Please.'

He hesitated. 'Well, I suppose so, for Max's sake. After what Marilyn did, it would be pretty harsh for you to suddenly disappear out of his life too. But it may have to be when I'm not around.'

I felt suddenly desperate to hug Adam, to hold on to him. I was already missing the contours of his solid, reassuring body. I'd loved that body so much – he was right when he said that we fitted together well.

'I'd like to say goodbye to him before I leave, if that's OK.'

'Before you go back to your husband, you mean?'

I bit my lip. 'I'm only going back to tell him it's over between us.'

I meant it, too. I couldn't continue with Ken in the knowledge that I'd felt so much for another man.

'You can pick Max up from school today if you want.' Adam extracted a hard lump of tissue from the front pocket of his jeans, and managed to uncrumple it enough to blow his nose into. He looked old and miserable, the red rims around his eyes making them seem even bluer than ever. Then he put his arms around me – but politely, like a formality.

I nodded into his shoulder. 'Thanks,' I said, wondering how I'd be able to cope knowing that it might be the last time I'd ever see Max burst out of the classroom door, laden down with artwork, lunchbox, swimming things, bookbag; yet still dancing across the big yellow snake painted onto the tarmac of the playground, hopscotching across its numbered segments towards me, with his stuff flapping about him, his very existence a miracle.

I'd always visualized collecting Holly from school like that, waiting for her in a huddle with the other parents in the playground. It had been such a joy to have Max running into my arms, walking him home to play, sometimes with a friend, giving him juice and biscuits and then cooking supper for him, sweet-talking him out of waffles and into broccoli. The small rituals of pre-meal pees and handwashes, rations of children's TV and liberal applications of glitter glue. I'd felt just like a real parent.

I was going to miss it all so much. And I was going to miss the man with his arms still around me, the scratch of his beard rubbing against the crown of my head. I closed my eyes and thought of Ken. Maybe I should at least try and make things work with him now: to get reaccustomed to brown eyes instead of blue, tennis instead of the *Tweenies*, the lonely nights in instead of the cheerful chaos of the supper-bath-bed routine. I was so afraid of being on my own. Perhaps, I thought, I could bend the truth a little, just to save his feelings? Perhaps I could make out that Adam and I were just friends, and I'd only rented the flat to be close to Max? But the thought of telling yet more lies felt like the scratchy fibres of a rope noose tightening around my neck. I *had* to start telling the truth, no matter what the cost.

Adam dropped his arms back to his sides, and moved away from me, looking at his watch.

'We'd better go. I'll ring Marilyn and tell her not to pick up Max today; that you'll bring him home. And then you're leaving, right?'

It sounded like an order. I'd lost him, and Max.

36

Normally, when I picked Max up from school, I stood in a cluster with the waiting mums, many of them with smaller children straining to escape from pushchair harnesses or snoozing in papooses against their still-distended bellies. It had been the first time since Holly died that I hadn't resented other mothers in general; since I'd almost, by proxy, become one of them, I had learned to pity them instead: not so much because of their complaints of sleepless nights and non-existent sex lives, but for the tangible marks of their suffering – the violet shadows under eyes they'd had no time to make up; the misshapen but comfortable clothes; the tangled hair; the defeated expressions when their toddlers took not a blind bit of notice of what they said. We'd chatted in a desultory fashion, about the weather, nits, colds, E numbers, cake sales. I'd loved every minute of it.

On that last day, however, I stood apart from them. It would have been nice to continue the charade one final time, but I was too afraid of breaking down. Unfairly, I imagined their censure: 'Look at Max's dad's girlfriend – Max isn't even hers, and she can't take the pace . . . she should try having three!' Although they may have realized that Marilyn was back on the scene, so perhaps they pitied me instead. They were probably thinking, Well, my ass may be halfway down the backs of my legs, but at least I've got a husband and a child of my own.

I put on my shades, even though the sun was behind a thick bank of grey-blue cloud, and fixed my eyes on the room Max would come out of at three o'clock. There was a Blu-Tacked sign on the classroom's outside door announcing that the letter of the week was C, and that they would be talking about Carpets, Corn and Ceilings. Not in the same sentence, I hoped for Max's sake.

He was the sixth one through the door. As I mentally named the classmates in front of him, I wondered how they would all turn out, and felt sad that I might never see them again. Dominic was out first – face of an angel, blond cherubic curls and cupid's bow lips, but a mouth like a sewer and far too handy with his fists. Then came Natalie, who was a sweetheart. She'd been round to play with Max a few times, and he bashfully referred to her as his girlfriend, and surreptitiously stroked her brown pigtails when he thought nobody was looking. Although she'd been the one who'd told him that boys put their willies into girls' dinkies to make babies, so perhaps she wasn't as innocent as she seemed either. She was followed, in a huddle, by Katy, Gracie and Amy, the 'y' girls. They were far too cool to hang around with the likes of Max.

Then Max appeared, laden down like a packhorse like all the other children, but distracted and too upset to even hopscotch down the painted snake. 'Anna!' he cried, hurling himself at me and breaking into tears. 'Look!' He yanked down his lower lip and showed me his bottom front tooth, which that morning had merely been wobbly, but was now hanging on by the thinnest of threads.

'Miss Taylor wanted to pull it out, but I didn't want her to,' he wailed. I wrapped my arms around his thin body, almost glad of his tears so I had an excuse to hold him. There was a splodge of blue paint in his hair, yogurt on his tie, and his fingernails were black. I contemplated kidnapping him; running away somewhere with him and starting a new life. Just me and Max.

'It just needs a little tiny twist, Max, and it'll be out,' I whispered. 'Want me to do it for you?'

'No,' he said, wriggling away from my grasp. 'Mummy can, when we get home.'

I released him. I knew I'd have to let him go some time. I prayed that nobody would speak to us on our way down the alley out of the school's side entrance, walking at a snail's pace behind a woman holding a staggering baby's hand. I couldn't even talk to Max, to ask him about his day as I usually did.

'Anna, is it Friday?'

'No, sweetie,' I just about managed. 'It's Wednesday.'

'Could we have Bun Day on Wednesday, just this once?' he said hopefully, but without real conviction. We came out of the alley, and he hopped up on the low wall alongside the old people's home, skipping along it with his arms outstretched like a tightrope walker. He seemed to have forgotten about his tooth again.

'OK then. Just this once,' I said, and he whooped with delight.

'I want a gingerbread man!'

'But what about your tooth, Max? You can't bite into a gingerbread man!'

He was crestfallen. Then he stopped and faced me. Standing on the wall, he was almost at eye-level with me, and his serious expression was so like his father's had been when Adam had faced me on the towpath less than an hour earlier, I caught my breath.

'You can, then, Anna.'

'I can what?'

'Pull out my tooth. Go on. I won't even cry – not if I can have a gingerbread man, and the tooth fairy comes.' He thrust his open mouth at me, pushing the tooth forwards with his tongue.

I thought of a conversation I'd overheard at one of

Ken's work dinners a few months back. I'd been down the other end of the table, stuck with another executive wife and some radio plugger, not listening to what they'd been saying, but trying to tune into the conversation in which Ken and an attractive red-haired woman had been engrossed.

'You just pinch it between your thumb and forefinger in a tissue, and twist it out,' the woman had explained earnestly, and I had been desperate to know what she was talking about. Eventually I'd decided that she must, for some reason, have been explaining to him how to pull out a child's milk tooth, and it had moved me. I knew it to be one of those nuggets of information I'd store up, and hope that I could use one day. Even though afterwards Ken had told me that what they'd actually been discussing was the way to stop lily pollen from staining everything – you pulled out the stamen – I still believed that I now knew the correct method of extracting a wobbly tooth.

Max's tooth dangled in front of me. Taking a deep breath to try and dispel my queasiness, I reached into his mouth, grasped the tiny white square, and yanked. It felt like the most intimate thing I had ever done for anybody else. I felt a split-second's resistance, and Max's face turned pale. I held the tooth up, and blood began to flood into the space in his gum.

'There it is! Your first ever tooth to come out – what a big brave boy!'

'Anna, I'm BLEEDING!' he moaned, clutching his mouth.

'Spit it out, darling. Have a sip of water and spit that out too.' Helping him off the low wall and handing him his water bottle, I instantly regretted my impromptu extraction. I didn't even have a tissue, for heaven's sake. I should at least have waited until we'd got home – although then Marilyn would have taken over. At least this way the moment had been mine. I would, for ever, be the person who pulled out Max's first tooth.

344

One of the passing mothers – Natalie's – stopped. 'Are you OK?' she asked, more to me than to Max.

'You wouldn't have any tissues, would you? I've just pulled out his tooth, and it's bleeding more than I thought it would,' I said. Max had taken the tooth from me and was showing Natalie, who was duly awestruck.

'Is that his first one to come out?' asked Natalie's mother, handing me a small pack of Kleenex. I couldn't remember her name, and there didn't seem much point in asking.

'Yup,' I said, beaming with as much pride as if the tooth fairy had left a pound under *my* pillow.

'Ooh,' she replied, 'Isn't that great? Natalie can't *wait* to lose her teeth!'

I handed Max a tissue, and he dabbed at his gum, although it had already stopped bleeding. 'Come on then, Maxie, let's go and get a bun,' I said. 'Want me to look after your tooth till you get home?'

He passed it across to me like a jeweller handling a valuable diamond, and I wrapped the bloody stump of it in another tissue. 'Thanks for the tissues,' I said to Natalie's mum, and she smiled cheerily.

'No problem. Well done, Max,' she said. 'See you both tomorrow.'

Well, you won't see *me*, I thought, plunged back into depression again as I watched her walk out of my life, with Natalie holding the handle of the buggy containing her baby brother.

Max hammered with his fists on the front door of his house, calling through the low letterbox: 'Mummy, Mu-ummy! Guess what?' His voice was muffled because he'd stuck a soggy half of gingerbread man into his mouth to free up his hands.

But it was Adam who opened the door, and my heart still jumped when I saw him, familiar in his checked shirt and jeans, his crinkled eyes and the wide smile which was only there for Max's benefit – it dropped from his mouth when he looked at me.

'Where's Mummy?' Max pushed past him. 'Anna, I need my You Know What, to show Mummy.'

'She's not here at the moment, sweetheart, she's just gone to Tesco's,' said Adam.

His face fell, and he laid the mutilated trunk of the gingerbread man on the hall table, all interest in it lost.

'Show Daddy instead,' I said, passing the precious tissue over to him. Max unwrapped it slowly, his big blue eyes anxiously scanning his father's face, waiting for the appropriate reaction as each layer was drawn apart until the tiny tooth lay there.

'Max! That's never your . . .' began Adam, switching his gaze from the grisly tooth to the gap in his son's smile.

'Anna pulled it out for me so I could eat my gingerbread man,' Max beamed, and Adam hugged him.

'Oh, Max, that's so exciting! We'll have to put it under your pillow for the tooth fairy, won't we?'

'It was only hanging on by a thread, and he did ask me to,' I said, not wanting Adam to think I'd pinned Max down against his will, like some kind of re-enactment of the dentistry scene in *Marathon Man*. 'If it's OK with you, I'll just nip upstairs. I've got a few bits and pieces to collect before I go,' I added.

'Why, where are you going, Anna?' Max plucked at my arm, a slight tone of panic in his voice. He knew, I thought.

I crouched down to him. 'Max. Now that your mummy's back, there's . . . well, there's not really enough room for me to be here too.'

'You could share my bedroom,' he said, clinging to me. I hugged him back.

'Thank you, darling, but that might not work out. You see, I'm moving out of my little flat, and back to' – I nearly said 'my old house' – 'back to where I used to live. But I'll still be in touch, lots, I promise. I'll write, and email, and talk to you on the telephone, and if Mummy and Daddy don't mind, maybe we could go out together for the day sometimes? The zoo, or the

346

park – or perhaps even a sleepover, when you're on school holidays?'

I wouldn't have to worry about what Ken thought about this – he'd probably be long gone by then.

'You're leaving?' His face was desolate. 'Anna, please don't go!'

Adam turned away. I held Max to me, committing to memory the feel of his thin body against mine, in the same way I'd done with his father. I could not think of anything to say. After a few moments, I prised him gently away from me.

'Want to help me get my things?'

'No,' he said, and ran away from me, up the stairs to his bedroom.

'This is horrible,' I muttered to Adam, but he'd walked away too, into the kitchen. Max's door slammed, and I felt utterly alone.

Going into Adam's bedroom was horrible, too. I'd spent so many nights there, was so familiar with its contents: the crooked Japanese print on the opposite wall which no one ever straightened; the woodworm-pitted antique pine wardrobe; the powder-blue walls which we'd painted ourselves. And now Marilyn's nightdress was thrown casually on my pillow, and her unzipped suitcase oozed tights and T-shirts across the floor. I felt angry, that Adam hadn't sheltered me from those sights – it was one thing to hear that they were back together, but I didn't want to see the evidence. As if he'd read my mind, he appeared in the doorway.

'Sorry, Anna,' he said. 'It's not like it looks – I've been sleeping on the sofa-bed downstairs. I told her that I wouldn't share a bed with her while I was still involved with you. It wouldn't have been fair on either of you.'

'I really hope you two will be happy together,' I said, fishing my Timberlands out of the bottom of his wardrobe, still flaking dried mud from a walk in the country with him and Max. Even opening the wardrobe door felt intrusive. 'You deserve to be happy.' I did mean it, but I sounded totally insincere, as if I was just trying to overcompensate for what I'd said on the towpath.

Adam sat down on the bed. 'Happy,' he said. 'I don't know. Well. I suppose I could be happy, even when I feel like my heart belongs to someone else.' He grabbed my hand and pulled me down next to him. 'Oh Anna, why did you—?'

I burst into tears, still clutching my boots, rocking back and forwards with the pain of mistakes, of wrong decisions and regrets. 'I'm sorry, I'm really really sorry.'

Adam stroked my hair. 'Don't cry.' He pushed me gently down onto my back; the mattress yielded under our weight. 'One last kiss,' he said, kissing away the tears which were dripping an uneven path into my ears.

Our tongues met, salty and passionate, and I felt a pang of indecision. Perhaps I ought to be fighting harder for him, begging him to give us a chance – but no, Adam wasn't mine any longer. Or, rather, never had been.

From Max's bedroom came the sound of a tinny little keyboard, pre-programmed to play 'She'll be Coming Round the Mountain', very fast. I sat up, pushing Adam off me. I badly needed to blow my nose, and besides, if I'd stayed there kissing Adam, I knew I would just have wanted to take off all my clothes and get into bed with him. Then I'd never have left.

'I think that's everything,' I said, picking up the boots, a jogging bra, and a British Airways travel kit which I'd kept in the bathroom. I noticed the boots' treads had disgorged narrow rectangles of dried mud all over the carpet, and I churlishly hoped it would annoy Marilyn. 'I'll leave you Lil's address, so if you find anything else, could you send it on?'

'Sure,' said Adam miserably, sitting up and running a hand through his hair.

I tucked my stuff under my arm, and plucked a tissue from the box on the mantelpiece. It felt wrong, like taking liberties in a stranger's house. I blew my nose, and lobbed the tissue in the wastepaper basket. One of Max's drawings was in there, scrunched up, and I felt angry with Marilyn. I'd never thrown away anything that Max drew or stuck or made, however cursory the effort had been – I had a thick folder of it all at the flat. The maps we'd done together when he got ill that time were my favourites, though. The 'naps'.

'Max,' I called, outside his bedroom door. 'I'm leaving now, darling. Will you come and kiss me goodbye?'

Hold it together, Anna, just for a while longer. I hoped my eyes weren't red from the last fit of crying. There was silence in the room.

'Max? Please?' I didn't feel I could enter. I was a stranger again.

I heard a shuffling from inside, then the drag of the door over the carpet. Max appeared, clutching Spesh under one arm and a football under the other. He hadn't switched off his keyboard, for it was still parping an allegro version of 'We Wish You a Merry Christmas'.

He thrust Spesh at me, his mouth turned down at the corners. I kissed the matted fur of Spesh's nose. 'Bye then, Spesh,' I said, trying to be jolly. 'Look after Max for me.'

'No, Anna, you can keep him.'

My mouth fell open, and from inside Adam's bedroom, I heard an exclamation of surprise. Adam appeared next to me. 'You're giving Spesh to Anna?'

'I want her to have him, Daddy. He's my most favourite thing, that's why,' said Max matter-of-factly, tears gleaming in his eyes.

'I can't,' I said, trying to give him back. 'Oh Max, not your Spesh.'

'Don't you like him?'

'I love him. I love you. I – I know how precious he is to you, that's all. You'd miss him so much!'

'I'm going to miss you more, Anna,' said Max, so

grown up that I could picture him as an adult, same eyes, deep voice, bristles, big feet . . . breaking girls' hearts left, right and centre, just like my heart was breaking then.

'Are you sure?'

'Yes. But I can visit him when I come for sleepovers, can't I?'

'Definitely.' I looked at Adam for confirmation, and he nodded and ruffled Max's hair.

'Baby, that's so kind of you. I'm sure Anna will love looking after Spesh.'

'I'll think of you every single time I look at him,' I managed tight-throatedly. 'Thank you so much.' I dropped my little bundle of possessions on the carpet – now including Max's treasured toy – knelt down, and Max ran into my arms. Once more, Adam walked away, and I thought, Right, now I really do have to go. Stringing it out is just making it harder.

Just then, we heard the sound of a key in the front door, followed by the rustle of plastic carrier bags. Max ripped himself away from me and bounded down the stairs, still holding the football. 'Mummy, Mummy, guess what? My tooth comed out!' he called, and I was left on the landing, my arms empty and my womb aching.

I didn't see Max again. When I left the house shortly afterwards, he was kicking the ball about in the garden with Marilyn. Through the open back door, I heard him excitedly speculating about whether the tooth fairy would fly or walk into his bedroom, and how much he'd get for his tooth. He appeared to have forgotten that I was going.

37

I drove home that same afternoon, very slowly, numb with sorrow and on a cocktail of Day Nurse, Strepsils and vitamin C tablets. All the goodbyes had really taken it out of me, and I felt weak as a kitten. Accelerating shakily away from Wealton with Spesh in the passenger seat, I felt a strange, hollow sensation of loss and regret. It was a cross between bereavement, and the feeling you got after a really good holiday, when you left knowing that you would most likely never see that place or those people again. Even though Adam said that I could still see Max, I sensed that it might easily not happen – and that in the long run it might be best for all concerned if it didn't.

I'd left a note for Dora, my landlady, giving a month's notice on the flat, and I knew I'd have to go down again with a transit van to move my stuff out – but I wasn't sure that I'd have been able to see Max and Adam again so soon. Or rather, to see Marilyn reinstalled in full flow as Mother and Wife.

I couldn't face going to Lil's straight away, so I went home first, planning to unpack the things I'd brought back with me, but not having the energy to do any more than crawl into another cold empty bed, feeling like a nomad. A nauseous nomad, I thought, as ten minutes later I had to dash for the bathroom, my insides churning afresh. Perhaps it was just life which was making me sick: sick of the deception, the lack of stability, the house built on sand. It felt like the tide had come in, and fast. Well, it was done now. No more Max or Adam or escapism. The rest of my life started here. It felt horrible.

I put on my nightdress and was about to climb back into bed, wrung out and just wanting sleep, when the doorbell rang. I ignored it. It rang again. I was plagued by people who kept their fingers on the buzzer, it seemed. I trudged downstairs, sighing heavily.

I opened the door, hanging on to it for support, expecting a delivery or perhaps Vicky or Lil, but a strange man was standing there, squinting uncertainly at me in my tatty nylon Tigger nightdress. Ken hated that nightdress with a vengeance. I'd bought it for £5.99 in a market, to wear after Holly was born, figuring that it wouldn't matter if it got covered with milk and blood or whatever, I could chuck it away afterwards. But in the end I hadn't been able to part with it. It was all bobbly, and so static that I gave Ken electric shocks when I wore it in bed. He used to say that it was made of some kind of special sex-repelling fabric; and I'd laughed, while privately thinking that Ken didn't need any special sex-repellent, he seemed to be perfectly repelled by me without any assistance.

'Anna?'

The man was in his sixties, with a large belly and pale grey hair, swept over his forehead in a vaguely familiar David Soulesque style. He seemed to know me, and I frowned at him.

'Really sorry to land on you unannounced. After nearly twenty years.' Suddenly he grinned, and looked almost rakish. The penny dropped.

'*Greg*? Good grief, is that really you? I didn't recognize you.' I felt too wrecked to summon up anything other than astonishment, but he didn't seem perturbed by my lack of enthusiasm. He spread his arms wide, but I didn't move.

Greg, my would-be deflowerer. Dad's friend Greg, the catalyst for me causing Dad's heart attack. Greg, whom I really hadn't ever wanted to see again, after the funeral. Thank heavens I hadn't run away with him, I thought. Whatever other sort of a mess I'd made of my life, at least it hadn't included a failed marriage to Greg.

'Yes, it's really me! I bumped into your brother behind the leather goods counter of John Lewis in Oxford Street, and he gave me your address – did he not tell you? Nice outfit, by the way.'

He nodded into my cleavage, and I pulled the front of the nightdress up to cover my chest better, mentally cursing my brother.

'Has he worked there long?'

'Um. Well – off and on. He's just got back from a year away travelling round Europe.'

'Isn't he married, then? I did ask him, but he acted like I'd said something funny. Bad divorce, was it? Needed to get away for a bit?'

'No. He's gay.'

Greg's jaw dropped, so far that I could see all the crowns and fillings cluttering up his mouth, flashing gaudy brightness among his grey teeth.

'Gay? As in, a homo? He can't be! Didn't he have that nice little girlfriend when he was a kid?'

I sighed. This, I could have done without. 'Yes, he had girlfriends. He didn't come out until he was twenty-five. He's got a very nice boyfriend now.'

Greg appeared to find this news utterly earth-shattering. He shook his head. 'A homo! Little Oliver . . . who'd have thought . . . Well, actually, it does kind of make sense – but still, what would your dad have said?'

'I'm sure Dad would have just wanted Olly to be happy, like Mum and I did,' I said stiffly, thinking it very bizarre to be standing on the doorstep discussing Olly's sexual proclivities in my Tigger nightie, when my entire life was turned upside down.

'Right. Well. Anyway. I didn't come over to ask you

about your brother. I need to talk to you,' he said, his face in creases of seriousness.

Good grief, I thought, now what? 'Oh?' I said cagily. 'What about?'

'Can I come in?'

I hesitated. 'It's not a great time. I've got a flu bug, and I feel horrible.'

He looked me up and down again. 'Yes, you do look rough, don't you?' he said cheerfully, and I was affronted. *He* could talk, with his beer gut and peppery stubble. He'd grown old-man ears, with hair sprouting out of them and everything; and the dimple in his chin which had been so cute all those years ago now seemed angry, as if someone had been conducting regular and rather careless excavations in there with a screwdriver. I shuddered at the thought of what we used to get up to on my parents' kitchen floor. It was staggering, to think I'd been so impressed by a pair of jeans and Dunlop Green Flashes.

I stood aside to let him in, and reluctantly ushered him into the kitchen. Flicking on the kettle, I gestured for him to sit down on one of the stools at the counter. He obeyed, his large bottom swallowing up the stool's surface; which reminded me of Peter, that time he'd come over to have a go at me about falling out with Vicky. I would have to ring Vicky and see Crystal, soon, I thought guiltily. That day at the spa had been months ago, and since then we'd drifted even further apart – so far that I wasn't even sure if our friendship was redeemable. I hadn't wanted to get in touch in case she'd seen through my deceptions, and I was pretty sure she'd been keeping her distance so as not to rub my nose in her pregnancy. She'd nearly be due by now, I thought, with a pang like a small contraction.

I waited for Greg to extract his pack of Silk Cut, light up, and *then* ask if I minded, as had been his wont, but his hands remained on the counter in front of him, fidgeting and restless. I remembered those hands, the way they used to cup my breasts and slide around my waist. They were still a smoker's hands, the lump on the index finger hardened into a nicotine yellow callus. I felt queasy again.

'Not smoking any more?' I asked.

His face settled into a smug expression. 'Two and a half years since I last had a fag,' he said proudly. 'Gave it up when I gave up the booze.'

'Congratulations,' I said politely. 'Tea or coffee?'

'Tea, please, love. Three sugars.'

I wondered if he'd always been this . . . rough. If Dad and he would still have been friends. Now I looked back, Mum and Dad's friendship with him and Jeanette had been odd, really. They hadn't had much in common. Mum liked gardening; Jeanette liked Bingo. Dad was into golf, and Greg played snooker. There had definitely been a touch of the *Abigail's Party* about their little set-up: the cosy nights in drinking sickly seventies drinks and handing round the nibbles. Paper tablecloths, cheesecloth dresses, kipper ties. I wondered what the attraction had been. We'd had plenty of other neighbours that Mum and Dad could have bonded with. Although that wasn't to say they would have lacked the broderie anglaise and bad ties . . .

I remembered, with shame, the way I'd seduced him: leading him on, then letting him believe he was making the first move. It seemed so sleazy, when at the time I'd kidded myself it was romantic and passionate. I looked at him, at the grizzled mass of chest hair poking out of his V-necked shirt, and thought, Oh the mistakes we make in our youth . . . And then I remembered my current predicament and thought, Oh the mistakes we make as adults.

It was all Greg's fault, I decided, viciously throwing two teabags into mugs as the kettle danced to the boil. If he hadn't told Dad about me and him, Dad wouldn't have keeled over and died; of that I was certain. If Dad hadn't died, I wouldn't have felt quite so fearful for Max's continuing survival. Losing Holly had been bad enough, but the thought of my bone-marrow donation failing Max had been horrendous, and of Adam knowing. Of feeling responsible for three deaths. But that meant that I'd lied to Adam, and now I'd lost him.

'So how're things with you, Anna?' he asked, staring at the marble surface of our kitchen counter as if he wanted nothing more than not to hear the answer. 'Apart from the flu, I mean.'

'Great,' I said, practically banging his tea down in front of him, ungraciously shoving over the sugar bowl. 'Just great. My life is a total . . .' I was going to say 'breeze', but unaccountably what came out was: '. . . disaster.'

'My life is a total disaster,' I repeated, a catch in my voice. To give him credit, Greg did look at me with concern.

'What is it, love?'

'I'm sorry,' I said, sliding onto the stool next to him. 'You don't need to hear all my problems – and to be honest, I don't really want to tell them to you. I'm just feeling a bit low at the moment, what with this bug. You've just happened to turn up at the wrong time, that's all. I'll be fine.'

He patted my shoulder sympathetically, and I managed to swallow down the tears pricking my eyes at the realization that I really had lost Adam and Max.

'So!' Greg said brightly. 'I hear you're an actress now. That's great. That's what you always wanted to be, wasn't it? I remember coming to see you in that school play that time. Weird sort of thing, about gangsters, weren't it? It had a funny name.'

'*The Resistible Rise of Arturo Ui*,' I said, managing to smile. 'By Bertolt Brecht. I had the main part – Ui.'

'Yeah, that's right. Dead proud of you, I was. Wanted to boast to everyone that you were my bird – but obviously I couldn't, you know?'

I thought of Adam, how he'd never met any of my

friends, or my family, and never would. Poor Adam –
he'd been having an affair with me without even
knowing it. I was no better than a bigamist. No wonder
he was shattered when I'd told him.

Then I looked at a photograph on the bookshelf of
Ken as a little boy, not much older than Max, holding
up a large pike with more teeth than he had. That little
boy had no idea he'd grow up and marry a woman who
would cheat on him. I felt so sorry for both of them.
They both deserved better than me.

'How is Jeanette?' I asked weakly.

Greg shrugged. 'Dunno. We divorced ten years back.
She went off with the barman at the bingo hall.'

'Oh. Sorry. Were you upset?'

He swiped a hand across his forehead. 'Gutted.
Devastated. Words can't express . . .'

Where had that adoration for his wife been when
he'd been trying to get into my knickers, I asked
myself?

'Did she ever know about us?' I'd always wondered
that. I assumed not, because otherwise my mother
would probably also have known.

'Yeah. I told her after your dad's funeral. After you'd
gone off to university. I felt so bad about it all.'

I looked at him in amazement. 'Really? I don't think
she ever told my mum.'

'No, she didn't. She was a gem, that woman. I broke
her heart, and still she was thinking of other people. She
said, "Eileen's been through enough. She just lost her
husband. She doesn't want to hear that her daughter's
been screwing a married man twice her age."'

'But they were friends.'

It was Greg's turn to look at me. 'Yeah, exactly. She
didn't want to give your mum any more grief. She never
told a soul.'

I felt a new respect for Jeanette, whom I'd always
secretly rather despised, with her loud floral tent
dresses, eyebrows plucked to oblivion, and careful
perms. It was such an incredibly juicy piece of gossip,

especially when she was the injured party. I'd never have been able to keep it to myself, in her position.

'We muddled on together, though she never really trusted me after that. Thought we was over it, to be honest, and then she met . . . *Ricky*.' He spat the name out like a mouldy strawberry.

Ken would never trust me again either, if I did tell him about Adam. I couldn't tell him. I just couldn't. I pushed away my mug of tea.

'I'm sorry, Greg, but I'm really not feeling well. What was it that you wanted to talk to me about?'

I wanted him gone. I wanted my bed, my haven, the only place I could go to escape. What a sad life I had, that I had no distractions stronger than a couple of plump pillows and the oblivion of sleep. I wished I really had got that job on the soap. If I'd had regular work, I wouldn't have had the time to obsess about Max and Adam. My energy could have been diverted into learning lines for real, instead of concocting lies.

'Well. Thing is, Anna, like I said, I haven't touched a drop for over two and a half years.'

'Of alcohol?' I asked, somewhat stupidly.

He nodded. 'Been going to them AA meetings. Twelve Step, you know?'

I pictured Greg, perched on a hard wooden chair in a circle of other hard wooden chairs, sharing.

'Bloomin' marvellous, it is. Never thought anything could keep between me and my pints, but it really works. And I feel so much better for it, too! Weight's falling off me. Complexion's improved, too.' He patted his veiny cheeks playfully and winked at me.

Crikey, I thought, taking in the considerable gut and the greyish pallor; if he looks good now, what sort of shape must he have been in before he quit?

'Are you familiar with the Twelve-Step programme?' he asked earnestly.

'Not intimately, no,' I replied. 'Vaguely, I guess. Don't you have to acknowledge your Higher Power, and that sort of thing?'

'That's it. That's Step Two. "We come to believe that a Power greater than ourselves could restore us to sanity." Anyhow, I'm up to Step Nine now. That's about making direct amends to all persons I have harmed through my alcoholism. Which is where you come in.'

'Me?'

'Yup. You know I always liked a drink or two, Anna. And it was wrong of me to go after you the way I did, when you was only a schoolgirl. Not to mention what I did to Jeanette, of course.'

'Of course,' I said faintly.

'And then all that stuff with your dad. I never stuck by you the way I should've. It was easier to have a few drinks and forget about it.'

'All that stuff' with my dad. 'All that stuff' seemed an odd way to describe a fatal heart attack, induced by Greg's bad news. I thought of Dad's funeral, of the two geese that had swooped joyfully, squawking with indecent volume, over our heads as we were all gathered by the small hole in the ground which was about to receive his ashes. I remembered that Greg and Jeanette had been there, but that I hadn't once been able to meet their eyes, and I'd wrenched my arm away from Jeanette when she'd put a sympathetic hand on my elbow, as if she wanted to help me across the road or something.

I missed Dad then, with a low twinging ache like a period pain. It wasn't fair. And Mum too, although her death had been much less of a shock.

Greg was talking again, although I'd tuned out. 'Sorry, what was that?' I had to say.

'I'm asking if you forgive me,' he said, turning to me and looking in my eyes. For the first time, I saw the essence of the Greg I had fancied so badly and had yearned to be with. 'And I hope your dad would've done, too, for the liberties I took with you. He was my pal, your dad.'

There were tears in Greg's eyes, and in mine. We

reached out and clasped hands simultaneously, seventeen years too late. I didn't recognize Greg's smell. I supposed that without the cigarette smoke and alcohol component, it wasn't the same. But for a moment, I closed my eyes and went back to being eighteen, when the most consuming thought in my mind had been whether or not to allow Greg into my pants; or in other words, to allow 'that' to go in 'there'.

'I'm glad we never actually had sex, though,' I said. 'I think that would have been worse.'

I felt him nod. 'Yeah. I'm glad too – much as I wanted to. I hope you managed to save yourself for someone more worthy of you, love.'

I shuddered. I wouldn't exactly have called Colin Baxter, a third-year drama student at Reading when I was a fresher, 'worthy'. After too many brandies with Stone's Ginger Wine in the student union bar, we'd spent one night in the narrow single bed in my hall of residence, memorable less for its passion than for its pain (mine), flatulence (his), hangovers (both of ours), and the sight of his grey Y-fronts, draped jauntily over the spout of the kettle, greeting me when I'd opened my eyes in the morning. If it hadn't been for the guilt of Dad keeling over and dying, then Greg would have been a much better bet in the deflowerment stakes.

'So, do you?'

'Do I what?'

'Forgive me?'

'I don't think there's anything to forgive. I've never blamed you, only myself. I've blamed myself ever since,' I whispered.

Greg looked at me with surprise. 'Why, love?'

It was my turn to look astonished. 'Because I'm sure he wouldn't have had that heart attack if you hadn't just told him you were leaving Jeanette for me. And I led you on in the first place.'

'Oh love,' he said, leaning across and hugging me. I found I didn't mind his embrace. I rested my chin on his shoulder, because right then, he felt like the closest thing I had to a father.

'You've really thought that, all these years? But I *didn't* tell him. He was clutching his chest before I'd said a word . . . It was nothing to do with us.'

I couldn't believe it. 'You swear you didn't tell him?'

Greg shook his jowls vehemently. 'I promise you, love. I didn't say a dickie bird, beyond getting the drinks in. Just turned round to hand him his pint, and there he was, on the floor.'

My stomach flipped over. 'Excuse me,' I said, sliding hastily off my stool. 'I'm going to be sick. Again.'

When I returned, some time later, Greg was gazing at the lone pot plant on our kitchen windowsill, a poor sickly parched thing with dry brown ends. Ken and I were useless with houseplants. We watched them slowly dehydrate, then stopped seeing them altogether, leaving their corpses littering our house long after they ought to have been thrown out. Every time I went to Lil's house and saw her plants, perky with health, their plump sleek leaves deep green and shiny, it reminded me to water ours – but by the time I got home, I'd usually forgotten again.

'You all right?'

I nodded. Even though I could still taste the faint bitter taste of vomit over the minty tang of toothpaste, my stomach had finally settled.

'Yeah. Actually, I feel better than I've felt for days.'

'You still haven't said if you forgive me.'

I smiled at him. 'Of course I do. I'm so glad you came over.'

We hugged again, briefly but with feeling. I realized that not only did I forgive him, I forgave myself too.

It was a start.

38

After Greg left, it wasn't just my stomach – or 'tummy', as Adam would have said – which felt less churned-up. In all the confusion of the past days and weeks, at last something positive, something definitive, had occurred: some kind of line had been drawn underneath Dad's death. Such old history amid such present turmoil, and I was surprised that it had hung around for as long as it had. But it was closure, a release from the noose of guilt.

I peeled off the sticky Tigger nightie and went and stood under the shower, letting my body go limp in the stream of water, idly watching it splatter off my shoulders and arms, and off the belly which I saw as nurturing nothing except regrets. Then I put on a summer dress and sandals, tied my hair up still wet, and brushed on enough blusher to hide my pallor.

As ready as I could ever be, I drove over to Lil's house, feeling nervous, sensing that Lil would coax truths out of me with the same ease that she used to deliver babies . . . but I wasn't even close to being prepared for what those truths would turn out to be.

'Hello, my darling Anna,' Lil said, giving me one of her reassuring hugs at the front door. I hugged her back, relishing the familiarity of thin shoulder blades under fine wool and inhaling her scent. When she released me, I picked up the two pint cartons of milk from her doorstep, their wobbly cardboard sides cool and slippery to the touch, and handed them to her.

'Oh good. The milkman was terribly late this morning. I thought I'd have to offer you black tea, but we'll be all right now. Come in.'

I sat on my usual stool in the kitchen whilst she made the tea. I could see her shooting sharp looks at me, taking in my drawn appearance.

'Have you recovered from your illness now?'

I nodded doubtfully. 'I think so. I was sick this morning, but I feel much better now. It keeps coming and going.'

'Have you seen the doctor?'

'No. What's the point? He'd only tell me that it's a bug, and I need to rest.'

Lil handed me a cup and saucer, then tipped a bronze stream of steaming tea into it from a large china teapot. Her hand was steady as a rock, and I watched with an almost greedy pleasure at the sheer relief of something as unchanged in my life as Lil pouring tea. She passed me a milk carton to open, and an empty milk jug, and pushed over a sugar bowl containing lumps of sugar and silver tongs. I hadn't seen sugar tongs anywhere else for years.

I was considering telling her about Greg's visit, as a sort of softener to any further admissions of adultery she might worm out of me. Break it to her that I'd long been the type of girl who cheated with other people's husbands. Funny how I'd never thought about it like that before. As I opened my mouth to speak, she beat me to it: 'Anna, could you, by any chance, be pregnant?'

Instinctively, I laughed. 'No, of course not, Ken and I haven't—'

Then I froze, mid-sentence, the wings of the milk carton in my hand gaping as wide open as my mouth was. Ken and I hadn't. *Adam* and I had. The precautions that Adam and I had taken had been perfunctory, to say the least.

'Anna? Are you all right, darling?'

My hand was shaking so much I had to put down the milk. When the hell had my last period been? Why hadn't I noticed? Was it really possible? No, surely I wasn't. My breasts weren't sore. I didn't have itchy shins, which had been a sure sign in my other pregnancies. I *had* been vomiting, but I hadn't been at all sick with Holly . . .

'No, I can't be. I've just had this bug that Max had.'

'But his only lasted twelve hours, didn't it? Yours has dragged on for days.'

'I've just had it worse, that's all. I had a sore throat and everything, not just sickness.'

Lil stroked my hand. 'Why don't you pop out to the chemist's and get a test. Just to put your mind at rest, if you're in any doubt? You could do it now. I'll be here with you.'

I loved her for not judging me. For not asking what was obvious: if I hadn't slept with Ken, then how could I even be wondering if I was pregnant? She could tell from my face that I'd realized it was a possibility.

'OK,' I said. '

I was pregnant; of course I was. Sitting on the lid of the toilet in Lil's old-lady floral-sprigged bathroom, I stared with incredulity at the pink line on the white wand. It felt so different from all the other times I'd found out that sperm and egg had fused. The first time had been sheer joy. The second: a large measure of joy, and a little fear. The third: equal feelings of both. The fourth – well, that had been Holly. I'd been terrified when I found out about her, but the terror had slowly diminished as my belly grew, month by month, my tentative happiness blossoming as my toes vanished from view.

But this . . . how was I supposed to feel about this? It

was impossible to feel anything at all except craven panic. I thought of Vicky then, and for the first time ever began to understand her predicament. I wanted a baby so badly – but not like this; not on my own and with all the pain it would cause Ken. I'd already decided to confess to him about Adam and the fake job, but how could I tell him this too? He would be so upset, and it would put paid to any remote chance of working things out between us. He would divorce me, without a doubt, and I couldn't blame him.

I was somehow not at all surprised at the prospect of ending up on my own, doing penance for all my crimes and petty deceits. Adam had already dumped me, and there was no way I'd use the baby – assuming I didn't lose it first – to blackmail him into taking me back. Besides, Max needed his own mother. It almost felt like a relief, as if God had taken the decisions out of my hands. I slumped back against the toilet cistern, exhausted with grief and confusion.

There was a tap at the bathroom door. 'Anna? May I come in?'

I slowly stood up and opened the door. 'I'm pregnant,' I said, and we gazed at one another. I thought about how, in all her experience of obstetrics, she'd never known how it felt to look at a positive pregnancy test of her own, that first whoosh of realization. I had a vision of her fifty years ago, at my age, grieving the way I'd grieved every month when her period arrived. She had been a slim, beautiful young woman then, with chestnut curls and laugh lines, neat blouses and scaffolded underwear. I bet she'd looked great in her midwife's uniform.

They hadn't had these neat, widdle-on-sticks pregnancy tests then, though. She'd have just measured out her child-bearing years in anticipation of an absence of the blood which let her down every single month; having to buy bulky sanitary towels instead of knitting baby clothes; listening patiently to numerous women weeping about the agonies of childbirth, the pain of breastfeeding, the hardship of motherhood. Now *that* must have been hard.

My dad had been to her like Max was to me, I supposed, a substitute child, her favourite nephew. I always had the feeling he'd been closer to her than he had been to her sister, his mother. Funny how I'd been closer to Lil than I had to my own mother, too.

'Come back into the kitchen. I've made a fresh pot,' she said, steering me gently by the elbow out of the bathroom. I was so glad that she was there.

'It's not Ken's, then,' she said, almost conversationally, as we went through the tea-pouring ritual again. She spooned two sugars into mine, although she knew I didn't take sugar.

I shook my head, treacly shame pouring over me at having to admit it.

'He'll be devastated,' I whispered. 'I was going to leave him for Adam, Max's dad, but that's not happening now. I was still going to confess though, about Adam and Max, to see what would happen from there; whether Ken still wanted to try and make a go of things. But a baby will just make him feel a million times worse about the betrayal. He wanted to be a father so much.'

'So you do still want to be married to him?'

'I'm not sure, really. I suppose it would have depended on his reaction when I told him the truth, because I don't see how I *could* continue to be married to him after everything I've done, unless he really wanted me to.'

'What changed with you and the other chap?'

I sighed, unable to stop my eyes from filling up. 'Well, for one thing, Adam's estranged wife came back on the scene. He'd phoned her in a panic when Max had that bug – it was my fault, I was in such a state. She turned up that night, just after I'd told Adam I was the person who gave Max his bone-marrow donation. *Then* I told him that I was still married to Ken, and he dumped me. Understandably. He and his wife –

Marilyn – are going to give their marriage another try, for Max's sake.'

I gazed at a framed cross-stitched alphabet on the wall by Lil's fridge, but it was so blurred that I couldn't make out any of the letters. I missed Max with a pain almost physical. Lil handed me a tissue and I blew my nose, thinking, Well, if I'm giving birth to his half-brother or sister, I'll have to be able to see him, won't I? So much for saying I could never have this baby. I'd never felt so confused.

'That day, the one Max was ill,' I said slowly, 'was when I really realized how much they both meant – mean – to me. I'd so wanted to be part of their family; and then at the beginning when Adam was attracted to me, I couldn't resist. It all seemed so perfect . . . although I didn't expect to fall in love with him the way I did. And I wanted to be near Max, to look after him, somehow.'

'There's a proverb, isn't there – that once you save someone's life, you become responsible for them? Is that how you felt?'

'Yes. It's an old Chinese saying. I did wonder about that before – and I suppose it was, although not consciously. Max felt – feels – a lot like my own son.'

'And what about Ken? He really has no idea?'

'I don't think so, no. Or else he's been having an affair too, and it's suited him that I've been away, and we haven't really talked about what we get up to when the other isn't there.'

Lil frowned at me. 'That would be convenient for you, wouldn't it? Do you really think he's got someone else?'

I paused, and shook my head sheepishly. 'No.'

'How on earth did you manage to fit these two men in, between filming your soap opera?'

I gazed at the floor. Here goes, I thought. I took a deep breath. For some reason, it was almost harder to confess than the adultery.

'There is no soap opera. I made the job up. When Ken

367

thought I was filming, I was with Adam. And vice versa.'

I saw the surprise, and censure, in her eyes, and it made me want to slide under the breakfast bar and huddle there, crouched over with shame, as I had done on occasion as a small child. There was a long, long silence.

'How will Adam react to the news of your pregnancy?'

I thought of Adam's bright blue eyes, imagining how, if I'd only found out two weeks earlier, before Marilyn had returned, those eyes would have opened wide with delight at the news that we were going to have a baby. For a second, my own heart jumped with the news, too. I was pregnant! Maybe this time it was meant to be, and this one would stay . . .

Two weeks earlier it would have been the kick up the backside to make me leave Ken and start a new life, with my new family, of which I'd have become a legitimate part and not a hanger-on any more . . . But then I remembered that I'd still have had to tell Adam that I'd cheated on him. Perhaps knowledge of our baby might have made him more forgiving; perhaps not. It didn't matter now anyway.

'Oh Lil, please help me,' I begged, not answering her question because I didn't know how to. 'I don't know what I'm going to do.'

'First you have to find a way to tell Ken.'

'I know. He'll never forgive me.'

'He might. I suppose you just have to decide whether you're telling him in order to ask his forgiveness and move on, or to simply explain why it has to be over between you.'

'Yes,' I said weakly. 'But I've treated him so badly; him, and Adam . . .' My voice began to crack. 'All I wanted was to be part of a family.'

Lil rubbed my arm sympathetically, and stroked my hair.

'It would take time, of course, for both of you. You

couldn't expect Ken to adjust overnight. But you could have counselling, perhaps?'

'To help him come to terms with bringing up another man's baby? That's so not Ken. He'd never do it. No, I have to tell him, so that he can divorce me.'

Lil's phone rang. We both listened as the machine picked up the call, and a quavery old lady left a very long and self-conscious message about the flower-arranging rota in the church. She appeared to be reading out the entire rota over the telephone. Lil tutted, and spoke over the top of it.

'Dear Edith. She always does that. I feel like telling her simply to post it to me but she clearly thinks I can't contain my excitement and absolutely must know which dates everyone's doing, the minute the rota is printed. Some of these poor old dears have such empty lives.'

I managed a weak smile. It was quite nice to pause for a moment, a commercial break in the tortuous drama of my own life – which, at that moment, I *wished* was empty enough to care so much about flower-arranging in the church. Edith carried on creakily reciting dates and old-fashioned Christian names such as Ivy and Doris and Marjorie, until the tape ran out and her voice stopped, mid-word.

'Thank heavens,' said Lil, before coming back to the question I'd left unanswered earlier. 'And what about Adam? When *are* you going to tell him about the baby? Do you think your news will make him alter his decision to stay with his wife?'

'I don't know. I don't think so. I've hurt him too much. And besides, it isn't fair on Max, or any of them. She's Max's mother . . . No, I'm not going to tell him, at least not yet. I'll have to at some point, but I don't want Adam thinking I'm using the baby to make him choose me.'

I've done so many selfish things, I thought. Surely I could manage this one unselfish one. Max needed his mum. I thought of a song about mothers which he had once sung to me. He'd learned it at school, and I'd felt annoyed with his blonde, baby-faced teacher – not much more than a child herself – for her lack of sensitivity. She must have known that Marilyn wasn't around.

The song, sung in Max's off-key childish voice, went:

'There are hundreds of stars in the sky
There are hundreds of fish in the sea
There are hundreds of people the whole world over
But on-ly one muvver for me
But on-ly one muvver for meeee'

He'd beamed with self-satisfaction at his word-perfect rendition, but then a frown had clouded his face. 'Where *is* Mummy?' he'd asked me, in a 'where did I leave her?' kind of way; as if Marilyn had been a lost pair of swimming goggles, or a once-favoured toy which had scudded out of sight under the sofa and was now barely remembered.

'I don't know exactly, honey,' I'd replied, stroking his hair back from his face. 'But I'm here. And I love you.'

I shouldn't have said that; I had no right. There *was* only one 'muvver' for Max, and it wasn't me.

'Would you consider having an abortion, to save your marriage?'

An abortion. Even the word made me cringe. Lil certainly wasn't mincing her words – more like slapping them on the table like raw steaks.

'No,' I said. 'I absolutely would not have an abortion.'

However much of a mess this was, I thought, it was imperative that I divested myself of all the secrets and came clean. An abortion would have been the worst secret of all. Besides, I could never have voluntarily got rid of a baby. No way. The idea was abhorrent to me – to throw away the chance after all those years, desperate for a child? Not to mention hypocritical, after the hard time I'd given Vicky for considering the same thing.

'I'm glad,' said Lil. 'But Adam does have a right to know.'

'Yes. I will tell him. Only once I'm past three months, though, and maybe even not until the baby's born . . . just in case.' There would be no point in dropping that kind of a bombshell on Adam and Marilyn, were this pregnancy to end like three out of my four other ones had. And it would give them time to work on their own relationship, without the spectre of me hovering over them.

'But you will tell Ken before then, won't you?'

I sighed, dread already collecting at the pit of my stomach. 'Yes. I have to get it over with. I can't stand keeping anything a secret for a minute longer than I have to.' It was true. After months of seemingly effortless deception, I now felt toxic with deceit. I wanted to be clean for my baby, not choked up and rancid. I wanted to know my fate. 'When he throws me out, could I come and stay with you?'

Lil put her arm around me. 'He might not. But of course you may, if he does.'

'Even if I did want to stay with him, he would never bring up another man's child.'

'So you said before. But it does happen.'

'Does it?'

'Yes. My friend Betty from the Choral Society, well, she died in eighty-nine, but her husband still idolizes her, even all these years later; and it turned out that he knew all along that their youngest son wasn't his. She'd been having an affair for years. The natural father was the boy's godfather.'

'What, he knew even before the baby was born?'

'Apparently so. So you see, it does happen, if the relationship is strong enough to start with.'

'That doesn't make sense, not in my case, Lil. If my relationship had been strong enough to start with, none of this would have happened.'

'Perhaps. Perhaps not.'

It felt quite odd, discussing my sordid personal

relationships with Lil, but I knew that she was more objective than, say, Vicky would have been. I would obviously have to tell Vicky at some point, but not until I knew my fate as far as Ken was concerned, I decided. I couldn't handle another person's input.

Lil busied herself watering a miniature rose plant on the kitchen windowsill. She used a small, immaculately polished brass watering can with a long slim spout, and I could see her reflection in the side of it. It reminded me of when Adam and I first got together, seeing our distorted chrome faces in the kettle and realizing how complete I felt.

'I'll be praying for you, darling. I'm sure it'll be all right,' Lil said briskly, but she didn't know that I was watching her expression reflected on the watering can and, despite her words, she looked every bit as desperate as I felt.

39

Ken scrutinized the photograph of Adam, Max and I, and, not for the first time, I regretted the decision to use 'props'. That wordless, studied consideration felt far too much like evidence being passed around a censorious jury.

I had to keep reminding myself to breathe. There was something unbelievably surreal about the whole experience. I wished Lil was there with me, but of course she couldn't be; this was something I had to do by myself. Over the past two days I'd wondered, many times, if I would still have confessed without the incriminating evidence of the baby. I knew I couldn't have lived with all the lies any more – although perhaps, by confessing, I was still being selfish. Perhaps Ken would have rather not known at all.

So far, he had remained very calm, although at the sight of the photograph his brown face took on a grey, ashen appearance; almost a texture, as if one good puff would disperse it, dust to dust, into the atmosphere. It frightened me more than if he'd been contorted with rage, screaming at me.

He handed the photo back, although my hand was trembling almost too much to hold it. There was no disguising the way in which Adam and I had been looking at one another in the picture.

'So,' he said. 'That's the boy?'

'Max.'

'And does his dad have his arm around you for any particular reason?'

I gulped. I'd thought sarcasm wouldn't be far away – Ken was using the voice I imagined he used when firing employees who raided the CD cupboard.

I dropped the photo, reached back in the box, and passed him Spesh, Max's battered tiger. Ken took it by one ear, with an expression of distaste which I found offensive, even under the circumstances.

'What's that?'

'He – it – is called Spesh. He was Max's most treasured possession. He was in hospital with Max the whole time he was there. It's why he's so knackered-looking.'

For a second, alarm flitted across Ken's face, and I loved him for it. Even in the midst of all this, he was concerned about Max's recovery. 'So why have you got it? Max hasn't—'

'Max is fine. I've got Spesh because . . .' The tightness in my throat compressed my voice down to a croak, '. . . Max gave him to me. He told me that I was so special, he wanted me to have what he loved the most. And that was Spesh.'

'Because you saved his life.'

I gazed into Ken's dark brown eyes. 'No. He didn't know that I'd saved his life. Nor did Adam, his dad; although he does now.'

'I don't understand.' Ken handed Spesh back to me.

'They didn't even know my real name. They thought I was Anna Valentine . . . I just wanted to meet him, so badly,' I began.

I had the weird sensation of a dam beginning to crack and burst; the initial drip drip of information was about to become a flood. Here I go, I thought. The point of no return. Like when my waters had broken. I'd only been about ten feet away from where we sat now.

The world had changed that day, not just for Ken and I, but for everyone: Holly was born on September 11th 2001.

And she'd died, along with all those other innocent people. After it was all over and we were sitting stunned next to the birthing pool full of cold turquoise water, I'd felt guilty for my grief. Even though part of me knew it was perfectly understandable for me to feel this much pain, a less rational part thought that my pain should be reserved for the people in those towers and their families. For the wives watching their loved ones jumping to their deaths. Not for one little blue dead baby.

Perhaps I never had allowed myself to grieve properly.

But I couldn't remind Ken of that day, not now. It wasn't fair to bring Holly into it, like some kind of excuse. Although perhaps if we'd talked about her more since she died, I wouldn't have been sitting there trying to explain what I was trying to explain. I wouldn't have had to watch Ken's face going through twenty shades of emotion, most of them involving undiluted pain.

No matter how I tried to focus on other things – fallen bleached-out petals from a vase of blown roses, rivulets of wax frozen into the side of the candles on the table, an upturned flowerpot in the garden, earth and feathery roots spilling out of it – nothing seemed to be able to pull my eyes away from the pain on Ken's face. The pain that I alone had caused him.

He was staring at the back of a postcard of John McEnroe, trying to take in the words I'd printed in capitals because I was too much of a coward to say them out loud: 'MY SOAP OPERA DOESN'T EXIST. THERE WAS NO JOB. I MADE IT UP. I WAS WITH ADAM AND MAX WHEN I SAID I WAS WORKING.'

I felt so sorry for him. Knowing Ken, a lot of what he was feeling was the shame of the cuckold: the loss of pride that he hadn't been enough for me;

the foolishness of the duped. Even though that was utterly missing the point, I knew that was what he'd be thinking.

All of this, and I hadn't even told him I was pregnant yet. The day seemed endless, as if the weak March sun had been shining relentlessly for about thirty-six hours non-stop. I wanted it to go down so I could go to bed and stay there with the covers over my head. Hibernate like a tortoise until my baby was due, and then start living again. The baby was the most important priority.

'So, you're leaving me for this guy Adam,' said Ken, staring at a smear of birdshit on the glass roof of the conservatory. The heating was on, and the stifling atmosphere added to the guilt already making my scalp prickle. A bead of sweat ran down Ken's face, and I thought for a moment it was a tear. But although his eyes were red, he wasn't crying. He hardly ever cried. After Holly died, he'd once said to me, 'I'm not very good at crying in front of other people,' and I'd thought, How odd, as if crying were some kind of skill he needed to practise until he was up to performance level.

'No. It's over between me and Adam.' I suddenly wanted to put my hand on his knee, wrap my arms round his neck, beg him to forgive me – but I didn't dare. A blackbird dug around for a worm in the gravel outside, oblivious of next door's horrible cat stalking along the fence, eyeing it greedily. I hated that cat.

'Why are you telling me all this then? You've gone to such lengths to hide it from me for so long, I'd have thought the last thing you wanted to do was confess.'

'I couldn't stand the lies any more.'

'So you ended it with Adam?'

I hesitated. 'Well. Not exactly. I told him I was already married.'

Ken laughed, the most excruciatingly laboured laugh

I'd ever heard. 'And he dumped you, didn't he? So you decided that you'd have to settle for second best after all, the boring workaholic at home whom you just happen to be married to. What a drag, eh? What a nuisance, that you foolishly promised to stay with me till death did us part. Bet you're regretting that now, aren't you?'

'No,' I said, thinking that this was a touch unfair. After all, Ken had promised the same thing to his first wife, until I'd come along. 'I'm not. I just regret . . .' Tears fell down my face onto Spesh's matted, patchy fur. I couldn't hold them in any more, and words gushed out of me in fits and starts.

'. . . I just regret everything since. The babies. Holly. Not being able to talk to you about it all. It shouldn't have been like this. Holly would have been eighteen months by now. If she was still here, none of this would have happened.'

It seemed that I couldn't help bringing her into it after all.

'It's my fault then, is it, because we don't talk about Holly?'

'No! I'm not blaming you . . . although it hasn't helped that you're away so much.'

Again, that hollow laugh. 'Wondered how long it would be before you got around to my job.'

I swallowed hard. It was tempting to get into a row about it, to wail that Ken was married to his job and not to me; but I had to stay calm if I wanted Ken to do the same. Making excuses wouldn't advance my cause.

'So that's the only reason you're telling me now, is it? Because you want to be honest with me? It would be much easier if I'd never known.'

I sent up a fervent prayer, to God, to my guardian angel, to the heavens above, that they would have pity on me and help me, a stupid weak human. Help Ken, too.

'You'd have found out sooner or later.' I reached

377

into the box and handed him the final card: Andre Agassi.

'I'M PREGNANT. IT'S ADAM'S.'

Ken sprang out of his chair with a howl of pain so intense that it was almost a scream, and started to rip up the postcard. I had never heard a noise like it, and I hope I never will again. The blackbird flew off in a panic, and I saw the cat's tail vanish over the fence.

I thought he was going to hit me, and at that moment I wanted him to, if it would have helped him. He was crying, finally, as he flung torn pieces of card at me, and swiped the cardboard box off the table onto the floor, scattering my pathetic little props. A chunk of Agassi's hairy leg got caught on the sleeve of my T-shirt, and I brushed it off.

'I'm sorry, Ken,' I pleaded in panic. 'I'm so, so sorry. I didn't plan any of it, I promise. I just wanted to meet Max and it all got out of control . . .'

Ken finished tearing the card into bits. He stood directly opposite me, hands clenched into fists at his sides, his face dark with rage and grief, so incongruous in the hot sunlight. When he finally spoke, his voice was a controlled whisper.

'Pack your bags and get out of this house, Anna, you evil slut. I never want to see you again. We're finished.'

I arrived at Lil's clutching Spesh in one hand and my overnight bag in the other and, no doubt, a haunted expression in my eyes. All I was missing for the complete evacuee impression was a cardboard box containing a gas mask slung round my neck and a luggage tag on my lapel.

I'd already packed the bag earlier that day, in grim anticipation of Ken's verdict: pyjamas, washbag, change of clothes. It had reminded me of packing a bag to go to the hospital to have Holly – even though I'd had a home birth, or tried to, I'd still been told to have a bag ready, in case I had to be whisked off in an emergency. Which I had been, although it was too late by then, and Holly was already dead.

Still, at least I'd had my toothbrush.

Lil let me in without a word, sorrow on her face, and stood at the foot of the stairs while I ran straight past her and up to the spare room. The room was already made up for me, with a discreet box of tissues on the bedside table, and a little posy of flowers from her garden in a vase on the dresser. It felt too neat, too white and floral-sprigged for the emotion I was about to pour out in it, as if the worst thing that had ever happened in there was nobody dusting the skirting boards for a fortnight.

I sat on the candlewick bedspread and sobbed and sobbed until I felt desiccated and hollow, a receptacle emptied of everything, except my baby, its little peanut-shaped body sprouting flappers of limbs and eyes like a tadpole's in its big misshapen head. At that moment I really believed it was the only thing worth staying alive for.

Lil came up and sat with me, holding me, only breaking away to get me a fresh tissue or a cup of tea. We didn't talk for a long, long time.

There was a small figurine on the mantelpiece above the fireplace, a shepherdess holding out her china white skirts in a swirling dance of happiness, a dreamy smile on her face and immaculate porcelain curls. I'd admired it since I was a child, and remembered how I used to pick it up when Lil wasn't looking, holding its slim, cold body in my hand, reverentially stroking the flowing dress and the bumpy hair, feeling as if they ought to be warm to the touch. The shepherdess had the tiniest, reddest Cupid's bow lips, and spots of pink on her cheeks not much bigger than pinheads. I'd wanted her so badly. Hinted at Lil on countless occasions to let me keep her. Even, several times, gone so far as to hide her about my person and smuggle her out of the house, where she would spend a dusty fortnight under my bed, brought out for furtive inspections at night. But my conscience would always prevail, and on the next visit to Lil and Norman's, I'd smuggle her back again. She never looked the same away from their house, because I always felt too guilty.

What had happened to my conscience? I'd had such a strong sense of right and wrong when I was a child. I'd have expected that to increase with age, not dwindle away until I couldn't even see how wrong it was to sleep with a man not my husband; to ruin lives with my selfish behaviour. When I was a kid, I'd been desperate to be an adult. Now that I was an adult, I wished for nothing more than the pleasure of that shepherdess's smile, and black and white moral boundaries which could be stretched, but never broken.

When I could finally speak, I pointed to the shepherdess and said, thickly, 'I used to steal that ornament from you on a regular basis.'

Lil smiled and stroked my hair. 'I know, darling. Norm and I used to joke about it. We half hoped you'd start sending us postcards from her, the way that people who steal garden gnomes sometimes do. We'd say, "I wonder where she's gone this time?", and imagine her like Julie Andrews up the mountains in Switzerland, or in a meadow somewhere, singing.'

'Sorry,' I said. 'She was always just under my bed.'

'You always brought her back with never so much as a chip out of her, so I didn't mind.'

'Do you still miss Uncle Norman?'

She nodded, gazing at the shepherdess. 'Every day.'

'Was he your soulmate?'

I used to think that Ken was my soulmate. But then I met Adam, and wondered if he was. Now I wasn't sure whether such a thing existed.

'I don't know about that. He was my friend, my companion, my . . . protector, I suppose. I loved him very much. There's not much else I can say, really.'

I got the strangest feeling that there was a lot more that Lil wasn't saying.

'Do you believe that there's one ideal person for everyone?'

She looked me in the eyes. 'Yes, I think I do. But I also think that you have to be incredibly blessed to find them. I – well – I did find mine, but he was married to someone else.'

I held my breath. 'Is he still alive?'

'Oh no. He died in the sixties. His wife later became a friend of mine, actually. You might even remember her – Doreen? Of course she never knew about me and Lawrence. It would have killed her.'

'You had an affair while you were married to Uncle Norman?' I couldn't believe it.

She nodded again, and in her eyes I saw the young woman she once was, frustrated in love, grieving for what she couldn't have.

'Nothing physical, of course, not like it all is these days,' she said. 'I believe we only kissed half a dozen times. But we saw each other infrequently for years and years, until he died. He was the one for me. I used to dream that Norman, or Doreen, would run off with somebody else so that we could be together. But neither of them ever did, and neither Lawrence nor I wanted to hurt them that badly.'

I put my hand on her arm. 'That's so sad.'

She smoothed her skirt over her knees in her characteristic gesture. 'Goodness, no, not really,' she said more briskly. 'Norman was so kind to me. I had a happy life, apart from . . . that. It's all ancient history now.'

'But he never knew?'

'No.'

'Ken knows about me and Adam now . . . I've ruined everything.'

Lil took my face in her hands and squeezed my cheeks gently. 'You don't know that yet. Just because he's reacted very badly, it doesn't mean that he won't have a change of heart later. Whether that will be weeks later, or months, or even years, nobody knows.'

Just don't give up on him, if you feel that you and he should stay together.'

'But I *don't* feel that we should stay together,' I said miserably. 'I want Adam, but he doesn't want me. I can't settle for Ken just because Adam won't have me – that's not fair on Ken.'

'Even if he agrees to try and forgive you? You've told him the truth, now you have to give him space to come to terms with it, and then you will both need to decide how to go ahead with your lives, together or not together . . .'

I yawned, suddenly overwhelmed with a massive, bone-crushing exhaustion. I felt wrung out, empty, and all I wanted was to sleep.

Lil stroked the hair back from my face. 'Have a nap, darling, you look worn out. You're going to need all the rest you can get now, aren't you?'

She stood up, picked up our empty cups and saucers and left the room, closing the door softly behind her. The shepherdess and I were alone. Her painted eyes remained wide open, gazing at me indulgently as if to say, 'Well, you've really done it this time, Anna,' but mine closed within seconds. Lil's words, 'have a nap', echoed in my head; and I badly wanted to see Max draw one of his 'naps' – the one which showed 'REALLY REALLY REALLY ACTUALLY HEAVEN'; 'THE AIRPORT'; and 'THE PLACE WHERE STORIES ARE MADE'.

Then I fell asleep. I dreamed about my baby: he was a little blond boy; Max's little brother. He looked like Max. He was peering through a low picket fence at me, gurgling and chortling, pointing skywards at an aeroplane crossing the wide blue sky which I realized we knew contained Ken, jetting off on a business trip – or more likely just out of my life for good. 'I'm sorry,' I told him again, but 'sorry' didn't quite seem to cover it. The plane was represented on Max's 'nap' with a moving dotted line, like they sometimes used in films to denote a flightpath. It flew over 'THE BIG BAD WOLF'S HOUSE', and on, past 'OUR HOUSE', and towards 'WHERE THE PEOPLE DIE'.

The shepherdess was still smiling at me when I woke up, five hours later.

'Please stay,' I said out loud to my baby, my hands on my belly. If I couldn't see Max again, I wanted to see his brother.

Part Four

40

SEVEN MONTHS LATER

George Valentine was born by elective Caesarean section. My obstetrician suggested it, and I agreed without hesitation; it wasn't that I was 'too posh to push', as common parlance had it, I just liked the idea of knowing the exact date and time when he'd come into the world. It somehow made me feel that there was less margin for error.

I couldn't stop marvelling at how quick it was, either; so sterile and painless. I felt the blunt unzipping of my abdomen, and the weirdness of gloved hands reaching into me, but I didn't look at their green-gowned bodies bent over my stomach behind the curtained-off area which bisected my body. I looked instead at the people holding my own hands: Vicky on one side of me, Lil on the other, their anxious masked faces peering into mine until I felt like a lab rat pinned out on a slab. None the less, if I kept eye contact with them at all times, it helped keep the waves of terror under control.

I'd secretly worried that having Lil there would remind me of when Holly was born, but it hadn't, not really. It was so different. And I couldn't have done it without her; without the lifeline of her cool, thin hand. She didn't say much, other than the odd muttered word of encouragement, preferring to leave the talking to Vicky.

Vicky, in contrast, hardly stopped talking, her mask wobbling up and down until I became transfixed by the movement. She and her six-month-old baby Chloë had accompanied me on all my ante-natal visits, whilst Shock-headed Peter had minded the other two children – remarkably uncomplainingly, it seemed. He'd really pulled his finger out since Chloë was born, and had cut his working week down to four days, to allow Vicky a whole day to herself. I wasn't sure whether the salutary tale of me and Ken had had any impact on them, but they seemed much happier together.

'Wish I'd known how easy Caesareans are; I'd have done it for all of them. Nobody staring at your parts. No stirrups. No midwives having to strain your poo out of the birthing pool with a sieve . . . That was sooo humiliating, even with the contractions coming every thirty seconds, I still had time to be mortified . . . And after three of 'em, my pelvic floor's like the stage trapdoor now. I always thought that your stomach muscles would never recover after a Caesarean but they do if you work at it, don't they, I mean, look at Victoria Beckham, her tummy's like an ironing board . . .'

Tummy. That word always reminded me of Adam. Adam was never far from my thoughts – how could he be, when they were taking his child out of me? I still missed him and Max badly, but for the past few months all my energies had been focused on growing George.

Vicky was still wittering on: '. . . My stomach's terrible at the moment – when I lie down on my side, it lies next to me, like a puppy or something. We'll do millions of sit-ups together after your six weeks is up, you wait, it'll be torture . . . The babbas can play together while we sweat – Chloë needs a mate. She's grown out of her baby gym. It's funny how six months will seem like a big age gap between them for the first year, and then there'll be no difference, will there? Besides, poor little Chloë's going to need an ally of her own age, what with Crystal and Pat torturing her whenever I take my eyes off them . . .'

At first I'd felt like telling her to put a sock in it, but after a while I found it oddly comforting, and focusing on her words helped take my mind off the wholescale rummaging occurring in my stomach. I also realized that she hadn't talked about her previous labours to me before, nor about the future relationship between her new baby and mine, for fear of upsetting me, or in case it all went wrong again. It was a good sign, I thought.

Then Vicky finally did shut up, because the doctors were tugging out my baby, and then they were holding him aloft and cutting the cord, and I saw him for the first time, purple and bloody just as Holly had been, but outraged and squawking at the rude interruption to his peace and quiet, his tiny arms punching and flailing in the air. I knew then that he was going to be fine. His mother's son, I thought; I bet he'll love his sleep. They put him on my chest and he quietened down immediately, gazing into my eyes as if to say, 'Well, and wasn't I just worth waiting for?'

'Oh,' sobbed Vicky, tears running over her mask. 'A boy! Boys always look at their mums that way. He adores you already . . . Oh Anna, I can't believe it! Congratulations. He's just perfect.'

George just stared and stared at me. There was a patch of my blood on his cheek, and it made me smile to think of all the other patches of blood to come in future, his own blood, not mine, a boy's grazes and scrapes and cuts. Tree falls and playground skirmishes, bike accidents and possibly worse. I stopped smiling at the thought, never far from the surface of my mind, that maybe, God forbid, he would have a serious fall or a terrible illness – but then seeing him in my arms, so real and solid and human, made me think, well, maybe he wouldn't. And if he did, I'd get him through it, like Adam had got Max through his. We'd get through anything together. Whatever happened, he was his own person, on his own path, and nothing I could do would affect that. All I had to do was to be there for him, and I knew I always would be.

'Hello, my darling boy,' I said to him. 'Meet your great-great-aunt.' I passed him over to Lil and she cradled him to her chest, his skinny little legs dangling comfortably over her forearms. I tore my gaze away from his ankles, smaller than marbles, and still-pliant shins – I'd grown those inside of me! – and watched the tears falling unrestrained down Lil's face, as she pressed her lined parchment skin gently against his soft red cheeks.

My darling son. He had Adam's eyes.

41

Anna Valentine
C/o Rosemead
21 Seymour Road
Hampton TW11

Adam Ferris
43 Hardcourt Road
Gillingsbury
Wilts.

31 October 2003

Dear Adam,
I hope you won't be upset to hear from me, and that
everything is going well for you and Max and Marilyn.
Please tell Max that I miss him, and I miss his emails.
I know I haven't written many to him over the past few
months either, but – well – the reason for that is also
the reason for this letter . . . which I'll come on to later.
Anyway, I'm dying to hear what his latest pinball
score is, and how many teeth he's lost now. Tell him
Spesh is fine. He sleeps with me at night and guards
my bed every day.

I'm living with my great-aunt, Lil, and have been
since I last saw you. My husband and I split up,
and are just waiting for the decree absolute to come

through. Seven months ago I told him about you and Max, and his reaction was not dissimilar to yours, when I told you about him. But it's OK. Lil has been amazing to me, and I've been spending a lot of time with my best friend Vicky and her children. I'm not working, but Vicky and I are planning to set up some kids' theatre workshop groups – Wigwam Drama – in a few months' time.

Ken, my soon-to-be ex-husband, has found a new girlfriend. Her name is Nadine, and she's twenty-seven, a County tennis player (he's mad about his tennis. Did I ever tell you that I can't stand tennis?!), fit and tanned and gorgeous – Ken is over the moon. And I'm surprised at how happy I am for him. After me treating him so appallingly, he deserves it. He was so angry with me when I told him, but since he and Nadine got together, he's being more friendly. We have to talk regularly, about finances and selling the house and stuff, and it's a lot more pleasant now that he can be civil to me again. Like you, he won't ever forgive me completely though.

I miss you, Adam. I think about everything we did together, and, unless I'm looking at it through rose-coloured glasses – which I don't think is the case – I realize how perfect we were for each other. I know I shouldn't say this, but I miss everything about you: waking up with you, making love with you, playing with Max. Being part of your family, which was all I ever wanted. Every day I hear your words in my head: 'I can't quite believe how spectacularly you've blown it, Anna', and you were right. I did blow it, didn't I? I was such a colossal idiot, not to be honest with you from the start. Oh well. I won't say any more – this is probably making you feel really uncomfortable, and I don't want that. However much I miss you, I do genuinely wish you happiness too, and I know that I was always the cuckoo in your nest. Regardless of the bone-marrow donation, I had no right to try and take Marilyn's place. I'm sorry.

There's something else I have to tell you now . . . I remember that letter you wrote to me, telling me that I'd saved Max's life. You said you were crying as you wrote it, and how could you not. Well, I'm crying too now, over what I'm about to say. I'm crying because I have to tell you in a letter, and I'm crying because I messed everything up; because 'I blew it'.

Anyway, here goes . . . I suppose the best thing to do is just let you have the facts: I've had a baby. Your baby. His name is George Adam Valentine, and he's now nearly four weeks old. He's utterly beautiful and looks just like you. ('Valentine' is my maiden name as well as my stage name.

I didn't tell you I was pregnant; partly because I wanted you and Marilyn to have a real chance to work things out without this potentially complicating matters for you both; partly because I didn't – and don't – want you to feel responsible for us; and partly, on a more practical note, because I was afraid that history might repeat itself and even if I carried him full term, something might have gone wrong at the birth like it did with Holly. I couldn't bear to tell you, and then have to 'untell' you.

But nothing went wrong. He's healthy and gorgeous, and I'm fine. I don't want anything from you, Adam, so please don't feel under pressure even to respond if you don't want to. I understand that Marilyn might find this a little difficult to cope with, and I've caused enough problems for you already. Perhaps you're planning more children of your own – perhaps Marilyn's pregnant again already. You just have a right to know that you've had another son.

I haven't enclosed a photograph because that somehow smacks of emotional blackmail – although, if you want to know what he looks like, just email or write and I'll send you some of the several hundred thousand pictures I seem already to have accrued . . . the poor child thinks that his mother has a camera glued to the end of her nose.

But seriously, Adam, I mean it: I'm not telling you this because I want anything from you. I know that what I did to you was unforgivable, and how much I hurt you, and I will completely understand if you don't even respond to this letter. Perhaps when George is older, you might want to get in touch, but it's up to you and, like I said, I will understand if you don't.

I think of you and Max all the time. Even after the total mess I made of everything, I can't help feeling that we've each given the other the best gift of all – I gave you Max back, and now you've given me George. Like you said in your letter to me, 'I could fill pages with thank-yous, but that still wouldn't come close to expressing my gratitude.'

With much love,
Anna xxx

42

'Auntie Anna, look, both of George's noses are blocked up.'

'Well, Crystal, he's only got the one nose, but let's see what we can do about it, shall we?' I extracted a tissue from my sleeve and attempted to swab out George's crusty green nostrils, but they were so small and so full that it was a futile exercise. My son had a stinking cold and, it was true to say, was not looking his best. He peered wearily at me from between pink-lidded eyes and shot me a look which said, *Please just leave me alone.*

'This dust probably doesn't help either,' I added anxiously in the direction of Vicky's backside. She was up a stepladder in Ken's and my old house, wielding a feather duster and coaxing an extended family of spiders out of their homes along the cornicing in the hall.

She and Crystal had come to help me give the place a thorough clean. It had been on the market for five months now without a bite and, on the phone to me at Lil's the other day, the estate agent had used the word 'tired' to describe it; which I knew and he knew meant 'filthy'. Ken and I had never really bothered to keep it nice when we lived in it, let alone since we both moved out. But there was to be a rare viewing that afternoon, some woman who'd already sold her house and was keen to buy, so I was hoping to show it off to its best possible advantage.

I really wanted to get a smaller place nearby for George and me to move to with our half of the proceeds – Lil had been fantastic, but I was ready for a bit more independence, now that I'd recovered from the birth and seemed to be getting the hang of being a mother for real.

Ken was being very reasonable about the divorce settlement, and had on several occasions conceded that I'd need a decent-sized place for me 'and the baby', although he could not bring himself to call George by his name, let alone see him.

'Oh, don't worry about it,' Vicky called down. 'A bit of dust won't make any difference. Crystal, why don't you play with George in the front room for a bit, now that it's all hoovered?'

'I don't want his bogies on me,' said Crystal, eyeing poor George with disdain. 'I want to carry on with my colouring.'

She flapped a booklet at me, and I took it from her. 'What are you colouring, Crystal? It looks really nice.'

'It's not *nice*, Auntie Anna, it's King Rat from *Dick Whittington*. Look, there's a picture of my mummy in here.'

'Let's see?'

Crystal flipped importantly through the pages of the pantomime programme until she found the black-and-white head shot of her mother, looking considerably younger, all corkscrew curls and dimples, under the caption: 'VICKY DYER, *Fairy Bow Bells*'.

I laughed. 'Oh, the dreaded panto. What year was that?'

Vicky craned her neck at it from the top of the stepladder. 'Ninety-four. I'd almost forgotten about it, until I found that the other day under the sofa – it must have been there for years. I thought it would be a good thing to keep Crystal busy while we cleaned. It's got all these activities in the back for kids: mazes and word searches and so on.'

I scrutinized the blurb under Vicky's picture.

TRAINING: it said. *Vicky studied Drama at Reading University, and in 1989 won the Laurence Olivier Award for Most Promising Newcomer of the Year in Theatre, for her performance in* A View From The Bridge. THEATRE: *Other credits include Susan in* No Sex Please – We're British! *(Bournemouth Pier);* Comedy of Errors *(Theatre Royal, Nottingham);* Mother Goose *(Derby Playhouse);* Stripped *(Riverside Studios, London)* . . . etc., etc. I scanned on down the list. TELEVISION: *Appearances include* Holby City, The Bill, A Touch of Frost . . . The usual fare.

'Doesn't look much for a career, does it?' said Vicky glumly.

I imagined my own blurb: *Anna studied Drama at Reading University. Her acting career was very unremarkable and she never won any awards, although she did successfully manage to dupe both her husband and her lover by pretending to have a job on a West Country cable soap opera.*

I remembered the blind, hot panic of deception, all those months of knowing that the crunch had to come, that at some point I was going to have to make a choice; knowledge which shark-circled continually under the surface of my consciousness, tormenting me and petrifying me when everything else felt so good. To lose Adam and Max had been unthinkable, but so, it seemed, had been the idea of telling Ken that I'd lied and cheated, and was abandoning him and the life we'd so painstakingly constructed together . . . Having to choose between two good men, both of whom I loved in different ways for different reasons, neither of whom deserved to be treated so appallingly. It had been horrible.

Then I looked over at George in the car seat, his adorable fat cheeks wobbling gently as Crystal rocked him, and my heart melted. I'd got through it, after all that dread. The sky hadn't fallen in when I'd confessed to Ken, and he hadn't fallen to pieces. And, as much as it still hurt, I was coping without Adam and Max. Plus it was such a relief not to have to tell any more lies. I concluded my imaginary blurb, feeling better: *Anna's roles included Davina in the BBC's* Butterfinger; Les Miserables; The Bill, Casualty . . . *but the only role she's ever really wanted was her present one: Mother to George, aged four months.*

'I think that's a lot to show for a career,' I said to Vicky. 'Not to mention three gorgeous children, and the imminent launch of Wigwam Drama. You should be proud of yourself – we both should be proud of ourselves. Want a cup of tea?'

Vicky glanced at her watch. 'Thanks, Anna, but we're going to have to go now. I said I'd take over from Peter at three so he could go into work for a bit. He'll be climbing the walls after having Pat and Chloë all morning.'

'Well, thank you for all the help,' I said, hugging her and Crystal. 'I'm just going to clean the door knocker and the letterbox, then I'll call it a day as well. I want to get back to Lil's for when George has his nap so I can finish off my emails. I've got to write to my accountant – some query about pensions for the divorce settlement – and I wanted to email Max, too.'

Vicky looked at me, gently wiping a smudge of dirt off my cheek with her knuckle. 'Have you heard from him lately?'

I shook my head, the pain welling up again like tears. 'Not for ages. He hasn't replied to my last four emails. I keep telling myself that he's busy at school, but I think it's more likely that Adam told Marilyn about George, and she's decided to try and make Max forget about me. I don't blame her – I mean, wouldn't you? Even if Adam never gets in touch, her just knowing that George exists is bound to freak her out.'

'Nothing from Adam either, then?'

I picked up George in his car seat and plonked him

on the rug in the front room, so I could dust the banisters without worrying about him inhaling the grime of years of neglect. Also so that Vicky couldn't see my face. It had been over three months since I'd written the letter to Adam, and he hadn't responded.

'No. I keep telling you, Vic, there won't be. I didn't really expect there would. Even if he wanted to, he'd know how much it would upset Marilyn. It's fine. I've got George, and that's enough for me. More than enough.'

And it was true. George was the best blessing – more than I deserved. I'd have liked Adam too, but I knew that was too much to hope for.

My mobile rang from where I'd left it in George's car seat. I extracted it from underneath his fat little legs. 'Hello?'

'Hello, dear, it's me, I'm just ringing to—' Lil's voice was suddenly swallowed up and then belched out again in undecipherable fits and starts. I heard 'up' and 'coming' and 'house', but that was about it. The line went dead.

I tutted. The mobile coverage in our road always had been rubbish, much to Ken's irritation. He'd hated having to conduct important negotiations with tour managers whilst either standing in the middle of the street, or at the bottom of the garden next to the compost heap.

I tried to ring her back, but it was engaged. 'Oh well,' I said to Vicky, who was stuffing Crystal's arms into her coat sleeves and gathering up colouring pens. 'I'm sure she'll call again if it's urgent. Thanks for coming over today. And Crystal, thanks for looking after George so beautifully for me.'

Crystal beamed. 'I won't kiss him,' she said, 'in case I get his germs.' I thought it prudent not to point out that he'd caught the cold from her in the first place.

After I'd waved them off, I lifted George back into the hall, out of the draught, gave him some toys to play with, and set to polishing the brass on the front door. It had been ages – years, probably – since anybody had done this, and in just a couple of minutes my hands were black and sweat beaded my forehead. I could hear little rattling and lip-smacking noises which reassured me that all was well with my son inside the house.

My son. Being able to own those two words *almost* made up for everything that had gone before. It was sublime just knowing he was there, existing; being able to chat to him from the other side of the door, picturing his fists wrapped around a rattle as he gummed it mercilessly. I thought of the numerous times I'd come through this front door, alone, wishing I had a baby to carry instead of the dead white weight of full supermarket bags straining my arms or, worse, my hands hanging empty at my sides. I wouldn't miss the house when it was sold, I thought. Too many sad memories. I couldn't wait for me and George to have a place of our own.

A small haystack of used and blackened Brasso lay on the doorstep at my feet as I attacked the house number, polishing with gusto, feeling satisfaction as the digits became shiny once more. I was fine. My son was fine. My house was clean (ish), my ex-husband seemed happier, and I was ready to move on to whatever came next. I didn't know what it would be, except that it would *not* involve deception.

Since George was born, the enormity of what I'd done to Ken and Adam – and Max – had sunk in in a way it never really had when I'd been caught up in the heady tangle of the lies. I didn't blame either man for their reaction when they found out. It seemed so preposterous that, were it not for the permanent reminder of George, I could almost allow myself to imagine that the whole thing had happened to someone else.

I stopped polishing to go round and give George a kiss, kneeling down next to his car seat and bending forwards, my dirty hands held away from my sides, as if I were apple-bobbing. 'All right, sweetheart? Mummy won't be long. I'll just finish the door, and then we'll go back to Auntie Lil's.'

I heard the crunch of footsteps coming up the gravel driveway towards the door. Blast, I thought, straightening up and making a face at George, who grinned snottily at me while still gumming away at his toy. It's the estate agent, and I haven't cleared away the step-ladder or any of the cleaning things. I really didn't want to be there when he showed the potential buyer round either – I didn't want to see him turn up his nose slightly at the rotting window frames, or hear him mutter superciliously, 'It needs cosmetic updating', and 'The vendors have split up . . . Yes, I'm sure they'd take an offer.'

'Sorry,' I said, as I leaned forward to pick up the pile of dirty Brasso bits off the front doorstep. 'I wasn't expecting you till—'

I stopped, gaping, my hands full of oily black fur. It was Adam.

If it hadn't been for the familiar blue eyes, I'd have had difficulty recognizing him. He'd lost weight, cut his hair really short and shaved off his beard.

'Hello,' I stammered, feeling as if the Brasso had been stuffed into my throat. I was knocked sideways by how gorgeous he looked. He was wearing his faded old Levis, and the mere sight of his hard thighs in them made my muscles think they were dissolving. I had an inappropriate flash of memory: us making love in the heat of summer, stuck together with sweat, our torsos making gentle sucking, lapping sounds like waves washing over a rockpool.

He smiled hesitantly at me. 'Hello, Anna. Sorry to turn up unannounced. Did your great-aunt tell you? She sent me round here after I called at her house.'

'She did ring, but I couldn't hear what she was saying. There's no landline in this house any more, and bad mobile reception.' I was still paralysed with a potent cocktail of emotions: shyness, shame, shock, lust – one glimpse, and I wanted him.

George snuffled and cooed behind the door, and I wondered how best to introduce them. I was worried that I might have to sit down on the spot, my knees were shaking so much. What if he said he didn't want to meet George at all; that he couldn't face it? Maybe he'd only come because he was still furious with me. Or – far worse – maybe it was Max; what if he'd come to tell me that Max . . .

I did sit down then, hard, on the doorstep, not caring that my jeans would be covered in greasy black stains.

'Please tell me that Max is OK,' I blurted out, all of a sudden smothered by a dark conviction that this was why Adam was here.

But Adam's face relaxed, and he half stretched out a hand towards me, before letting it fall again awkwardly. 'No, he's fine, don't worry. He's great.'

There was a long, difficult silence, tense with expectation.

'Nice job,' said Adam eventually, gesturing towards the gleaming door brass. 'So this is your house?'

'Not for much longer,' I said, dumping the Brasso into a black binliner next to me on the doorstep. 'Someone's coming round in a minute to look at it. I'm buying a place for me and George . . .' I had a terrible thought. 'You did *get* my letter, didn't you?'

He leaned against the wall by the front door, looking down on me, a little shamefaced. A dry twig of winter-bare wisteria got tangled in his hair, and I itched to pick it out.

'Yes. I'm really sorry I didn't get in touch. I wanted to get a few things straight in my mind first, without doing anything impulsively.'

'Oh, don't worry, that's fine, honestly,' I said falsely and airily, as if he were saying sorry for spilling tea on the carpet. It embarrassed me to hear him apologize at all – it was I who could never apologize enough. And now that we'd established that Max was OK, I was convinced that Adam was still angry, that he'd come to tell me that I'd ruined his life. I felt as sick as if he'd already spoken the accusatory words. Every instinct in me wanted to gather George up and run away, as fast as I could.

George coughed delicately, as if to bring our attention to him.

'So . . . ?' said Adam, smiling suddenly, bringing my negative train of thought crashing to a hopeful halt. 'Could I . . . I mean, is that him? Is that George?'

He was *really* smiling: Adam's beautiful warm beam, the one I'd missed so much. I found it difficult to reply.

'Yes, yes, of course – sorry. He's got a dreadful cold at the moment, that's why I kept him out of the draught. Hold on, just let me wash my hands, they're all black – No, on second thoughts, come in, and I'll wash my hands while you meet him . . .' I got up from the step. I felt like wrapping my arms around Adam's knees and *begging* him to forgive me; to love my son as much as he'd once loved me.

Instead, I pushed the front door wide open with my elbow, and George sat there, blinking at the sudden extra daylight in his face. Adam followed me in and knelt down almost reverentially before him, putting his large hands on either side of the car seat in an instinctive protective gesture.

'Hello, George,' he said, and the emotion in his voice immediately set me off. He leaned forward to kiss him, just as George sneezed mightily, spraying snot all over Adam's face.

'At least you got rid of your beard,' I said, laughing and crying at the same time. I looked down at Adam's broad shoulders, hovering over George like a guardian angel, hiding him from my view, but in the knowledge that he was perfectly safe where he was. In a way, I didn't mind that I couldn't see either of their faces when they met for the first time. I wanted it to be private between them, to try and help them forge their own relationship regardless of the mess I'd made of everything prior to that one, unsullied moment.

'Have you got a tissue?' Adam asked, in a strangled sort of hiccup.

I fetched him some kitchen paper and washed my greasy hands in the sink, not caring that I left the soap black and the sink in a complete state – so much for cleaning the house – then dashed back, not wanting to miss a second.

'And could I pick him up, please?' he added.

'Of course,' I said, handing him the kitchen towel and moving to help him unclip George's harness. But Adam had already lifted him out and hoisted him up in front of his face, staring at him with an almost painfully intense loving expression. George gurgled with pleasure at the unexpected liberation, kicking his arms and legs.

'Oh Anna, he's just gorgeous.' He hugged George to his chest, stroking the back of his neck with a thumb.

I remembered the way he used to stroke me with his thumb, and felt a renewed pang of the loss I'd gradually learned to live with. But this moment wasn't about me, I thought, as I gazed at the pair of them. I was just grateful that Adam was there, holding his son. I watched the tears run down Adam's cheeks onto the top of George's chick-fluffy head, and I wanted to keep that exact image for ever. I pictured the two of them as a complicated mosaic, chips of shiny smashed emotions stuck back together with the grey cement of circumstance, in an utterly lifelike reality. What once was fractured could be reassembled, differently but permanently.

Please let it be permanent, I prayed silently.

'Did you say you were expecting someone round?' said Adam, looking at me properly for the first time. I tried to pull myself together, realizing what I must look like: tear streaks in the dust on my face, black finger-nails, dirty clothes . . . but then suddenly knowing that it didn't matter; that Adam was looking at me as

404

George's mother, not appraising my physical attractiveness. It felt oddly comforting.

'Yes. A woman's coming to look round with an estate agent. I don't want to be here when they arrive, actually. I'll just put away this ladder and the hoover, and then— How much time have you got? Do you want to go for a walk or something? George's pushchair is in the car.'

There it was again, Adam's big smile. 'That would be great.'

43

Ten minutes later we were walking along an avenue of naked chestnut trees in the park, two parents bumping their baby in his buggy over frosty ground, on a cold February day. It was the scene that I'd craved for so long and imagined so often. It still wasn't mine, but as the fresh air pinkened George's cheeks and his eyes became drowsy with the effort of staring up at us in the rear-facing pushchair, I thought, I'll settle for this.

It occurred to me that this was the first time I'd ever had the chance to speak to Adam completely honestly, now that the revelations had all sunk in. There was so much I wanted to say, to tell and ask, that for a while I couldn't say anything at all. We walked in silence, both of us gazing at our son's face, watching him slide into sleep.

'Does Max know you're seeing me?' I eventually managed. 'Does he even remember me?'

'Of course he remembers you. I'm sorry he hasn't been in touch lately, but Marilyn thought . . .'

'Don't worry. I can imagine what Marilyn thought.'

'So, no, I didn't tell Max I was visiting you, otherwise he'd have insisted on coming too. He's gone to stay with Marilyn for the weekend.' Adam looked sideways at me, waiting for my reaction.

'*Gone* to stay with . . . ?'

His lips twitched, but whether with amusement or sorrow I couldn't quite tell. He cleared his throat. 'Yes. Um . . . things didn't work out between us. She moved to Southampton shortly after Christmas. It's only about twenty miles away, so she sees lots of Max. We did ask him if he wanted to go and live with her, but he said he'd rather stay with me.'

I stopped so abruptly that George almost jerked awake. 'You've split up?'

My legs started shaking again. I squeezed the buggy's cold black rubber handlebar so hard that it yielded slightly in my palms, like one of those executive stress toys Ken had periodically brought home, promotional red rubber balls emblazoned with band logos. Ken's promotional items seemed like relics from a past life.

Adam and Marilyn had split up.

'We tried, really hard. But we both knew that it wasn't working, and that we were only doing it for Max's sake. Going through the motions. We thought it was the right thing to do, but in the long run we realized that if neither of us was happy, he wouldn't be happy either. So we gave ourselves until Christmas. But the truth is, our marriage collapsed the first time she left.'

'Oh.' I didn't know what to say. I thought of George being unzipped from me, and the purple scar I bore. 'I wish you could have been there when George was born,' I blurted, thinking, what a selfish and inappropriate thing to come out with.

'So do I,' said Adam, putting one hand over mine and stroking it gently. 'I'm sorry.'

'But it was my fault, for not telling you. I shouldn't have said that. I'm sorry about you and Marilyn, too. I know you wanted to make it work.'

Adam rubbed his chin, as if he was taking comfort in a phantom beard. His free hand still covered mine, and even the touch of his warm fingers aroused me.

'Well, I did and I didn't. I couldn't forget you, Anna. That was the problem.'

'Couldn't forgive me, either.'

'That's what you said in your letter. And yes, I admit that at first I thought I wouldn't be able to forgive you. But as time went on, and I thought more and more about what we had, and how close you were to Max, and how I really felt about you – I realized that I'd overreacted. That you hadn't set out to hurt me; far from it.'

'No.'

'I was angry for a while – at least, I thought I was. But really, I was more angry with myself than you; at first, for what I saw as having been tricked. Then for letting you go.'

'Really?'

'Yes. The more I thought about it, and the more Max and I missed you being around, the more I realized that what you'd done was . . . well, brave.'

I laughed, painfully. 'Brave is the last word I'd have thought anyone would use to describe me.'

'You *were* brave. You'd just lost your baby, you were scared of getting close to Max in case you then lost him too, but you still came down and met him. Us. It all made sense, afterwards, how freaked out you were when he was ill that time, the day Marilyn came back.'

'I thought he was going to die,' I said, my eyes filling at the memory.

'You carried all that responsibility for him by yourself. I had no idea. You met us only months after you lost Holly; it was still so raw for you. And there was I, constantly boasting about Max and how wonderful he was. I had Max – thanks to you – and you didn't have Holly . . . But you gave yourself to both of us, without a murmur.'

I was crying so much that for a long time I couldn't speak at all. 'But the lies,' I managed eventually. The tears seemed to be searing my cold cheeks, and it felt as if this was the first time I'd ever cried, properly, for Holly; as if all the past tears had just been practice ones.

Adam took me in his arms. 'No one's perfect, Anna. We all make mistakes. And, for what it's worth, I think you're still being incredibly brave. You've just endured pregnancy and childbirth without a partner; and after all you went through before – that must have taken guts.'

Shattered with emotion and discomforted by the undeserved praise, I broke away, and busied myself checking that George was wrapped up well enough.

'Are you still sleepwalking?'

I blew my nose on one of George's wet wipes and looked at him, puzzled. 'I don't sleepwalk.' How embarrassing for him, I thought. He's got me mixed up with Marilyn.

'You do. You did, anyway, several times, when you were living with us. I used to wake up in the middle of the night and have to go and look for you. You were usually in Max's room, sitting with your back against the wall by his bed.'

I remembered sitting with my back against the wall in *Holly's* bedroom once, reading Adam's letter; but nothing about any nocturnal visits to Max.

'I was a little bit worried that Max might wake up and find you there, and not realize that you weren't awake.'

'Oh. Sorry.' I was confused and mortified, and still crying. 'Why didn't you ever tell me, the next morning?'

Adam's voice wobbled a little and he looked away. 'I always intended to. But the thing was, in the night, you were so . . . unhappy, like a different person. You were often in tears, and sometimes you said things, about Holly mostly. Then you'd wake up in the morning as your usual happy, wonderful self, and it just seemed . . . cruel, almost, to tell you. I loved our mornings together so much. I suppose I just thought that it might be better to let your subconscious get on with grieving, without having to put you through it during the day as well as at night . . . I don't know. It was probably wrong of me. But you shouldn't be sorry; I should. I knew how much you were suffering, and yet I didn't even really try to talk to you about it.'

An icy wind swirled through the park, making the branches tremble and numbing my ears. Adam stopped to do up his jacket. He bent his head over the zip, and his words came out muffled at first, and then clearer once he straightened up again.

'I'm sorry I didn't contact you sooner, but I needed to make sure that it was completely over with Marilyn; that there really was no chance for her and me. I had been thinking that, even before I got your letter, but I still waited. Got Christmas out of the way; made sure Max would be OK with Marilyn leaving again. And I wanted to think about my own feelings for you, as well; to take time and to check that they were real feelings, and not just a sense of responsibility.'

He slid his hands up the sides of my arms until they gently held my neck, and I remembered how his hands had always felt as if they were supporting me: cupping my breasts, encircling my waist, holding my bottom. Keeping me together. Lucky George, who could have his whole body supported by those hands.

I couldn't speak at all now, although I just about managed to raise my eyebrows.

He continued. 'Do you know what I did, the day I got your letter? I went down to the canal, where we talked that time, sat on that bench – the one you were sick behind – and I cried. For hours. I just read the letter over and over again, and cried more than I've cried since Max was ill. Nearly gave myself frostbite. But I wanted you so badly. I wanted to jump into my car then and there and drive up to you and grab you and George and take you back with me and never let you go . . .'

I wiped my eyes again. 'And now?' I asked, hoping I knew the answer.

He paused.

'I suppose what I came to say was this: I miss you,

Anna. I miss the way that you light up a room when you come into it; and the way that everyone who meets you is fascinated by you. I was so proud to be seen out with you – I miss watching people watching you, and seeing the admiration in their faces. I got such a kick, knowing that it was me who got to go home with you at the end of the night. I loved that Max adored you so much, and the way you made us both laugh – we haven't laughed like that since you left, and I miss that too. I miss your lovely body, and the shape your mouth goes into when you say certain words, and the way you always sing harmonies of songs on the radio . . .'

'Which words?' My hands instinctively slid around his waist and down into the back pockets of his jeans. I had finally managed to stop crying. 'The shape of my mouth when I say which words?'

Adam pretended to think about it. 'Well. Say: "Yes".'

'Yes . . .' My mouth didn't feel as if it was doing anything out of the ordinary.

'Mmm, that's it. That's one of them. Now say: "Adam".'

'Adam,' I said obediently.

'You look *very* sexy when you say "Adam". Say "I want".'

'I want?'

He tucked a stray strand of my hair away behind my ears, and gazed into my eyes, smiling. I could barely breathe with anticipation. I glanced down at George, but he was lost in his baby dreams, wispy clouds of his own breath floating up as if he were donating it to me.

'Good. Now say "to be with you for ever".'

I opened my mouth to speak, but he carried on. 'Anna, I've missed you so much, and I really want you and George. Please can we try again? Perhaps you'd consider moving back to Gillingsbury, but if that's something you wouldn't want to do, then perhaps Max and I could move up here . . .'

I hugged him so hard that we both nearly toppled

over, and had to grab the pushchair handle to steady ourselves. George flailed and snored, but didn't wake up.

'Yes, Adam, I want to be with you for ever,' I said, slowly and deliberately.

I remembered the day I first cooked for Adam and Max. The scraped-off pasta tubes, chilled wine and sticky tabletop. Adam's warm body against mine. Then all those weeks afterwards, Max winding his thin arms around my neck, and waking up every morning feeling as if I was in just the right place.

'And I'd love to move back to Gillingsbury,' I added, visions spinning joyfully through my mind like Max's Beyblades. Vicky and the kids could come and stay, and so could Lil. Lil would *adore* Max. I hoped Vicky wouldn't mind, but perhaps I could set up Wigwam Drama in Gillingsbury simultaneously – it could be a franchise. I saw us all discussing it in Adam's – our – house: Vicky and Adam deep in conversation, Crystal bossing Max and Pat about, Chloë and George running their fingers down the mesh walls inside a playpen and chuckling at the gentle zippy sound. George would be wearing one of Max's old sleepsuits. It would be too big, and the empty feet of it would flap about as he kicked and cooed . . .

We were back at the park entrance. A car pulled up at the zebra crossing at the park gates to let us cross, a song blasting out of the open windows like heat thawing the cold air; Jackie Wilson, 'Sweetest Feeling'. The music serenaded us across the road, my hand in Adam's, our baby's lashes fluttering on his cheeks, and by the time we reached the pavement on the other side, we had become something different: a new, fledging family. I felt reassembled, like broken china, into something lasting and beautiful.

'I can't *wait* to see Max again,' I said ecstatically.

THE END

Acknowledgements

Lifesaver was inspired in part by my own experience of almost becoming a bone marrow donor for someone with leukaemia via The Anthony Nolan Trust. Unfortunately, I wasn't a close enough match, but I thought a lot about that mystery person, and hoped that a suitable donor was found for them in time for their life to be saved.

The Antony Nolan Trust always needs more potential donors (especially men aged 18–30). All you need to do is to get a blood test, and then your name goes on the register. It's not all that likely you'll ever get called to be an actual donor (I'd been on the register for fifteen years before I even got asked to go for a further test), but if you do, it's not a major operation, and it could well save somebody's life. Contact them at www.anthonynolan.org.uk, or tel. 020 7284 1234.

Thanks to Selina Walker, Diana Beaumont, Judith Welsh and all at Transworld; to Vivienne Schuster and all at Curtis Brown; to Angela Martin; Jo Frank; Vicky Longley; my indispensable Girly Writers friends – Jacqui Lofthouse, Linda Buckley-Archer, Stephanie Zia and Jacqui Hazell; to Mark Edwards; Marian Keyes; Louise Harwood; Jane Landymore; Sharon Malrooney; Claire Harcup; Clare Jackson; and (for the country music joke and fairy/finance director comment) Freya Pace. And to the inspirational Save The World Club for their community mosaic project in Kingston.

TO BE SOMEONE

Louise Voss

'BEAUTIFULLY WRITTEN . . . BY TURNS COMIC AND
POIGNANT, ABOUT FRIENDSHIP, LOVE AND
REDEMPTION. I LOVED IT'
Marian Keyes

Helena Nicholls – ex-world-famous pop star and prime-time DJ –
wakes up in hospital to find her looks, her career and her
personal life in tatters. She has been abandoned by her
boyfriend, and the person she loved most in the world – her best
friend since the age of five – is dead. She feels that she belongs
nowhere, and her sense of identity, fragile at the best of times, is
in pieces.

As Helena begins the painful path to recovery, she casts her
mind back over the events in her life which have brought her
here. Those memories, good and bad, combined with the songs
forever associated with them, are milestones on her journey.
When her world is rocked by a chance meeting with an old
friend, she sees a glimpse of the future she could have. But if she
is to have a chance at that happiness, she must first conquer her
troubled past and work out what it means to be someone . . .

'A SAD, FUNNY BOOK ABOUT FRIENDSHIP, LOVE AND
GETTING A NEW LIFE'
The Big Issue

'A GREAT FIRST NOVEL. LOUISE VOSS IS AN EXCITING NEW
NAME WITH A REAL TALENT FOR STORYTELLING. HER
BOOK IS DEFINITELY A MUST READ'
Woman's Journal

'IT IS LOUISE VOSS'S VOICE THAT YOU REMEMBER AT THE
END: CONTEMPORARY, FEMALE, AUTHENTIC'
Independent

'A STUNNING DÉBUT'
Heat

'MY FAVOURITE BOOK THIS YEAR. A BEAUTIFULLY
WRITTEN STORY WHICH I DIDN'T WANT TO END'
Cerys Matthews, Catatonia

0 552 99902 4

BLACK SWAN

ARE YOU MY MOTHER?

Louise Voss

'AN EXHILARATING EMOTIONAL RIDE THROUGH LOVE,
FRIENDSHIP AND LOSS'
New Woman

From the age of nineteen, Emma Victor has had to bring up her
much younger sister Stella. It has shaped both their lives. Now
Stella is almost grown-up, and Emma's nurturing instincts extend
to her work as an aromatherapist, and inform her relationship
with the unreliable but irresistible Gavin. But something is
missing, and Emma has to confront her deepest need – a
need she's been denying for years – and embark on a
search for her birth mother.

Are You My Mother? chronicles Emma's search for her birth
mother and for a sense of her own place in the world in this
compelling, funny and profoundly moving novel about love,
identity and the need to belong.

'A HEART-WARMING STORY WHICH COVERS THE
COMPLICATED AND EMOTIONAL THEMES OF BEING
ORPHANED AND ADOPTED AND SEARCHING FOR
BIRTH PARENTS'
Hello!

'STRONG CHARACTERS, A MEATY PLOT AND A
SATISFYINGLY UNEXPECTED TWIST TRANSFORMS EMMA'S
JOURNEY OF SELF-DISCOVERY INTO A VERY GOOD READ'
Woman & Home

'UTTERLY BELIEVABLE . . . HIGHLY EMOTIONAL . . . IT'S
ALSO A COMPLETE TEAR-JERKER'
Heat

'VOSS'S TENDER AND MOVING TALE IS A SEARCH FOR
TRUTH, AND QUESTIONS OUR NEED TO BELONG, OUR
ABILITY TO FORGIVE. AN EXCEPTIONAL ACHIEVEMENT'
What's On in London

0 552 99903 2

BLACK SWAN

A SELECTED LIST OF FINE WRITING AVAILABLE FROM BLACK SWAN

77083	3	I'M A BELIEVER	*Jessica Adams*	£6.99
77084	1	COOL FOR CATS	*Jessica Adams*	£6.99
99822	2	A CLASS APART	*Diana Appleyard*	£6.99
99933	4	OUT OF LOVE	*Diana Appleyard*	£6.99
99950	4	UNCHAINED MELANIE	*Judy Astley*	£6.99
77185	6	SIZE MATTERS	*Judy Astley*	£6.99
99734	X	EMOTIONALLY WEIRD	*Kate Atkinson*	£6.99
77105	8	NOT THE END OF THE WORLD	*Kate Atkinson*	£6.99
77097	3	I LIKE IT LIKE THAT	*Claire Calman*	£6.99
99947	4	CROSS MY HEART AND HOPE TO DIE	*Claire Calman*	£6.99
99826	5	TAKING THE DEVIL'S ADVICE	*Anne Fine*	£6.99
99898	2	ALL BONES AND LIES	*Anne Fine*	£6.99
99801	X	THE SHORT HISTORY OF A PRINCE	*Jane Hamilton*	£6.99
99890	7	DISOBEDIENCE	*Jane Hamilton*	£6.99
77110	4	CAN YOU KEEP A SECRET?	*Sophie Kinsella*	£6.99
99859	1	EDDIE'S BASTARD	*William Kowalski*	£6.99
99936	9	SOMEWHERE SOUTH OF HERE	*William Kowalski*	£6.99
77103	1	BLESSED ARE THE CHEESEMAKERS	*Sarah-Kate Lynch*	£6.99
99938	5	PERFECT DAY	*Imogen Parker*	£6.99
99939	3	MY SECRET LOVER	*Imogen Parker*	£6.99
99909	1	LA CUCINA	*Lily Prior*	£6.99
77088	4	NECTAR	*Lily Prior*	£6.99
77095	7	LONDON IRISH	*Zane Radcliffe*	£6.99
77096	5	BIG JESSIE	*Zane Radcliffe*	£6.99
99902	4	TO BE SOMEONE	*Louise Voss*	£6.99
99903	2	ARE YOU MY MOTHER?	*Louise Voss*	£6.99